The Price of Blood and Honor

Tor Books by Elizabeth Willey

The Well-Favored Man
A Sorcerer and a Gentleman
The Price of Blood and Honor

Elizabeth Willey

The Price of Blood and Honor

WILLE

TOR®

A Tom Doherty Associates Book · New York

HUMCA

This is a work of fiction. All the characters and events portrayed in this novel are either fictitious or are used fictitiously.

THE PRICE OF BLOOD AND HONOR

This book is printed on acid-free paper.

A Tor Book
Published by Tom Doherty Associates, Inc.
175 Fifth Avenue
New York, NY 10010

Tor Books on the World Wide Web:
http://www.tor.com

Tor® is a registered trademark of Tom Doherty Associates, Inc.

Library of Congress Cataloging-in-Publication Data

Willey, Elizabeth.
    The price of blood and honor / by Elizabeth Willey.—1st ed.
        p.   cm.
    "A Tom Doherty Associates book."
    ISBN 0-312-85784-5 (alk. paper)
    I. Title.
    PS3573.I44722P75   1996
    813'.54—dc20   96-18273
                                                        CIP

First Edition: September 1996

Printed in the United States of America

0 9 8 7 6 5 4 3 2 1

⌐Acknowledgments ⌐

THE AUTHOR IS THANKFUL FOR THE patience of Deborah Manning, Betsy Perry, Mary Hopkins, Greer Gilman, Patrick Sobalvarro, and Delia Sherman, all rich with insight and generous with criticism and encouragement. The edifice of the Palace of Landuc and its furnishings was constructed from plans (modified) provided by Barbara Ninde Byfield. Valerie Smith performed the remarkable feat of being both a buttress and a fire wall. The author's husband provided all those vital things without which not a word would have been written.

The Price
of Blood and
Honor

— 1 —

IN THE CAREER OF EVERY SORCERER comes a time when he must assay the price that sorcery shall exact of him and choose, if it be not too late, whether the Art be worth the price. Sometimes this choice appears early, as in the case of a certain sorceress who dedicated herself to her Art at the age of fourteen years, renouncing the joys of liberally offered love, the diversions and dominion of society, and public paeans for her great beauty, in order to cloister herself under the frequently unpleasant tutelage of a succession of arid masters of sorcery. On concluding her apprenticeship with the then-customary duel, she mounted an ass, who had but an hour before been her most recent master, and rode to Noroison, where sat King Proteus, to claim her former master's territory; and Proteus, impressed by her ability and affected by her beauty, granted her this boon, though the territory was one he desired himself, situated on a powerful Nexus and with several Nodes of the Stone's power rising there. He offered her the honor of marriage as well, which she refused, displeasing him; but the boon was granted and he could not withdraw it without risking a challenge and a duel, which risks the King forbore to undertake, with a view to the ass who had once been this sorceress's master. So the sorceress dwells there still, uncompanioned in her pastoral realm, served by her creatures, warding her secrets, feeding her knowledge, and waiting.

And sometimes the choice appears late, as in the case of a certain mighty Prince, who commanded all the Elements and held a Source alone, as only Primas, Proteus, and Panurgus have done before in the history of the worlds, and who has lately discovered, in his prime of potency and pride, that there is something he values more, though the discovery shall gall and gnaw his heart and cause him much pain hereafter. He has ransomed his blood with his sorcery, and this seems a surpassingly high price; he thinks, as he rides through an untrodden wood, of precedents in which others have sacrificed blood for sorcery, and cannot but wonder if he has not been a fool; he bites his lip and grinds his teeth, self-doubting. But lurking in memory are the commentaries on those who have bought sorcery for blood: and the truth of the matter is that they have paid as high as he, or higher; for vengeance and Fortuna have already turned on most, and they are dead or worse. It is as if, he thinks, an unexpounded natural law acts to balance, somehow, blood and power; but there is no profit to him in philosophy now, and he turns his mind to matters of planning and defense.

And sometimes the choice only seems to appear, as in the case of a certain prodigiously talented young sorcerer, who has thrown his lot in with his recently-found, dispossessed father, and who enters now his father's demesnes in company with that gentleman; he congratulates himself, as he rides, on choosing well, and on having chosen both blood and power in one sweep, but he disregards the lady riding behind him and it has not occurred to him that the price he pays to perfect his Art may not be as simple as supporting his defeated sire. The young sorcerer has forgotten, in the momentary exhilaration of the filial bond, that his father had already renounced much of his power, in vows taken all too lightly, and given it to the lady, his daughter; and therefore she holds that power already, though she uses it not; and thus he has made only a down-payment on the Art he would claim, with high principal and interest yet to come due.

And sometimes there is no choice. The lady who rides behind her brother has been heaped with power and wealth, none of her desiring; rather than choosing, she must accept, for, try as she may, she cannot refuse; and she must pay regardless of her own desires, and make the best of everything bestowed upon her.

—2—

BESIDE THE SCATTERED COALS OF A dying fire, two people sat on their heels and one stood. Above them in the night sky were few stars—so few they might be counted, were anyone so inclined. The place was neither here nor there, or perhaps as much there as here: it lay between two realms, no-man's-land in the truest sense. The ground rolled, nowhere level, a rippling maze of low mounds, hard and dry, punctuated irregularly by tufts of dry grass. The air was as empty as the land: arid, waterless, windless, without warmth. The people, like the place, were between: they were resting in a moment between one movement and another, between to and from, between be and become.

"We can't go. They can barely walk," said one, rubbing at her red-edged eyes. She was leading two horses, salt-flecked weary animals; a third, taller and fresher, followed them. "Papa? Dewar?"

The two men were staring at each other, with none of their attention to spare for her. One nodded once and said, " 'Tis a bold resolution, and I'll not test its limits; for though blood's strong-binding, 'tis bounded by the heart. Come then, and welcome."

"If you will have me there," said Dewar, offering a last demurrer. "Sorcerers are not known for keeping company, as gentlemen do. Blood may carry weakness as well as strength, Prospero."

"In but little time I'll be no more a sorcerer," said Prospero, "so there's an end to't, and the tragedy's a comedy, rounded with reunion. Hah!" He rose to his feet, slapped dust and ashes from his knees. "How go the horses, Freia?"

Dewar, released from scrutiny, the hanging tension of the moment resolved, let his heels roll from under him and sat back with a slow exhalation, closing his eyes. At his boot-toes, scattered coals from the fire with which he'd Summoned Prospero brightened with his breath and subsided, dimmer than before.

"They're too tired to go, Papa."

"They can walk, and so should we. They've had fodder and water?"

"We didn't have much left, and they've eaten it all."

"The more reason to begone: but let us consider ourselves as well as the beasts; this is mortal weary country to cross, and some refreshment will shorten the distance. Dewar's near-dazed with working."

The truth was that they were all tired. Dewar was tired and hungry from the exertion of Summoning Prospero, and Prospero was tired and straining to keep a smooth surface over his agitation, and Freia was tired and unsure where she stood in the world. Before they went anywhere, it seemed wise that they should eat. So they stirred up the embers of the fire, which Prospero had nearly extinguished in his precipitous involuntary arrival, and wordlessly shared a meal from Prospero's saddlebags; the horses were given a portion of Hurricane's ration of grain. Then, at Prospero's urging, they walked slowly away from the site of their late reunion.

"I've never felt fearful in these hinterlands, nor had reason to, yet I'm apprehensive," said the Prince. "There's a safer place for us all to rest. Dewar, I know thy sorcery's drained thee; an thou canst sleep a-horseback, Hurricane will bear thee."

Dewar stretched, his joints creaking and snapping. "I can walk a ways," he said.

Prospero nodded, and so they went.

The resting-place was four hours' plod distant, in grey-skied darkness, through the hillocked desert and the dry grassland that fringed it. No visible blaze marked the route, but Prospero guided them confidently through the waste, leading Hurricane. Dewar stumbled from time to time, and Freia walked by him and lent him her shoulder to steady him. The horses Epona and Torrent trailed behind, lag-footed, but willing to follow Hurricane from habit.

There were no clear-cut roads to or from Argylle; tracks, paths, streambeds, and sometimes no marks at all on the landscape showed their direction. The grassland was a thin band where Prospero led them across; it sloped up steeply, broken by black, glossy lines of outcropping rock, to scrubby trees and thin-leaved, resilient bushes. The slope came to a peak, and the other side, less steep and wetter-smelling, held fewer bushes, larger trees, lusher grass, and none of the linear outcrops. There Prospero stopped to make a light at the top of his staff. Color returned to the world, the trees' long dark-olive needles and red-veined black bark startling the monochrome-lulled eye. Long, black, columnar shadows swayed and fell back drunkenly as he guided them onward.

Freia paced along steadily, nearly light-footed, and Prospero's staff swung in time to his longer steps. Dewar concentrated on getting there, pushing through bushes and slogging up hills. He felt himself to be dangerously overtired; he reached, with his sorcerer's senses, for the Fire of Landuc's Well to sustain him, and could not fasten on it, yet he would not demand respite of Prospero. When at last, at a mud-daubed log hut, Prospero said, "Here 'tis," Dewar went in and lay down without speaking. A single long sigh, and his body slumped on the hard-packed dirt floor.

"Asleep already," Freia said, and adjusted his cloak around him. He had slept in the instant.

"Aye," her father said. He touched her head, stroked it. "Puss, make up a fire. I'll see to the horses. Thou'rt showing wear thyself."

"You sleep too, Papa. You don't look well."

" 'Tis worry wears me. Let it not weary thee. Sleep." He kissed her and went out.

Freia built and lit the fire on the rough stone hearth and waited for Prospero to come back, gnawing her grimy fingernails, dozing and starting herself awake. She trembled from time to time, exhaustion's grip, but refused to rest until she knew he was indeed still with them. She had not seen him for so long—three years in Argylle and then the uncounted captivity in Landuc—that she had forgotten parts of him, how angry he could become, and how suddenly calm. Her head clamored with things she had to say, though she was too tired to tell her father anything now. It would be enough that he was there. Anyway, Dewar, even sleeping, was an intruder, and she wanted to talk to Prospero alone, at home in the evening firelight after supper, so Freia held her words in and looked forward to the time when she could let them out.

Returning, Prospero was unsurprised to find her waking and forebore to chide her. He smoothed her tangled hair again. "Time to rest," he told her softly.

She nodded, another tired shiver running through her.

They shook out their cloaks without speaking again and lay down, and Prospero put her between him and dreamless Dewar, thinking to keep her warmer so.

Under the spreading, clogged canopy of the forest, as they rode on together, toward and away in every step, Freia's mood lightened; Prospero's darkened. Dewar rode between them on the invisible track that Prospero followed, watching his father's straight back. Prospero had his sword again, the blood-stained one he'd surrendered to Gaston on the battlefield; Dewar wondered briefly how he'd gotten it, and concluded that either it had been returned to the Prince in Landuc or Prospero had purloined it somehow. The sorcerer shrugged and looked around him.

These were old trees; the forest ground was free of undergrowth beneath them, with a scattering of delicate greenery over many years' accumulation of dead needles. The smallest trunks might be circled by three men's arms; the largest were four times as large, or larger, silently alive and thriving on their own litter. There were no branches protruding from the trunks for most of their height, or so it appeared; only a few bright green tufts dotted the rough black bark far below the radiating boughs that interwove between the trees. Prospero was leading them along a slope, swerving up or down around the trees, trying to neither climb nor descend. From time to time their steps coincided with deer-trails, but there was nothing else: no cuttings, no gradings, no human mark on the wood.

Prospero rode half-attentively, choosing their way by instinct and habit, the greater part of his thoughts fixed resolutely on the future. Despite his defeat in war, he had thus far been able to conceal Argylle's location and its nature from the Emperor Avril, but on his return to Landuc he might no longer be able to do so: the bargain he had made to free his daughter demanded he yield all. Therefore Argylle's defensibility must be assured. He did not mean to allow Landuc to have the Spring; in all honesty he could make a case for it being impossible, leading inevitably to the mutual destruction of the realms, of vast Pheyarcet and the Spring's small environs. But Avril, who understood nothing more of sorcery than a trained organ-grinding monkey understood of harmony, could not be relied upon to see this distinction. Prospero considered the grim possibilities of this and planned.

Dewar rode preoccupied by the problem of the Well. He could sense its hot pulse here, weak and distant, ebbing exponentially as they travelled away from it: a disturbing, dizzy sensation, now that he attended to it. It had been stronger in the desert area, strong enough to support his Summoning Prospero; here, it was only a trace of itself, a memory of what it might have been at one time. This Spring of Prospero's, he surmised, banished the Well. The antithetical Sources, Water and Fire, could not meet or mix. Could it be, Dewar posited to himself, that only the Well's present unnaturally quiet state (which had prevailed since King Panurgus's death) permitted the Spring to arise and flourish? They were undoubtedly now in an area that had once been only the Well's, though the Well had been but a small presence here, its power withdrawn inward by Panurgus to sustain the inner realm and leaving a vacuum-like waste at this outer edge of Pheyarcet, not unlike the artificial Limen dividing the Well's Pheyarcet from the Stone of Morven's Phesaotois. Dewar could not perceive the Spring, but he began reckoning, recasting old formulae and equations in his mind, and soon he saw nothing of the wood around him, wholly self-absorbed.

Freia rode or walked, collecting new spring greens to eat, some distance back from the other two, in such a turmoil of emotion that she could not be sure what she thought or felt. She was happy to be going home, truly home to stay, with her father, at last. The enormous joy she had felt when Prospero appeared still reverberated in her heart. Yet her joy was dulled by manifold griefs: by her anguish at having caused him such trouble, by the terror and misery his wrath had struck into her, and by her own private burden of woe. His storming frightened her. She had not expected it, had never imagined he might be angry with her for escaping Landuc, for returning home, for finding him. She ought to have stayed in Landuc and waited for him, the Emperor's prisoner, but she had been half-maddened by captivity and desperation, and the few words she had had then of Prospero had been inconclusive. She ought to have stayed, she chided herself, she ought to have stayed, and Prospero would have fetched her home soon and she could have found the poisonous fungus she'd craved. She had failed him by mistrusting in his return. How could she have thought he would not return for her? Now she could not remember what he had said, what she had said, when he had seen her in the Palace; she remembered only that he had been curt, and that she had wanted to go home with him so much that her heart might have burst. Prospero had gone, and had not come again; Dewar had come, and she had gone with Dewar.

Now Dewar rode before her, at times beside Prospero, at times behind him. Prospero wanted him to come home with them to Argylle. This too bewildered Freia—despite the help he'd given her, Dewar was a foreigner, one of the Landuc people of whom Prospero had always spoken so harshly. What would he do there? When would he leave her father's side, so that she could talk to Prospero alone and tell him of her journey with her gryphon, tell him what violent Golias had done, and be comforted? She tried to imagine Dewar in the cave with them and failed; it was their place, not his. There were two chairs, two beds, two goblets. She and Prospero, she decided, would go there and have supper, and after supper it would be cool enough for a fire (for spring season was still young), so they would sit together at the hearth. . . . Freia gazed at Prospero's blue-cloaked back and dreamt of what they would say.

Utrachet greeted them outside the walls, which were two courses higher than when Freia had last seen them. Prospero sent his son and daughter on ahead to the gate and spoke privately with the Castellan; Freia watched them over her shoulder, afraid Prospero would vanish again.

A light but steady rain had gusted in from the southeast early that morning, now carrying a fresh-earth smell from the ploughed and planted fields. Freia and Dewar left the horses with a woman at the paddock outside the half-built walls and, as Prospero had directed, went through the clumps of mist and rain to the stone house above the river where they had stopped before.

In a flat, beaten-down grassed area within the walls, a whirling vortex of naked and near-naked children played some game of speed or pursuit. Distracted by the arrival of the travellers, the vortex broke into confused eddies, coalesced briefly into staring faces, and then, with a few high-pitched shrieks, began moving again after they had passed. People Dewar didn't know greeted them both in the strange local language, sober as if Prospero's mood had already touched everyone; Freia returned the greetings soft-voiced, almost shy, and answered questions scantly or not at all.

She had nothing to say to Dewar, either, as they waited for Prospero together. Dewar took a book from his bag and sat near a window, reading. Freia looked out the window, but there was only the scaffolding and walls; the rain and mist hid the forest, so she sat with her head on her folded arms, her eyes on Dewar without watching him. Prospero himself joined the two, in the low-roofed upper room with the long table, as they were brought a cold luncheon by two young women. With a nod, he accepted the wine his daughter poured for him. She poured for Dewar too after a moment's hesitation.

The rain thinned as they ate, then halted. The wind backed to the northwest, dried, and began to break the clouds and scatter them.

"There's no ground to delay the blow," Prospero said when he had picked at a platter of meat and a plate of winter-kept fruit and cheese. "This night I'll accomplish what be needful and on the morrow hie to Landuc with—"

"Father—" The word tasted so odd that Dewar had to stop after saying it.

It was odd to Prospero too; they stared at one another a moment before both smiled with embarrassment.

"I read that treaty," he went on, his smile fading. "I wondered how you intended to comply with it."

"I've sworn already. Shall kindle a bonfire of books and trinkets, fine instruments o' the Art and sorcerer's toys," Prospero said gruffly.

Dewar nodded and steeled himself. "I don't mean to be impertinent, sir, but it seems a terrible waste that all your life's work be destroyed," he said, and caught a look from Freia: startled and grateful.

"I cannot call it all," replied Prospero; "I have left to me what would make, should make, *shall* make a lesser man content enough."

"Papa, don't," Freia said. "You love your books. All you do is sorcery."

"Have told thee not to speak of't, baggage."

"Father," said Dewar, hoping the storm rumbling in Prospero's voice could be averted, "all know you to be the Master of Elements, of Elementals; none has ever approached your knowledge of the subject. That so much of learning, of your original, definitive work, be cast away, is—"

" 'Tis the terms of my vow!" Prospero shouted, pounding the table and addressing them both, "and I'll not hear another word from you!"

Dewar held his tongue. Freia, to her brother's surprise, did not.

"Papa," she said in her sweetest, smallest voice, and got up and went around the table to him. She put her arms around his broad shoulders, her cheek against his hair.

He growled, "Cease this; thy pity strangles me."

"Papa," Freia repeated. "Could one or two books not be forgotten?"

"Nay," he said curtly.

"A few pages?"

"Nay."

"Suppose I took away—"

"Nay."

"Papa, you are difficult to help." She hugged him.

He drummed his fingers and then patted her arm. "And thou'rt a stubborn and persistent wench." Further surprising Dewar, the Prince looked up at his daughter, fond, not angry, and squeezed her hand. "Nay. It cannot be, child. I have given my word; I have told thee greater ill should follow, harm to thee belike and thy brother, and I be forsworn, and I shall not be forsworn. Thy scheming's for naught, but kindly meant, and kindly taken."

Dewar saw his moment and spoke. "What about copying," he said softly.

"Na—" Prospero began, and Freia looked up, wide-eyed.

"Of course! A copy's not the original," said she. "Papa, is it not so? You didn't say—"

"Silence," he commanded her, and removed her arms from his neck. She sat beside him. " 'Pon my honor I'll be harried to death by you, a brace of cannibal hounds," he said after a moment, glaring at her and then at Dewar. "Shall I rend out my lights and liver, and—"

"Prospero," Dewar said, "if it is your preference that all your lore be forever lost, so be it. But I'd ward it well and it would not be forgotten, a life's labor wasted, if you give me what you deem the most important parts and let me copy them. Surely there's time for some. I shortened your journey hither by Summoning you."

Prospero's glare did not drop, but the expression in his eyes altered slightly.

"Prospero, it is your very life's work I would preserve. Would I ask otherwise? No. It is an exceptional idea, for an exceptional time, a time no one would ever have thought we might see, when an honorable sorcerer is robbed of his sorcery by an Art-blind clerk's cheat! Yet still you have a will, Prospero, and you can thwart Avril's theft in a small way."

Prospero studied him, his son, his heir in more vital ways than his daughter. The notion of letting the boy even look at the books was to be vigorously, instantly denied, and yet—it was truly not Prospero's will that they be burned. Better to burn them than let them fall to Oriana's hands, or Esclados's. But his son, his own son—his daughter was worthless for sorcery; she must have an earthier destiny—he was an able young fellow, and disliked Avril, and his alliance would be useful. And Prospero's pride reminded him that sorcery comparable to his would likely never be seen again in this age of the world, and why not let his name live on, in some small way?

"So be't," he said.

Dewar breathed again, his head pounding with disbelief.

"Come with me instanter," Prospero said, rising, "for there's but scant time for such a labor as thou shalt have. Come. Son," he added, glancing back, and Dewar jumped up, and followed him out.

Freia watched them go.

Pens, ink, paper, lamp, and words.

Prospero had selected the texts for Dewar to copy. Dewar, surreptitiously browsing when the Prince had left him, gleaned a few others Prospero hadn't indicated. The places were marked

with slips of paper, the books piled on the floor and table beside the sorcerer, and now Dewar wrote.

Oh, the books were beautiful; at first he wasted minutes at a
time raging silently at their imminent loss. Prospero's life-work,
centuries of sorcerous research and information collected from
other sorcerers, was set out in neat, legible, unvarying pen-
work. He had employed the Art in dozens of disciplines, and
as Dewar comprehended the scope of his father's erudition, his
respect for the man grew, as did his pain at the loss of so much
knowledge. Among the books of sorcery which Dewar could
not copy were anatomical dissections, physiological treatises,
herbals; books of medicine and music and cookery, books of
venery and poetry and trade; building-plans, geographies, ce-
lestial and oceanic charts; scores of volumes treating every
branch of the Art; and the books were only a part of the whole
treasure. Dewar looked at, but dared not touch, ingenious devices of polished brass and steel, gems glinting in their oiled
works, stored under crystal domes; draped circles and ovals on
the walls, which must be Mirrors for Summonings and Ways;
a pair of disused orreries, high on the shelves, enamelled in
brilliant colors, their sharp-edged hoops and lines blurred by
dust; stacked trays of crystal lenses and metal lozenges and
disks; four sturdy scales and their sets of brass weights; shelves
of bottles, crocks, jars, and boxes, with neat-written paper la-
bels naming each herb, distillation, or unguent contained
therein.

Dewar did open cautiously one slender drawer in an ebony
cabinet of uncountable drawers, from thumb-sized to large bins
at the bottom, for it was unlocked, unwarded. In the drawer lay
shells, hundreds of pale spindle-shaped sea-shells, and as he
closed it in puzzlement he saw that each drawer was labelled
with a tarnished silver plate. He opened another and held the
light near it, first glancing over his shoulder. *Cyclones, Aesti-
val,* these: conical brown-and-cream spiralled shells, their ends
stoppered with red wax. Another drawer held *Clouds, Cumu-
lus, Autumnal, Nocturnal:* small mussels, thumbnail-sized and

mated, moon-white on one paired edge, fading through indigo to black at the other. *Zephyrs; Boreal Blizzards; Sciroccos; Fair Sunsets; Wet Dawns:* tiny winkles, each differently striped and scratched; spiny white whelks, colder than ice to the fingertip's touch; large fat sand-brown land-snails, near-meaningfully scribbled in white; tight-closed whole scallops, stained every hue from palest gold to dark storm-crimson; thumbprint-sized cowries, polished to watery purple, their toothed mouths, like the rest, sealed with red wax. Dewar moved away reluctantly; then he turned, and looked again at the first drawer, just to know. *Clouds, Cirrostratus, Vernal, Diurnal.*

His heart aching with envy and admiration, he sat down to work.

Though the sorcery books on the table were but Prospero's own pick of the harvest, meagre to compare, yet they were rich beyond Dewar's dreams. There were clean, precise diagrams in dozens of colors. There were doodles here and there in the margins, which proved to be not doodles but miniature notated force-diagrams, Prospero's innovation which Dewar despaired of duplicating. Prospero hadn't stayed to watch his son work, and so Dewar could not ask him about the diagrams he imperfectly understood. He copied them as well as he could, deciding not to waste time puzzling over them now, and his pen raced on across the pages. Freia brought him food and smoky, stimulating tea. He thanked her the first three or four times, spoke to her, and then forgot her; the food appeared, the plates vanished, the pots of tea refilled themselves, and Dewar saw nothing but black ink looping, rising, falling on white leaves.

Scudamor and Utrachet were counting swords, bows, and arrows, armor, spears, and shields, setting aside the damaged ones. All had been stacked helter-skelter in an old thatch-roofed long-house usually used for winter food storage, dumped there by the remains of Prospero's army and untouched since. Prospero had commanded that the weapons be set in good order for use again, and thus these two were picking through splintering pikes, nicked swords, and shields with broken straps. All the Argylle-made weapons that they had brought with them had been taken in Landuc on Prospero's surrender; these were mostly things that had been seized by the prisoners when they escaped from Perendlac.

Freia wanted a bow, and so she found her way to the warehouse where the Seneschal and the Castellan were taking inventory. She hesitated in the doorway, but Scudamor saw her and smiled at her.

"Welcome, Lady," he said. "How may we serve you?" When the Seneschal spoke, Utrachet turned from a basket of vexatious arrows which had been forty-six and forty-nine the first two times he'd counted them; he smiled and bowed as well.

"What are you doing with the bows and swords?" she asked.

"Lord Prospero commands that they be tallied," Utrachet said. "He wishes to know how many there are of each thing."

"There is only one of each thing," Scudamor said, "but of each class of thing, there are many."

"Twig-splitting," said Utrachet; Scudamor laughed. "Lady, I'll guess you desire a bow."

"How did you guess that?" Freia wondered, tipping her head to one side and eyeing the bows that hung on the wall.

"Because you have none," he said, grinning, "and it's turned fine bright weather for the hunt."

"I have lost my good crossbow," she said, not smiling. "They took it from me, in Landuc, and I need a bow of light pull, because my arms are grown watery in idleness." She crouched in front of a basket of arrows and began taking them out one by one, squinting along them.

Scudamor nodded. "It is an evil place," he said. "May we never hear of it again."

"Prospero thinks we shall," Utrachet said, "and for that we must have the walls around us."

"I don't like those walls," Freia said, pushing aside the arrow-basket. "They shut things out. There is nothing here to shut out, or in, not like Landuc, where they have only walls; everyone in

Landuc is shut out, or in. These are poor arrows."

"They are from Landuc," said Utrachet. "There are some of our own arrows, Lady, somewhere in this burrow; and the bow I made that Miruin's daughter got too tall to use."

"Utrachet told me of the walls in Landuc," Scudamor said. "Our walls will be better."

"There are no good walls," Freia disagreed, standing.

"Ours have doors in them," said Scudamor firmly. "And they are made well."

"We don't need walls," said Freia. "Please show me Sherlon's bow and the arrows. I am going to hunt something for Prospero for supper."

They went all three to the back of the warehouse, and among a clutter of discarded children's bows and tools Utrachet found Sherlon's bow, which Freia tested; the string snapped, so they found a new bowstring for it, and Scudamor rummaged out a basket of shorter Argylle hunting-arrows. Freia chose sixteen, put them in an oiled leather quiver, and thanked Scudamor and Utrachet for finding them and the bow. The bow was a lighter pull than she wanted, but it would do for small game, and small game was all she meant to take. She had already provided herself with a knife and a net, some thongs and a water-bottle, and thus kitted she set off for the forest.

Utrachet and Scudamor returned to their counting. Utrachet's arrows were forty-seven, and he tagged them so and turned to arrowheads.

"The Lady's much altered," Scudamor said in an undertone to a tangle of bowstrings.

"It is that place, Landuc," Utrachet said. "It changed us all that were there."

"You, not."

"Yes, me too: for now I know that to be a pard in Argylle is better than to be a man in Landuc, and to be a man in Argylle is the sum of joy. But it is a hard way to get wisdom. She has changed. Lord Prospero must mend her. All changes in his hands."

Freia's path took her past a pack of children excitedly building rock-and-mud walls in the dirt, which walls meandered and ambled without closing on themselves. They sat back on their heels and looked at her, nudging one another; Freia glanced at them and one of the older, less-shy ones piped, "Best of the day to you, Lady."

It caught her off-guard; she said, "Thank you—keep well," and hurried on. The children nonplussed her, as ever; she didn't know what to say to the bigger ones, although the smaller ones, carried about and petted and cuddled, were more approachable, though given to alarming noises and incomprehensible demands. But playing in the mud was difficult to understand as well. What was the point of it? Had she played in the mud the way the Argylle children did, modelling buildings and walls with sticks and soil? She didn't remember it. What would it be like to be so small, a suckling grub, and to become larger? She could not conceive of being other than she was. Her earliest memories were green and quiet, looking into grass, at flowers, at insects, studying the shapes of leaves; in the background ran Prospero's voice, a comforting wordless bass rumble. The Argylle children always seemed to be running everywhere, imitating the adults, giggling and rolling about like cubs and pups, engaged in enjoyable but alien play.

Crossing the puddled, bare-dirt square, passing the roofed-over fountain in the middle, she caught Prospero's eye, and he shouted at her from the staging where he was talking to some nearly naked, grimy men from the wall-crews. Freia hesitated, and Prospero waved at her impatiently: Come here, she guessed, and so she changed her path and stood at the bottom of the staging. Prospero, cloakless, wearing a padded, plain vest over a smoke-blue shirt with its laced sleeves rolled above his elbows, climbed down a ladder from the top of the wall.

"Now whither goest thou," said he, his hands on his hips, looking down at her.

"Hunting."

"Did I not say to thee, tend thy brother as he writes?"

"I made him ink and tea, and he has paper," Freia said. "He needs nothing more."

Prospero shook his head. "His work beareth great weight of consequence; thy sport's but petty play thereto. Go thou, stay his wants, however trifling they be they're of much moment to us now."

"Papa, please, I do promise I'll be gone only the day—"

"No larking i' the wood for thee! Not today, not these twelve most precious days to come. Let nothing stay his hand from its work of preservation! Be thou devoted to his progress only. I enjoin thee, put by thy unmaidenly pursuits and be a true lady; serve him, forgo thy toys and whims. So would Lady Miranda do; so would I have thee do as well."

Freia shifted from one foot to the other. Protest was useless; she knew Prospero's tone of finality and command. No appeal would move him.

"Freia?"

"Very well, Papa," she said, low-voiced, and turned away, walked toward the clutter of coracles and rafts, to row one over the water to the island. She was dazed, in a fresh turmoil of confusion and unfathomable pain. What did Prospero want of her? When she passed a group of women with baskets and babies going out to sow seeds in the fields, one of them, Dazhur, greeted her merrily and begged her to come with them, but Freia shook her head, called back "I may not," and went on to the boats.

There on the riverbank she paused a moment, struck by a thought that had not before occurred to her: she could not have had supper with Prospero in their cozy cave, as she had so wanted to do. Prospero had removed most of the furnishings from there—everything but his sorcery books and tools, and the heavy table and chairs—to the square stone house on the mainland, and now Dewar was in the cave, copying the books. She had not brought him there when they had come to Argylle together the first time: Prospero had, now.

Rowing, a sudden spasm of startling anger boiled up in her,

and she thought to throw the bow and arrows into the river outside the framework of hide and wood; but she still had them
when she arrived at the cave where Dewar looked only at the
book and paper before him. She dropped Sherlon's bow and the
arrows in a corner.

Three of the women she'd just seen were round-bellied with
children. Still she had not had an opportunity to tell Prospero
about what Golias had done to her, nor about what she had
done to herself in the strange place Dewar had taken her: the
memory of it all felt nearly like a delirious dream, now, but she
knew it had been no dream, and that she carried no other legacy
from Golias than that of nightmare. The marks on her body
were gone, except for the scar across her chest, which would
fade. Freia sat down outside the cave, against the rock face,
clasped her knees with her arms, and crept her thoughts away
from the chasms of pain and fear that riddled them.

On the third day, Freia found her brother asleep and left him
there. She went to Prospero, who had accelerated the work on
the city walls and other structures and was rushing about, over-
seeing the construction.

"Papa, how long should Dewar sleep?"

"Sleep?" repeated Prospero. "Doth *sleep*?"

"His head's on a book and his eyes are closed. I think he's
asleep."

"Sooth, 'less 'a learns the book by osmosis. Wake him; can
sleep when 'tis finished. When I'm finished," Prospero added
in an undertone. "Wake him; give him tile-tree leaves, a de-
coction of a handful in a quart of water boiled to half-a-pint.
The white crock on the third shelf, behind the tall blue cordial-
bottles."

She nodded. "Yes, Papa. I want to talk to you about something tonight—"

"Puss, needs must finish these walls. I've a mind they'll be
needed."

"After dinner—" Freia began, in a small voice.

"Freia, thou hast no sense of time," Prospero snapped; "the hours are precious, and there'll be none beyond to accomplish what I must do now. I'll sup as I work, with the men. Go thou, mind thy brother's pen moves on; 'tis vital to us as these walls."

"But I—"

"Art deaf? He dallies in dream as we speak! *Go!*"

Freia went.

HARVEST-TIME HAD COME TO AïË.

Seed-heavy golden grasses nodded on the slopes below the ideally proportioned temple, where Odile of Aïë lived with such attendants as pleased her. Yellow and scarlet leaves flashed bright, then dried to crackling brown, fluttering on the branches and twigs of the mauve-grey thickets around the cleared lands. The pigs that lived in the forests rooted urgently for nuts and fungi and anything edible, knowing that the fair days would soon end, that the season of cold and fear would soon be on them, when they'd become winter food to their fellow-woodlings, the wolves of Aïë, running before teeth that would slice hamstring and slash throat. Smaller prey was hard to find in Aïë in the snow; most of the lesser animals hibernated or hid themselves well from the wolves. Hart and hind dined on the years's late bounty too, desperately, and mated and danced and fought in full knowledge that the wolves' jaws might tear throat and belly in a month's time. Stags whetted their antlers on stones.

In the fields, cattle dragged sheaf-laden travois through the stubble toward the low, thatch-roofed stone barns. Other cattle were lifting the sheaves from the field and loading the travois that returned empty from the barn. Among all the animals, a lone human figure could be seen, a bent young-looking woman whose task it was to bind the sheaves; she labored blank-eyed with weariness, but not daring to rest, gathering the scattered stalks and tying them with a straw twist, stooping and straightening, again and again, her arms criss-crossed with red: the marks of her mistress's displeasure. The grain was cut by horses pulling awkward mowing blades, like scythes on clumsy roughrounded wheels. Some of the more agile dogs supervised this work and helped with the sharpening, running on a treadmill that drove the grindstone to sharpen the wheeled scythe.

The shepherd-dogs began keeping the sheep closer to the fold at night and watched them jealously during the day: counting. Two of the rams, newcomers comprehending for the first time the full scope of their condition, attempted to break away. They killed three dogs before being pulled down themselves, and the wolves watched from the undergrowth and laughed.

From the steps of the temple, from time to time, one of the white-gowned maids might gaze over at the laboring beasts, but dared say no word to any. On the mistress's errands, the maids came and went, sometimes (but rarely) beyond the bounds of Aië itself. From time to time in any season, the mistress, Odile herself, might walk abroad at twilight, followed by her white maiden-fowl, and the animals would fawn and kneel, trembling with their fear: it was ill with them, true, but they knew it could be worse. The wolves would come from the forest then, and the coarse-bristled swine and the deer, and all of them would bow to her and quiver beneath her gaze. She was capricious. Sometimes she selected one and changed it again: wolf to sheep, pig to dog, hart to man (oh, brief, happy reprieve, worsening the affliction) to hart again, or to cow or ass or anything that pleased her, that day, that hour.

She changed many of them afresh after the sorcerer swept away from Aië again on his black horse that was no less than a true horse. Each creature in those days knew greater dread than before; a chained dog became a chained bear, and the yellow-eyed wolves tore it apart as she watched, perhaps amused, and played further games with her subjects, bestowing and removing favors whimsically, unpredictably. Some had (the few survivors) memories of her rages many years ago when the cold-eyed sorcerer had left the temple after his long sojourn, but more recalled the night that the sorceress's son had fled Aië, and of the punishments visited on them after, conspirator and innocent alike. The maids had had more liberty in those days, and one had whispered to a spit-dog, who had told the other dogs, who'd told the sheep and cattle and a wolf, who'd spread word in the wood, that the boy might free them all someday: their only chance. When the boy, joining their number for a few days, had stood transformed, chained and terrified, they had despaired, every soul, but Odile had relented and in the end the boy escaped her. The panting wolves had lagged in their pursuit; he had outrun the deer, and had taken refuge in a thorn-thicket impossible for even the strongest boar to penetrate. For that, they had all suffered.

Now the tall sorcerer had come and gone again, and Odile was restless, her cruelties quicker and cruder than usual. The subjects of Aië abased themselves before her and received her anger on dumb, but not insensible, heads. Through the summer she shut herself away in her sanctum, dedicated to her sorcery, brooding indolence displaced by passion-fed activity.

She transformed various of them to horses, then back again, seeking some particular look. At last two suited her. A maid worked in the stables, grooming the horses and preparing their tack and a little-used high-wheeled black phaeton. The maid said nothing, but they all knew: Odile was going to travel. None of them could recall such a thing happening before. Odile never left Aië, her seat of power and pride, had never stirred from the precincts of her black-pillared temple from the hour of her possessing it and gathering its forces in her hands. Never, indeed, did she leave, until one night, in the hour before moonrise, she swept down the wide steps and stepped into the carriage held by the maid and took up the reins of the two black horses. A ball of fire followed her, lighting her way. The beasts crept forward on their bellies, bowing in farewell. The sorceress turned and her fingertips grazed the head of the silent maid who had prepared the carriage and horses: now a bird bobbed away from the carriage and crouched with the others.

Odile of Aië stung the horses with her whip and set out on the Road.

Dewar's pen moved on. On his surrender, Prospero had gotten eighteen days from the Emperor, concerned not so much to complete his vow as to complete his walls. The Prince had reckoned eight days' travel from the Palace to the Spring, six days to work and one to burn the books, and then three to return to Landuc by leaving the Spring's domain at a desperate pace and opening a Way as soon as he'd entered the Well's influence. Then, by the terms of his surrender, would Prospero be at the Emperor's command, stripped of earthly wealth and sorcerous power and every title save that inalienable one of Panurgus's son. But Dewar had Summoned him less than a day into his journey back to Argylle, they had spent another three going from the desert to the city, and thus Prospero had twelve days to build his walls, Dewar twelve days to copy his father's words and save what he could from the fire.

The tile-tree leaves kept him bolt-awake. His hand cramped and he sent Freia for hot water and a towel to rub it back to flexibility. He sent her for cold water, too, to splash on his face. At his curt, preoccupied commands she mixed ink for him and found more pens, filled the lamps and trimmed their wicks, gathered all the paper and parchment there was in Argylle, sharpened quills, and bound the loose pages together with red thread when he handed her a stack saying "This is done."

Freia said nothing more to him than "Ink," "Tea," or "Here." From the shore of the island, where Dewar scratched away in the cave where she'd once lived with Prospero alone, she watched as Prospero's walls rose and trees were felled, conspicuously idle in a beehive of industry. She said nothing to Utrachet or Scudamor either, the few times she saw them, nor to anyone else. The whole population of Argylle was an army of workers obeying Prospero's commands, digging, raising, lowering, chopping, chiseling; the work went on night and day, drums beating and pulley-crews chanting, and the walls went up.

On the seventh day of the twelve, they began felling trees on the island. Freia flew at Prospero, argued with him furiously, and was hotly rebuffed. Father and daughter didn't speak to one another after that, and Prospero oversaw the building of the walls with trees from his island as his son scribbled on, oblivious of the alterations around him. Freia had slept outdoors on the island, under a favorite tree; now she slept in the cave, outside the sphere of Dewar's lamplight, in the corner where her bed had stood before Prospero had moved the beds out to the first house he had had his men build on the mainland.

A curious alchemy began to work on Freia. The pressure of Prospero's changes heated her sad heart and aching soul, reforming the pain there to the first true anger she had ever felt. She seethed with hot energy, but, confined to the island to serve Dewar, could do nothing, could not run through the dark forest and cool herself with distance and exercise, so she sat pulled into a clenched knot and raged within. She could not be angry at Prospero; he was the primum mobile of her existence. She could not be angry at Dewar; was he not helping Prospero, had he not helped her as well? Thus she directed her anger at the Argyllines, who did Prospero's bidding and ravaged her world and changed it. Prospero had made them, but they were intruders and aliens who did not belong; and left with nothing to hate but them, Freia hated them as well as she could: which was not very satisfying and not very well done, by the standards set in Landuc, but sufficed to disturb her peace and make her unhappy and ill.

She slept in wrath and awoke wrathful, and her brother sat staring red-eyed at the books and papers, writing like a madman at the table she and her father had used for every meal, for cutting cloth, for counting seeds, for kneading bread, for her lessons, for everything, for years.

Dewar was blind to all save books and words. He had no means to follow the time, and so he wrote as if every page he turned might be the last he'd see of the knowledge his father had spent a lifetime assembling. But it never was; he turned page after page and wrote page after page and the time passed word by word.

The flyleaf of the book said, in Prospero's neat hand, "On the Quickening of Life in the Inanimate. Toward the Reshaping of the Animate (after the manner of Aië)."

This book was one that Dewar had added to the pile himself, after Prospero had left him; the word "Aië" had caught his eye, and he began looking through it furtively to find what Prospero said of the place. Freia never looked at what he had written, so he did not think she would notice; and Prospero had not returned since he had left him to the copying.

His eye strayed on the words *to shape a human form* and he was caught.

It was a journal, of a sort, written in tight-clustered lines; scattered throughout were references to other notebooks by number. He flipped to the beginning.

In this book I note effects of mine early efforts in creating a folk native to this place to dwell and serve here.

I. Caliban (added later, in a darker ink)

That man is shaped of mortal matter is evident for in decay the Elements sunder; to Water and Earth, Air and Fire being lost with the breath and spark of life. Moreover the infant man is shaped in the womb of what matter the woman taketh in, thus be she starved so be her offspring, and be she well-nourished so be the issue taken of her body and of her body made.

Yet man is ill-shapen for many things and I would have a more durable and essential creature here, thus have I worked in stone and clay, made a creature man-shaped and infused it with a Sammead.

It moveth well through earth and upon it, but lacketh much wit, being dull and cowardly, and though it be strong and easily bent to my will I do not deem it a success, for it cannot bear the full light of the sun. Moreover its appearance is loathsome to me, which I regret mightily, my sculpting of its form being indifferently done. It hath a great terror of water for which I cannot account. Yet it labors unceasingly once compelled to do so, though its labor of necessity be done in dark of night or deepest shade. I do not consider this creature much good and I shall destroy it when I have made some further study of it.

Dewar skimmed onward, past Prospero's observations of the creature's behavior.

Though I am still dissatisfied with Caliban I have found it to be of great use to me. It delveth most excellent well and I therefore set it to enlarge my cell here to more commodious aspect. That accomplished well and to my satisfaction I have made it understand the pattern of the works within the earth which it was my intention to shape with sorcery. The creature's digging and burrowing are so fluently done as to suit it right well for this labor, and I have ordered it to commence thereon.

What works within the earth? Interesting. Dewar made a note in his mind to investigate this, and paged onward.

Caliban continues his labors below. Quarrels with Ariel when they encounter. Disaffinity of Earth and Air.

Well, but that was obvious, thought Dewar; any apprentice would have guessed it. Caliban wasn't terribly interesting. Where were the Prince's notes on Aië? He flicked pages.

My discontent is great enough to have set me to another attempt. His surly nature ill-pleaseth me and other things (not least his uncomely shape), therefore shall I next attempt to form a female being, which shall be more tractable and docile as females are. I take a different approach (see notes in Vol CL) which is slower to show result but perhaps better suited. My own haste hath undermined my building of Caliban; this creature will I better make.

Dewar stared at this passage, which was boldly written at the top of a page, as if Prospero had turned over a new leaf and begun this thought fresh. A female shape. Sweat pricked Dewar's hands. He turned pages, reading a few lines on each.

The skeleton is complete. I must use greener wood for the ribs; felled the smaller apple tree and bent its wood thereto, steaming and forming them; truly Water is ever the means by which Earth is shaped, more so than Air.

[. . .]

Today the fourth failure in carving the jaw. It goeth ever awry in my hands.

[. . .]

A coating of beeswax to the joints was all that was lacking to the skull; it regardeth me now from the dresser, its jaw at rest from all my work. The wax maketh the movement of the jaw smooth and natural. I am pleased.

[. . .]

The preliminary experiments on the clay and sand are ill-ended. I must find other matter to work with, some better way of fleshing the bones. Cragiolo by his evidence did use human flesh fresh-killed. I mislike it; and had I men to slay for the work I need not undertake it. Animal flesh?

[. . .]

Today's labor's a most repulsive carcase-mess, half-animate and corrupt, that I needs must blast with fire. Animal flesh serveth not; for the base essence of the creatures lingereth. It must be done with clay.

[. . .]

A fool was I not to think of it, but Cragiolo's errors misled me; his notes seem to show blood as much a culprit in his early failures as dead flesh, but 'twas blood alone kept his works from utter barrenness. This morn I did admix as much of mine own blood as I dared let into the white earth, reddening it; 'twas not sufficient and I put a deep entrancement on a young gryphon that hath harried the horses earlier, then bled the beast for the rest. It is but a small portion and it will do no harm as my blood dominates, and as the beast is an admixture of Earth and Air it will provide reconciliation of the two, which do not naturally compound. A fine dovetailing of purposes in circumstance.

The wet clay cannot be let to dry; I have worked rapidly and as nicely as I could and shaped and placed the organs and vessels of the body in the cavities, then molded muscles and flesh on the skeleton, exerting all my skill to shape a human form. I did not care to make the creature barenobbed and bald-felled as Caliban, and so I pressed grasses to the body for hair.

I must rest an hour or two before the sun rises and I take the final step.

It went most excellent well. I am pleased; at least, no flaws can I see. As noted the body stirred as I infused it with vitality; the transformation to flesh was uncanny to see, coming from within the torso and not from the extremities as I had looked for. The blood-clay paled and flushed with the color of live flesh, first over-ruddy and then full natural; I waited until the hands and feet were ready and then drew the body from the Spring where I had submerged it as described in Vol CLXIII. It did not breathe. Fearing failure after such success I knelt to test whether breath stirred; there was no breath nor pulse. I seized the head and moved it back to open the passages, then blew past lips clay-cold and dead to inspire life as is done to new-born babes and the drowned.

The breath took; the creature—she?—trembled once mightily, gasped, and her lips touched mine again as she clutched at air. I saw the eyes move beneath the lids, then open. The pupils shrank at the light. Verily it was a wonder to see them turn in synchrony and fix on me.

I rose and completed the spell; the creature watched me dumbly, bestirring little, beginning to move more surely as I concluded, touching her body. I was full weary when I finished but drew in the Spring's flow to sustain me.

I shaped as fair a creature as I durst, not desiring to make a paragon, yet I observe that in mutation the form hath grown smoother, the lips softer and the eyes' shape somewhat altered, the coloring of the skin delicate and pleasing. The hair hath darkened to a shade not unlike mine own, due I warrant to the dominance of my blood, and hath curled. I cannot account for the curl, but it is a full comely effect.

The creature—she—touched my face when I smiled; the fingers are sensitive and light, and the touch was well-controlled, not clawing or rough. I permitted her to finger my beard, my cheek, my throat and ear, and then she touched her own smooth chin, then mine again, most cunningly and visibly comprehending that we differ. She touched my mouth and then her own, then mine again, parting my lips, parting her own, and her brows came together—a charming expression of perplexity, full human and genuine.

I stroked her hair and forehead, and she leaned to the touch, turning to try to see my hand touching her; I took her chin, examined her face—I erred somewhat, the chin is not symmetrical, though the jaw is small and the cheekbones finely shaped, and the flesh floweth smoothly over them. Her expression was serious and her gaze intent on me. I took her hand and moved its fingers; all articulated perfectly, and the joints of wrist and elbow pivot smoothly and easily within the flesh. I moved her shoulders; she was docile and made no opposition as I circled the arms to be sure the joints were mobile, for that I met such difficulty with the scapulae. There is no impairment. The back is nicely shaped, the spine neat and fine, the throat graceful and the torso handsomely feminine.

I desired to know whether she was able to walk, and thus I stood and, holding her hands, tugged upward. At first she sat, not comprehending, and then looked at my legs, the vague perplexity again upon her brow. I spoke encouragement, but she did not rise, though she flexed her feet. I knelt again to assure myself that her legs would bend, and moved them and her feet and toes and she again was docile and unresisting. Then did I lift her bodily to her legs, and she made a startled cry and swayed, letting her knees bend, would have fallen but that I caught her and supported her. Well: she could not walk, then, and must learn, and so I shifted my hold on her and took her wholly in my arms to carry her forthwith. She was frightened now, whimpering, and grabbed at me as if afraid of falling, and I must soothe and coo to her as to a babe until she was quiet.

I bore her to the cave and set her in the chair, and she would not release me until I had spoken to her gently again; as I spoke she watched my mouth and eyes, the sound reassuring her so that she let me take her arms from my neck. I was famished with hunger by then and must sup, and set honey forth and bread, slicing the bread and spreading the honey, eating without nicety. She watched this—never did she take her eyes from me—and I seeing this dipped my finger in honey and offered it to her, to see what she might make of it. She looked at it; I licked my finger and offered it again to her, touching her lips, and she licked cautiously and then with interest, finding it much to her liking. I sat on the stool beside her to try it again, and she put her fingers in the crock and got a great gob of wax and honey in them.

I did not stop her; she sought to remove her hand, but the neck was too narrow, and so she drew the hand forth without the wax, all coated well with honey now. And then she most violently surprised me: she did offer me her honey-covered hand. Is it possible that a human creature uncultivated, in basest natural state, understands generosity? Or is a human creature by nature generous? 'Tis counter to my observance of the coarser run of man. I thanked her and licked a finger clean, not to fail in courtesy, and then gave her her hand back so that she might lick it herself. This she did, honey dripping on her legs and breast, and I ate more bread and we watched one another the while.

Full weary was I from my long working, for this making hath taken me five days, and I desired to sleep, but must not let her wander alone. Therefore I rose, took a cloth and wet it and wiped the honey from her, then lifted her again. She was not so frightened this time; I set her in the bed I had made in hopes of success enough to need it, where I have kept the bones of the skeleton well-wrapped until they were required, and I laid a sleep over her with the coverlet and now go to mine own rest.

Dewar looked at the corner where Freia had been sleeping as he worked through the nights, sometimes distracting his attention by whimpering or crying out in her dreams. Her bedding was neatly stowed there in a wicker basket, a fur spread over the top.

To have transmuted earth to flesh and living bone . . . Dewar was stunned. He would never have guessed. Prospero had surpassed every sorcerer in the history of the Art. He had constructed an intelligent creature indistinguishable from the natural. He had no need of Aië. Odile was a rank dabbler by comparison. Aië. What said Prospero of Aië? Dewar sought through the text, paused again to read snatches.

He flipped through the close-written pages wherein Prospero told of teaching his creation to speak, to walk, to eat, to bathe. A passage caught his eye:

> . . . then did I say to her, Hast thou a name? And she looked in the glass I had set before us and touched her image, then mine, then her own again. This is Papa, she said, putting her hand over my reflected face. I took her hand and placed it on my head saying, Nay, here is Prospero, that is but the image of him, no real man. Prospero is what I am called, what thou and all others call me. How art thou called?
>
> I did wish to discover, if she hath some sense of name for herself innately.
>
> She said, Child, and I said, Nay, child is but a label for thee, not a name, and I curst myself that I had not addressed this subject with her instanter she could speak somewhat, for she drinketh swift and thirsty of such knowledge as I set before her and thereby hath diluted her original state. Maid, she said, Nay, said I, maid is but a label also. I am Prospero, my name; I am a man, a Prince, a sorcerer. All these are labels save Prospero. I am, she said. I am not-Prospero.
>
> So all that is not Her, is Prospero, and all that is Prospero, is not Her. The self needeth no label for it knoweth all, that which is itself and that which is not itself.
>
> How shall I call thee, then? I ask her. She maketh no answer, as if not comprehending, and beholdeth me owlish, all eyes and ears. 'Twas in my mind to name her Miranda, for Gonzalo's bright daughter, though she's but an irregular, discolored image: yet meseems perhaps 'twere insult, to so use the dearest of names. How to call thee? I ask again, of myself more than her, for she hath no answer, methinks; yet again doth she astonish me, and saith, I am not Prospero, what am I?

Right quickly say I, Thou art thyself, and who art thou?

Freia, says she, and I did not understand at first and said, A maid? And she said, That is a label, I am Freia.

So hath she a name, but I am unsure whence it cometh, or how she knew it, and it is most exhausting to question her, for she learneth apace and betimes giveth answer far distant from the question to my mind.

[. . .]

. . . sensitive to smallest pressures, and though this maketh her biddable and complaisant, she cannot endure displeasure long. An she trespass again, I must have done quickly, and give her comfort anon, lest it canker her tender heart.

Dewar was nearly at the end of the book; the last pages were in his fingers, and the word Aië had not leapt forth at him. His eye rested at the top of the final leaf and he read:

. . . hath swum to the mainland, with but a knife and her good bow and some arrows. I am sore wroth and loth to pursue her lest we do one another harm.

The creature is so willful and contrary I will not have her here, and in her heat she is best off in the wild. In all men doth lie concealed a beast, but in her 'tis by her base nature more like to dominate. Meseems she goeth to seek a mate, and shall find none here, I know, therefore shall bide alone away or return to reconcile herself to me.

—Later. Mine anger abated, I feared lest she come to instant harm. I Summoned vision of her this night and looked upon her as she slept in the grasses by a mothflower bush. She is uninjured, placid in repose, and I gazed to be sure she had taken no harm and then dismissed the sight.

I have mused upon the business and I know myself better; I have fed her wantonness subtly, overfond and indulgent, and there is a piece of me, animal and rude, that straineth for her maidenhead even as she pants in first heat of lust. Poor fool, that knoweth not herself. Did I not shape her sweet body with my own hands, to please my own taste? I do not want a wife; and I ought to have destroyed her after some few days or months, but I cannot, now. Though half-beast in her blood and shaped of wood and clay, she hath grown too human, unlike vild Caliban, a creature of will and whim and desire, and were cold murder to do away with her now.

This is an unreliable way of making men and taketh overmuch of me, and I am weary of it. I shall investigate the methods of the Countess of Aië, but better creatures would I have than those she keepeth by her.

There came a step outside the door. Dewar slammed the book shut, put it in the pile of books to be reshelved, and had his pen in hand as Freia entered with a wooden bowl of cooked meat and grain. She set it wordlessly beside him; he did not look up, but he could not keep from watching her sidelong. Prospero had truly transformed the lowest class of being to the highest. There was nothing to her to divulge that she was not human-born, that her bones had been wood and her flesh blood-clay ensouled with breath and life, and that she was nothing more than a curious experiment Prospero had kept about the place from sentiment.

Freia went out again, glancing back; their eyes met for an instant. Dewar said nothing, but watched her as he would a wild animal caught unawares at its business, and she dropped her gaze and left.

⟞ 4 ⟝

ON THE EVENING OF THE TWELFTH day Prospero saw the last course of stone laid down upon his broad walls. He smiled, and his smile faded as quickly as it came.

"Well done," he told the Argyllines, who stared, amazed, at

what they'd wrought. The earth-filled wood-braced walls were thirty feet high, ten thick; they were roofed with logs, to be topped with slate later; outside, a ditch twenty feet wide added to their height. "Done swiftly, done well; you shall be glad of't ere long, I fear. Now rest you, and bide, and toil by day and sleep by night as men prefer. I've other work to complete."

He walked slowly to the riverside, surrounded by the walls. Smokes were rising here and there from the communal hearths, cooking-smells and evening-sounds coming to him weakly, as from a great distance. Wooden buildings would be replaced with stone, he planned, mud streets with paved. A square, in the center of the city. Fountains, public places, private homes. And the isle—

Prospero paused on the mainland shore and looked at the island. At its crown still stood the huge tree at whose foot the Spring surged, filling the basin Caliban had made and spilling out to cut a little channel for itself after mossing the stone around it. A few squat trees, Freia's orchard, remained on the lower part of the isle; the giant was fellowless on the height, a naked pale-green-wreathed obelisk. On the slope, the ends of stumps were white and stark against the drying leaf-mulch.

Freia was just visible sitting in the long grass at the downstream end of the isle, arms around her knees. Her garden was overrun with weeds; her budding fruit trees wanted pruning. Prospero frowned. She was sulking, and it liked him little; she had squalled and sulked at all his labors to keep both her and Argylle safe, trying his humor. He'd turn his hand to correcting her megrims later.

The sun stretched long deep-gold arms over the land. It was time Prospero was about his last task. He chose a shallow rowboat and, alone, crossed the satin-surfaced water slowly, but with long strong pulls.

Dewar's hand and arm were the only parts of him that moved as his father entered the cave.

"Make ink," Dewar said, voice hoarse, eyes on the lamplit paper.

"Nay," Prospero said, unoffended. "Thy labor's o'er, thy rest before thee. Shalt have no more need of ink for thy task."

"No," Dewar said, writing still faster.

"Aye," Prospero said. "Finish that page, and 'tis done."

"I'm not ready!"

"Alas. Nor am I. All things must end."

Dewar cursed under his breath, spared a glance for Prospero. Prospero nodded. His son's eyes were red-rimmed and too bright; his movements too quick, drug-fed. It would take him several days at best to recover from the effects of sleeplessness and work.

"One more," Dewar said, his eyes on the book again.

"Sundown cometh," Prospero said, "and with it my time, and thine. Hast done more than any other could, and it must suffice."

"Not enough," Dewar said. "This next—"

"No more," said Prospero, finality in his voice.

Dewar cursed again, and Prospero said, "I'll return, and when I do, thou'lt leave this place, this chamber and the island; go with thy sister to the mainland, the city, and there await me, resting."

"Another hour—"

"Nay, son. All the hours have gone." Prospero left, hearing Dewar's cry of frustration behind him.

He walked slowly to the other end of the island, and on the way he spoke to the men and women working on the logging and clearing and sent them away to the mainland also, leaving piles of brush and lumber on the shore, whence they were to be rafted. Freia he found seated between the skirted leg-like roots of one of the still-standing woodnut trees. She was feeding birds; there were seeds and bits of dried fruit on the ground, and several dainty songbirds perched on her fingers, supping from her palm. All fled save his daughter as he approached.

"You drove them away."

"Must drive thee too. Come, take wing; 'tis time I must fulfill my vow. I'll send thy brother over with thee to the house.

Do thou attend that he lieth down ere he sleep standing 'gainst a wall."

Freia shrugged and stood, folded her arms, and followed Prospero without another word.

"Ariel!"

"Yes, Master!"

Prospero lowered his uplifted arms slowly. The first stars were becoming visible overhead, topazes and diamonds and aquamarines studding the pure, distant heaven's vault, a piece of the moon cast among them. The sorcerer breathed in power, breathed out serenity, and with that draught of power came to him also a feeling of fixedness, a feeling of inevitability. It seemed to him, in that moment, that all Time had proceeded to this conclusion, that in the beginning it had been set as were the stars' courses that he should stand thus now: the very spheres required it so. Whirled up by Fortuna, he had forgotten that all she raised, must fall.

Eager Ariel spun dry leaves up and down, waiting; his whirlwind-column rippled Prospero's cloak at his heels and rustled in the foliage overhead. Prospero cleared his throat. "Good Ariel," he said, "the hour hath come for us to part. Thou hast served well, and thy devotion doth merit my full gratitude to thee."

"Part, Master?" Ariel asked, puzzled. The leaves drifted to the ground. "Am I not bound to you?"

"Bound thou art, and unbound shalt thou be."

"Unbound?" Ariel repeated.

"For the Lady's liberty shall be paid by thine, swift Ariel." He lifted his silver-chased staff and struck the ground three times. "Caliban!"

"Aye," boomed a voice from far below, a thick and distant sound. Slowly, the earth thrummed and trembled, and at last the ground before Prospero broke. Caliban's mottled rough head, like lichen-crusted stone, lifted; he raised an arm and then the other, pushing aside a boulder thrown up by his arrival. "Master."

Prospero hesitated, looking on him in the moon's slender silver beam, and then said, "How fares thy great labor, Caliban?"

"O Master, it is near complete," said Caliban. "What task today?"

"No task for thee," Prospero said, and in his voice was a gentleness, "but holiday, O Caliban, that hath toiled long and long at labors none to thy liking. I shape a sorcery this night that shall open the pents I have placed on thee, and leave thee at liberty to go where thou list, do as thou wouldst, e'en as before I shaped this crude form that prisons thee."

Caliban was stone-still, stone-silent.

"But, Master," said Ariel, diffidently, "what would you have us do?"

"When I have lifted my bonds on you, may go where you list, do as you would," Prospero repeated. "I shall call on you no more. You twain shall be free from association with such mutable and mingled creatures as men, free to ride the gales and sound the deeps, released from servitude. I'll lay no command on you again."

"No—more—tasks?" Caliban said slowly.

"Sluggard-wit," Ariel hissed, "what hast thou done, to so displease our Master—"

"Nay, nay, you have served well, both and always," Prospero said heavily. "This night shall I renounce sorcery, and ne'er more Summon Sylph and Sammead to my bidding. The hour's come: I cannot eke it longer."

So saying, he turned from the small, uncertain dust-devil that was Ariel and the stony mass of Caliban, and he paced to the edge of the Spring. He laid one hand upon the bark of the great tree that gripped the Spring in knotted roots, roots that stretched over and pierced through a worn shield-shaped stone that capped the rocky isle. "I have in mind to make," he whispered to the tree, "some alterations in our life," and recalled a long summer's afternoon when Freia had gainsaid his plans, her protest rounded with the sleep of sorcery he had laid upon her. Did he regret? Nay, he swore to himself, and hurried on to his work, his last best work.

Well: the tree waited; the Spring bubbled quietly up and sank back to earth; the moon had passed the fifth degree of her ascent and floated toward zenith. Let it be done quickly. Prospero stood on the hilltop, above the Spring, and lifted his staff, drawing a quadruple-circle in the air. He spoke a Summoning, and a Salamander swirled and roared above him, stretching and straining to escape. Now Prospero, holding staff and Salamander aloft, an oriflamme above him in the darkness, went quickly down the slope to the cave which stood, its door ajar in the dark.

Prospero paused and shouted "Freia!" at the cave-mouth, a quick suspicion touching him; but nay, she was not there, she had bided at the mainland with her brother, though he'd feared she would disobey yet again and return here against his word. The cave was empty, but not empty: within were assembled all his books, his notes and works of craft and Art, his sorcery complete. Would it not destroy him to destroy it? He hesitated, and the Salamander roared and writhed.

Yet an oath-breaker's end would be worse than to endure without sorcery. Prospero closed his eyes a moment and lowered the staff. "Dost see the Bounds within this cavern," he said to the Salamander.

"Issseeeeeee," it sizzled.

Prospero's hair was frizzling with the heat.

"Within those Bounds mayst burn," he said, "and when thou hast devour'd all within, destroyed all to the bare stone of the walls, be thou dismissed, replete with that which lies within the Bounds and no more."

"Sssssooo," it sizzled, and Prospero swung the staff and cried a word of release, hurling the Salamander into the cave. It exploded, an incandescent ball of white heat. By the harsh light he saw books and instruments knocked down by the explosion, saw his winged table and his chair—ah, the table, the chairs, he should have taken them away, too late—Freia's chair carved with flowers, that he had made for her—they charred and coaled and burnt, and the books glowed and ashed, and the astrolabe and geoplane melted—

Prospero fled, his heart wrenching in his breast, striding back up to the Spring; the zenith was nearly upon him, he must be a true sorcerer this night or all was naught. He put the sight of his burning library from him and concentrated on the future. The Salamander's roar was a dull throb in the air and its furnace-glow lit the end of the isle, casting misshapen shadows of the rocks and stumps out to the waters.

The sorcerer turned his back to the cave and addressed the Spring and the tree. Winds were beginning to rise, odds and ends of gusts tugging his cloak or chilling, then warming, his face and hands: winds breaking free from the Salamander's destruction. Prospero muttered a few words, shooing the liberated airs away. The moon soared into her sixth degree above him. He lifted his arms and his head, and his staff stood of itself above the Spring, the silver double-spiral that wound from heel to top beginning to glow in the Spring-light as the staff turned slowly around and around like a spindle.

"By this hallowed Spring I stand and by it I command thee, staff, made by mine Art, be unmade by mine Art, be changed by mine Art to this standing tree's heart . . ."

Prospero gestured, herding the staff, continuing his invocation; light rained up from the Spring, scattered by the staff to brighten the moon and the undersides of the tree's trembling leaves. The staff seemed to swell, its silver coils shrinking and stretching in the brilliant light, and it hovered beside the tree now, spinning faster and faster. Prospero's hands shone. He added to his invocation. "By this hallowed Spring I stand and by it I command thee, tree, nurtured by Spring, be changed by Spring . . ."

The tree took on a faint luminescence. It expanded within the glow, then filled the glow, and the glow moved outward and the staff disappeared, merging into the tree. It formed a brilliant streak in the heart of the wood, which streak now turned but slowly, ponderously, weighty with sorcery. Prospero closed his eyes as the tree's swelling substance engulfed him. It moved over the Spring, and the Spring became a tree-shaped fountain, no longer shining softly and spilling water but drawn to the cresting moon above, a column of swirling light.

Within, Prospero's arms were above his head, and he felt himself becoming tree-substance, the heavy element within him seeking union; he resisted and cried to the Spring, and the Spring began to sink, or the hill to rise, informing the tree-shape with the stone of the hill, enclosing the Spring.

The staff moved around and around Prospero now in a tight orbit. The tree's rotation was ponderous and gradual, slowing as its substance changed from wood to stone, yet still it swelled around Prospero. The Spring rushed upward and outward, sinking, the substance of the hill flowing and the Spring brightening and concentrating as it did.

". . . wood to stone," Prospero was shouting in the stream of the Spring, "strengthened by all mine Art borne within my staff to tower's heart . . . ," but he could not hear himself, only what he thought he said, and he was no longer sure where in the spell he was, carried on and down by it as its deep boneshaking music plummeted away from the moon. He shouted descriptions, visions, and charms; he recited every spell he had ever known, recalled and forgot them one after the other, gathered all the power he could grasp to him and spent it, pouring his sorcery into the earthly construction that ground and groaned around him.

One last thing—

". . . do I loose thee, Ariel, and never shall place Bound on thee again, go where thou list, do what thou wilt; and thee Caliban do I likewise unbind from the form which I shaped upon thee now to go where thou list, do what thou wilt—"

The Spring cried a single sweet high note and ebbed rapidly, dragging him with it. Prospero felt himself fall and he felt the sorcery explode around him, and the only light in the darkness of the world was the Spring.

"Master?" whispered Ariel, pushing a breeze before him as he wound around and around a long spiral darkness. But it went down and down, and Ariel misliked the oppression of earth around him. The Sylph whispered, "Go where thou list, then, Ariel," and whisked about, hissing in the stone passageway, up and out, higher and higher, starward and beyond.

"Master," murmured Caliban, throwing off the hateful constraints of the crude humanoid shape into which Prospero had forced him, and he dove down, flying in his cold element as rapidly as Ariel, away from the Spring and its clammy constraints, away from Prospero's long chores—away from the Lady, from flowers—a geode popped as he passed, and Caliban chortled at its sharp-budded crystals, and he thought of taking it to the Lady. But the depths called him; he was already deeper than ever he had delved since Prospero had Summoned and enmeshed him. He went down.

The moon slid down her arc and away behind the mountains; the stars ticked in circles above. Freia slept in a chair by an unshuttered window, her head on the rough wooden sill, an old cloak wrapped around her. The midnight lights and explosions had been too alarming to permit rest. The people Prospero had made, the Argyllines, huddled in frightened knots in their houses by cowering fires, afraid of the sorceries and strangeness that flowed around them in the dark. Freia watched, trembling, and behind her Dewar snored raspily, oblivious of the destruction and danger in the world. Wild, brief windstorms blasted and thundered over the town, then gusted and screamed away to all points of the compass; patches of rain, fog, and snow of every description whipped past Freia's window. Swift clouds skimmed over the moon and cleared it again, so that the light twisted and changed too much for her to see anything. Shutters banged erratically on the wall nearby, and from the forest came splintering and crashing sounds: great trees were falling. Things smashed into the side of the house, then were blown onward. Her ears ached and rang and popped with the noise, and her eyes stung with wind-carried grit and dirt.

A final explosion had deafened her and thrown her to the floor; when she stood, ears ringing, the great bubble of fog and light that had covered Prospero's isle was gone and so was the ruddy-gold glow from the cave. She had guessed that he had lit a fire there and burned all his things, his things and a few of hers too that she had not thought to take away; but they belonged there, for that was home: her chair, her feather-bed, her little bark box of stones with water-worn holes in them. And then the prickling, singing feeling of the Spring coming out and out had distracted her from the pyrelight, and the shifting occluded shapes in the Spring-light, and the trembling of the earth.

Silence had come after that final explosion, but Freia had watched still, and had fallen asleep on watch curled tense and tight, her hands fists. The sun warmed her hair and she relaxed a little, drawing an arm beneath her head, and she slept on until the light was fully day-bright, dreaming of explosions and dark dungeons.

"Lady!" called someone into her dream.

Freia woke with a quick, frightened wrench.

"Lady," Scudamor said more softly, "Lord Prospero—where is he?"

"I don't know," she said, wiping huge grit-grains from her lids. Her eyes hurt, sandpapered and salted. "He doesn't tell me," Freia said to Scudamor. "Didn't he come back?"

"From the isle? No, Lady Freia," Utrachet said from the door, a stage whisper.

She couldn't think; she was so weary she wanted to push Dewar from the bed and lie down. "We must go look, he might be hurt—the fires," she suggested disjointedly.

They nodded, and Freia followed them out. Why did she ache so in every bone, every muscle, as if she had been wrenched from head to foot? She stumbled on a step, and Scudamor caught her arm and kept her from falling. Utrachet rowed them to the isle, just the three of them in a flat-bottomed rowboat, his chin on his shoulder as he pulled. Freia half-lay in the bow, pillowing her head on her forearm, and nearly dozed before the boat scraped gravel at the landing-beach.

"Lady, should we look in the tower?" Utrachet asked.

"Tower?" she repeated, clambering out of the boat.

"The tower," Utrachet said, and pointed.

Freia looked and gasped. She had been so tired as to be blind to anything more than an arm's-length away, but here on the rocky shore of the isle she could not miss the tower.

The island's shape had changed. The tall stone outcrop from which had sprung the Spring, to which had clung a film of soil and shrubs, was gone. In its place was a low rise, gentler and bare of trees. Bare of tree—the great tree was gone, too, the Spring's companion, and in its place stood a mighty tower, the kind of tower Freia had seen in Landuc's fortresses. Prospero had described such things to her, before ever she laid eyes on them, when they had been mentioned in such works of poetry, history, or literature as he had seen fit to set before her. In Landuc, where everything had been strange, where everyone seemed to be immured in hollowed-out stone, such towers, variously tall or squat, round or square, had been scattered everywhere, on nearly every sizable hill. Prospero had been prisoned in such a tower, in a castle on a stony mountain. Here, this tower hung over them, louring and dark, casting a shadow as hard-edged and empty as the blank blade of a knife.

She gaped.

Sheer, high, stark, the tower stood there as if it had plummeted from heaven.

Prospero had made it, Freia knew. He had done this thing, had removed the last lovely tree from her island and stuck this stone monstrosity in its place with his magic, a last evil thing to create in the world before he gave up sorcery forever. With the candor of exhaustion, Freia was suddenly glad that Prospero had lost his Art. Now he would always be Papa, her father, no more to throw sudden sleeps over her when he tired of her company, no more to raise storms, nor summon creatures and visions fair or monstrous, no more to vanish and reappear without a word of reason. There were so many things to do in the world besides sorcery, and he had never had time for them. Perhaps now he would let her guide him to the cliff in the Jagged Mountains where the gryphon's nest was, to the ocean-wide plain below the flat-topped hills where teeming uncountable curly-horned deer grazed, to the swamps in the north where the beautiful blue-and-white birds fell to the water like pieces of broken sky.

But where was Prospero? Nowhere on the island. Without speaking the searchers stalked the tower, circling round and round and drawing nearer. Freia looked for the rivulet that had been the Spring's overflow, but it was gone; the ground was so altered that she could not even find its course. They went three times around the wall at last, Freia leading, and halted at the stone doors.

Freia put her hands on the doors. At that light touch, the two thick halves swung easily inward. Coolness rushed out from the dim interior. She stood uncertain on the threshold. The place was alive, yet not alive; though made of stone, it breathed and stirred with life: like a forest, but unlike. There was no feeling of danger, but she was afraid.

Prospero had to be somewhere within. She must find him.

She turned to Scudamor and Utrachet. "He must be here. Wait for me."

"Let me go with you, Lady, and Scudamor wait here for us both," Utrachet said.

"No. If I don't come back, you had better close the doors and, and stay away. This isn't right. It doesn't belong here. It's dangerous."

"If there is danger—" Utrachet began.

"We shall wait for you, Lady," said Scudamor. "Today, tonight, tomorrow."

Freia shrugged, abashed by his ready obedience. "It is up to you whether you wait or not."

"We shall wait," agreed Utrachet, unhappy.

She nodded and edged past the doors, suspiciously looking up at the lintel, at the doors, at the stone floor. Nothing moved but air, past her, as if the tower exhaled a long, chill breath of relief. Utrachet and Scudamor stood on the threshold, watching her.

Past the reach of the doors her eyes began to adjust to the dark stone. She saw another wall before her, a curving wall that seemed to be in the center of the empty space. She looked up; the space was higher than the doors; she couldn't see where its ceiling was. It felt enclosed, though, not as though the whole tower were hollow all the way up.

"Prospero," she whispered.

The whisper echoed, but not far.

Freia walked cautiously to the wall inside the tower; yes, it was curved, and she began to follow it around, but stopped. Away from the door, the darkness was so complete that she backed away and then half-ran to the door again, terrified of the stone-enclosed feeling: it was like Landuc, like the dungeons of Perendlac and Chasoulis where Ottaviano and Golias and the sorceress Neyphile had kept her, and her remembered fear and horror made her stumble in her haste to be away.

Utrachet and Scudamor met her, tense, ready to pounce on anything. Freia composed herself; some unconscious urge made her desire to show courage before them.

"There's nothing there. It's dark. It's very dark. I, I need a torch."

They all three left the open doorway and walked around the tumbled earth and rocks of the isle, looking for something she could make into a torch. No piece of suitable wood did they find, so Utrachet loped to the boat, rowed to the riverbank, and fetched back a lantern, one of the best in Argylle, made of pierced copper with panes of thin-polished shell, and half a dozen tallow candles. On the threshold of the tower, Scudamor lit a little pile of tinder and touched the first candle's wick to it, then placed the candle in the lantern. Freia nodded thanks and took it from him.

The doors hadn't moved; the cool air was still pouring slowly past them. It smelled wet to Freia. She said, "Remember, don't go in," and left the Castellan and the Seneschal behind, forcing herself to walk around the rounded wall. The lantern-light was unheartening, weak after the sun's brilliance. She circled fully around the tower, inside, then halfway again.

Exactly opposite the door was another door, set into the inner wall. It was open. There was nothing else. Freia lifted the lantern and saw that it was open because it could not be closed; there was no door in that doorway. Stairs led down and up, the same black stone as the tower.

The cold, moist air flowed from below, contradicting the behavior of proper air. Freia decided to go that way, and again she whispered "Prospero?" unanswered. So, deliberately slowly, her scuffed sandals slapping on her heels, she went down. Just a few steps took her out of sight of the doorway; that unnerved her so that she backed up to assure herself that it was still there, and still open, and it was, so she turned again and went unhappily down, against the current of air.

Sometimes her nose twitched as she descended: ghosts of scents drifted past. The sharp smell of crushed leaves, the dry, dusty scent of late-summer grasses, the rich scents of ripe fruits and turned earth, the salty decay-tang of the coastal marshes and the cold scent of the Jagged Mountains to the west, all these and others, unidentifiable, unaccountable, she smelled as she descended. She sniffed for Prospero, for the astringent herbal smell that combined with his sweat to make a lively, vivid aura around him, and she could not smell that at all. Her footsteps patted around her. She had not thought to note the number of stairs and she had no certain idea how long she had descended. The grade was easy, and her legs were more bored than weary.

The stairs coiled around and around. She stopped once and sat down, replacing her candle. That worried her. How long had she been here? Could these steps go down indefinitely? She was cold, and she had forgotten to eat in the turmoil of the morning.

"Prospero," she called, but in a whisper, afraid to make a loud noise in the confined space.

The air stirred, purling around her, enough of a flow to make her blink. Freia stood and let gravity draw her down, step by step, and twelve steps later she stopped.

The stair ended, and another doorless opening was before her. The rush of air was strong here.

"Prospero!"

Her voice bounced, boomed and echoed, rattled off an unseen roof, and clattered into the hollow space around her where she stood in the opening.

She listened to the echo until it had quite gone, and then, with a sudden surmise, called "Caliban!"

Again the word was lost, shattering and fading in shards. No answer came.

The air stirred against her face, and it brought her a quick whiff of the moist darkness under the overarching arms of trees that covered streams. Wet stone, wet leaves, moss, water.

Freia turned her face, following the scent. This had to open somewhere, then. She took a hesitant step from the doorway and then stopped to light one of her candles from the lantern and balance it there in a corner, at the base of the steps, a lone flame-beacon to guide her back. The light guttered in the draught, but stayed lit. Then she found the scent again—a sniff of sun-warm roses preceded it—and struck out into the dark.

Dark it was, and that was all. Dark above, dark below, and nothing else, not for many steps until she passed a huge black pillar like the one that held the stair. The stone beneath her feet was cold and flat. Freia paused, looked back; her candle was a spark. Well. She set another candle down at the foot of the pillar and went on, but the scent was becoming more complex. It had acquired a bloody undertone and a cold edge of ice. And flowers came and went, bruised petals and leaves, and the scents of herbs she knew well, always moist and damp.

Freia stopped again and looked back: she saw only one spark now, the second; the first was lost in darkness and distance.

To come so far, and turn back— Not yet, then. She looked ahead, and then turned her head carefully to not-look ahead. At the corner of her eye was a gleam. She moved toward it slowly, carefully; in three dozen paces she could see it straight on, a distinct light down low. She began to hurry, not checking her candle-beacon, and the sounds of her steps became a confusion of haste-noise in the darkness, a clutter-clatter that masked the other noise until she was nearly at the light.

The light was a round hole in the floor, which was full of soft-shining water, and as she slowed she heard a sound like rain. Water was falling into the hole from nowhere.

"Prospero!"

He lay on the other side of the luminous pool. The water made a pleasant pattering sound. Freia skirted it, knelt beside him, pulled him gently onto his back. He had a scrape on his cheekbone, but seemed unhurt otherwise.

"Papa, wake up."

He was limp, breathing through his slack mouth; his eyes were rolled up beneath his lids; pulse slow and strong, hands cold. He'd been stunned, she thought. Freia swung round and cupped her hand, dipped it in the pool.

The pool erupted. With a boom, water shot straight upward, and droplets showered Freia and Prospero as it fell back; a brilliant white mist spread out from the pool. Freia knelt, immobile with surprise. She felt no danger, only startlement.

"Prospero," she said again, touching his face, and he snorted, sneezed, coughed, and jerked his hands. Freia trickled the remaining water in her palm against his lips. He licked, tasted, coughed again, and now his eyes opened.

They looked at one another; the water subsided into its pool, as if satisfied. The mist condensed and dripped. Freia shook drops from her hair.

"Freia . . . Freia. What dost thou here, child?" Hoarse and uncertain, his voice frightened her.

"Looking for you."

"And where—" Prospero tried to rise, but his arm wobbled

beneath him and Freia caught his shoulders, moving behind him, to help him sit. He looked around him. "The Spring," he said then, rubbing at his elbows and his back.

"It's gone now."

"Gone? 'Tis there."

"Gone from the isle. We're—there's a tower now. I came down stairs inside it to find you." Freia studied the shining pool, understanding belatedly what Prospero had meant: this was the Spring. He had changed it. She scooped water from it again, and again it erupted, startling her as much as the first time. Freia drank the water in her hand under the strange rain; its taste was familiar and it refreshed her greatly. It subsided, as before, and she felt its subsidence deep within her, as an ebbing of some part of herself. "But," she began to say, leaning toward it, to look in.

The candle in her lantern guttered and went out.

"Oh, no!"

Prospero ignored it. "Down stairs," he repeated, a blurred face in the faint light from the water. "Stairs," he muttered to himself.

"A long stair, stone, this kind of stone. They go around, like a sea-shell, a spiral."

He nodded.

"Come, Papa. Let's go up again. I can find the other candle." Freia stood and tugged his arm, but she had to kneel again and put her shoulder under his to help him stand. They rose together, unsteadily. "Papa?" Certainly he had hit his head on the stone, she thought.

He nodded, taking his weight from her to sway unaided. "Very tired, Puss. Nay—leave me. To myself. Here have I buried my heart."

This made no sense to Freia; she disregarded it. "We'd better go up now, Papa. Before the candles I left there fail. I'll help you."

Freia guided him around the pool—the Spring, he had said—and stared into the darkness for her beacon. She thought she saw a glimmer and set off toward it, but lost confidence and returned to the Spring. The air had settled; the outside-smelling currents were gone, and only damp, enclosed stillness remained.

"Hast lost thy way," Prospero said.

"I—I'm not sure where the way lies," she admitted. "I cannot see my candle."

Prospero looked into the darkness also. "The way," he said in an undertone.

The illuminated Spring burbled up again, sending a jet of bright water from its middle in a single burst; the jet fell sideways, splattering the black stone, and the water was quiet again.

Freia felt Prospero lean, and thus prompted she took a step. He moved with her, stiffly. They walked in the direction pointed by the Spring, and many slow steps later the candle gleamed lonely before them, and she hurried as much as she could. It was a knuckle-sized stub when they reached it, but she lit a fresh candle for the lantern and sighted the first candle from there too, and Prospero said nothing, leaning on the pillar with eyes closed. In the lantern-light, his face was lined and weary. Freia nudged her shoulder under his again and he whispered "Yes, yes," and so they went on. The first candle went out before they reached it, and Freia froze a moment in terror when it vanished. But Prospero kept going, and she carried on in as straight a line as she could. Lifting her lantern high after a few dozen steps, she saw the darkness-in-darkness of the doorway ahead, to the left, and nearly wept with relief.

The stairs were difficult. Prospero stumbled, knocked her down, muttered that he could climb alone, insisted she leave him and he'd climb alone when he'd rested, and Freia must wrestle him on and up, grim, saying nothing. She dared not argue with him; he was not like himself, which frightened her, and she wished now she had brought Scudamor and Utrachet, who could have carried him more easily. He would not let her lift him across her back as she carried elk carcasses from the forest, but insisted that he walk on his own legs, and they ascended slowly, until the last candle was consumed. They went up in darkness, and Prospero said nothing at all now, but he became heavier and heavier, and Freia dragged them both upward until the flat floor tripped her feet. Then Scudamor and Utrachet rushed into the tower to help, and they were home.

The simply-built table had been scoured smooth and white with sand, then polished with beeswax; its pale wooden top was decked now with a clutter of platters and bowls and the remains of a meal that was not supper, nor breakfast, nor anything usual in the cycle of the day. Here the sun, bright and hard through a deep-silled unglazed window, made a glowing jewel-pool beside a wine-bottle; there it made a sparkle from the tip of a black-handled knife. A pair of roasted fowl had been denuded to the bones; a slab of meat, red and bloody within, black with char and pepper outside, stood in its dripping, a last carved but uneaten slice moist in the juices. Beside a soft, oozing cheese, a flat brown dish of yellow apples shone fair as gold in the sun, and Freia, one of the three for whom the meal was spread, selected one and bit a white circle in its sweet flesh. Prince Prospero cracked nuts from a broad-rimmed bowl that also held a mound of dried blue-black grapes, and Dewar, making slow concentrated effort, tore a piece of bread from a hard-crusted brown loaf, as though separating each crumb from its fellows with regret. The table was unclothed, but white napkins lay crumpled here and there, three of them, beside the clay plates and goblets of the table's company.

"We ride now to Landuc," Prospero said, pushing away his plate, scattering nutshells. "Thou, Freia, prepare for the journey; we must away within this hour."

"I don't want to go back there," Freia said. She lowered her apple half-bitten.

"Thou'lt come," Prospero told her. "Thou shalt come with me, and cease this eternal contrary. I've had a bellyful of thy sour naysaying and heavy foot-dragging these days past, and thou shalt come with me, and swallow thy draught of the trouble thou hast so diligently brewed for us. If I cannot command gratitude in thee, I shall at least have obedience."

Freia jumped to her feet, walked toward the door; Prospero rose and stood in front of her, blocking her departure.

"Nay," he said, and they locked gazes. "None of thy running to the Threshwood." Prospero shook his head slightly.

He was taller than she, broader than she, and Freia, looking up at him, saw only hard determination in his face. She waited a few heartbeats, but his expression and stance did not change. He had never struck her, but she had been beaten hard and long of late and Prospero's anger frightened her; he had never been so angry before, and he still would not see her alone or listen to her. They had returned from the island, they had slept a few hours, he had closeted himself with Scudamor and Utrachet, he had roused Dewar to eat, and in all that time he had not spoken to her kindly, when he spoke to her at all.

Her shoulders went down. She turned away and left the doorway and Prospero.

Dewar did not look at them. Freia's eyes rested on her brother as she hoped for an instant that he might take her side, but he remained silent.

"Papa, I don't want to go there," she pleaded in a whisper. "I'm afraid."

"Hadst thou proper fear of the place the first time, 'twere not needful now that thou go there again," Prospero said coldly. "A curb to thy whimpering, baggage, ere thou drivest me all out of patience with thee. Hast been of little aid; beware lest thou become an impediment. Be ready to ride in a turn of the green glass." He watched his suspiciously submissive daughter closely, her bowed head seething, he was sure, with schemes to give him the slip; and with his hand he flicked the glass, that stood in a rack of timing-glasses on the sideboard.

'Twas an echo of the days when she'd first quarrelled with his judgement, she fractious and sullen in the face of his adamance against her demands on him, and she'd run away into the wood then for seven years and more. To be fair, she'd returned from the wild less feral herself and had sought to please him since, but he knew he had never wholly tamed her—as her flouting and pouting had demonstrated. This time she'd not flee the consequences of her disobedience; too long he'd left her to her own direction. This time she, being of his blood, must and could take her part of the burden of trouble she had brought on them. "Haste thou, gather what's needful for our journey, provender and gear, and I'll seek thee out presently."

Another tense, overlong moment stretched and snapped. Freia turned and, without looking up at Prospero as he stood aside from the door, left him alone with his son.

The Prince sat down across from the sorcerer, whose eyes were closed. In his right hand was a cheese-laden knife, resting on the bread on his plate; he held up his head with his left hand, elbow on the table.

"Dewar."

"Mm."

"Art hungry still?"

Dewar sighed. His eyes opened a crack. "Don't think so. Was I asleep? Sorry. You were saying about . . . about . . ." He couldn't remember.

"Thou'rt best off sleeping again," Prospero said gently. "I'll be riding with thy sister back to Landuc."

Dewar couldn't remember for a moment that he had a sister. "Sister."

"Aye. Come. Best lie thee down again. 'Twill be some three or five days ere the drug's illness leaves thee. Sorry I am to have given it to thee, but 'twas worth it."

"It was," Dewar agreed. The books. His vision still ran with words when he closed his eyes, Prospero's handwriting graven inside the lids. His mouth moved to make a segment of a smile. He let go of the knife with an effort.

Prospero looked at him affectionately—bleared red-rimmed eyes, crumb-dusted beard. "Come," he said again, and slid his arm under Dewar's, lifting him to his feet effortlessly.

"Never been so tired."

"Wert long without rest and must pay the debt." Prospero

walked him from the room, along the high-windowed, wide hall back to the bedchamber where Dewar had rested insensible for nearly a full day already. He was a solid young fellow, muscular and not run to fat the way so many of the better ones from Noroison did, Prospero thought, becoming toadlike at an early age. A Prince's son indeed. And could use a sword as well as the staff. Wherever the boy learnt that, Prospero thought, 'twas well-taught. That physical strength had made it possible for Dewar to copy for twelve days and nights without halting, though the toll was high.

Dewar was sleepwalking now, stumbling, letting his father half-drag him, flop him onto the bed, cover him with a homespun linen sheet and a woollen blanket. He sagged, sighed, and slept.

THOUGH MARRIAGE HAD, AT LEAST IN theory, made the Countess of Lys and the newly dubbed Baron of Ascolet one flesh, it had not brought their respective land-holdings closer together: which lands, though not the most extensive nor the most desirable of the realm of Landuc, were still sufficiently broad that the Baron, upon his formal dismissal from the war-service of the Emperor by the Prince Marshal, found himself in a riverport town in Upper Ascolet, a good four hundred miles from his lady wife of less than two years' standing, who waited for him in her city of Champlys. Faced with a forbidding journey through the mountains along the whole length of his lands, in wintertime, the Baron can surely be forgiven for hesitating in his warm inn. His small, illicit knowledge of sorcery did not extend to the blind opening of Ways between points, and so he must travel overland by some route. True, the winter thus far had been dry, but this meant that only sixteen feet of snow lay in the passes of Ascolet instead of the usual thirty-two feet or more. True, his command of the Well was sufficient that he might shorten his journey by riding along Leys or the Road; but as he sat and swotted over his Map and Ephemeris, which he knew to be unreliable at times, he found that such a journey by Ley would be little easier than forging ahead without benefit of the Well's guidance, and the journey by Road would require him to travel so far, and so circuitously, away from Landuc into wide Pheyarcet through Eddy-worlds and outlands, as to consume entirely the brief interval of time between his dismissal and the date on which he was to present himself in the city of Landuc, at the Emperor's throne, to swear publicly his vows of allegiance and fealty. What benefit to him now his clandestine, dear-bought initiation in the Well's fire? He dolefully cursed Panurgus, who had shaped the Roads thus, and fretted after his wife in a fashion she would have found most gratifying, had she been present to witness it. As the world stood, however, she was not present, and the Baron dissipated his exigent fretting on a plump flaxen-haired chambermaid who bore some resemblance to the Countess in the dark.

Baron Ottaviano spent some days reckoning and re-reckoning the ways to and from Lys and finally concluded that it could not be done. Moreover, by now, he thought, Luneté would have received her own summons to the great midwinter court, via an imperial courier, and he regretted the bravado that had inspired him to refuse Prince Gaston's offer to enclose a letter from Otto for the Countess in the courier's pouch. "No, thanks, sir, I'll be there before the courier," Otto had declared, and Prince Gaston had said only, "Very well." Now the Countess would have received that summons to court, with no word from him on what he was about, and as she had recently been eloquent on the subject of correspondence, Otto understood that it would be well for him to contrive some consolation, or conciliation, quickly.

His solution was not quite so perilous as the snow-filled passes of Ascolet, but was nearly as toilsome in its way. Otto gathered together a handful of the Ascolet men who had supported him through his travails, tallied up his ready money and then cheerfully reckoned that a baron had credit enough to travel on a light purse (for the collection of tax revenues had been—perhaps willfully—confused by the late alterations in Ascolet's status from imperial possession to independent kingdom to barony), and set out back toward Landuc, on a well-travelled king's highway. Prudently, he appointed a burly man a handspan bigger than himself as his Chancellor of the Exchequer for the duration of the journey, and although this soldier was inept at figures, he was proficient at diplomatically explaining to innkeepers and hostlers that His Excellency the Baron of Ascolet would pay later. And therefore they made good time and were well-housed and well-entertained each night.

They crossed the rolling lowlands at a good pace and reached the city of Landuc with sixteen days to spare before the court, and so Otto did not even pause at the Palace gates (he did spend little more than a quarter of an hour in a jeweler's shop, with his Chancellor, selecting a rope of pearls to grace the throat of the Countess of Lys), but set out immediately again on the king's highway southward, along which he reckoned the Countess must come. Now that he was struggling against the road's current, Otto noticed how much traffic there was. Every noble in Landuc who could move was travelling to the midwinter court for the spectacle of Prince Prospero's formal surrender; the highway was snowless and frozen solid in the dry deep cold, and caravans of painted coaches and horses and baggage rumbled rapidly along, sweeping into inn-yards and occupying every room in a place. The expenses were much higher on this leg of the trip, and the innkeepers were far less receptive to the idea of the Baron's travelling on credit: there was so much good solid gold and silver flowing along the road that they had but to hold out a hand to catch a fistful, and so the Baron's ethereal money bought him nothing. Thereafter, he and his party travelled incognito; they did not declare themselves and slept in stable-lofts; and they breakfasted, dined, and supped on onions, coarse bread, hard cheese, and sour beer or cider, all these cold comforts bought dearer than Otto's rustic Chancellor could believe. The chambermaids and serving-girls were all busy with the cash-rich customers, too, and the Baron consoled himself with the reflection that it would be prudent to keep a low profile going out, in order to avoid embarrassment on his way back, with his wife.

It was therefore with sincere joy that, on the sixth day of their journey from Landuc, Ottaviano espied the Countess of Lys's arms on a coach at a crowded inn where, it seemed, most of the nobility of the southern part of the realm had halted for food and fodder. He and his party clattered into the inn-yard, and Ottaviano made his way through a throng of gentlemen and ladies to inquire of the preoccupied host where he might look to find the Countess of Lys.

"Lys! Back there," said the host, jerking his chin toward the stairs and back. So Otto, leaving his men to forage in the public room, went upstairs and intruded on three other private parties, largely composed of ladies, until he found the right door.

"This is not the public dining-room, sir," said a hawk-faced lady he didn't recognize, as he stepped into the chamber, but Otto did recognize Luneté, with a little leap of his heart, before she turned to see him. "Sirrah—!"

Otto took two more steps and put his arms around his wife, giving her a squeeze by way of greeting, and kissed the back of her neck soundly. "Hello, Lu!"

Without a sound, Luneté spun around on the bench (the older lady had taken the only high-backed chair) and leapt to her feet; her maid squeaked with surprise, and the fourth woman, who must be the hawk-faced lady's maid, gasped. The Countess's hand was lifted and she was very close to boxing his ears, but Otto caught her wrist, laughing.

"I've been looking for you," Otto announced, grinning, and kissed his wife again before she had quite caught her breath.

"Otto!" Luneté said then, drawing back as far from him as she could, encircled still by his arms.

"Yours to command, my lady."

"I, I, I did not know you—you sent no word that you would meet me on the way," she said.

"I missed the courier and came myself, as fast as I could. Had some work to do in Ascolet first." Otto kissed her once more. "You're a sight for sore eyes, Lu! And who's this?"

Luneté turned, extricating herself from his embrace as she did, and introduced him to the Countess of Surluse, her neighbor south-west of Lys, who held herself starchily and disapprovingly aloof from the Baron of Ascolet.

"Liker a highwayman than a prince's son," said the Countess of Surluse with a meaning-laden sniff.

Ottaviano disregarded the sniff and found another bench along the wall; he pulled it over to the table and joined them in their lunch, which was an unidentifiable scrawny fowl, a few chops, pickled crabs, white bread that tasted of other things than meal, and a greasy pudding. The ladies were drinking the fortified and fortifying hot punch known as glog, which Otto found to be a great improvement over the thinner brews he had been served on this trip. Likewise, the chops and pudding were welcome after the onions and black bread he had been travelling on, and he did them better justice than they deserved. The ladies dined, as ladies will, delicately, and with little conversation. Laudine was dispatched to chivvy the kitchen sluts (as the Countess of Surluse referred to them) into providing them the coffee they had ordered with their food, "for they've charged us for it, sure as sundown, my dear; these highway innkeepers are sharp as skewers, specially before a court."

Laudine was reduced to carrying the coffee up herself, which agreed poorly with her idea of the sort of service the Countess of Lys ought to have in an inn. The rest of the small Lys party—a footman, a page, and a coachman—had dined in the common room, which was so crowded and tumultuous with arrivals and departures that there was no seating the Emperor himself there, should he have come. Otto found the coffee, although weak, to be an excellent completion to the restorative meal, ignoring the dry biscuits with it. Those the Countess of Surluse wrapped up thriftily in her handkerchief for later, giving them to her maid to carry. "They have charged us for them, certainly," she said, as if daring either Lys or Ascolet to think anything of it.

The reckoning had been paid in advance, an unusual practice prompted by the high volume of traffic coming through the inn's dining-rooms. The Countess of Surluse muttered approvingly that they should not have to pay anything extra for Otto, at least, although he had eaten more than anyone, and Otto handed her and her maid into the rugged old Surluse coach with all the grace he could muster before attending to Luneté. "Where shall you stop the night, sir?" the Countess of Surluse asked him, before closing her coach door.

"I guess that'll depend on how much progress we make," he said.

"I have sent one of my boys on to Savarin's, at Galisbridge, to take rooms for my party and the Lys people," she said. "He won't rob me as badly as some of the others. He knows me."

"I'm sure he does," said Otto. "You've been very kind to my lady wife, and thank you. We'll see you at Galisbridge, then." And he bowed, stepped back, and closed the door before she could say anything else.

Luneté's coach was being brought around from the stubbled, muddy field where vehicles had been left in ranks and rows, owing to the impossibility of fitting them all in the yard.

"How about if I come ride with you to Galisbridge?" Otto suggested to his wife, leading her to her coach-door.

"Um," said Luneté.

"There's room," he said, opening the door. It was a six-seater, and only Luneté, her maid, and her page were there to occupy it.

"Laudine, Dinas, get in," said Luneté, and moved back a few steps with Otto.

"What's wrong?"

"What in the holy Fire have you been doing?" she whispered.

"What do you mean, doing?"

"You smell like, like a brewery and a midden! When did you last shave? Your clothes—"

"Oh," said Otto. He shrugged, rubbed his hand over his raspy coppery-bristled chin, slapped at his leather leggings. "I hurried to get here, that's all. I didn't know you were friendly with Surluse."

"We met on the way," said Luneté, sighing a little, "and she was very thick with my parents, or so she says, although I rather think she didn't like my mother. She means well. And she has been very kind to me."

"Tough old bird. Wouldn't be surprised if she came over with Panurgus," Otto said. "I'll clean up when we get to Galisbridge, all right?"

"I wish you'd told me you were coming. I'd have been able to put off the Countess a bit. She's arranged our stops all the way to the city."

"That's no bad thing, believe me. The road's only going to get more crowded."

Luneté nodded. "Otto, dear, I'm getting cold standing here. I'll see you at Galisbridge."

"If I take a bath and shave first." He laughed.

"At least change your linen," Luneté said, and kissed his cheek. "There. I am happy to see you, you know: you just look as though you've come from the battlefield. Now hand me up."

Otto did so, closed the door on her (she lowered the shutter and blew him a kiss) and the coach rolled out of the yard.

"My lord," said his Chancellor of the Exchequer, "this stop here done cleaned us out, sir."

"Don't worry about it," said Otto cheerfully. "From here on we'll be travelling with the Countess of Lys. Get the horses out here and let's go!"

Dewar slept, dreaming lucidly that he slept on the soft bosom of an ocean, rocked and carried up and down his sleep by its rising and falling waves. He dreamt of coolness, and dim twilight-blue light, and a feeling of still serenity unlike anything he had ever attained waking; he dreamt of the warm, supporting embrace of sweet water, deliberately sinking deeper into his dream, refusing to wake yet, swooning with the pleasure of his surrender to the enclosing element. And sleep he did, deeper and darker and without dream, until he turned in a wave of sleep and woke all at once.

He had no idea where he was. He lay on his side in a bed with rough linen sheets and a scratchy brownish woollen blanket, looking at an unpainted, plain wall made of wide boards. There were no curtains around the bed; they were drawn back to the bed-posts, that were also plain and undecorated. The window was covered by a wooden shutter; there were bright cracks and chinks in it, and a door was open enough to let light in that he could see these things. The air was close and stuffy. Dewar tried to think where he could be. It wasn't his tower; wasn't any house of Oren's he could recall; wasn't Lys; wasn't any of the tents he had lived in during the Ascolet and Chenay campaigns with Otto in Landuc; wasn't his round-walled spiralling house by the sea . . .

It felt wrong to be anywhere he had ever been.

Dewar rolled onto his back, groping for the Well, for the Stone, feeling the one distant and the other somehow muffled or blurred.

Seizing on that feeling, he remembered where he had been: in Prospero's place. They called it—what did they call it? Prospero had a Source here, that was why he couldn't sense the Well or the Stone clearly. He had come here with poor Freia, left again, yes, a forced march to the Well-forsaken outlands of the place, where he had Summoned Prospero—

And returned. Copied Prospero's workbooks in a cave. Freia had fed him some drug to keep him awake for he knew not how long, and for all those hours he had copied Prospero's workbooks. Yes. Where were the copies?

Dewar sat quickly upright and had one foot on the floor before dizziness rushed over him, a sparkling giddy near-faint, and he flopped back onto the bed panting, breaking into cold sweat, his heart racing. Some effect of the drug, he guessed. Where were the books? He stared at the ceiling—more rough boards and beams—and racked his memory. Copying the books.

Words, pages, diagrams flashed before his mind's eye. Yes, all that, all that, and then what? Someone had taken the work from him as he completed it; who? Prospero? He tried to sit again, slowly, by propping himself on an elbow.

Quick steps pattered in the hall, and the door was pushed open. A woman whose hair was so dark as to be nearly black came in and spoke to Dewar in a lilting language. He understood not a word, which made him feel further disoriented. She wanted him to lie back, pressing his shoulders, speaking on, and he let her settle him in the bed again. She wore the scanty pinned-and-draped linen clothes they favored here when they bothered to dress themselves, and when she straightened he could see that she was pregnant. The woman sat on the side of the bed, looking at him. She asked him a question.

"I don't understand you," he said, frustrated. He had forgotten about the peculiar language they used.

She put her head on her side for an instant, birdlike.

"Where is Prospero? Where is Freia?" he asked.

"Prospero," she repeated, and "Freia," and with those were other words.

Dewar shook his head. The woman sighed, said something, squeezed his hand (surprising him) and smiled, and was up and out of the room in a trice. Dewar put his feet out of the bed again.

This time he managed to stand, holding a bed-post, and let the dizziness pass by. When his head had cleared, he went to the door slowly and glanced up and down the hallway. It was lit pretty well; there were small windows high up, like a clerestory, and all the doors up and down it were open, so that squares of warm sun fell on the floor or wall at regular intervals. No hanging or carpet softened the raw wood; it was all plain, unworked. He recognized the place now as the house where he had come with Freia and Prospero on first entering this wilderness—Argylle, that was what it was called.

He was hungry and he wanted to relieve himself and wash. And he wondered what had become of his clothing, for he stood there in nothing but skin. A breeze tickled his legs as he looked back into the room for clothes, but he saw none, nor any box or cupboard that might hide them. He remembered that the latrine in this rough house had been at the opposite end of the hallway from the stairs, and went and found it, then prowled the hall. The other rooms were empty of all but a few pieces of furniture: another bed like his, a very fine bed of dark, carved wood with beautiful hangings, the long table at which he had dined with Prospero and Freia, a few chairs and benches and smaller tables, some linen-cupboards. By the bed like his stood a hunting-bow. Wrought-iron gratings pierced the floors here and there in these rooms: for ventilation and heat. The windows were unglazed.

Voices preceded people coming up the stairs; Dewar waited in his doorway, folding his arms. There had been one man here at least who spoke Lannach, he recalled. Perhaps the woman had gone to fetch him.

She had. Talking without stopping, she led the rangy blond man Dewar remembered to the sorcerer. The two of them finished their conversation, and the dark woman shook her head and pattered off.

"She's of a nesting mind," said the blond man, who was wearing a single length of reddish cloth over one shoulder, fastened by a braided leather belt, "and wants to fuss over you like her chick. You look steady." His Lannach was heavily accented and fell into a singsong rhythm. Dewar found that he must pay close attention to follow; he was unpracticed at deciphering accents.

"I feel steady. But I'm hungry. And where's Prospero?"

"He's taken the Lady and gone to Landuc. He said we must see to you, Lord Dewar, and so we shall, now that you wake." He grinned. Scars flexed on his suntanned face.

"Thank you. I am sorry, but I have forgotten your name."

"I am Utrachet. I am Lord Prospero's second, his Castellan he calls me. We met on the beach, after the fight at Perendlac."

"I remember that now. Did I sleep long? Where are my clothes?"

"Tauvis stripped you to wash the clothes, Lord Dewar, and so they are somewhere about, only she knows where, and I shall find them."

"Thank you. I was working at writing, on the island before I slept. I know I wrote many pages of notes. Where are they?"

The Castellan nodded wisely. "The Lady gave them to Scudamor, who keeps things for Lord Prospero. She said they are very important, and that you would want them. He will have them."

"I must see them right away."

Utrachet looked perplexed. "Scudamor is not here, Lord Dewar, and I do not go into the things he keeps in his storeroom: they are all ordered in his way. He will be here tomorrow. Is this well enough, or shall I look?"

Dewar hesitated. "You're sure he has them safe."

"Oh yes. She said he must keep them for you."

"Then it can wait, just one day," Dewar said. "It has waited a few days already, I think."

"You have slept through the last of winter, four days since Lord Prospero left us. Today is the first day of true spring. Everyone is swimming. Come to the river with me, and then we shall eat, if you will have it so."

"All right," said Dewar, for the day was very warm, and he followed Utrachet out of the house and through the empty square of the walled town, outside the walls to a fallow field that stretched to the river.

Utrachet had meant "everyone" when he said it. Dewar thought that the whole town must have taken a holiday. The riverbank was a solid mass of bodies, men and women and children sunning, grooming one another's hair, tickling and teasing and playing love-games, wrestling and taking turns throwing a stone and running footraces, and just talking and talking in a pleasant singing hum. The river itself was full, too; people were falling out of boats, having swimming-races, playing more lovers' games, splashing, laundering clothes, washing their hair, washing a handful of children who had had a mud-throwing contest, and talking and talking. The trees at the edges of the fields were out in their newest green foliage, that stirred in the sweet air. The sown fields were dusted with sprouting leaves, and the green fallow field they walked on was speckled with pink, white, and yellow flowers. Utrachet undid his leather belt and bundled up his half-tunic. Tauvis was ahead of them, naked now, carrying her clothes over one arm as she walked upstream to the area where the laundering was done. A leggy brown-haired girl ran to her and they went on, arms around one another.

Dewar stopped, staring at the island that lay across from the walled city site.

"Prospero made the tower," Utrachet explained, in the same tone he used for weather.

"Oh," Dewar said, and walked on, still staring at the black, monolithic-looking tower. A tower. Why would Prospero put a tower there, away from the city? He must see it himself, and soon.

But there were other things to do first. Dewar waded into the cold river and was pounced on by a trio of bold children, who pulled at him under water, teased him, and shrieked with delight when he chased them and threw them into the water; he swam farther and faster than anyone else, and he could stay under water longer, too; he amused a toddler with round black eyes, who was sitting on the shoulders of a burly reddish-haired man, by spitting water through his teeth in a stream, which became a coveted skill among the slightly older children. Then he left the river to dry off, because the afternoon was fading, and on the riverbank a dark-skinned man combed his hair and beard for him. Trying to fit in with the local standards of social behavior, he borrowed the comb to unknot a young woman's curly locks for her while she fed a child at her breast. The woman smiled and hummed a little as he combed, clearly pleased. Two younger women—more girls still—took the comb from him, giggling, and dressed each other's hair with elaborate braids under the first woman's direction. Dewar watched the crowd. A great number of them had gone up to the flowery field, where they were cheering three runners on.

A little way away from him, two women lay in the sun touching each other slowly and dreamily, occasionally glanced at by those around them, and Dewar lifted an eyebrow and politely looked away, stirred nonetheless: but they weren't the only ones doing so, he realized, and he tried to ignore the movements and noises, and wondered instead whether it was immodest of them, or whether modesty was a false notion where there was no shame—and there was indeed no shame. He was unclothed, and so was everyone around him. The sun and the warm air lay on his body like a blanket, as it did on all of them. He observed that the population of Argylle was composed entirely of young women and young men and children, and there were no grizzled beards or grey hairs among them: a favored group, he thought, Prospero's favor. Most of the men were scarred, and some were maimed or limping: souvenirs of Prospero's war with Landuc. Most of the women were either nursing or pregnant.

This led him to think again of Prospero's Spring, which Freia had not wanted to show him when he first came here with her, and of the Well and the Stone. The absence of those forces, on which he was accustomed to draw to strengthen or sustain himself when he needed strength or sustenance, was very noticeable to him now in his weakened state. He was gnawed by hunger and could not dull it by the sorcerer's method of living on pure power; he needed food, and as cooking smells began drifting his way from open-air hearths, the need became annoyingly distracting. Dewar tried to blunt his hunger by thinking of this Spring, which he thought must be somewhere not too distant. Prospero's notes had seemed to put it very close to where he lived, but Dewar could see nothing hereabouts that might be such a power source, either concealed or open. He swallowed on his empty stomach and recalled the indirect approaches to the Well of Landuc and the Stone of Pheyarcet.

Soon, though, people rose and went toward the cooking-fires, and Dewar joined them, for the supper was ready. A man who had only half a right hand gave Dewar a large, shallow bowl and a wooden spoon. The food was mostly winter-food still, but there was salad made of sweet and sour greens and buds, peppery yellow blossoms, and a strong-flavored crushed root, all dressed with salt and verjuice; shellfish that were tossed into a big basket of stone-boiled water until they opened; coarse but flavorful flat bread, cooked on hot rocks around the fires; a thick savory vegetable stew that tasted different from every pot; and dried fruits that had bland, almost greasy nuts tucked into the seed-hollows. He ate ravenously. They drank water or weak-bodied beer from clay or wooden beakers, so that Dewar surmised that the wine he'd had at other meals here was Prospero's private stock. It was a pleasant meal, eaten outdoors. Someone handed Dewar a piece of cloth to drape around himself as the air grew cold after sunset, and he managed to get it to stay put after some fumbling. Everyone sat around the four cooking-fires, talking and laughing, shoulder-to-shoulder in the firelight, a warm tangle of legs and arms developing as the evening went on, and although Dewar understood none of the language, he found it a congenial experience nonetheless. He liked the Argyllines. There seemed nothing dislikable about them.

Soon a wave of yawns went around the company, and clumps of people got up, picked up sleeping children, and left the fireside for the darkness. Dewar rose when Utrachet did, with a handful of others, and strolled with them back to the city walls. There was only a thin moon; the starlight sufficed to see shapes, but not faces, and so Dewar could not see who it was that took his hand, pressed it, and then slipped her hand into his improvised wrap. Startled, he stopped, and his assailant rubbed against him, unclothed for all he could tell. Teeth nipped his shoulder.

"What—" said Dewar, making to move away, but couldn't with her holding on to him like that. He touched skin, curly hair, flesh. Were people so free and casual here? Well. He smiled. It would hardly do to insult her by refusing.

His faceless, nameless friend's warm hand was stroking him, accompanied by a hip movement that made the intention perfectly explicit. She tugged playfully, and he took a step and began to laugh, and so did she, a rich alto ripple lovely to hear. Dewar gave her his hand again and led her through the open city gate to the bed where he had awakened.

"And where are your lodgings?" asked the Countess of Surluse.

"We shall go to Lys House, of course," said Luneté of Lys. "I sent a letter by the Emperor's courier, telling the steward to open the place and prepare it for me. It must be in a sad state, though—it cannot have been used for more than twenty years."

"And all that time, the staff have been boarded and paid for no service! A bad business. Sarsemar would have been wiser to lease it."

Luneté pressed her lips together. "That would have been unseemly, I think," she said. Sarsemar had taken liberties in his position as it was.

"But it is in Firdrake Square, still a very favored area, and he would have had no difficulty finding a tenant. A careless man, Sarsemar. I am pleased never to have had much to do with him. Such people will chill the prospects of everyone around them." The Countess shot as significant a glance as possible at the Baron of Ascolet, of whom she had formed an opinion that he was rackety, an upstart, and not at all what he claimed to be.

Luneté caught the insult, though Otto, who was supervising the loading of the Surluse coach, did not, and Luneté's previous patience with the Countess of Surluse's sharpness vanished. Ottaviano had behaved entirely like a gentleman to the rasp-tongued lady, and she had no business disparaging him in the slightest matter.

"Madame," said Luneté, "I must remind you that I cannot hear such things said of a gentleman as close to me as my former guardian." And she added a significant look of her own.

The Countess of Surluse humphed, but wisely left the issue: Lys House was, to be sure, in a favored part of the town, and it would not do to chill her welcome there. The tumult of the inn-yard, their last stop before the city, prevented much more conversation between them, and the Countess of Surluse was handed into her coach not long after with great address by the Baron of Ascolet, and was wished farewell very gratefully by the Countess of Lys—who did, after all, bid Surluse to call upon Lys when she had settled herself, and Surluse in turn bid Lys and Ascolet come dine the next day but one, the day before the great Court assembled, and so they all parted as amiably as might be hoped for, for near-strangers who had shared a difficult and crowded journey in midwinter.

Otto rode inside the Lys coach with his wife, her maid, and the page on this last half-day's stage to the city. The Countess of Surluse had explained to them that, as desirable as it might seem to press on and arrive late at night at one's own house, in practice a house that has only just been opened for one's arrival is usually less ready to receive one than an inn, no matter how many preparatory commands have been sent in letters. And since many did press on to reach the city in the weariest hours of the night, the inn was not as crowded as the worst they had seen on the trip; and Luneté in particular, wondering what sort of servants the Lys House steward might have been able to hire in such a brief time, saw the wisdom of this approach. They halted thrice—once to let Dinas out to climb onto the box beside the coachman, once to rest and care for the horses and themselves, and once to stand on Hunter's Hill outside the city, the famous panoramic view of land and harbor spread before them on this very cold, very clear day. A weathered kingstone smiled over carved numbers telling them that it wanted but ten miles to the city center. Otto, who had been to the city more than once before, pointed out an assortment of monuments, arches, and towers to his wife, who really wanted to know where Firdrake Square was and how much longer she must rattle along to get there. And over the whole city, behind it as it were, backed by the tongue of the great forest that was part of the Emperor's own preserve, watched the Palace, whose angled high white walls were clearly seen, and the golden-domed building within them glimpsed behind trees and lesser buildings. Within those walls was the Well: Luneté did not think of this, but Otto did.

Firdrake Square lay near the Palace. Luneté realized she should have guessed that, and wished, as her coach stopped and rumbled and stopped and rumbled over the cobbled streets, that Lys had been just a little less favored—just a little, so as to be closer to the city gates, sparing her this last, most fatiguing piece of the journey. Otto had left the coach and was riding, leading the coach and deploying his men to push through the crowded streets when such was possible. Laudine had a headache and was as out-of-sorts as Luneté, wondering that the Emperor would put up with such conditions in his own city. Dinas was in raptures, having a grand view of more houses, more shop-windows, more fine horses, more carriages, more chairs, and more people than he had ever imagined there could be in the world, and the coachman and footman were reminding one another that there would be some kind of punch, and some kind of food, and a good welcome generally, at Lys House when it opened its doors to the long-awaited new Countess.

They made one last, climbing turn; they left, of a sudden, the clamorous traffic behind them; the horses put their shoulders to it and drew the Countess of Lys's coach up a curving street that led into a closed loop of road, which was Firdrake Square. Otto tapped at the window and told Luneté so, and she could not resist leaving the shutter down and leaning this way and that, looking at the houses of her neighbors and their carriage-entrances and the trees that curved over the street. Everything looked very tidy and well-kept: she saw a child playing hoop, with four attendants; bare tree-branches reaching above high garden walls; a pair of liveried maid with covered baskets followed by two liveried footmen with greater baskets, all march-

ing along decorously quiet; she saw window-boxes of late greenery and a muffled-up gentleman in a light, dangerous-looking
open carriage. They all glanced at the coach, at the Lys shield
on the coach-door, and looked away, not staring. A very good
neighborhood, thought Luneté. Outside one door, across from
her own, stood a horse and eight soldiers, the horse like a statue,
uncommonly still, and the soldiers ranked in neat order, four
and four to each side of the iron gate. But she hardly noticed
that: it was across from her own house.

"Lys House," said Otto, for it was carved, though not
painted, over the arched front door, and he sent his Chancellor of the Exchequer to bang on the closed door of the carriage-
entry.

There ought to have been people watching for her, thought
Luneté. She had written to them; they knew she'd be arriving.
It looked too quiet.

No one came to the door.

"Knock again," Otto said, and he sent the footman up to
yank the bell as well, and the page to knock and ring at the front
door.

"Why aren't we in?" Luneté demanded, sticking her head out
of the coach.

"Something's amiss," said Otto. "Did you—"

The Chancellor's hammerings had attracted some attention:
the muffled-up gentleman had turned his carriage back to them.
Now the house-door opened and a portly man came out, and
with him a handful of others, footmen and valets by the looks
of them. Otto seized the first fellow at once.

"Are you deaf? The Countess of Lys bids you open the door
of her house and has been so doing for the past ten minutes."

"Unhand my steward, sirrah!" said the muffled gentleman.

"Your steward? Lys's steward, I should think," said Luneté,
who had left her coach with Laudine. "Are you not Pometer?"

A small number of passersby, appearing as by magic, began
to take an interest in the proceedings.

"Pometer is my steward, and this is my home," said the muffled gentleman.

"Pellico Sarsemar!" cried Luneté, a peal of rage in her voice. "This is Lys House and it is mine! You will remove yourself in the instant, sir!"

"The so-called Countess of Lys, I take it," said Sarsemar.

"I remember you," said Otto, nearly snarling. "I remember that I saw you in the stables buffling that dairy-maid on your last visit to Sarsemar. What the hell are you doing in the Countess of Lys's house, and how fast can you run?" He too had been seized by a rush of anger: to have come so far and find the Baron of Sarsemar's oily son squatting here was too much.

"Otto!" said Luneté.

"The pretender of Ascolet, as well," said Pellico. "I must ask you to leave; you are blocking the street before my carriageway, and I have no intention of receiving such distinguished company. The neighborhood is slipping as it is," he said, gesturing toward the house guarded by eight of the Emperor's soldiers, "and I am sure no one would desire it to go any further."

"It's gone already, if you're here," said Otto. "This is Lys House; Sarsemar has no more business with it than Sarsemar has with the Countess of Lys."

"The house has long been an emolument of Sarsemar, by the Emperor's grace," said Pellico Sarsemar, "and—"

"It has not," said Luneté.

The bystanders began to offer opinions and histories among themselves.

"You lie," said Otto, and he bounced up and lifted Sarsemar out of his carriage, onto the pavement, releasing him. Otto's men pressed around him, as much as they could. A certain amount of shoving began among the Sarsemar men and the Ascolet men.

"You jack-knave," said Sarsemar, and struck at Otto with his stick; Otto caught it, tore it from him, and broke it on his knee.

"Pometer, give me your keys," said Luneté, drawing herself up and holding out her hand. "You are relieved of your duties."

Pometer fidgeted from foot to foot, pale with fear, wringing his hands. "Your Grace, with greatest respects, I cannot, I—"

"Kester" (for this was the Chancellor's name) "relieve Pometer of his key-ring," said Otto.

The Chancellor of the Exchequer of Ascolet seized Pometer by the collar, but Pometer showed exceptional spirit and wriggled out of his coat. Voices were being raised now among the bystanders, who were drawing back to give the confrontation breathing-room, and among the disputants, who were calling one another liars and worse and beginning to finger their weapons. It must go badly with the Sarsemar side, who were unarmed, save that more people were beginning to come from the house (though still the carriage-entry remained closed).

"This is outrageous," declared Luneté, angrier than she had ever been.

"You have no business here, madame," said Pellico. "Begone. The decent inns are no doubt full, but you can certainly find some doss-house suited to you and your company."

"That's it," said Otto, and began wading through the crowd with murder in his eye. Pellico backed around, separated from his carriage and trying to reach it.

On the other side of the square, the front door of the house guarded by eight soldiers and a patient horse opened. A tall man, crimson-cloaked, came out, and the movement and color caught Otto's eye as he lunged to grab Pellico. Otto froze, then stood quite still. Pellico sprang into his carriage.

As the attention of most present had been on Otto, their heads were turned by his distraction, to look at the guarded house and the man speaking to the soldiers outside it.

"By the Fire, it's the Prince Marshal," said Otto quietly.

Luneté of Lys, mortified beyond belief, wished the earth might open and swallow her: a wish unlikely to be granted even in former days of the Well's most overt potency and presence. That so august a person as Prince Marshal Gaston should see her in the middle of a street brawl ought to be a fatal humiliation. Laudine gasped and curtseyed, staying down.

"Bosh," said Pellico Sarsemar, uncertainly.

"Calling on old Valgalant, the traitor," whispered someone.

"The great fool he; should have stayed out of town."

The Prince Marshal had taken the bridle of his horse in hand and turned, and now his eye lit on the drama across the pavement, really seeing it for the first time. His distant, serene expression shifted slightly as he focused on the street and the coach and the people arguing there, whose voices had all dropped in an instant when Otto had said, "It's the Prince Marshal." For everyone knew who Prince Gaston was, and no one particularly desired to be singled out for his notice at the moment, not in the throes of an altercation they all felt to be crass and common, though of enormous importance.

Luneté prayed in her thoughts, a heartfelt prayer of but a breath's duration, that the Well might take pity on her embarrassment and send the Prince on quickly before he recognized the Baron of Ascolet, who had fought against and then under him in the recent wars.

But the Well was deaf, or busy, and instead of mounting his enormous horse and taking his regal self elsewhere, Prince Gaston walked toward them, leading the horse, and six of the eight foot-soldiers who had waited for him followed. The other two opened the ironwork gate of the house and took places to either side of the door.

The voices raised in argument in the street had fallen utterly silent when Prince Gaston had taken his first step toward them. Now the bodies fell as well, bowing. Despite the dirt, Luneté curtseyed, a presentation curtsey; so did Pellico's housekeeper, even deeper. Pellico managed some awkward repositioning of himself in his carriage, which he feared to leave. Ottaviano, however, straightened, his backbone arranging itself into the habitual military erectness it had learned to assume in the vicinity of the Fireduke or Prince Herne.

"Ascolet," said the Prince Marshal.

"Sir."

"And Lys."

"My lady wife, sir, Luneté, who comes to take oath for Lys."

Luneté dared look up and met the Fireduke's gaze on her.

"Your Highness," she said, dry-throated. He hardly seemed to see her; the Countess of Lys was no part of the deeper matters that held his attention at the moment; she was an ephemeral movement in the landscape around his thought. But the Countess saw the Prince Marshal, a being from whom all adjectives had long been burned away, leaving only the essence of what he was. She tried to picture him later, and despite the daylight, despite the clarity of her vision, she had only an impression of vast height (of course, she nearly knelt), of brightness, of a balanced and pensive soul pausing in its business to glance at her. A crimson cloak, and the pale horse beyond. She did not think he had spoken to her.

Prince Gaston looked away from the Countess of Lys; it had only been half a heartbeat that he saw her at all, perhaps. No one else in the pack of disputants raised his head, all waiting to be addressed or dismissed, all hoping to be overlooked.

"What's debated here?" the Prince said to Otto.

"Lys House has been wrongly given to kin of Sarsemar's to use," said Otto.

Prince Gaston nodded once, up, down; no further explanation was needed, as Otto had guessed. "Go to the Palace," he said. "Tell Lord Teppick to accommodate thee."

"Yes, sir."

"Whatever else may pass, th'art Sebastiano's son," said Prince Gaston, in a voice only Ottaviano heard.

Otto looked down. "Yes, sir," he agreed, the blood flushing over his face.

The Prince turned away; he mounted his horse; the foot-soldiers remained behind him, going to the house of Valgalant (four went in, no doubt to its back gates). Before the hoofbeats of the Prince's horse had faded in the air, Ottaviano had tugged Luneté to her feet, was wordlessly bundling her into her coach, pushing the stunned maid Laudine and the page in after her. Sarsemar's son and servants looked at one another, discomfited, as the Lys coach and the Ascolet horsemen clattered off down the street, following the Prince Marshal, and the soldiers that stood before the Valgalant house watched the knot of people dissolve into the afternoon's usual foot-traffic once more.

"Best of the day to you, Lord Dewar." Utrachet sat down, across the table from Dewar and the woman with whom Dewar had passed waking and sleeping hours of the night.

"And to you, Castellan." Dewar swallowed a piece of leathery brown dried fruit, the second course of his breakfast. The first had been a pot of porridge, enriched with interestingly pepper-flavored seeds, lacking salt. There was no third course. It reminded him of the food Freia had shared with him when they had travelled together on her gryphon, in Landuc, searching for Prospero.

"Tauvis is fetching the clothing you wore," said Utrachet. "I have told her not to fuss over you, that you are not an invalid though you slept long. She thought you were ill, but Sulishon has told her you are not. So had I told her, for Lord Prospero said you would sleep so."

"I was very tired, that was all," Dewar said, faintly embarrassed by the implied public discussion of his good health and its symptoms.

Sulishon, Dewar's bedfellow, said something.

"She would like you to come to her people tonight," said Utrachet. "They have gone up to the new fields, ploughing."

"I may go, but I may not too," Dewar said. "There are things I must do here, I think."

Utrachet conveyed this. Sulishon shrugged; Utrachet said something else, and she made a face at him, stood, and kissed Dewar's mouth (with a nip) and left them.

"I hope I haven't offended," said Dewar, a purposefully broad statement.

"Offended? No. She wants what she wants, and it will be or it will not be. Some would offend, yes. Dazhur would offend. Sulishon, not."

"Good, then. Utrachet, is Scudamor here now? You said he would be back."

"We can inquire for him. If he is not here now, he will be soon. It is early yet, but he travels quickly."

"I have thought of something else to find," Dewar said. "When I came here, with Prospero and Freia, I had a bag and a staff. I know I carried them to the island. Where are those now?"

"Scudamor will have them," said Utrachet confidently. "The Lady will have put them in his care."

Dewar leaned back. His greatest concerns alleved, he could relax. "When he has given me back those notes, I wish to go see that tower, the thing Prospero made." It must have been a mighty work, and he was chagrined to have slept through it. If only Freia had brewed him one more cup of that drug!

"There are boats. I will row with you, or Scudamor will. The river has gone down, but you do not know the current. The tower is a very strange place: I have been just a little inside it, and it is quite dark and empty. Prospero has desired that we move certain house-things there before he returns. But it is empty now."

"I thank you for your help."

"It is Lord Prospero's wish," said Utrachet. "He said you are his son, and we are to provide you with all you ask."

Tauvis brought Dewar's clothes to the bedchamber where he had slept. Through Utrachet, he requested water, soap, a towel, and a comb, and put himself in reasonable order while Utrachet went out to see if Scudamor could be found. He had grown a beard while he was working like a maniac and then sleeping, and there was no razor nor knife to shave with, so Dewar left it.

He did not have a conscious plan, beyond collecting his belongings and seeing the tower. A flow of action had seized him. There were things he must do here, things he must do elsewhere; he seemed to float effortlessly from moment to moment, with a feeling of predestination. Things would happen; he would act.

Someone tapped at the chamber door as he pulled on his

boots, and Dewar looked up and said "Come." Utrachet entered, and with him came Scudamor—whom Dewar knew, having met him before—and a very fair, very beautiful woman, a woman who wore the coarse clothing of Argylle with such grace and dignity as would distinguish her in any society.

Dewar wished he had met her last night.

"Lord Dewar," said Scudamor, "here is Cledie Mulhoun."

Dewar stood and bowed. "I am honored." He could not stop looking at her. Her features, her bearing, her gestures were all impossibly fine. She could not belong here: she must be some foreigner, some friend of Prospero's.

"Cledie asked me many questions, which I could not answer, about the Lady," said Utrachet, "and you, who travelled with her, might know more."

"I will answer if I can, madame."

All this time Cledie had been studying him, her bright, wide brown eyes moving over him and weighing him, her face alive with an intelligence that was uncommon anywhere. She spoke, and Utrachet nodded.

"She asks, Is the Lady well."

Dewar hesitated, and saw that Cledie saw his hesitation, and knew that even though they could not speak directly, she was not to be misled. "As to that, Castellan, you folk who have been here will know as much as I, nearly. The Lady was badly treated in Landuc. She was hurt; she was not ill, but she was weary and sore. I brought her here to mend and rest, but as I have worked steadily the whole time I have been here, and did not observe her much, I do not know how she fares."

Utrachet translated this. Scudamor looked grave. Cledie frowned and spoke.

"Why then did Lord Prospero take her away again?"

"I don't know—I do know, a little. You, Scudamor, you, Utrachet—you saw that treaty. It involved her, involved marrying her off. He had no choice but to take her back with him, if there were vows of that sort to keep."

There was a brief discussion following this answer.

"Cledie finds the idea of marrying off peculiar, as do we all," said Scudamor. "It is to mate people who would not?"

"Yes. It is not uncommon in Landuc."

"Will you be married off as well?" was Cledie's next question.

"No," said Dewar, smiling in spite of the seriousness of the conversation. "It is done to women, giving them to powerful men, and sorcerers do not bind themselves with marriage."

Cledie Mulhoun spoke again. "When will they return?" translated Utrachet.

"I am sorry. I do not know. Prospero has been defeated; he is under the Emperor's foot now, and so is Freia for she is his, and all that was his, is the Emperor's," Dewar said.

This caused another brief discussion, and Utrachet asked Dewar, "What then of Lord Prospero's declaration that the Lady must stay here?"

"He did not mean quite that, I think. He bestowed these lands on her, certainly, hoping to keep them from the Emperor. I don't know if that will hold water there. The Emperor will not be inclined to let her go, and Prospero ceded to him the right to choose her husband."

Cledie said something sharp-sounding when this was translated to her and left.

"She says, if Argylle is the Lady's, then the Lady is Argylle's," Utrachet said, "and she cannot be given or taken away."

⟞ 6 ⟷

THERE ARE AS MANY WAYS OF entering a Palace as there are visitors. The Emperor's Palace in Landuc, seat of a powerful man in a powerful realm, receives thousands of visitors through its doors each day, and each comes in the appropriate style. The preferred doors for entering the Palace, as with any Landuc house, are on the east side, and a loiterer at the top of the white stairs there, below the Proclamation Balcony and the great golden dome, may watch the world come and go in a morning.

The potentate might arrive in a sedan-chair shaded by lofty, rippling feathers dyed the hues of the rainbow, riding a high-stepping panoplied horse, or in an open carriage or closed coach discreetly or ostentatiously blazoned with arms and devices. The lackeys might be naked, or nearly so, or plainly dressed, or frothed with gold and silver lace; they might be men or not, armed or not, imposing or not, but they would be legion, and would affect to be unawed at the sight of the famous gold-leafed dome of the Palace, at the sweeping stairs leading to the impossibly tall white doors inlaid with gold flames, at the ranks of cold-eyed guards, never at ease, who watch the approach of all who come.

Beneath the eyes of the guards, even the potentate is diminished, for the guards know that all are subservient to the Emperor, from the mightiest to the lowliest, and that, be the petitioners ever so powerful, their petitions might be denied, their plans dismissed, their kingdoms taken from them and sucked dry as an orange, on the Emperor's nod.

The guards' eyes watch the arrival of lesser creatures too, as closely and as cynically as they watch the monarchs and magnificences who travel in state. Goldsmiths, jewelers, architects, armorers, usurers, playwrights, poets, portrait-painters, philosophers, fools, sea-captains, shipwrights, bankers, guildsmen, dwarves, landscape-designers, ladies' maids with messages, gentlemen's men with gifts —all pass to and fro in compact review of the realm before the eyes of the guards. Among them go counts and earls, barons and lords, knights and marquises, swarmed by their followers, friends, and companions, full of the importance of themselves and their errands and never admitting that the guards, at any instant, might step forward and seize any one of them, for any reason. It had happened once: Baron Beort of Gonlingfast had been taken on the third step—the very spot struck a thousand times a day by slippered soles and booted heels—taken and hauled to the sixth step and beheaded, and his body thrown to Prince Herne's yellow-toothed pack. Everyone knows it; but it is history now, and such things cannot happen to loyal supporters of the Emperor.

Not all visitors come to the Palace through the east door. Some come to the side doors with laces, linen, perfumes, poisons, gowns, gloves, shoes, hats, tapestries, carpets, furniture; some come to the rear doors with laundry, music, dogs, horses, candles, coal, wood, beer, wine, vegetables, poultry, meat, fish, flowers to sell, buttons to peddle, alms to beg, fortunes to tell. Some—a very few—scale ivied walls or copper-green drainspouts and slip in through the thousands of windows or down the hundreds of chimneys, and most of those are clever enough not to boast later if they succeed in leaving. And some of those who come and go thus furtively are as those who enter through the east door, but do not wish their calls to be noted by the gold-cuffed clerk who stands at a tall writing-desk inside the door and sets down names in his great ledgers.

The Princes of the realm come and go freely through any door or window they please, Prince Marshal Gaston or Prince Herne causing a nearly imperceptible straightening and stiffening of the spine to ripple through the guards; Prince Heir Josquin's leisurely arrivals and departures, borne along in a chattering cloud of noble admirers dimming their glories and giving their ears, eyes, and anything else he might desire; Princess Evote aloof and Princess Viola running an appraising eye over the ranks; blue-coated Prince Fulgens scowling over some slight new-minted (genuine or imagined); and, but recently after long absence, brooding Prince Prospero, unaccompanied save by his muffled daughter. A wave of alert apprehension had gone through the guards as the Prince of Air passed, his dark cloak floating and casting swirling shadows on the white stone, for although the guards saw everything and everyone come and go, all sorts, all day, if there was one kind of visitor they would gladly never have seen at all, it was a sorcerer.

For sorcerers arrive differently. They come unannounced, as Prospero did, alone and more dangerous than a phalanx of Lys pikemen, a crackling aura warning even the insects to stay away from them. Oriana of the Glass Castle had lately come in a chariot, drawn by horned creatures which had bitten the throat out of the groom who ran to hold them for her. Esclados the Red had liked to travel in a sedan-chair carried by wide-eyed near-naked virgins chained with rings of gold and ropes of pearls; the Spider King's method of travel was unnerving to the most stalwart of the guard; Acrasia the Foul came and went in a black, dark-draped closed coach which left a reek of corruption in its wake. But of these only Oriana had been to the east door since the Emperor's accession.

That a sorcerer had, very lately, been about the Palace, had burgled the place and carried off Prospero's Well-guarded daughter from under Prince Gaston the Marshal's very nose (the same girl who now trotted in Prospero's shadow), was whispered, but the subject displeased the Emperor and was not openly discussed. It had been a long time since the Palace Guard met sorcery head-on, and, when faced with a sudden explosion of flame and a hot draught of ashes beneath the portico, they reacted with admirable aplomb.

As this explosion occurred, the guards ducked and shielded their faces even as they brought weapons to bear on the source. The flames and cinders blew away as suddenly as they had come. Their source, the sorcerer, stood on the white, unscorched marble, nonchalantly brushing ashes off his handsome turquoise-blue cloak's shoulder cape with a hand gloved in matching leather. He doffed his black hat and blew ashes from the blue-green-silver cockade, then donned it again at a jaunty angle. His other hand held a long black staff. He ignored the guards; he ignored the gasps and a cerise-cheeked baroness swooning on the steps; he stood in a perfect silence, turning on his heel to look over the place with an appraiser's perspicacious eye. He had not been to the east door before and was wondering how to proceed.

"Let go of me, wolf!" someone cried, and then, "Dewar!"

He whirled.

Some distance below him on the steps was tall, frowning Prince Herne, and Prince Herne's left hand gripped the upper right arm of a woman whose brown cloak was thrown back to show her gold-and-brown brocaded dress. The woman was struggling, pushing at Herne, who was as little troubled by her resistance as might have been one of the columns under the portico.

The visitors to the Palace discreetly and prudently drew back, out of the way between Herne and the sorcerer. Herne's choleric humor was famous, and one never knew what a sorcerer might do.

"Why, Prince Herne," Dewar said, smiling.

"Take him!" Herne ordered the guards.

The sorcerer spun around again, drawing a line on the white marble with his staff-end; a sheet of fire leapt up, rippling in the cold winter air. The guards tried to flank it, and it danced before them, hissing. Dewar descended toward Herne.

"Hello, Freia," the sorcerer said.

"Let me go!" cried Freia, prying at Herne's hand, wrapped round her arm as a root grows round a stone.

Herne drew his saber from its scabbard slowly, caressing the air with it. "In a clean fight I'll gut thee, turncoat," he said softly, with a joyless smile.

"I'm not interested in fighting with you or anyone right now, Herne. What are you doing trolling young women around by the arm?"

"The baggage sought to steal a horse," said Herne. "The Emperor's hospitality is not to her liking. We've other things to discuss. Draw." The steel of his blade flashed as he gestured at the hilt of Dewar's sword.

"I couldn't dream of duelling with you, Herne, not with you incapacitated so," Dewar said pleasantly. "You're far too honorable a man to, for instance, use her as a shield, eh? Yet you can't let go of her; she's quick, she'll take to her heels and be-gone."

Herne laughed. "Aye, I'll turn her loose to go. And whither?

She's not been to the Well, not passed the Fire. How far to thy earth, tender pretty vixen? Where's thy Map, thy Ephemeris?" He shook Freia. She kicked him, hampered by skirts and manure-stained cloak.

Dewar's staff swung in his hand, a glowing haze trailing it, cometlike. "Come, Freia," he said to her. "Bring me to your father. Herne, I strongly suggest that you release her, now."

"Take her," Herne suggested, and moved up a step closer to Dewar, lifting his sword, dragging Freia.

"How now, Herne; what's toward?" someone called from above. A whisper passed among the onlookers who had not slunk inconspicuously away, fearful of sorcery.

Herne glanced past Dewar. His eyes narrowed. "A horse-thief and a traitor," he said. "Beneath you, Gaston."

Dewar's shoulders prickled; he heard Gaston behind him and glanced around. The guards were still fenced with flames; the Prince Marshal approached alone, passing indifferently through the fire.

Gaston paused in mid-step, met Dewar's look, and his brows drew slightly together.

"What's thy errand here, Dewar?"

"A professional call," Dewar said. "On this lady's father."

"On her father," the Marshal repeated, eyeing Dewar thoughtfully.

"I've a prior call upon thee, bastard," Herne said.

" 'Ware thy tongue, Herne; what know'st thou of his parentage?" Gaston said. "Meseems the lady finds thy arm little to her liking."

"The wench was in the stables trying to steal a horse," Herne said.

"He's Papa's horse," Freia said. "Liar!" She landed a kick on Herne's high-booted shins.

"Trying to steal thyself away, then," Gaston said, "and couldst not go a furlong ere wert taken again. The Emperor desires that thou shouldst stay, Lady Freia, and—"

"He's nothing to me! Nobody orders me!"

"So 'tis seen," Gaston said, "yet hast no choice but stay. What's thy office with Prospero, Dewar?"

"It is domestic in nature," Dewar said, and they regarded one another again.

"Th'art acquainted with the lady."

"Well enough to guess that she prefers my arm to Herne's," Dewar replied in the same dry tone.

"Herne, release her, and I'll see them both within," Gaston said.

"A fine guard wert thou aforetimes," Herne said. "She's a very vixen, and he's cunning and without honor—"

"Watch it, Herne," Dewar snapped.

"Herne, release her," Gaston repeated.

With a glare, Herne opened his hand. Freia stood still for a heartbeat; Dewar smiled at her, and she sprang up to stand at his side. He slipped his arm familiarly around her waist and embraced her. Freia clung to him, hugged him trembling around the neck.

"Well met," said he. "Glad to see me?"

"I hoped and hoped you'd come," she said, low in his ear. "I was afraid you wouldn't."

"I had vital matters of my own, elsewhere, but it would have been ungentlemanly not to come. Your fears were baseless, madame."

She nodded. "I thought so," Freia whispered, and leaned against him, relaxing. "I trust you."

"Thank you." He looked down into her strained face, then pressed her against him, a reassuring squeeze. *Was* she his sister? Could a blood-clay construct be properly called sibling to those born of the body? Well, Prospero named her daughter; he had made up his mind to claim her as his own, and since Dewar was Prospero's son then Freia must be his sister. It certainly accounted for her devotion to her father. But it was a queer notion. He looked up at the Princes again, the corner of his mouth quirking.

"Gaston, thou chivalrous blockhead," Herne snarled, and stalked away.

"Perhaps," Gaston agreed indifferently, and he turned and looked down at Freia, at Dewar. "Herne is no friend to thee, Dewar, but I am not thy enemy. Nor would gladly be."

"I understand," Dewar said, half-smiling. "Freia," he said, lowering his gaze from Gaston's, "I have some unfinished business with Prospero."

"He's here," she said, straightening and moving away from him a little.

"I know. Will you take me to him?"

"He's with that weaselly Emperor," Freia said, and her look became colder.

"Perhaps I should speak to this Emperor also," Dewar mused. "Yes. I think that might be best. It's time."

Freia folded her arms, pulling her cloak tight around her. Her expression had changed, closed and cooled and become inward-looking, though she watched Dewar and Gaston narrowly.

"I'll escort thee, Dewar, but must first extract thy word of—"

"I won't kill anyone if I'm not attacked," Dewar said, smiling, glancing significantly after Herne.

" 'Twill serve. Come with me. And thou, lass," he caught Freia's eye, "come also, for th'art too precious to cast lightly loose."

Dewar drew her hand through his arm; she went with him, her face an unsmiling mask. The flames he had conjured fell down and extinguished themselves as he approached, and the guards saluted Gaston and let them pass.

Count Pallgrave, to his own great humiliation, had been expelled at Prince Prospero's behest from the chamber where Prince Prospero and the Emperor were now having a loud, but unintelligible, argument. He sat stiffly outside, waiting until he should be called again to advise and annotate points of discussion and agreement. The Emperor's secretary Cremmin, who had taken his portable desk out with him into hallway exile, sat busily polishing his minutes of the meeting thus far today. They were not a pretty sight, full of blasphemies and ad hominem slurs from both parties, and the Emperor's remarks about Prince Prospero's daughter, the Lady Freia, really ought to be struck altogether. Cremmin instead filled them in, perhaps embroidering slightly. Even so, His Majesty's invective came off a poor second to Prospero's.

The hall leading to the chamber was long, its floor of cold polished white marble and its walls decorated with cameolike, allegorical white-and-salmon bas-reliefs of Panurgus's nonmilitary conquests, each panel picked out with gilding on fingertips, arrow-heads, nipples. There was light from thin windows between the bas-relief panels and from freestanding candelabra; the arm-thick candles were lit, though storm-tinted late-afternoon winter sun was making the hall as warm as it ever could appear. The approach of Prince Gaston with two persons in his wake was thus immediately visible, as well as audible.

Cremmin rose, as did Count Pallgrave. The four guards to either side of the salmon-and-white door squared their shoulders and set their eyes resolutely forward. The Marshal was accompanied by the very Lady Freia whose name had arisen in discussion and by a bearded, cloaked young gentleman whose air of insouciant superiority could not be due to the metal-shod staff he carried like a sceptre.

"The Emperor desires not to be interrupted, Your Highness," Cremmin said respectfully, bowing. "I will announce you when—"

"Don't bother," said the young gentleman, somehow lightly sidestepping Prince Gaston and nearly getting to the door.

Two of the guards stepped together in front of it, shoulder-to-shoulder.

Count Pallgrave inhaled, a hissing sound. "Young man, this is not—"

The Marshal interrupted him. "Aside," he said. His mouth might have twitched in a faint smile. Was Gaston amused at Pallgrave's discomfiture? The guards stepped aside as precisely and impassively as they had stepped together.

The young man inclined his head courteously to Prince Gaston, smiling sardonically.

"Your hat, sir," Pallgrave growled, placing his monocle in his eye for a better look at this would-be jester.

The gentleman, who was clearly no gentleman at all, opened the door, hatted still. "Hello, hello," he said, "I do hope I'm interrupting something."

"Pall*grave!*" shouted the Emperor.

Lady Freia, startlingly, giggled, then sniffled and sighed. She turned away from the door and went back down the corridor alone. Two of the guards followed her at four paces' distance after Gaston paused in entering the conference room and ordered them softly to do so.

Count Pallgrave drew himself up stiffly as the door was closed in his face. Cremmin hid a smirk and sat down again.

Lady Freia didn't look back at the guards escorting her, but her shoulders hunched as she crossed her arms and she walked with her eyes on the floor.

Prince Prospero had turned from giving the fire a wholehearted kick as the door opened; the Emperor, seated at the table, started to his feet.

The smile on the face of the man who opened the door was anything but deferential. "Hello, hello," he said insolently. "I do hope I'm interrupting something."

"Pall*grave!*"

Prince Gaston stepped in, closing the door on Pallgrave and, merely fortuitously, setting his shoulder blades to it. The handle turned frantically, unheeded behind his back.

"Gaston, we hope this jackass is a prisoner who has slipped from your custody. Get him out of here and have him hanged."

" 'Twere ill-conceived of thee to pick a quarrel here, Avril," Prospero warned, watching Dewar. "What's thy errand, sir?"

"You left me incapacitated," Dewar said, deliberately oblique, "and we left matters between us in some suspense."

"Time pressed me to leave thee and hasten hither, to waste time," Prince Prospero said. "We'll make an end of our dealings anon."

"Who is this?" demanded the Emperor.

"So you're the Emperor," Dewar said, regarding him. "Hm."

"Get—him—out," the Emperor ordered Prince Gaston.

"No man orders such as he," Prince Gaston replied.

"Indeed," Dewar agreed, "though had you bargained with me in the past, brought me under contract, Emperor, you might be able to bargain now. As it is—"

"You're that Dewar of whom we've heard."

"There could be more than one man of the name about," Dewar said. "What have you heard?" he inquired, in a tone of mock-dismay.

Prospero laughed outright, a dark sound.

The Emperor glared at him, and Dewar shook off his flippancy. "My errand's mainly with Prince Prospero," he said to the Emperor then, businesslike. "But since you're here I may as well tell you a thing, one that may benefit us all."

"And what is that," the Emperor said.

"Prince Prospero's welfare is of dear concern to me, and if he were to meet with mishap here—for example, dine upon a meal that disagreed with him, or cut himself shaving in the bath or fencing, or perchance an accident with rope—I see you take my meaning. Be his well-being less tenderly cherished than your own, Emperor, I shall take your blood for his in filial vendetta."

"What—" began the Emperor, and stopped.

Prince Gaston closed his eyes a moment, then looked at Prince Prospero, who had folded his arms and stood watching Dewar with half-raised eyebrows, his expression betraying only calm interest and perhaps a touch of pride. There it was. Avril's and Prospero's feud had just become broader and more dangerous.

"Your Marshal here can assure you that I'm well able to do so," Dewar said.

"You knew of this," the Emperor accused the Marshal, rising from his seat as his anger rose.

"Your Majesty, I did not," Prince Gaston said sharply.

"Of course he did not," Prince Prospero snapped.

"How not?" demanded the Emperor.

"I'm not in the habit of announcing my lineage, nor are most sorcerers," Dewar said drily. "However, Emperor, I make an exception in this case. You crow over the defeat of your brother. Take your delight in moderation this time, or you'll find yourself facing me—and you're not competent to do so, ignorant as you are of the Art. You're undefended, unshielded here, even though hard by your own Well. You have relied on oaths and old treaties to protect you from sorcery, but I have sworn no vows to you or the Well. I could kill you now. I will not. And you shall remember that you are hostage to your own good conduct toward my father."

"You dare to stand here and threaten us—"

"I could extinguish you before Gaston could draw, and his sword is of no use against me," Dewar said, motionless but tense. "But I have no real quarrel with you. I do not involve myself in politics, and I shall not take sides in Prospero's dispute with the Empire. That's his, not mine. Just remember that I'm here, Avril, Uncle Avril, and that I have an interest."

"We shall certainly remember that, sorcerer," the Emperor said, narrow-eyed, "nephew."

"Good," Dewar said. "Free for dinner?" he asked, turning to his father.

"Not free, but available," Prince Prospero said, the corner of his mouth lifting in half a smile. "Aye, let us dine; thy uncle hath much to chew on and digest ere we fare further with his reprehensible ideas."

"You demanded a judge," the Emperor said.

"Aye, and a clean one, if there be such in the realm, which I doubt."

"It will be settled by the Imperial Court," the Emperor said, smiling, "as it is a lofty matter."

"Imperial Court?" Prince Prospero repeated derisively.

The Emperor continued to smile. "Tomorrow afternoon," he said.

Freia knew the guards were there. Since arriving in the Palace, she and her father had been under house arrest. The guards were always there.

She closed the door to her apartments and left them outside. She'd managed to lose a pair today, and had crept out of the Palace with no clear destination beyond not-there, but Herne had caught her in the stables. Freia felt a taste of despair in her throat; she swallowed it. Dewar was here now. He must have come to get her out, to get Prospero out, away from the cruel Emperor, from Prince Herne who made her tremble when he looked at her, from raging Prince Fulgens, from Golias. Prince Gaston was a cipher, a background figure, always watching, as he had watched before. He wasn't on her side, though she thought he wished to be kind.

Dewar would help them.

Freia left the door. The room was dim, though its tall windows were uncovered. On the unfavored north side of the building, it overlooked a fir-ringed ornamental lake which was frozen and dead for the season. Rushes poked through the ice at broken angles, yellow against the black. The hearth was empty; the fire had gone out and there was no wood. The servants were as ungracious as their Emperor. There was never any wood; they'd built a fire once, on the first day, and it died of starvation. She was always cold here. She had been warmer in that snowbound house in Chenay, where she had met Dewar, where her gryphon Trixie had barely fit into the barn. There'd been firewood, anyway, and better food than the overdone, inedible messes they served here.

She stopped at the narrow black table which stood like a bar to entry in front of the door, noticing that it held something new: flowers. Yellow roses, the edges of their furled petals blushing peach, and cream-white lilies were joined by soft, trailing gossamer ferns that spilled over the edge of their silver trumpet-vase and brushed the table. It was midwinter here—where could the flowers have come from? Freia sniffed cautiously at a half-opened rose: its perfume was spicy-sweet and sharp, weak in the cold chamber. The lilies cupped a heavy, drowsy scent. The lush flowers were nearly too rich, nearly cloying; drawing back, she carefully stroked a fern's delightfully soft frond.

Under the frond was something white and sharp-cornered. Freia's fingers knocked it down; she lifted it and found it was an envelope. She looked at it, puzzled.

In a book of Prospero's, she had read about people in Landuc sending one another messages in bouquets of flowers, but in the book there had been meanings in the flowers themselves, which ones were chosen and how they were arranged. Prospero had said it was a fool's tale and that nobody did that, at least nobody of sense, although he'd not answer for idiotic fops and flirts. The people in the poem had all been shepherds and shepherdesses, not courtiers, and Freia had concluded that they sent messages with flowers because they couldn't write. But why send both flowers and a letter? Who would do that?

Her name was on the envelope: *Lady Freia.* She had never had a letter before. Prospero had lately received letters from acquaintances and men of business, but she had neither. This must be for him. She picked at the wax carefully: her name *was* on the outside, and she could give it to him after she had looked to see who had sent it by mistake. The wax resisted her fingernail, and finally she had to tear the envelope to open it.

Inside was a piece of paper folded once. On it was written:

> To the worshipful Lady Freia, with most respectful greetings. We have met and parted in vile and harrowing circumstances, and since then my heart is deeply weighed by my trespasses against your liberty and by the sufferings you bore after being removed from my hands. Alas, had I known that leaving you in care of Golias would redound so to your harm I had never done it. For I do love you as my cousin and as the most courageous and right noble lady in the Well's great realm of Pheyarcet, and I would never that so fair a creature should be so basely used as you have been. I beg you grant me some sign of compassion that will redeem my unhappy soul from its wretched

perdition. I would prove me to you a more courteous gentleman and more loving friend than I have shewed myself hitherto. I am yours to command to any task and any favor of notice from you would be treasured by your most miserable cousin and devoted servant Ottaviano.

The ornamented Court-hand in which the letter was written took some minutes for Freia to read, and as she deciphered its meaning her hands trembled and her face became pale.

When she had reached the end and Ottaviano's swashing signature, she stared at the letter again, frozen with fear, and then crumpled it and threw the ball of paper into the cold hearth. The envelope followed, and Freia flew to the gloomy corner where the bed, festooned with brown curtains and dull crimson tassels, stood high and square. She kicked off her muddy shoes and spread her muck-hemmed cloak across the bed for an additional blanket, her outer dress on top of it. Shivering, she pulled the covers down, tugged the heavy, cumbersome bed-hangings around, and got in, wrapping the blankets and pillows around herself to make a warm nest.

Here. He was here. Ottaviano was here in the Palace—he had been in her rooms—he was here, and Golias was here too. She had seen him in a hallway when Prospero brought her to meet his sisters and then had glimpsed him that very morning in the breakfast-room and fled without eating. Now Ottaviano was here also, and with fear-sickness she wished she had been able to get away from the Palace today.

She had stopped attending the formal Palace luncheons and dinners days ago. People stared at her. They whispered, but no one talked to her. Prince Josquin was courteously distant, but she never knew what to say, and after a few empty politenesses he had said no more than "Good evening" to her. The Empress Glencora had an odd accent, and she spoke quickly and brightly, and Freia couldn't quite follow what she said. The others didn't try. Prince Fulgens bellowed at her once when she'd failed to understand his "Heave it here, girl" to mean "Pass the salt" and after that Freia had deserted the Emperor's table. Prospero had scolded her about that. He scolded her about everything. He had lectured her as they rode here on the Road, and he had chivvied her relentlessly since arriving. Their every conversation had revolved on her behavior, her disobedience, her folly; any word she spoke to Prospero brought a scolding. All the ill-hap and evil that he now suffered was her fault, according to him.

Was it her fault? Freia had no notion of her own blamelessness. She had had no chance to tell Prospero what Golias had done to her; it had hurt her deeply, true, but perhaps it mattered less than what had been done to Prospero, which would hurt him longer and more than her transient physical pains. Hitherto unaccustomed to hypothetical cases, Freia had hours now to teach herself their construction and bitter use. Had she but remained at home, waiting, while Prospero went to war—but she still saw no wrong in having followed him. Had she not sought the place where she could free herself of the burden of Golias's rape, had she instead insisted that Dewar carry her directly home to Prospero—why, they would have arrived in Argylle in time, before Prospero left again for Landuc, and all would have been well for Papa. He would have kept his sorcery even though he'd lost his war.

But it was his war, Freia thought. His war. She hadn't wanted anything to be different and he had.

She squeezed her eyes shut. It was harder and harder to imagine herself home again. Home was gone; Prospero had changed; she was as much a prisoner as she had ever been, but her father had joined the enemy.

For perhaps an hour she worked on being asleep, achieving only a dreamless, unrelaxed doze that was often the best she could do now. The sound of someone saying her name made her startle awake, clammy and disoriented. It wasn't home; the voice wasn't quite Papa's—

"What?"

"Freia? You're in bed? Hell, I'm making a light," Dewar announced irritably, and light flared, a bright line between the curtains. Freia pushed one aside, sitting up, pulling the blankets around her.

"Hullo."

Holding a triple candlestick, Dewar came around the bed and sat on its edge. His eyes were black in the candles' wavering light; he wore different clothes now—snug-fitting silvery-grey breeches; blue stockings; a waistcoat embroidered with seashells; a sea-blue coat, deep-cuffed, silver-buttoned, silver-laced. Fair Prince Josquin wore such garb, and the other men of the Court; Freia could not quite fathom Dewar so dressed. He nearly glowed. He said, "Hello yourself. Are you being spartan for any particular reason?"

"Spartan?"

"No light, no fire, no maid, no dinner." Dewar gestured at the cheerless chamber. "And a surpassingly hideous tapestry," he added.

"This is where they told me to stay. There isn't any wood."

"Tell your maid to bring it to you. You do have a maid?" He looked around: clothes on the floor, general disorder in the room, and Freia's tangled hair something less than fashionably dressed.

"The Empress sent one. She was nasty; she pulled my hair and pinched me. I told her to go away and she did," Freia said. "I can comb my own hair. Nobody brought wood ever. Maybe they're afraid I'll set the room on fire."

"Would you?"

"I'd burn it piece by piece in the fireplace," she said, wanly humorless.

Dewar grinned, white teeth flashing in his dark beard. "Start with that tapestry, and I'm with you all the way. How are you? What's news?"

She shrugged. "Nothing."

"Nothing?"

"Prospero talks to the Emperor and nobody tells me what about. I don't know what's happening. I'm afraid to ask. Papa's

so angry all the time, and I'm—Dewar, I'm afraid. This is a bad
place. I don't know what's going to happen." She stared at
him, pleading in her heart for him to offer her a way out.

"Ask Prospero."

"He won't answer. He—he growls at me."

"Ask Josquin or somebody. He'd tell you if he knew. He's
not a bad fellow."

"I don't know anybody. I—Dewar, I want to go home. I
don't want to be here," she whispered, her throat tight.

Dewar frowned. "Then you shouldn't have come."

"Tell Papa that! He brought me. Dewar—"

"I can't help you leave," Dewar said. He looked down at the
candles and pinched a bit of soft wax from the side of each one.

Freia didn't finish speaking, forestalled.

He went on, "Prospero asked me not to."

"Oh."

"Freia, this is not, not— It is not an unpleasant place. You
could enjoy yourself. You could be of great assistance to Prospero if you tried being charming to some of the people who have
it in for him here. Admittedly that's most of them, but you could
try. And this is me telling you this, not Prospero speaking
through me." Dewar rolled his wax into a ball. "Jos, as I said,
is really very pleasant, and Ottaviano's not bad—just ambitious. Gaston's quiet, but he has a mind of his own, and he has
a lot of influence on the Emperor—if only because the Emperor
can't afford to lose his support."

"Ottaviano . . . he's here," Freia said.

"Have you seen him? Spoken?"

"No! Oh, no. No. But he's *here*. What if—he can—"

"He's not going to hurt you." Dewar gestured, brushing the
notion aside.

"Golias is here," Freia whispered, drawing her knees up. "I
saw him."

Dewar looked at her over the flames, waiting. "Did you—
say anything—to Prospero?" he asked hesitantly when she said
no more.

"He won't listen to me. I—I tried to tell him. He never let me. He's so preoccupied. His horrible war. —It doesn't matter. It's over."

Dewar nodded. The subject made him uncomfortable. He shifted, turning away.

"Why did you come here?" Freia asked, hoping he wouldn't go.

"I fear someone will try to kill Prospero. The Emperor had someone ready to poison him when Gaston captured him the first time, and I wanted to be sure nothing of the kind happened here. I told the Emperor that I'll kill him if anything happens to Father."

"Would you?"

"Yes."

"He didn't think he'd be—executed, he said," she said.

"Indeed he did. He may not have said so, but he knew it was highly probable. But he's safe now, at least from the Emperor, because the Emperor is an ignoramus and dares not pick a fight with me." Dewar smiled, pleased with himself. "Simple, eh?"

Freia nodded.

"I'll leave you to rest," Dewar said, standing. "And perhaps I'll see you in the morning."

"Good night."

"Good night," he said, and the little constellation of the candles' light moved away, reflected in the black windows, across the room, and stopped. She saw him open the door and the candles went out, pinched or blown. The door closed.

"Gonzalo," whispered Prospero.

His whisper fell into the footstep-metered silence of the long cloister. In the early days of Panurgus's rule of the Well, this had been small cell-like clerks' chambers opening onto a courtyard; the Palace had devoured the courtyard over time, and now it was covered and enclosed, starved of daylight, though still paved with mosaics of swirling flames. There had been a time—Prospero recalled it well—when this had been known as the Poets' Court, for Queen Diote had smiled on poets and artists; and they had held little courts, reflections of the great Court, exclusive gatherings of the devotees of eight or a score of poets clumped among the arches and columns, seated on the mongrel assortment of chairs, tripod-stools, and divans that had furnished the place, declaiming, debating, drinking, delaying, deifying. It was silent space now, a between-place unseen by its transients, and forgetful centuries had passed since the last poem hymning Diote's beauty was composed here.

Lord Gonzalo turned, shadowed; the oil lamps that lit the place were not spaced widely enough to brighten it. He leaned upon his stick, then straightened, squaring his thin shoulders as Prospero's quiet feet bore the Prince to the Lord of Valgalant.

"Old friend," Prospero whispered—three footmen on some errand hurried past—"Come, step aside, or if we shall not speak, say so."

"Old friend," Gonzalo replied, a low creak, "how, not speak? Have we forgotten the words men use, our tongues dumbed of intelligence, our intellects numbed of sense? Not speak, and hear naught, no tidings nor comforts nor joys? Ah, the world is retrograde; time's past when an hour's parting furnished meat for three hours' conversation, when a month's absence fed a year's vigorous debate. But with long fasting, the appetite dieth; the belly forgets that it must have food—and when it hath, betimes it swoons. So I, when your voice came again to my ears. My lord." He bowed.

Prospero closed his eyes, opened them, smiled sadly, swallowed. "They have silvered thy head, Gonzalo, but they cannot tarnish thy tongue; robbed thy estate, but not thy wit. Let me embrace thee; I have lived in barbarity, Gonzalo, I have famished of conversation, and I prithee forgive my empty silences, my unsavory words, my ill-chosen condiments of wit."

"I was brazen and gilt," Gonzalo said, "and I have blessed Fortuna's alchemy that gave me silver for my pains, not steel. She hath transmuted us all, in her inconstant way: I see you have become a father, and twice over, that grudged an hour from your books and sorceries to dine, and never a day for dalliance—I e'en now recall you saying, 'twas business for the morrow. And some fair morrow caught you at last and you are become flesh withal. How is she called, this morrow?"

"There is no morrow such as you envision. I'd fain not speak of my daughter," Prospero replied, bitterness tinting his tone; "she is base motherless matter, a rocky field to my cultivating and a stone ear to my will, that hath brought us into such peril as you witness. And for my son: in shaping yon piece of work I lifted ne'er a hand, and a very marvel, is he not? I scantly know him, nor doth 'a know himself; he's young, my eye tells me, and quick, my ear tells me, a prodigy of sorcery and an elegant fellow with a sword—and more I cannot say, naught knowing. Let us speak rather of your daughter, thereby to brighten our souls in her reflection."

"Of my daughter," said Gonzalo.

"Miranda, aye; how fares she? Came she hither? Avril consented to lift the sentence of banishment 'pon you both, though 'twas little to his liking."

Gonzalo looked away, past Prospero's shoulder at the line of long-flamed lamps that led to the doorway, to the side at the scuffed, once-brilliant tiling of the floor. "Nay, my lord, she is not here."

"Is she returned home to thee? I know not the particulars," Prospero lowered his voice, looked about them quickly—no one there now, the dinner-hour had come, "but here's my ring, that I gave thee, and got of my son in Chenay, that said he had it of a lady there—Miranda, she—with news that mattered nearly to me. 'Twas a great thing, a deed worthy of herself and her house."

"She's—returned, aye," Gonzalo said. He placed his hand on

Prospero's shoulder. "My lord, I cannot spare thee pain, save by quickly wounding, taking no delight as some do in ascending the gradients of agony. I'll say it, then: Miranda's dead."

The stillness of the cloister hung; it seemed to Prospero that it expanded, and pressed into him, and pressed outward and silenced all the world to its outermost wastes, the Well itself stifled: and then he breathed again, and looked on Gonzalo's sad lean face, recognizing there for the first time the burnishing of new grief.

"Dead," Prospero repeated.

Gonzalo bowed his head.

"How? Who? When?"

"These things I too ask, and asked, and no answers have come; she was brought to Valgalant, encoffined, enshrouded, and there I consigned her to her tomb. The Emperor's men that brought her told no tale of how this ending came, and I thus have only grief to tell. Yet if she did give that ring to your son, which I lent her to lead her to you, then I know she was in Chenay. Therefore shall I apply to those who were there, to tell what was betided. 'Tis possible a general silence will prevail, from the Crown's wish to rule in darkness, without the Well's truth to light the world. But I shall ask."

They stood in the flat silence. Prospero's heart sank in him: Miranda, dead; hope, dead. How cunning Avril's evil was—as subtle as the Well—insinuating itself everywhere, leaving nothing untainted.

"This is heavy news, old friend," the Prince said. "The very life is gone from the world with her passing. What good is left, I cannot see."

"It wounds you as it wounds me, my lord, a death so nigh the heart to leave it stone-still with surprise: how could a cold husk hold such vitality? We are but vessels; the vessel destroyed, Miranda's gone, her essence sublimated to purer form. You spoke of your daughter as base matter a moment past; we are all base matter, unrefined, while we eat and breathe and soil the world around us. Surely that essence within your daughter's form is nothing base."

Prospero snorted. "There is no cure for this in philosophy. I have no daughter, Gonzalo; heard you not the clack o' the day?"

"Is aught befallen your daughter too? O Fire of my soul!"

"Naught's befallen her; she's arrogated from me, a puppet-judge hath so decreed. Understand that afore I began this past battle of the war, I did wish to assure me of her freedom, were I taken, and her of good estate, thus filed an endowerment and emancipation."

"Ah. Fidelio."

"E'en he, good fellow, but never say his name again, that he may continue among us. In her I vested title and rights to all my lands and holdings, to keep them from th' usurper's claws. I knew no glimmer of the boy, else I'd have made them to him, and 'twere a better thing, for 'tis done oft enough that a son cometh to his father's estate afore his father's death. For this very morn hath th' Emperor's judge decreed that a daughter may not be emancipated, which hath been done before three times in my memory and doubtless others; by nature's law he saith the blood-bond must be inviolate. And therefore hath Avril the right by treaty, a treaty forced on me by her own ungrateful folly, to seize her of me and bestow her on his corrupt Madanese heir, and to seize likewise mine earthly holdings. I have a daughter, and no daughter, by a legal wonder that no honest hedge-magistrate could countenance. An ill day was she shapened."

Gonzalo nodded sagely. "I do recall when Fensdarggan's estates were so confused, by reason of the second wife's children—"

"E'en so, Lord Fedo took counsel and emancipated the two daughters of the first wife, to simplify the inheritance of his sons by the second—dowered 'em richly and the thing withstood three challenges from the sons, 'twas legal as the King's will would have it. And 'twas done again thereafter: but Avril's puppet hath purblinded himself to serve the dark-witted fool."

Prospero's jaw clenched; Gonzalo shook his head, his shoulders falling. "Yet still I have a son."

"Prince Prospero's son?" the Countess of Lys repeated, wide-eyed, as that individual entered the Emperor's throne room. Her breath caught as she saw him, and an involuntary chill of recognition and remembered excitement rippled across her skin. Dewar wore deep sea-green, a sheeny mutable brocade dark and cold, and a handsome emerald glittered in his ear. He carried a walking-stick, too, silver-knobbed and slender.

"Indeed, if you can *imagine* any woman having *anything* to do with Prospero," Princess Viola said, "oh, but you haven't met *him* yet, well, you shall; *I* will introduce you, certainly. It sounds *utterly* untrue to me, but Prospero says so and so does Dewar, or should one say *Lord* Dewar—although the Emperor has not granted him any *formal* title—and certainly they *do* look alike, although it is *unfortunate* that his daughter takes after him, *especially* in her bad temper."

"Lord Dewar's daughter?" Luneté asked, bewildered by the Princess's fount of wisdom and by her own memories of Dewar's breath on her neck, of her hands on his body. She had not imagined he could be here. She had told herself they would never meet again. He was Prince Prospero's son. He was here.

"No, no," Viola said impatiently, wondering what kind of country goose this Countess was, "Prince Prospero's daughter."

"I do not believe I have met her," Luneté said, grabbing at safe ground, tearing her gaze from Dewar, who had not seen her, barely registering the existence of Prince Prospero's daughter. "But I have met so many people, you have been so very kind—and yes, they are very like, aren't they. Tall."

"*Exactly,* although he doesn't have Prospero's *nose,* which frankly one must hope *never* appears in the family again. Really, he's a *very* pretty fellow, and he dresses well and dances *ever* so nicely. *Such* legs. You wouldn't imagine him a *sorcerer* at all, he's a perfect *gentleman* at Court! I cannot *wait* until he's called into a duel."

"A duel? Why? Has he quarrelled?" Her heart thudded: she could imagine a quarrel, oh, yes.

"No, but—well." Princess Viola suppressed some interesting speculation involving the Baroness of Broul, Lord Dewar, and a closed carriage. The girl was quite green, much too easily shocked, but she was trying very hard, much more promising than Prospero's unpleasant daughter, and the Empress was particularly interested in her, having been close to her mother. "I suppose you *must* meet her, eventually," Viola said, "but *I* don't think she's right in the head, and it doesn't seem *wise* to me that His Highness the Heir should wed her, really, not until we've seen *more* of her, it wouldn't do for him to marry a *madwoman* or a *commoner,* and she is *very* common, common as dirt. Oh, dear me, yes—I've *shocked* you again, but you'll see her, my *dear* Countess, *you'd* be a fitter match for His Highness, more nobility in *your* ancestry and bearing, than that staring, shivering rat. We wonder, you know, if she isn't *lying.* I can't *imagine* her being connected with the family at all. Really. Golias at least is *courageous,* and has a sense of *style,* one can see that he's a Prince. And she has the most *peculiar* habits—isn't that the Baron your husband there?"

"Yes, he—"

"A *very* handsome fellow, and the image of Panurgus. Really. You haven't seen the Gallery? Oh, it's *frightfully* tedious, *nobody* ever goes, but in winter, you know, one can at least take exercise by walking there, and I can *never* count the portraits, I declare they move around, I never find the one I want *twice,* but they all laugh and say I'm just being silly. Really. I suppose I am. There are more *interesting* things to do than count portraits here, I *assure* you. The conservatories are *very* pleasant, Princess Evote and I often have— Oh, here's Prospero." Viola's voice dropped; her fan went up; and Luneté turned to see the Princess attempting an expression of faintly veiled disdain. On her plump face, it appeared as a pout.

The Countess of Lys looked back toward Prince Prospero, the man whose ambitions had so disrupted her own life. She had already decided she loathed him, and she viewed his nose with particular intent to dislike it, but his nose was inoffensive—aquiline, but inoffensive—and his eyes were intense and intelligent, his brow high and his mien all that befitted a son of the great King Panurgus, princely and austere. He wore a black-sheathed sword, and Luneté remembered from her etiquette book that the Princes, initiates of the Well, could bear arms in the presence of their ruler. His severely-cut clothing was restrained, of near-black blue satin unornamented with jewels or laces; his bearing was dignified, and he surveyed the company coldly, detached and above them.

The Countess was reminded forcefully of Prince Gaston, whom she had met but three days before as she and Ottaviano arrived, who had looked through her in a glance and, she thought, comprehended her at once. He too had seemed remote, preoccupied with more important things than the Countess of Lys, though the Baron of Ascolet had gotten a few low words that had made him look down, words which he had declined to repeat to his wife.

Prince Prospero was inclining his head, speaking to Dewar, and Princess Viola was whispering behind her fan with someone else now, so that Luneté watched undistracted as her husband the Baron of Ascolet was presented to Prince Prospero by Prospero's son. They straightened, Otto's bow decently formal and deep, the Prince barely nodding (but princes need bow to no one); Dewar said something, smiling with one side of his mouth, and Otto nodded and looked around them. The room was becoming crowded, but there was space around Prospero and his son, an arm's length at least. Prince Prospero turned his head and gazed straight at Luneté, into her and through her, just as Prince Gaston had.

She felt her face growing red; it was rude to stare so, unless one were flirting in the most obvious way—she knew that much about Court manners—but Prospero was staring too, calmly, assaying her with the eye he might use for a landscape or a fine ship.

Luneté looked away, lowering her eyes and recollecting her fan; and as she lifted the silly feathered thing, she met Prospero's eyes again. His mouth was quirking at the corner, just as Dewar's did. She liked him in the instant, her prejudice overthrown. Prospero returned his look to Otto, who was still craning his neck, trying to see through the crowd, and Luneté realized that he was searching for her.

There was space around Prospero and Dewar, but little elsewhere; Luneté sidled through clouds of scent and jostled fragile hothouse posies, brushed silver- and gold-laced sleeves and detoured around wide, expensive gowns shimmering in the candlelight.

"Countess," said Dewar, touching her sleeve, and suddenly she was out of the crowd, in the bubble of silence around Prospero and his son and her husband. Her eyes crossed Dewar's; she knew she spoke, faltering, some word of greeting, but he only bowed to her and turned his attention back to Prospero. She was trembling. She held herself still: Otto was right there.

"There you are," Ottaviano said; "I'd begun to think you'd left."

"I'm not about to leave now, I assure you," Luneté replied. The food at the Palace had been disagreeing with her, and she had jokingly threatened to go to the nearest ale-house and seek better fare.

Otto said, "Uh, sir, my wife, the Countess of Lys, daughter—"

"Bors's girl," Prospero said, and he took her hand and bowed, more deeply than he had to Ottaviano. "Thou'rt the image of thy gracious mother, madame. It is a pleasure to behold thee."

"Thank you," Luneté said, amazed, and a smile joined her blushes, embarrassing her further—she would be the laughingstock of the Court, she thought, if she could not better govern herself. She wondered for an instant if he were mocking her—her gown had been her mother's, made over in newer style—but the Prince straightened, releasing her hand, and gave her an approving nod.

"But thy good father's eyes betray his wit in thee," said Prospero, fixing her with his cloud-grey gaze, "and thy deeds as well. Blend thou thy mother's grace therewith and Lys shall thrive in thy hand."

Otto was wearing a face Luneté had known well in Sarsemar: neutral, opinionless, hiding his thoughts.

"Thank you, Your Highness," Luneté murmured, curtseying.

"No thanks are due," Prospero replied, " 'tis simple truth. —Dewar, hast seen thy sister?"

"Hm. No," Dewar said apprehensively.

"Comes the Emperor, led by his dogs and trained apes," Prospero said beneath a brassy fanfare of trumpets, "Dewar, do thou go to her chamber; ascertain that she's gowned and fetch her hence."

Luneté backed away, dismissed; the hard note in his voice as he spoke to Dewar was utterly different from the kindness she had heard. It was just as well; she did not know what to say to Dewar, how to look at him without blushing to think of what she had done, and her husband was here.

Otto caught her elbow. "Court's opening," he whispered, "you go there, see, and that guy in the curly hat will tell you where you stand. We don't stand together."

"I know," she said, although she hadn't, and went to find her place alone in the stir of the crowd.

People jostled and pushed as if they were in the market-square. Luneté tried to be polite, but her patience failed her and she began nudging and shoving like the rest, all of whom were hurrying to sort themselves into the proper ranks. She found her place between a very tall, thin old man in unrelieved ash-grey mourning and a cask-bellied wine-smelling fellow whose wispy beard did not enhance his leering smile. Luneté remembered her fan and used it.

"Pardon my forwardness," murmured a dry voice above her, "madame . . ."

Luneté looked up. The gentleman in mourning addressed her; his face was lined and his eyes sad, yet she thought he looked good-humored though terribly old—how old must he be, if he lived here in Landuc, where a favored man could live forever blessed by the Well? Or was he out of favor?—and so she smiled a little, still screening her face from the gentleman on her left.

". . . yet when we are forced into such close quarters, as cattle in the slaughter-pens, we need must take some note of one another," the ancient man said in the same dry, low voice.

The simile was startling; Luneté's eyes widened. Maybe he too was drunk, she feared.

"You are the Countess of Lys," he said.

Luneté blinked. How had he known that? Gossip travelled fast here. "Who has told you that?" she whispered.

He smiled, barely. "Why, you yourself, Countess, standing there. For there did Bors your father stand through many an hour in Court, beside me for many a year. And the place hath been empty long and long. Welcome."

"Oh, I see," she said, understanding. There was a place for everyone, and everyone stood in his proper place, and if no one was there, the place was vacant.

"The Count of Punt hath taken advantage of the vacancy to flood himself and o'erspread his allotted banks," observed the man in mourning, in the same emotionless undertone, "yet I misdoubt he resenteth your intrusion. The ranks be not so rigid that we may not change our places, you and I, should you find that such a small alteration would please you."

Luneté unravelled the courtly speech and smiled, warmly this time. "For now I will hold my father's place," she whispered, "but if your courtesy will allow it I may beg the favor of you later, should it be needful."

He nodded a hair's-breadth and looked away, up the ranks of people and along, toward the empty throne. Luneté looked too, between the exceedingly high hair-sculptures of two outlandish noblemen in front of her who were muttering gutturally to one another and shrugging often. She saw Prince Marshal Gaston in blood-red unadorned with frills, without jewels save his sword and a dagger; dark Prince Herne, green-coated, who glowered toward the other end of the room; and, dwarfed by his brothers, Prince Fulgens in frothing diamond-dewed lace and pale blue. But where was Prince Prospero? Luneté could not see him at the throne, with his brothers, where she supposed he ought to be. These were the four great Princes, the four eldest sons of King Panurgus, who had endowed each with dominion over an Element and set them above his other children forever.

Luneté of Lys shivered, moving from side to side to see them. She had never thought of Court, when she had thought of being Countess of Lys; she had thought of the castle in Lys and its gardens, the high-walled city and the long plains. But never had she thought of going to Landuc, seeing Princes and Emperor and people whose names were in histories and ballads. She felt small and insignificantly young.

A little distance from their mightier brothers stood the Princesses Evote and Viola and new-made Prince Golias; Golias wore no sword. Panurgus had had other sons—dead Sebastiano, exiled Esclados the dabbler in sorcery, and long-vanished Hyetos the Philosopher Sublime. What would crude Golias do, Luneté wondered, to distinguish himself in such a company? Had he passed the Well's fire yet, as the children of Panurgus were entitled to do? She supposed not, or he would have been permitted the privilege of bearing arms. Even rattle-tongued Princess Viola had stood that test; what would it do to Golias? She studied him, looking for resemblances between him and the other sons and daughters of Panurgus, and gave it up; she saw none. Sometimes it was obvious even to Luneté that members of a family shared features, but, she thought, as often as not strangers do as well.

A stir at the other end of the hall—Luneté looked that way, toward laughter and a murmur of voices. With a shock she recognized Prince Prospero there—as far from the throne as one could stand and still be in the room. Disseized of his estates, out of favor, the fallen Prince's position in the world was shown by his position in the Court. The untidy crowd of the least-favored there gathered parted, bowing deeply and obsequiously. Prince Josquin the Heir emerged, all in cloth-of-silver, shining and fair as a fountain, and strode quickly down the hall, smiling, greeting his Princess aunts with bows and hand-kisses, slapping Prince Golias on the shoulder, moving like quicksilver upward toward the dais. The Master of Protocol intercepted him and (with respectful gestures and bows) directed him to stand above Gaston, on a step; Josquin rolled his eyes comically (even Luneté could see it), smiled indulgently, nodded condescendingly, stood with one hand on hip, bent slightly to conduct a whispered conversation with Fulgens, smiling still. Luneté thought she had never seen anyone so elegant in her life.

The Master of Protocol seemed twittered about something; he paraded down the length of the room to approach Prince Prospero skittishly and Prince Prospero glared down at him and shrugged, very slightly, as if the gesture were not worth the energy to make it. As before, there was an empty space around Prince Prospero, despite the crowd: as though the Emperor's displeasure might be catching.

Something was wrong, Luneté guessed, and she remembered that Dewar had been sent to find Prince Prospero's daughter—his sister—and the chief spectacle of the evening's ceremonies was to be the girl's betrothal to the Prince Heir. Under the circumstances, Luneté supposed that she'd be late herself, dressing, putting on cosmetics and jewels, getting her hair to go right. She patted it; the ribbons and the aromatic hot-house flowers Otto had brought her were still in place, and if the whole elaborate pile hadn't fallen down by now she supposed it wouldn't. Laudine had anchored everything firmly with pins and tight curls, and it felt more like a strange hat than Luneté's own hair.

She wondered what Dewar's sister, Prospero's daughter, might be like. Luneté had never heard of such a person before, but she had never heard of Prospero's son until recently, either. It seemed to be the custom here not to mention one's offspring until they were well grown.

A sweet trumpet sounded, high and long, and a cascade of

notes followed. Luneté straightened and told herself to stop gaping. It was Court, not a mummers' show. She managed not to gape, and even, she thought, to look blandly respectful as everyone else did, lowering herself as everyone around her did, as even more courtiers and footmen and guards streamed in to fill the room and the Emperor led the Empress past the kneeling Court (Luneté, not daring to crane her neck, saw only the top of Her Majesty's crowned head) up to the dais and left Her Majesty at the bottom and seated himself slowly, surveying the Court assembled with, it seemed to Luneté, a cold and calculating expression, all as wonderful sweet music such as Luneté had never in her life heard before played on and on. She felt light-headed with excitement.

The music crescendoed and stopped, and a man whose title Luneté couldn't recall cried out, in a long and involved way, that the Emperor was here and Court assembled before him, which Luneté thought must be plain to a blind idiot. And then she remembered that she was here to take her oath, and she panicked that she had forgotten it, and a great deal of Court business and trumpeting and music went on while Luneté stood, looking fixedly at nothing, running over and over her words. She would have to say them in front of everybody, everyone important in the world, she, Luneté of Lys, and she would have to get them right, and she was certain she would get them wrong like the princess who jumbled her prince's name in the wedding-vows and the marriage was cursed thereafter—

Luneté wished very much she had not come to Landuc.

A "hm" from the sad gentleman in mourning-clothes beside her started Luneté out of her iteration of the oath. A stir in the crowd up near the dais; heads turned, all along the room with a gust of whispers; Prince Gaston moved slightly and then resumed his hands-behind-his-back watchful stance. Prince Herne tossed his head and snorted; Prince Fulgens scowled and looked coldly, and Luneté could not see the Princesses or Golias. The towering hair-sculptures moved together, apart, together, conferring.

The Emperor himself bestowed a searing glare on the disturbance and then on the Master of Protocol, who had stepped forward—to sort things out, Luneté supposed. He stepped back so quickly he trod on someone's foot. Luneté glimpsed Prince Josquin, whose face was immobile and bland as a porcelain statue's.

The man kneeling before the Emperor rose and stepped back, bowing deeply, and with a shock Luneté recognized Ottaviano. She had missed his oath! She blushed with guilt. Why, that meant she had missed Prince Prospero's oath as well, she had been so preoccupied with—

"Luneté who claimeth the County of Lys, approach the Throne," cried the Master of Protocol, consulting a list.

Luneté went ice-cold and red-hot and stepped forward, murmuring excuses to the tower-headed gentlemen, who parted with ill grace before her. She remembered the approach. Deep curtsey. Walk. Curtsey again. She hoped by the Well she was getting it right. Nobody was laughing, anyway. Walk. Now she was at the dais. Curtsey and stay down.

She felt herself sway, almost faint.

By what right did she claim the title of Countess of Lys and the lands and privileges and forces and duties thereto pertaining?

She claimed the title of Countess of Lys by the Fire of Landuc that leapt in her father and now in herself and the lands and privileges and forces and duties thereto pertaining. Oh, she had muffed it, would he say anything?

The Emperor acknowledged that the Fire that leapt in Luneté and in Lys were one.

Approach the Throne.

Stand, not falling over, up the steps (hold the long heavy gown correctly), kneel on the flame-patterned carpet where Otto knelt a few minutes ago. That was heartening. Look up— oh, one isn't supposed to, or is one—

The Emperor folded Luneté's hands in his. He leaned forward, his eyes bright and sharp-pupilled. "Very like your mother," the Emperor observed. "Uncanny." He studied her a moment longer, nodded. "We receive Luneté daughter of Bors of Lys in our Presence," he said more loudly, "and do countenance her claim to the County of Lys and do consent to grant to her the governance of the County of Lys for so long as our Well shall sustain her, in exchange for her devotion of her person to the office of Countess of Lys."

Now for the hard-to-remember part. Luneté took a breath and said, "I Luneté do solemnly swear by the Well of Landuc that nourishes me to devote my person to the County of Lys and to the Well of Landuc that sustains it, and to undertake no act against the Well. . . ." It wasn't difficult at all; Luneté listened, amazed, as her voice pronounced all the words in the correct order, vowing her person and her life to the service of the Well, the Emperor, and Lys.

The Emperor accepted her fealty and appointed her Countess of Lys with all the rights honors and obligations pertaining thereto, and Luneté's mind skipped ahead and recalled the formula for thanking the Emperor, backing away from him, descending the steps and returning to her place—more curtseys, careful small steps down, curtsey, back away, be dismissed from the Presence, rise, back to her place.

When she was once again standing between the dignified man in mourning and the bibulous glutton, Luneté felt suddenly hot and giddy. She had done it, she had taken her vow, she had escaped Sarsemar, no one could take Lys from her now, the Emperor had granted it; Lys was hers at last, and she was Lys's; she was suddenly homesick with a throbbing, resonating pang. . . .

Something touched her right arm; she shook her head and jerked herself. The elderly gentleman was supporting her.

"Oh, pardon me," Luneté whispered, horrified. Had she swooned? She tried to stand alone, and he insisted on holding her arm.

"Madame, I recommend you breathe slowly," he said, and Luneté, ashamed of her weakness, did so, closing her eyes and concentrating. The swimming feeling left her head. Someone else was taking a vow. She listened; it was a child's voice piping the words, some boy requesting the Emperor's guardianship on the death of his father. Luneté licked her lips and opened her eyes, smiled at the kind gentleman in mourning gratefully.

"I was nervous," she whispered. She shouldn't have had Laudine lace her so tightly. The rich food here and the lack of exercise had had an immediate and annoying effect on Luneté, discovered as she tried on sleek-fashioned gowns that had fit perfectly in Lys. She would have to be mindful at meals or she'd end up as round as Princess Viola.

"Still in these ashen days, to some few it cometh hotly on," said the gentleman cryptically. He patted her hand gently, nodded once, and looked back at the Court proceedings. Music was playing; a whisper ran through the room. Luneté heard someone whisper "Josquin," and sure enough the Prince Heir's expression of polite inattention had changed to something more alert. The betrothal, Luneté guessed.

Yes. The Master of Protocol was talking about Prince Josquin, his titles and radiantness and the strength of the Well in him and on and on.

"Blether," muttered the old man contemptuously, very much under his breath.

"They do go on," whispered Luneté as softly as she could.

"Words have no power in his mouth."

Luneté wondered what that meant, but now the Master of Protocol had paused for breath. He went on to say that the Emperor (another tangle of titles and radiance and eternities) had decided to bestow upon his son (more improbable descriptions of Prince Josquin) the hand of his ward Lady Freia (who had not a single title, eminence, or radiance to her name) in union of the Well.

The corpulent man snorted to himself, not quite laughing.

"But," Luneté murmured, puzzled, not aware she had spoken aloud.

Lady Freia was apparently supposed to present herself at the dais. Luneté sensed, rather than saw, some movement at the front of the room again; everyone was leaning, looking, and a few people gasped and shook their heads, whispering again; and all she could see was the Emperor, and he was smiling a small and unhumorous smile with no warmth of the Well's blessing to it.

"I will not," Luneté heard a woman say, low but intense enough to carry far. Luneté couldn't see who had spoken, there at the foot of the dais.

Silence followed. The jostlings and whisperings were stilled, dread-struck.

A murmur from the Master of Protocol, who was visibly distressed—Luneté saw him come down the steps, pale-faced and indignant.

"I'm not your ward or anybody's!" Lady Freia cried.

Luneté, who had thought Lady Freia was Prince Prospero's daughter, glanced up at the man in mourning, who seemed to know things. He was watching with a Court-face that did not conceal anger.

"Carry on," the Emperor said, icily, not smiling. Luneté could see him clearly; people had drawn back, away, and the Emperor's face was narrow-eyed, looking down with anger—or was it contempt?—at Lady Freia, out of sight to Luneté. She could see Prince Josquin, though, and his expression was the same polite mask as before.

"You can only pretend I'm your ward, it's all lies you made up for yourself!" Lady Freia retorted. "You cannot make something true just by saying it is so!"

The Court gasped.

The man in mourning chuckled. "From innocent lips," he observed, but did not complete the proverb.

"What?" wondered Luneté.

"Madame," the Emperor said, leaning forward, "you are a guest in our Palace—"

"A prisoner," Lady Freia hissed back.

A storm of whispers rustled through the assembly now.

"—and your status and your family's are precarious—"

A glove flew through the air to land at the Emperor's feet; Luneté craned her neck to see it. The whispers were silent. Prince Gaston moved a step forward; the Emperor gestured slightly to him and he waited.

"I remind you, Avril, that I have promised to avenge any injury to my father, and I shall champion my lady sister as well." It was Dewar who spoke, his voice melodious, even cheerful; Luneté couldn't see him either—he and his sister stood across from the Princes, on the same side of the room as she did.

The man in mourning was smiling thin-lipped.

The Master of Protocol was fuming crimson-faced, his ceremony in tatters.

"Lord Dewar, your filial and fraternal sentiments are to be lauded," the Emperor said, ignoring the glove, "though your enthusiasm is misplaced; no injury is offered your father or your sister."

"Take care that none is," Dewar said. "I warn you that in dispossessing my father of his daughter you have made a fiction which cannot be sustained by the truth of the Well, and which will annihilate you if you attempt to invoke it there. For example, by calling on the Well when you name her your ward."

"The girl's father," the Emperor said coldly, "has legally dispossessed himself of her, and of all his goods and chattels, by treaty, and since she cannot exist in a vacuum—"

"I'm not your ward!" Lady Freia cried out. "Papa! Papa, say so!"

Luneté glimpsed her then: a blur of brown everyday gown, loose dark curls trailing down from a thick, unadorned hairknot, and grim white face, springing a step toward Prince Prospero, restrained by Dewar who caught her arm and pulled her back.

"—in Landuc, the Crown stands, as it does for all minor orphans, in loco parentis, which is so established and precedented as to withstand, we imagine, even a sorcerer's logic," the Emperor concluded. "And since the Crown's ward cannot speak for herself, the Crown will speak for her in her nonage. Do you challenge the Crown and therefore the Well, sorcerer?"

"No," Dewar said. "You have Summoned the Well and its consequences on yourself. I remind you: I have an interest, and I will oppose any violence offered to either."

"Dewar!" cried Lady Freia, sounding frantic. "Papa!"

"Then let the matter be closed," the Emperor said, "with the understanding that, of course, no violence shall be offered the Crown's ward, who is not competent to speak for herself. The Crown appoints Princess Evote to appear before us in her stead."

Princess Evote came forward, in coppery silk satin and ivory lace, curtseying to the Emperor, and took a place where Luneté could not see her. There was a stir, and Lady Freia's voice rose saying, "Let go of me, let me go—" and a flurry of movement and murmurs, and the Emperor said, "Her presence is not necessary," and a door slammed.

The Court barely breathed as the ceremony of betrothal continued to its end, Prince Josquin's voice cool and detached, Princess Evote's formal and exactly enunciating every word on behalf of absent Lady Freia. The dowry was small: just four estates, of none of which Luneté had heard. It seemed very little for a Princess to have. Luneté listened, still astounded; how could anyone behave like that in Court? At her own betrothal to the Prince Heir? As the ceremony concluded with the Emperor's blessing on the union, the Count of Punt interrupted her thoughts.

"Reckon she'll stand in later, too?" He grinned. "Or maybe they'll get a stableboy."

Luneté stared at him, uncertain what he meant but shocked by the lewdness of his grin, and lifted her fan.

The Count of Punt leaned closer, though, and then leaned away with a faint sneer; the kindly gentleman in mourning turned and now looked at Punt in such a way as to repel his attention from Luneté.

The Emperor was blessing the Court and the Empire and Pheyarcet. Luneté knelt as everyone else did, and music played, and the Emperor and Empress went out followed by all the Princes and Princesses, and Court was over. There would now be a procession into the ballroom, Luneté recalled, and she was unsure whether they would go in this order or whether she should go with Otto. She thanked the gentleman in mourning, cut the Count of Punt, and was stepping into the milling, sorting collection of nobles when a page tugged her sleeve.

"Your Ladyship is requested to attend the Empress," he said.

"Oh!" Luneté exclaimed, "I—now?"

"Yes, Your Ladyship." He turned and ducked into the crowd, and Luneté followed him to a side door where they passed through a press of lords and ladies. Some frowned at Luneté as the page announced her brightly to the footmen; others scowled in annoyance as the doors were opened and the Countess of Lys went past them with the Empress's page into Her Majesty's drawing-room.

"Most regrettable," said Lord Gonzalo softly to Prince Prospero. They had met, not by accident, in a side-passage usually used by the butlers and other servants to provide service to the Coronation Hall; it was vacant, as the throne room would be used no more tonight. A single oil-lamp glowed over their heads. Prince Prospero gripped the long marble-topped counter that ran along one side of the passageway; he turned to Lord Gonzalo.

Prospero's face was thunderous with rage. "I regret it indeed; I regret the day, the very hour I—but it is done, in Fortuna's hands are we all for good and ill."

"She spoke the truth, and perhaps Justice's scales will sway."

"The truth weighs nothing here, and Justice is a pandered bitch, to woo with lies and pinchbeck promises like any other whore. Did you mark how the villain smiled, and *smiled*— Dewar."

"Father," said Dewar, joining them.

Prospero looked steadily at him, past Gonzalo, and Dewar blushed.

"I wasn't going to challenge him over that," Dewar said, defensively. "I couldn't."

"Hast done what was possible. Lord Gonzalo, I think my son Dewar is yet unknown to you—I present him to you, heir to the hollowness that remains of all my works and deeds."

Dewar bowed, pleased to be introduced. "Sir, I am glad to know your face at last," he said, "your name has reached my ears before, kindly spoken. My father is not wholly done, while he still has such friends as Valgalant."

"Alas, Valgalant is poor in everything, friendship not least," said Gonzalo, bowing also, smiling at the handsome young man, seeing in him Prospero's last best work. "Poets' flights aside, one friend is small riches nowadays."

"Do not undervalue so precious a jewel, sir," Dewar said, "even for the sake of good manners. Valgalant's friendship is double the value you state; for your daughter, Lady Miranda, is the loveliest setting ever to display friendship in this world."

"Ah," said Lord Gonzalo, "I had forgot—I knew it but today—you had met her."

"In Chenay," Dewar said, "we met and parted quickly, and I have hoped we might meet again with more leisure; we even promised one another such a meeting, at your house in fairer weather and better times. Yet I would hasten to meet her here, if she is here, and bend the intention for amity's sake, and, if the lady were so kind, for the sake of a dance."

Gonzalo sighed, looked away, and then looked back at Dewar's eager smile. "My daughter hath broken faith with you, Lord Dewar, and shall not meet you now or later, here or anywhere. She is dead."

Dewar halted in mid-breath to take this in. His mouth closed; he swallowed, confused by the bitter taste of the news; he looked at his father, whose grim face confirmed Lord Gonzalo's dry words. Of course—Lord Gonzalo wore mourning; Dewar had forgotten that here, mourning clothes were ash-colored. "Sir, I am sorry. I—I did not know. I have heard nothing of her since then." He glanced again at Prospero, gauging his words by the other's expression. "May I ask, if it is not too painful a subject . . . what happened? For I . . . it is inconceivable to me that . . . after such a journey as she . . ." He halted himself; he could not easily frame elegant words around such a tender matter.

"I do not know how, or when, or where," said Lord Gonzalo simply. "She was returned to me by Prince Gaston, and she resteth from her labors now lapped in stone, for death-fire is forbidden Valgalant by the Emperor's order."

"By Prince Gaston," Dewar murmured. "And he would not tell you . . ."

"He hath said, with regret, that he cannot. I do believe he hath been commanded not to speak of it," said Gonzalo.

Prospero, frowning, leaned against the long marble counter, folding his arms. "There's but one commandeth Gaston."

"The Emperor, then, ordered him to be silent," Dewar said.

" 'Tis apparently so, for I applied to him fervently for particulars, and have had only his courteous regrets that he cannot say," Gonzalo said. "And his counsel, that I press not too deeply into the heat of the fire." He shook his head. "Gentlemen, 'tis done, and 'tis the will of the Emperor that no more be known of it."

"The will of the Emperor is not the Well of the realm," said Dewar.

"You have your father's tongue, sir," said Gonzalo sadly. "Let us find some other news to occupy us, good friends."

Dewar bit his lip, held back his words. "I beg your pardon, Lord Gonzalo. I did not intend to dwell on a subject that surely grieves you." He bowed. "I too am grieved."

"Well and all, Gonzalo," Prospero said, straightening and coming forward, "shall you linger long round this unhealthy court?"

"Not so long, perhaps, as good courtesy would have me, though the Emperor did bid me attend."

Prospero snorted.

"But since you are here, old friend, perhaps I shall tarry here, beyond my limits, and company you an you would."

"I am on the Emperor's sufferance," said Prospero. "I may not leave nor stay save at his bidding; the spit-dogs have more liberty. Yet my son may go as he will."

Dewar construed this as a prompt. "Sirs, I must leave you, for I wish to watch the spectacle of Court here; I have not seen it before, and it is of some interest to me."

"Go, then, and see all," Prospero said. "I am ill-suited for follies and footing."

"Nor I," said Lord Gonzalo. " 'Tis but poor amusement to me, but a young gentleman will surely find diversion in it. I wish you well, Lord Dewar."

"Until we meet again, Lord Gonzalo, I wish you better cheer."

The Countess of Lys had spent hours poring over her father's copy of *The Boke of Elegant and Seemlie Decorum* by a Noble-Man of the Court, and therefore she knew that she must wait at the door, be announced by a footman to a lady or another footman, be announced by that lady to another, and be announced by that lady . . . well, it apparently could go on awhile, but the Empress was not being very formal this evening, and so Luneté must wait only a few minutes while Her Majesty was informed that the Countess of Lys attended as commanded.

Luneté watched, since the book had not said not to; the Empress Glencora was at the other end of the long green-and-gold room, seated, and some of the other ladies (among whom were the Princesses) were seated and some standing; they had cups and glasses and tidbits of food, and were chattering and laughing, attentive when the Empress or the Princesses said anything. Her Radiance's gown was unimaginably lovely—gold tissue over white satin—and she looked like a gilded porcelain sculpture of a person, all gold-and-cream, her diamond-crowned head tilted at just the right angle, her back straight. Luneté sighed to herself, feeling unbecomingly tall and ruddy-colored. The Empress was talking to two ladies, privily it seemed, and the others had drawn away. Her Majesty frowned a little and shook her head, then turned to the lady who bore word of Luneté's arrival and nodded, and now a message was relayed to Luneté that she might approach.

The Noble-Man of the Court's book had informed Luneté how to do this, too. She need not curtsey at the door, since the audience was not private; she approached within eight steps, paused, waited respectfully for the Empress's nod—which came at once, with a smile from the royal lips and "Come here, my dear, don't be shy"—curtsey, forward four steps, curtsey—

"Here, take this footstool," the Empress said, patting the one her own feet had been on an instant before, and Luneté blushed, fumbled her thanks, and sat down obediently. Without saying a word, the Empress now somehow dismissed the other ladies who hovered about; they all drifted off to the table where the wine and cakes were waiting.

The Empress looked closely at Luneté for a few seconds and nodded. "Well, my dear. I knew your mother very well; you resemble her wonderfully."

"Thank you, Your Majesty."

"But you've got Bors's temper, I fear," the Empress went on, "because Sithe would never have run off with anyone to get married, no matter how violently in love she thought she was."

Luneté went crimson. She opened her mouth to say something and then closed it.

"It is the privilege of an Empress to meddle now and then," the Empress said, "and I am heartily sorry, Countess of Lys, that I did not meddle sooner. Perhaps I should have had you brought to Court and reared here; but all was sixes and sevens. Perhaps if you had been here when the Count died, you would have stayed here. But that is all gone by, and you have shown a remarkably good judgement by at least postponing marriage until after you came of age."

Luneté's embarrassment was nearly mortal. She had lowered her eyes and was looking at the pattern on the rug, little flowers and fire-blossoms.

"Do you love him?" the Empress asked, in a tone that demanded Luneté look up.

"Yes," Luneté said, staring at the Empress.

"Love," said the Empress, "is inconvenient. You are aware that the Emperor did not receive news of your marriage with joy."

"I—Your Majesty, it seemed the—the best thing—"

"I don't doubt that, with Ocher panting on your neck," the Empress said. "A vow of chastity at the Shrine of Stars would have been inappropriate, considering your position as Lys's heir."

"I didn't know who he was really. I mean Otto," Luneté tried to explain, terrified. She had never considered becoming one of the Shrine's virgin priestesses.

"You didn't?" The Empress stared at her.

"No, Your Majesty," whispered Luneté.

"My soul, you fell in love with the fellow first and— This is what comes of rearing girls in places like Sarsemar," the Empress said to herself, more than to Luneté. "Indeed. Sun above, my dear, I quite understand, but do you understand that you must be very careful?"

"Careful?"

The Empress sighed. "My dear child, you cannot be so naive as to have ignored the possibilities of your army and your husband's ambitions."

"No, Your Majesty. I have not. We have discussed it. The army of Lys is the army of Lys, and it is not the army of Ascolet. And we have discussed—ambitions. He is the Baron of Ascolet and he has taken the oath to the Emperor."

"Very good. I have presented your case as favorably as I could to His Majesty, and I am pleased to hear you speak such good sense as shows I was right to do so. I pointed out to His Majesty that the present arrangement may well be the best, under the circumstances, and that the time to emend it is past. The Crown will recognize your marriage."

"Oh, thank you, Your Majesty," Luneté said, weak with relief.

"However," the Empress went on. "As you have no mother, and have displayed a certain willfulness, I shall be blunt: there is another possibility. Your husband may dust off his ambitions someday. If at any time the Crown suspects for any reason that Lys and Ascolet conspire, the Crown will exercise its right to annul your marriage ab initio. You must avoid not only disloyalty, Countess, but any appearance of it which could give rise to rumors. You must maintain your County and Barony separately. You must not lower tariffs or duties, favor one another in trading agreements, make one another large interest-free gifts of money to cover unexpected expenses— I believe you understand me?" And the Empress's look was very significant.

"Yes, Your Majesty," Luneté said in a small voice, nodding, guilty though not charged.

"I strongly recommend, Countess, that you find an advisor. Someone who is *not* your husband—the Baron is a forceful and persuasive man, and will sway you easily. Take counsel with your counselor, and not with your husband, in decisions affecting Lys."

Luneté nodded again.

"As you have led rather an isolated life," the Empress went on, "I shall undertake to find someone suitable for you. Sarsemar presents a reasonable alternative, or does to the Emperor's eye, but I suspect such an advisor would have entirely the opposite effect desired."

"My husband would cut Ocher's throat, Your Majesty," Luneté said, and then she blushed scarlet—had she said that? Oh, Well.

The Empress laughed. "He would be no son of Sebastiano otherwise, and therefore your advisor must be prudent, diplomatic, and—uninclined to wooing. Or a woman, but there are few who would suit and who could be sent to you in Lys. Will you dwell in Lys or Ascolet?"

"Both, Your Majesty, as opportunity or events require. We are discussing that. Still."

"I see. Kindly keep me informed, Countess, as to how your experiment proceeds. As I said, the Emperor has been persuaded that it may not entirely be a bad thing, but one must not tempt Fortuna."

"Indeed I agree, Your Majesty."

"Good. You are a sensible young woman. I wish—" The Empress stopped herself, made a moue with her pretty mouth, and smiled. "Now you have been browbeaten and the evening is spoiled."

"I hope not, Your Majesty. I am very grateful for your advice. It has been difficult to know what to do, sometimes."

"I am sure it has. You have chosen a hard road for yourself. My dear, I hope I will hear more of you than rumor and gossip from passing travellers. Indeed I heartily desire to see you at Court."

Luneté bowed her head, grateful. "There is much to do in Lys at the moment, Your Majesty, and I feel strongly that I must go back soon, but I hope to attend Court after I have settled myself at home."

"I shall remind you of that, Countess. Your mother was a great friend to me and I should think ill of myself if I allowed her daughter to slip away unnoticed. There is always a place for you here, and an ear. Remember that."

"Thank you, Your Majesty. Thank you very much. I shall." Luneté bowed her head again; the Empress was being very kind, much more so than Luneté had expected.

"I shall be annoyed if you forget. Now run and take a glass of wine—you look quite pale —and a bite of something, and ask Lady Elis—in the violet gown—to come here. We shall all go out to the ball presently, and of course you shall join us." And the Empress smiled on Luneté, who stood and curtseyed and took the extended porcelain-white hand, kissed it reverently, and curtseyed again and backed away.

— 8 —

"PRINCE PROSPERO!" SAID THE EMPRESS, RAISING her voice slightly, and the tall dark figure at the other end of the corridor paused, turned, bowed a fraction of an inch, and approached.

"Madame Empress," he said, giving a chill glare to the bevy of attending ladies as a group. The Countess of Lys stepped back a half-step. Princess Evote sniffed. The Empress flicked her fan and stepped forward, and the women hung back.

"It is unfortunate that your daughter is indisposed," the Empress said, failing to find a truly euphemistic way to describe the scene in Court.

"My daughter is unfortunately disposed," Prospero said coldly, "disposed of as the Emperor would, in such a way as to curdle the best of dispositions, which I freely admit she hath not, and to bring on indisposition most extreme."

The Empress shooed her ladies back further with another flick of her fan and walked a few steps with Prospero. "I cannot see it as so poor a match, Prince Prospero," she said, "though it is arranged hastily and without consulting the hearts of the principals. Good has come of worse pairings, and ill of better."

"This is true, madame, and rarely hath a marriage been so clouded from its inception, so that we must hope for favorable downpours from Fortuna in compensation. I would be hard put to find a peer less objectionable than your son, madame, nor objections stronger than my daughter's."

The Empress weighed his mood and hazarded more. "Do you not object, yourself?"

"To the manner, but not the matter, and let that stop at thy ears and never pass thy lips, madame. I believe you have some sway with your son, as do I with my daughter, and if they be subtly reconciled to the thing it may come off tolerably well. But Avril's blessing is a curse; he inverts all nature in his person and influence." He was looking at her shrewdly, and his voice was low.

"I did think it might be thus with you," the Empress said, equally quietly, "it is often so in these things, that a dislike is made where none need be, if all is not arranged properly. I told His Majesty it should not be hastily done, but it's done."

"E'en so. I shall wear at the one, and do you the other, and mayhap 'twill settle smoothly."

Heartened by her success thus far, the Empress decided to attempt another act of diplomacy. "Indeed," she said, smiling at him.

"I bid you good-night, madame. The conceit o' the dance ill fits mine," Prospero said more loudly, and he bowed and started away.

"Prince Prospero, a word more—"

He halted, looked back, lifted an eyebrow. The Empress realized with a twinge of annoyance that he was not going to come to her—the man's manners were arrogant in the extreme—and she moved to join him. She lowered her voice again. "I ask that you soften your evident hostility to Prince Golias—"

"*Prince* Golias?" repeated Prospero, turning toward her. "Hath come to pass a happy wedding of jackal and harpy? I marvelled at his face in Court." He stared down at her with a look of such steely coldness that she felt herself dissected, forced to speak.

"The Emperor has confirmed the title twenty days ago, remedying Panurgus's obstinacy, and Golias has sworn in return his fealty and aid," the Empress said. "He is to pass the Fire as soon as—as soon as the Emperor sees fit to arrange it."

Prospero still stared down at her, his eyes widening.

He began to laugh, slowly, chuckling softly, then more loudly, then giving in to full-throated mirth. Leaning against a pillar, he repeated "Prince! Prince!" between gusts of laughter.

Empress Glencora watched this display icily. "It amuses

you?" she said, when Prospero had begun to calm down, weakened but still chuckling.

He laughed harder again. "Aye, madame," he said after an indecently long interval. "It amuseth me right well. Ah, Avril, thou onager, blindly bent on hammering asunder any edifice of wisdom left behind by thy sire! Think you, madame, that Panurgus might willfully deny his own? Was he such a two-faced tergiversator as his self-raised successor? Nay, the pillars that ward the streaming Roads bear one face apiece, and that the King's; and the King's visage, though 'twas uncomely, wore truth upon its brow. Why, Golias is no son of his! Whose son he be his mother only knoweth, but Panurgus was a wise man and knew the Well's ways, and he knew by the truth the Well's Fire shows, as I know, that Golias was none of his get, no more than yon cub Ottaviano is Sebastiano's— Ah, Glencora, I thank you, for I had feared Avril showed some glimmer of intellect! Now may I console me that no wit, only Fortuna, hath turned the days so drear, for Avril hath all the wit of a woodbird that knoweth not the cuckoo's egg. *Prince* Golias!" Prospero snorted and was off again, laughing as he spoke. "I thought him a but mercenary turncoat, gold-lured, and now he's revealed a wool-clad wolf: and doubtless shall soon ravage the wolf-clad sheep that think to blunt his fangs. A fitting addition to this company of exalted scoundreldom and rascality! Prince Golias! Ah, dear me. I thank you, Glencora, it is long since I laughed so, and I shall cherish to my grave this hour that afforded me such cheer."

Glencora was dumbstruck. The ladies behind her were whispering behind their fans, a sibilant symphony of gossip and astonishment, except for the Countess of Lys, who was quite still.

Prospero, smiling yet (not wholly pleasantly), went on. "I thank you further, Empress, for I see your hand in't that Avril hath chosen to enrich my daughter with your son, not this illstruck coin Golias. And I bless Avril's arrogant ignorance, that would go 'gainst what he could of Panurgus's doing, for had he known how false and foul this Golias is, he surely had bestowed her there instead, poor maid, to torment me thereby."

"You say that Golias lies?" the Empress inquired in her chilliest voice.

"Aye! The bastard lies, else his mother falsely lies—rather, lay, for where she lieth now she lies no more—seeking to gild her folly. He's no son of Panurgus; weren't so, he'd be another man, no Golias. A false Prince made by a false monarch! All façades, no substance behind 'em: Avril seeketh his own kind."

"I do not understand," the Empress said after a moment of schooling herself deaf to the slurs upon her husband, "how you are so certain of the truth of what you say."

"Why, 'tis writ in the Well, Glencora, the very Well which Avril cannot control. The Well's currents flow true, and who knoweth their mark sees their working on the world as plainly as you see the flood cut the riverbank, the fire melt the iron bar. Aye, here's the great evil in Avril's ignorance: that he knoweth not the world he claims to rule. He governs it not; it floweth where it may, gnawing and breaking Panurgus's Bounds; in ages soon this mighty Landuc shall be naught more than a bright spot in an undistinguished cosmos, rather than a very sun to light the world's day, diminished for not being maintained." Prospero's merriment was gone; he was stonily sober now and looked on the Empress with an unsympathetic eye. "He ruleth no more than he can see, and that which he sees not, is unruled, lawless, unruly."

Dewar caught the Baroness of Broul's eye as she entered the ballroom with the Empress and her flock of women and the Emperor and his favorites, the procession winding around slowly to stately, brassy music. The Baroness smiled at him, her fan failing to screen the look from the Baron of Broul, who followed it with a glare of his own before recollecting that he ought to preserve his dignity by cutting the upstart bastard sorcerer. The Baroness puckered her lips and blew a kiss to Dewar and then looked forward also. The procession coiled in on itself; the Court knelt to the Emperor and Empress (Dewar remained standing at the side, behind the Emperor's back), and then the Emperor seated himself and his consort on a pair of low thrones at one end of the room. The music became livelier, and the formal order of the procession fragmented as people moved, chatted, and partnered.

"Careful," a voice at Dewar's ear murmured, "he has a short temper."

"Among other things," Dewar murmured back, without looking, "Your Highness. His face is rather red; has he a history of apoplexy as well?" He inhaled a little: musk and roses.

"If he doesn't, he will, especially if he hears what she has told several bosom-friends. But careful. He's one of the Emperor's favorites, first after Pallgrave."

"Women talk," Dewar shrugged. "Who listens?" He glanced at Josquin for the first time. "Husbands certainly don't," he said, "or they'd not be talked about. Good evening, Your Highness."

"Good evening, Sir Sorcerer. Lady Filday is giving you the eye from the north-northwest, and I advise you not to return it. She has a poor repute and minor wit, and I presume her inheritance is of no interest to an ascetic scholar like yourself."

Dewar smiled. "Sorcerers do not marry, my lord." He glanced back at the crowd in the middle of the room, arrayed in squares now; the music changed, and they began to dance. The Countess of Lys met his eye for a moment and gave him a disturbingly serious stare, no smile whatever on her face. She wasn't talking to her partner, either, though the ladies around her were gossiping and flirting in the prescribed pattern, complementing the dance's partings and approaches. Dewar lifted an eyebrow and returned his attention to the Prince Heir.

"I believe I'm not supposed to be seen speaking to you," Josquin continued in a private tone, "and at any rate I have something of an appointment, of a sort, elsewhere, but we really must talk sometime—privately."

"I agree. Until then," Dewar said, bowing, and Prince Josquin smiled charmingly and moved off among the crowd, graceful and shimmering, acquiring a cluster of duller satellites. Dewar gazed absently at the dance again, envisioning Josquin's appointment and wondering whether the Baroness of Broul had embroidered her account or bleached it. No one else spoke to him, though particular notice by the Prince Heir ought to be good for a few hours' social success, as hangers-on who hoped to capitalize on royal favor cultivated the new possible favorite. Dewar, in stance and expression, further discouraged approaches. Landuc's Court was a bore, compared with what he had known in Phesaotois under Oren. The women were abysmally stupid, the men were dung-licking lackeys to the Emperor (not a good plot or rebellion among them), and their wine—Madanese wine, in honor of the betrothal he supposed— was chokingly sweet and thick. And he was the only adept sorcerer in the room—Otto was no more than a journeyman— making it an inferior party by any cultivated standard. He would dance with Luneté, he decided; it had irritated Otto amusingly the last time he'd danced with her, at their wedding in Lys, and Dewar felt like irritating someone tonight, someone of more interest than the Baron of Broul. Freia had behaved abominably, Prospero had dismissed him without even thanking Dewar for keeping her under control for as long as he had, and Dewar wanted someone else to suffer inconvenience tonight.

The dance was closing; Dewar went round the perimeter to the place where Luneté, partnered with a weedy, adolescent-looking nobleman in ill-cut red velvet, must end. The music ceased; bows and curtseys followed, and Dewar moved in.

"Countess, may I crave the pleasure of a dance, or are you engaged for the next?"

Luneté looked at him with the same intense, peculiar expression she had used before, then glanced away, blushing. "Dewar— Lord Dewar, I— Where is Otto? I must speak to him."

"Around here somewhere. Ah, there—with the Baroness of Broul. Charming lady." Ottaviano was smiling and leading the Baroness to the dance. He asked her again, in a lower, more intimate tone, "Shall we dance, Luneté?"

"I must talk with Otto," she said, but she allowed him to lead her into the flow of the dance. "Could we trade partners?"

"It is a Court dance, madame, not a country dance. I think it is not done thus these days. The Emperor is very strong on keeping the same partner, unlike his father." Dewar watched Luneté. She seemed genuinely agitated. "Did the Empress say something distressing?" he inquired solicitously.

Luneté met his eyes for the first time, instead of gawking after her husband. "It was Prince Prospero," she said.

"Prospero has made a career of upsetting people at Court," Dewar said. "Don't take it to heart. Wherever did you meet him?"

"Dewar, would he lie?"

"Prospero?"

"Yes. Would he say something he knew wasn't true?"

Dewar considered. "I think not, madame," he said. "He has a gentleman's sense of honor and conduct and a sorcerer's Well-governed tongue: he would not lie, might omit a fact, but would not embellish one." He wondered how Luneté had run into Prospero and what Prospero might have said to her. It would require little priming to pump her dry; Luneté wasn't very cautious.

"So if he said something—outrageous—something incredible—something—"

Dewar led them off to the side gracefully, lifted a glass of the sweet red wine from a passing servant's tray, and offered it to Luneté. "Please drink," he said. "You're making little sense."

She glanced at him with dark, dismayed eyes, nodded, and sipped the wine. "I suppose I might as well tell you," Luneté whispered after a moment, glancing around; "it's going to be all over the Court in a few minutes. He—I went to see the Empress; she wanted to talk to me."

"Yes, I saw you go. Are we to congratulate you on being appointed a lady-in-waiting?"

"No. That would be dreadful; I know nothing about being a lady-in-waiting, and I have much to do in Lys, I am only now understanding how much." Luneté drank, glanced around at the glittering, chattering crowd, and lowered her voice still further. "Is Golias— There he is. No, the Empress just wanted me to know that they're going to be keeping an eye on us. On Lys and Ascolet."

"Kind of her. Of course you assumed they would anyway, I hope, but to tell you so is an uncommonly great courtesy." Dewar watched her; she was watching Otto and the Baroness, who were smiling and talking animatedly.

"Afterward she led us all out to meet the Emperor and his group, before coming in here," Luneté said, "and we met Prince Prospero in the corridor, leaving the ball."

"Ah," said Dewar, prompting her.

"He talked privately with the Empress; I couldn't hear what they said, and then she called him back when he was leaving and asked if he could not bear himself with better courtesy toward Prince," Luneté swallowed, "Golias."

"The Empress is an optimist," Dewar observed.

She drank and swallowed again. "He started laughing. He asked how Golias had come to be a Prince, and Her Majesty told him the Emperor had named him so, and Prince Prospero laughed and laughed— Dewar, he says Golias is not King Panurgus's son! That his mother lied! And he said—" Luneté stopped and looked for somewhere to put the empty wineglass. "Oh, good, the figure is over, I must speak to Otto!" She handed Dewar the glass; he deposited it on another passing servant's tray and followed her into the crowd as it rearranged itself.

Though obviously getting on most peremptory well with the Baroness of Broul, Ottaviano managed to conceal his disappointment at being interrupted by his wife and Dewar. "Madame, perhaps you are not acquainted with Lord Dewar, my cousin," he said, bowing, to the Baroness.

"Oh, we're acquainted," the Baroness of Broul said, and she smiled very warmly at Dewar.

Dewar moistened his lips with his tongue, smiled, and bowed, and the Baroness sighed slightly and then attended to Otto's introduction of his wife.

Luneté watched the byplay between the sorcerer and the Baroness with a flash of furious indignation born of sudden understanding. He was a flirt, she thought; look at him giving that beady-eyed blond hussy his eye and his hand for the next dance! How could he, in front of her? Not that she had any right—yet, it seemed in poor taste. The faithless, seducing rogue—and Otto had been flirting with the creature too. "Otto," Luneté said, "I must talk with you right away."

"She is bursting with words," Dewar said, "some very amusing. Someone finally told Avril that Golias is no son of Panurgus." He smiled very unpleasantly. "I daresay His Majesty will be a trifle red-faced."

"You knew this?" Luneté turned on him, still red-faced herself.

"My dear Countess, it is obvious to anyone who has endured the Fire of the Well and who has eyes to use and the brains to use them. The Well's children are distinctive among lesser beings."

"Why—let's get off the floor, they're starting to dance," Otto said, and they all, Baroness in tow, moved toward the side.

"You were saying, Otto?" Dewar said.

"Nothing."

"Of course, you knew also," Dewar said, smiling, looking at Otto with an air of condescending superiority. He was certain Otto had not, for Otto had said nothing of it to him when they had first spoken of Golias nor later during the wars.

"How might he know?" the Baroness of Broul interjected, eager for the gossip.

"Oh, ways and means," Dewar said, patting her hand. "Dear me, the Baron seems to be looking at Your Ladyship and beckoning. Perhaps you'd best see what he wants, and we'll meet again anon—the last dance, at least, and I'll see you to your very charmingly-appointed coach."

"I should be most grateful if you could be so kind, sir," said the Baroness, smiling, and she looked back with a little blown kiss as she left them.

"Her coach?" Otto repeated, ignoring Luneté's fingers digging into his arm.

"An heirloom of the Baron of Broul's," Dewar said, lifting an eyebrow. "Considerably older than his wife, I'd dare say, and heated, too."

Luneté glared at him. Insolent rake! she thought.

Otto chuckled; Luneté nudged him hard with her elbow. "Otto, I want to talk to you."

"Certainly, Lu. What's up? More gossip?"

"Alone," she said, giving Dewar a withering look.

"If it's something more Prospero said to Glencora in front of her ladies," Dewar said, smiling most annoyingly and bowing, "it'll be all around the room soon."

"Exactly," Luneté said, and she felt unaccountably close to tears. "Excuse us, please."

Golias smiled at Freia, showing his canines, and closed the door behind him, turning the lock.

Its thud as it went into place was the only sound in the library for a long quarter-minute.

"Fancy meeting you here," Golias said, moving toward her.

Fear clutched her stomach, made the bile rise in her throat. Freia circled away from him as he approached, at once watching him and seeking something with which to defend herself.

"Your father's been spreading a rumor," Golias said, "one I don't like, and you're going to tell him he's wrong. You're going to tell him my mother didn't lie. Cat got your tongue?"

She had nothing to say to him. Maybe a heavy book—she'd never have time to use it—a wine-bottle from the table, damn, he was between her and the table— she sidestepped him as he stalked her and put a sofa between them.

"Bastard bitch," he said.

Golias moved to her right, cutting off Freia's path to a stair that went up to a gallery. She backed away, moved to her left around a grouping of chairs and small tables. She thought she could throw an oil-lamp at him, but they were all lit and she feared that it would very likely start a fire, and fires had a way of getting out of control—

Golias was still smiling as he came rapidly around a long table, and Freia darted down to the other end of it, barely keeping it between them.

She was cold. Some part of her detached itself, thinking that she should have grabbed a log from the wood-box when she could. Or a brass candlestick—

He sidled toward her along his side of the table. Now she couldn't back away; there was a high-backed sofa behind her, so she went the same way, and he suddenly put one hand on the table and vaulted it.

Freia screamed once, reflexively, and sprang back. Golias grabbed her left arm, laughing, and spun her around to wrench it up behind her back, shifted his grip quickly and spun her again so that she faced him, her left wrist in his left hand, and stepped rapidly forward so that he pushed her backward onto the table. His right leg went between hers and his right hand caught hers as she tried to gouge his eyes.

He grinned.

As she inhaled to scream again, he kissed her, bending her further back, and released her hand, laughing in his throat as she writhed.

Freia screamed in her soul: *Papa!*

He put his right hand behind her, transferred his crushing hold on her left arm to it, and with his left hand grabbed Freia's hair and held her immobilized, still bearing her back against the table with his mouth on hers, chuckling as she tried to bite him. Bigger and heavier than she, Golias could use his weight to pin her and his reach to control her while she squirmed and sought weak points, degrees of freedom, escape.

She couldn't touch his sword; he wore it across his back and wouldn't let her reach high enough to grab the hilt. No dagger that she could reach, either.

An intolerable interval, but probably only a minute, later, Golias stopped kissing her and said, smiling, "With all this comfortable furniture around, it seems a shame not to use it, dear lady."

Freia attempted again to bite him, and he drew away, laughing, and lifted her up bodily. She landed several good kicks on his legs, sobbing and yelling, and Golias put her down on a divan, pinning her with knees and still holding her left arm— going numb now—behind her back. Kissing her again, he opened the front of her dress, cutting the cord.

Someone banged on the door, shouting.

Golias chuckled softly and strangled her yell with a wadded piece of lace-fringed cloth. "Such a lovely mouth you have too. Pity to stop it. There."

The banging became battering.

Freia tried to spit out the cloth and kicked, knocking over a small table—a mistake; Golias caught her skirts and, shifting his weight on her, began moving them up.

The battering at the door stopped and started again, then stopped with a last thud.

Papa! Freia wailed in her soul, *Prospero! This time don't fail me—* She twisted under Golias, impeding him, and he jerked her left arm so that it felt broken; the pain overwhelmed her and black spots hazed her vision. Something clattered, and a cold draft moved over her sweating forehead.

Golias glanced up quickly, tensing, and then resumed.

In his instant of inattention, Freia got rid of the cloth and shrieked. Golias slapped her, stunning her for an instant, and removed his right arm from beneath her, using it to cover her mouth as he continued getting her clothing out of his way.

Whissssh.

The unmistakable sound of a sword coming out of its sheath.

"Golias!"

Startlement crossed Golias's face; he let go of Freia's mouth, reaching up and drawing, half-rising off her.

"Freia, get thee gone!" Prospero ordered his daughter, and steel whizzed over her body to strike at Golias. With his left hand Prospero pulled Freia toward him, dumping her off the divan, as Golias parried and Prospero attacked him swiftly. Metal rang against metal—weeping, shaking, Freia huddled out of the way on the carpet, half-under the divan, until they passed into a more open area of the room.

Holding her dislocated-feeling left arm close, Freia rose to a crouch, watching them. She was afraid to pass anywhere near them and their flickering, clashing weapons. She looked at the closed door and didn't move—they were between her and it. Golias would grab her, stab her as he had before.

A cold draft stirred the room again; the draperies over the one of the tall terrace windows bellied and shrank on themselves as Prospero backed Golias past. Freia shivered. Prospero must have come through there. Yes. The door was still locked, but outside was so cold—

The gallery caught her eye, ill-lit and remote, above the fray.

Freia fled up the stairs and along. A door to her left fell open as she brushed against it; she went into the room she found there, a private workroom of some kind, its single window's draperies open to let the cold eyes of the Landuc stars see in. The door closed behind her. There were chairs, a table—she didn't make it that far, but folded, nauseated with rage, fear, and impotence, onto the floor, to sit there sobbing sickeningly.

Shouts and sounds of fighting, crashes, angry cries, and brief silences floated up; Freia stopped hearing them when she covered her ears and wept, keening softly to herself, rocking on her knees, and then cried a while longer in the dark.

The door moved. A light shone in through the first crack, striking Freia.

The bearer of the light said "Holy Well!" in a low, appalled voice. He quickly opened the door fully to enter and shut it behind him.

Silenced by the shock of what he saw, he squinted at Freia as she tried to scramble away.

"Lass, lass, come here," Prince Gaston whispered, and he set the light down on the table, bent, helped her up in one fast movement. He settled her on a wide, deep old leather sofa. "Sit here. Here. Whose hand hath turned 'gainst thee?"

Freia's guts were still liquid with fear. She shook her head, covering her face. Where was Prospero?

"Lady, good lady—" Gaston sounded nonplussed, and he touched her shoulder. She flinched, but wouldn't look at him. After a moment he went away, returned. "Drink this," he suggested, half-kneeling beside her. "Come now, lass. 'Tis over. Drink."

He was gentle and insistent, his hand weighing her arm down.

Trembling still, Freia lifted her face and saw that he offered her a glass of something—liquor, obviously—and she accepted it. Gaston had to steady her hand when a wave of heavy shaking went through her. It burned her throat and belly and made her cough, her eyes watering.

"Here."

A clean, plain white linen pocket-handkerchief was in his hand now. Her own was sopping. Freia nodded thanks and blew her nose.

Gaston's eyes moved over her as she did these things. He brought her another drink, putting a splash of water in the glass too.

"Tell me what's passed," Gaston commanded her, on one knee in front of her again so he could see her face.

Freia couldn't find a word for any of it.

"Wert attacked," Gaston prompted.

Freia nodded, shaky, convulsively fast. "He—" she choked out, and had a sip of the fire-and-water drink. She coughed again.

"Slowly. Take't slowly. Art safe now. Slowly," he reminded her softly, putting his hand on her left wrist, pushing the sleeve back to see the marks and deepening bruises there. "Who hath done this, lady?"

Golias, her mouth formed, and she could not say the word. But he had been watching.

"Golias," Gaston whispered, his face changing.

"Yes . . ." breathing out, the word fit in, and Freia shook her head. "I couldn't—I couldn't—He . . ." and she stammered, disconnected syllables.

"Slowly," Gaston whispered.

"Before—" Freia tried to say, and shivered, set the glass down abruptly to keep from spilling it. Breathing too fast, she closed her eyes and made herself breathe more slowly, thinking about each breath, fists clenched.

"Better," her interrogator encouraged her, and he laid his hand on her shoulder, carefully, the warm touch nearly weightless, reassurance without compulsion.

"When he—before—" Freia whispered, and she opened her eyes to look at him. "He said—he would—ag-g-gain," she forced out. If only Prospero had listened to her; had he taken but an hour to hear her tale of injury and outrage, surely he would never have brought her in range of Golias again.

Gaston asked softly, "Rape?"

Freia nodded.

"And 'twas again tonight."

"Yes—"

A hard expression came over Gaston's features, and he studied her a moment.

"I n-never—" Freia protested, beginning to weep, "I never— His m-mother, he s-s-said—"

The Fireduke softened. "Aye, I've heard that tale. —And Prospero came in."

Freia nodded again, quickly, using the pocket-handkerchief and successfully fighting down her tears. "Papa. Papa made him stop. Prospero. Yes. Fought him. I had to get away. Where is Prospero?" She swallowed a breath deliberately.

"I know not, lass. Thou hidst here because wert afraid?"

"Of-of G-G—" Freia stuttered. She shook her head, exhausted, shivering.

"Lass." Gaston shook her by her shoulders, but not hard, then moved up to sit beside her on the chill leather sofa. She drew away from him, but allowed him to touch her cold hand, his palm warm and hard, his sword-callous fingers pressing hers. "Lass, lass," he murmured to her, trying to comfort her. "Thou fearest him, his violence."

Freia nodded.

They stared at one another, she pale with grief and distress, he impassive as stone but for the intense light in his eyes.

"Lass, I swear it to thee by the Well that sustains me, this shall not happen again, it shall not shadow thee a day longer."

Another few heartbeats passed.

"Thank you," she whispered.

"Naught have I done for which thou couldst thank me," Gaston said in an undertone, to himself more than to her. "Let us get thee to thy father."

He assisted her to stand and kept his hand under her arm, supporting her as they went, she all a-tremble still, down the gallery and descended. There were overturned furniture, smashed glass, spilled wine, broken paintings, books on the floor. A small fire in one corner had been doused; ashes and water sullied the soft crimson carpet. The draperies were thrown back and the open window had been closed.

Freia drew her breath in. She tugged her ripped dress over her breast; Gaston picked up a silken chair-shawl and placed it on her shoulders. Freia looked gratefully at him and clutched it in front of her.

They stood a moment, their eyes meeting.

"I'm in thy father's bad books," Gaston said gently. "Go thou to thy rooms or his. He'll find thee anon."

She nodded, swallowed hard, gripped the shawl with both hands. His damp handkerchief was still in her fist; Freia handed it back to him. Gaston accepted it wordlessly. Freia turned and slipped out of the library, barely opening the door.

Gaston stood looking at the closed door for a long time. He unfolded the ball of tightly crushed linen in his hand and found that she had given him her own handkerchief too, wadded up with his and just as wet with tears.

"ALL RIGHT, LUNETÉ. WHAT'S GOING ON?" demanded Ottaviano. She had dragged him back to their apartment, through the empty, quiet Palace halls and corridors, sent the servants away, and now they two stood there face-to-face.

She looked at him searchingly. "Prince Prospero told the Empress that Golias is not a son of Panurgus," she said.

"Dewar said, yeah. What's so upsetting in that? I thought you didn't like Golias."

"I don't like Golias," Luneté said. "Otto, would Prince Prospero lie about that?"

"He wouldn't. As you notice, he didn't say anything about it—nobody did—"

"Who would know?"

"Golias's mother and anyone good enough at using the Well to see. Not many people." Including his Mistress in sorcery Neyphile, thought Otto, who knew about the ability and had not figured out how to do it.

"Did you know?" Luneté asked.

He hesitated and said, "No," softly.

Luneté steeled herself. "If he didn't lie about that, he wouldn't have lied about something similar, would he?"

"I don't think Prospero would tell an outright falsehood to anyone," Ottaviano said. "It would be beneath him. Even though it killed him, he wouldn't lie to your face. He'd lead you to come to a false conclusion on your own. What else did he say, Lu? I've never seen you so upset. Sit down—you look sick." He gestured to a pair of chairs by a small alabaster table. They sat, staring at one another, he puzzled and curious, she biting her lip to fight tears.

"Otto, he said Sebastiano was not your father."

"He said *what*?" yelled Ottaviano, standing.

Luneté spread her hands, helpless, horrified to hear the thing said again by her own lips.

"You misunderstood!"

"I didn't. I know I didn't. Otto, if he wouldn't lie, if he'd know it to be true, how—what—why would he say that?"

"He doesn't like me," Otto said, sitting down. "And he said this to everybody." He gazed at the low-banked fire, thinking. Prospero had said something when he'd had Otto at sword-point—something that had sounded like rhetoric at the time. Yes. *Cecilie was thy mother, at least. No man can be sure of more than that.*

"I heard. Certainly the others heard too. Otto—" whispered Luneté.

"Yeah." What would the Emperor do? Otto chewed his lip.

"Otto, I never asked you—where is your mother?"

He looked from the fire to his wife. "She died when I was born. They had to cut her side to get me out—they told me I was a big child, and there was something about the way I was facing, and she was a little lady like the Empress—and she died."

Luneté nodded. She had heard of such births, which always brought death to the unhappy mother, who often welcomed it. She touched his arm. "Oh. Otto, I'm sorry."

He shrugged. "I never knew her. I know my father Sebastiano better; he left a letter for me, a couple other things like that, and he had—some of his people hide me in Ascolet, other places too, and bring me up."

Luneté frowned. "Why? Why did he not bring you here to Court?"

"He was out of favor, far out of favor, and he didn't know he was going to die right then, Lu—he probably figured he could bring me to the King and acknowledge me any time, but hiding me again would be hard, and there were wars on and he was busy. I always figured he just didn't have time and I never held it against him. He did a lot for me, more than I can say."

Otto swallowed. His mouth was dry. He rose and went to a cupboard, got two glasses and a bottle of the Lys wine Luneté had brought with them. It cut sharply across his palate and took the nasty taste of apprehension out of his mouth. He brought the glasses and bottle back to her.

"What are we going to do?"

"Do? Nothing. What can we do? It's in the Emperor's lap. Sebastiano's dead; he can't be embarrassed by it and I'm not going to let it bother me."

"Otto," said Luneté, a little exasperated at his thickness, "if Sebastiano isn't your father, shouldn't you know who is?"

"Luneté, I have no idea. None."

"Can't we find out somehow?" She accepted a glass of wine.

"How? As I said, it's in the Emperor's lap. He can ignore it if he wants to, treat it like a dirty rumor the way he treats Prince Josquin's carrying on. And he can use it to dump me out of Ascolet if he wants to, or he can leave me there, having just confirmed me in the office. I don't know what he'll do, Lu. It's unguessable."

"We should talk to someone. Find out. Something. Somehow." Luneté drank all her wine quickly and tried to think; the wine steadied her, and she refilled the glass. Who would know? What would happen to them if Ottaviano weren't Sebastiano's son?

Otto shrugged. "I don't know who'd know. Most of the people who were that close to my parents died when Sebastiano died, in the battle with him."

"Would Prince Gaston know?"

"Why him?" Otto asked, reasonably enough.

"He just seems to know everything," Luneté said, wretched. "Somebody must know!" She drank half her wine in quick sips.

"Lu, stop thinking about it. There's not a damned thing we can do about it now. We'll have to follow the Emperor's cue. If he ignores it, we don't mention it. If he wants to make something of it, we can claim Prospero is being malicious."

"But you said he wouldn't lie."

"The Emperor would believe that he would."

"Could Prince Prospero prove you're not Sebastiano's son?"

"I'm sure he—no. He can't practice sorcery anymore."

"Could Dewar?"

Otto paused and then nodded reluctantly. "Probably, yes."

"But you can't."

"Well, no. It's— Luneté, I know a few tricks. That's all. Dewar—the kind of sorcerer Dewar is, is the kind of sorcerer Prospero was, and that's never been the kind of sorcerer I wanted to be."

"A competent one," Luneté said bitterly. "If they could, why not you?"

Otto's jaw clenched and he took Luneté's wineglass from her hand. "Because sorcery has its price, and the more a sorcerer you are, the higher the price goes—and it's not one I've cared to pay. Dewar paid, and he's a sorcerer now—a hot one—and he must have paid high for it, considering."

"Then let's ask him if there's some way to find out who your father is as well as who he isn't," Luneté said triumphantly.

"He'll say he doesn't engage in trade," Otto said.

Dewar was dancing with a sleek silvery-haired lady, who was entertaining him enormously with witty scandal from his father's days at Court. She danced well, also, and she had clearly read and done more than most of the other women of the Court, and he had nearly decided to accept her implied offer of a later, private, more detailed exchange of pleasantries. When the dance ended, he bowed over her hand, not touching it with his lips, straightened, and damned if Ottaviano wasn't standing there.

Couldn't he find his own partners? "Good evening, Baron," said Dewar, allowing his annoyance to show.

Ottaviano put on his best Court manners. "Lord Dewar, madame, I am sorry to interrupt you. If his lordship would be so kind as to accompany me, there is a dispute of some importance which he might be of aid in settling."

A duel, thought Dewar. It was inevitable; Otto was just inept enough to have stumbled into some such mess. "Madame, I must abandon you; if you can forgive me, perhaps we shall meet again later." He lifted his eyebrows inquiringly.

"Gentlemen often have disputes requiring settling," his partner said, "and they are always important. Indeed they are half the interest of the Court. I shall look forward to hearing about this one, if you would call on me tomorrow after the third hour." She smiled.

The sorcerer bowed. "Madame, I cannot guarantee that I shall have anything of interest to report, but I shall be honored to call."

"Of course it must be of interest! Why, all the talk of the court is that sorcerers are such interesting people; they must lead such interesting lives."

Dewar laughed. "Excessively so at times, madame. Until tomorrow," and he bowed over her hand again.

"You really move," muttered Otto, leading Dewar from the room.

"Move?"

"Broul's wife first, now Lady Keneage; are you using some spell?"

The sorcerer smiled superciliously. "Sorcery is wasted on these people. They are consumed with curiosity, however, regarding sorcerers. I cannot allow the opportunity to enlighten them with a few hours' interview to escape me."

"Be careful Broul and Keneage don't take notice of your interviews."

"Shall I introduce Her Ladyship the Countess to those two charming girls from Ithellin?" Dewar wondered. "Or to the blonde with the convenient mole on her—"

"Forget I mentioned it."

"Or perhaps to Lady Miranda of Valgalant?" Dewar continued, turning and fixing Otto with a cold, watchful stare.

Otto halted, halfway along the hall; Dewar stopped with him, still scrutinizing him.

"Lady Miranda," repeated Otto, as though he had never heard the name before.

"Lady Miranda," Dewar agreed, speaking softly but clearly, and somehow he drew Otto, without touching him, aside to an alcove. "You know her."

"I didn't, actually."

"You know she's dead."

It had not occurred to Otto that this might be something he ought not to admit. "Well! Everyone does."

"No, it's been kept mum," said Dewar. "I learned in a most awkward way myself. You knew her."

"I didn't. I did not know her, Dewar. Never saw her." Otto glared at Dewar, slowly heating to indignation. "Ask Gaston about it."

"Did he kill her?"

Otto's breath caught in his throat. Suddenly, he understood: Lady Miranda's father was Dewar's father's partisan. Keeping the lady's death hidden while the Emperor administered the final blow to Prospero's claim to the throne would be imperative; were it known she'd been murdered, there might be outcry, opposition, sympathy, who knew what.

"Did he?" Dewar pressed him.

"No. He was very angry about it; insisted on going to the old man himself," said Otto, deciding that the Emperor's advantage did not, in this particular area, serve his own.

"You know who did kill her."

Otto opened his mouth—halted himself—sighed, looked away.

"Tell me, Otto. Or I must conclude you have some shared need for concealment, and some share of the blame."

"Golias," said Otto—whispered Otto, a breath-word—to the frescoed wall, on which horses' and riders' heads were already turned away, attending elsewhere.

"Golias. Your boon companion."

"I had nothing to do with it and he's no particular friend of mine."

Dewar fixed Otto with a piercing, probing look; Otto felt warmth, the Well Summoned to the sorcerer. Dewar said, "You have entered a number of undertakings together, at least one of them bearing some similarity to this."

"I said I had nothing to do with it! The other business— I never meant—" Ottaviano tried to return Dewar's stare, but was weakened by his own feeling of culpability. No one had said anything, not yet, but there had been hints from Prince Gaston that the affair at Perendlac and Chasoulis might not be buried mercifully in the past. Freia was in the Palace; he had heard her spoken of, had seen her wild and angry in Court this very night. He would smooth that over if he could, but she'd sent him no word in answer to his conciliatory note and he'd had no opportunity to speak to her. "If you wish to take that up, there are formalities."

"I am inquiring about Lady Miranda of Valgalant, nothing else."

"Are you taking that on yourself, then," said Otto.

"No," Dewar said firmly, shaking his head once.

"Taking it elsewhere?"

"No."

"Then why in hell are you asking me about it?"

"My own reasons, Baron, which suffice for me. So you knew nothing, eh?"

"I didn't know her name, who or what she might be—she was a spy, he said. Seemed likely enough. She was picked up by some of his men, scouting. Golias kept her as a prisoner." Otto disliked this line of conversation; it might yet lead him into a very dangerous situation with the sorcerer. "If you want to make anything of it, go to Broul," he said. "He's got it in for Golias, or so I hear. Argued against confirming the title."

The sorcerer shrugged, seeing the redirection for what it was. For the moment, he needed no more than that name, Golias, and so he collected Otto with a glance and strolled along the corridor again, still talking, but not loudly. "From what I hear, his dislike is not unfounded; Golias was insolent to his wife, and the Baron was told of it."

"I'm told she only complains to him when—" Otto stopped himself. "But she's a friend of yours. Your pardon."

"The Baroness of Broul rather fancies the look of you. She asked me to tell you so," Dewar said, "and I add, on my own, that she is a thoroughly delightful person."

"With a warm coach."

"Also handsomely upholstered. Where are we going?"

"My apartment. Luneté's there. We have to talk to you. Have you heard the gossip?"

"What Prospero said to the Empress, very loudly? Yes."

Again they paused, now at the end of a hallway standing before a high, tastelessly gilt looking-glass, and Dewar looked at Otto in the reflection and Otto looked at Dewar.

"And?" Dewar prompted Otto. "You want me to curb the wagging tongues? Persuade Prospero to say it was a joke in monstrous taste? Either is beyond my inclination and my ability."

They still looked in the glass, studying one another. Dewar was serious, no hint of humor in him now. Otto swallowed, glanced to either side: no one around.

"Dewar, if Sebastiano wasn't my father, who the hell is?"

"Excellent question. I presume you're going to investigate it?"

Otto writhed. It galled him to admit he couldn't do something, and he'd faked his way through a number of things, at divers times, which he hadn't done before. But sorcery couldn't be faked, and it couldn't be fooled. "I don't know how," he said.

"So you'd like me to do so," Dewar said, still watching Otto in the looking-glass.

"If that's what it would take."

"May I offer some friendly counsel?" Dewar said gently.

"Sure." Otto clenched his fists.

"Stars above, you are distressed," observed the sorcerer. "Two points, actually. One: don't go looking into this unless you truly want to know. Consider the worst case, and ask yourself whether you could live with it being true. Two: I will only do this once. You had better get reliable witnesses, including the Emperor or someone he trusts completely like that wizened winkle Pallgrave, or all you will have is an allegation."

Ottaviano looked at Dewar: so cool, so unruffled. "How did you feel when you found out who your father was? You didn't know, did you, during the war."

"I did not. I was surprised. I was also pleased. I am still pleased. I was further pleased by your telling me what my father was about when we met in the forest that time," and Dewar's mouth lifted just a bit, "and that is why I have given you that advice."

"Measure for measure. All right. I can't imagine what the worst case would be, and I don't really care. I suspect that it won't matter to the Emperor—since I'm not Sebastiano's, I'm nobody but the Countess of Lys's husband and a rebellious upstart." Otto grimaced and turned to lead Dewar on down the corridor. "Come on, Luneté's waiting." He looked back.

Dewar was looking at Otto with a peculiar smile, his head tilted on one side. He began to laugh softly, shaking his head.

"What's so damn funny now?"

"If you cannot think of a reason I should tell you something else, you could be in for a shock," Dewar said, still laughing quietly. "Dear me, Otto, what *did* Neyphile teach you?"

Otto ignored the taunt and concentrated on the offer. He thought hard. "I don't think I have a reason for you to do me any favors," he said. "If you can't think of one, I can't either."

"I didn't think so. Pity. You're not in terribly good odor with my father just now, but I'm more easygoing," Dewar said, his aggravating smile still there. "Well, let us join the anxious Countess."

Prospero stormed.

"I'll tear his lungs out!" he cried. "Rend his throat with my hands, my teeth; skewer his heart and twist it on its cords 'fore his very eyes— And Gaston! Meddling, self-righteous son of the Sun! Ten thousand ills 'pon them both, that hinder and hamper my every deed! By what right doth he interfere in a just duel, O Emperor, in a duel that your own guards caused? Where were they that my daughter could be outraged and abused in your house, *Emperor*?"

The Empress sat very still. The Emperor leaned rigid against the mantelpiece, miming a casual stance. Glencora, not Avril, answered. "Prince Gaston said he thought Prince Golias would be killed. He—he did not know why you were—duelling Prince Golias, Prince Prospero. The Marshal thought it must be a quarrel of the war."

"*Damn* Golias to oblivion! Damn Gaston for his upright, noble, meddling conscience! And where in the eight Halls of Damnation were the guards set o'er her, Avril? Why were they nowhere near? And where in the Palace is she? Demons bugger thee, Avril, my daughter's suffered enough here! You dare claim her as your ward, and ward her thus? I'll brook no further harm to her!"

"We do not know where the guards were," the Emperor said stonily. "Herne is investigating. Calm down."

"Calm down! Calm! I find that false-titled bastard hound of thine forcing my daughter and I'm to be calm thereat? Shall I tap him on the shoulder and deliver a lecture on manners, per- haps, or technique? Excuse my interruption, bow, and leave? I'll see his head on a pike! Didst never wonder why the maid feared him, that dealt her such violence as Gaston himself, carnifex magnificus, hath admitted he found abhorrent, from which her health's not yet recovered? Didst never bridge doer and deeds, thou ass?"

"Prospero!" yelled the Emperor. "We did not know!"

Prospero replied with an explosive, hissed obscenity: "Shit- witted snail! My daughter is missing; hath been looked for; cannot be found. A vild upon thee!" He turned away and paced to the windows, back to the Empress. "I cannot find her," he said, in a nearly normal, strained voice. "She's run, fled—could be hurt, I did not see; Golias could have her again, by the Well! Let her be found!"

"Assuredly," the Empress said, and stood, and took his arm. "Prince Prospero, best wait in your quarters, do you not think? She may go there. Would she not seek you?"

He shook his head wearily. "Nay, was not there a moment past."

"Let us go there and wait. And the Emperor will find her and send to us when he does, and Golias, and the guards, and we shall all unravel it. It is terrible. Well knows, it is terrible. Have you been in her own chamber? Perhaps she's there. Let us look." Soothing, warm-voiced, the Empress coaxed Prospero out of the room, throwing a sharp look at the Emperor. "There's none but would agree with you, Prospero," he heard her say as the door closed.

Freia's rooms were out-of-the-way. Prospero, after a gloomy moment's reflection, decided that indeed, she might have run there, if anywhere in the Palace she hated; it was her own turf, such as it was, and Freia was ever one to run to earth when hurt. So he led Glencora and two of the Empress's women there, the women and Empress almost trotting to keep up with his long-legged strides.

No guards stood at the door. Prospero growled something uncomplimentary about Herne and lifted the handle; it was locked—no, jammed.

He stood, his blood going cold. "So 'twas at the library—" he whispered to himself, not to the ladies with him, and called "Freia!" at the crack of the door.

Silence met his ear pressed to the wood.

"Stand back," he ordered the ladies, eyed the handle, and kicked it so that the door danced and something snapped. The door had been wedged with a chair; it clattered down, broken-backed, as the door swung inward. The sitting-room was dark, faintly flower-scented from a large bouquet on a console-table before the door.

"Freia?"

The Empress came up beside him, offered him a lit candle from a sconce.

"Back," he told her and her women curtly.

The light was small. It lit him through the sitting-room to the bedchamber.

"By the dark Moon, 'tis hellish frigid here," he muttered. He lit more candles, light touches to wicks. "Freia?" he called softly, persuasively. "Puss, 'tis Papa. Where art thou hid?"

"Papa?" he heard, a tiny mouse-noise.

Prospero could not discern whence it came. "Aye," he said. "Puss, I'm not wroth with thee. By the Four Winds, nay. Where art thou?" He turned around, seeking, perplexed; the three women at the door peered into the dimness of the sitting-room.

"Papa," Freia said, the same tiny, brittle sound, and he whirled; she stood in the middle of the chamber, weeping, hugging some dark thing like a blanket round herself.

"Freia!" and Prospero clasped her to him, absurdly grateful and glad to have her. All his anger at her Court tantrum had gone. She could not dissemble, he reminded himself, she had never done; her surface showed her depths transparently, and she acted as her heart prompted her.

"You came, you came," Freia whispered again and again through her sobs.

"Aye, aye," he repeated, "aye, dear heart, aye, child . . ."

The Empress stayed in the doorway, watching. She turned and gave a soft order to one of her women, who left.

"Did he hurt thee, Freia," Prospero murmured.

"Not—" She gulped. "You came, you stopped him, O Papa—"

"Hush, hush, child—thy gown!"

"He t-t-tore it—Papa, O Papa—" Freia hugged him again. "You were there," she whispered.

"Hush. Shhh." Prospero stroked her undone hair, kissed her forehead and pressed her to his chest. "There. There. Fear naught, child, fear naught. I'll see him tree-tied and gutted for this, the bastard cur."

Prince Herne stood hard-faced before the Emperor and Count Pallgrave; the diligent pen of Cremmin awaited his answer to the Emperor's query.

"Is she gone?" Herne demanded.

"We asked you whether you had removed the guard from her," the Emperor said.

"Remove it? I'd double it. She's sly as her sire. Has she escaped?"

"So you did not remove the guard from her."

"Hell, no!" Herne, arms folded, waited for Avril to explain himself.

"You have a roster of the guard, I presume, Prince Herne?" Pallgrave asked.

"The captain does. You think I assign them myself?" The Prince looked down on the gaunt Count.

"Send for the captain," the Emperor commanded. "Now."

Herne stared at him a moment, then opened the door. "You," he said to one of the Emperor's guard outside. "Go get Captain Horun, and tell him bring his duty roster with him."

The guard saluted and left at once.

"What's afoot?" Herne demanded, closing the door.

"There has been a lapse," the Emperor said.

"Did the vixen run?" Herne demanded, a note of annoyance coming into his voice. "I'll ride her down."

"That will probably not be necessary," the Emperor said.

There came a tap at the door; it opened and a footman announced the Countess of Orasch with a message from the Empress. The Emperor nodded. The lady entered, curtseyed.

"Her Majesty desired me to inform Your Majesty that the girl is found," the Countess said.

The Emperor laughed, a short bark. "Where?"

"In her apartment, Your Majesty."

Count Pallgrave coughed lightly; the Emperor nodded. "In what condition?" inquired Pallgrave.

"Dishevelled," said the Countess, "discomposed, gibbering and weeping, wearing an antimacassar for a stole. Her father attends her."

"Doctor Hem shall go to them immediately and examine her himself. Inform him. Let him report to us when he has so done."

"Yes, Your Majesty," the Countess said, and she curtseyed

again and left. As she did, the Fireduke entered, and she bowed to him as well.

"Ah, our Marshal," said the Emperor. "About this quarrel between Prince Golias and Prospero, which you disrupted and then reported to us."

Gaston lifted his eyebrows and waited to hear what the Emperor would ask him.

"Prospero," the Emperor went on when he was forced to recognize that Gaston was being unhelpful, "accuses Prince Golias of attempting his daughter's virtue."

Herne snorted, the query clarifying much to him. Gaston nodded and waited to be asked a question, thinking, guessing, planning.

The Emperor glared at him. "We know Prospero has old quarrels with Prince Golias. Might you have heard anything supporting this new allegation when you halted their duel?"

Gaston frowned, considered, answered carefully. " 'Tis as I first told you. I heard their weapons. 'Twas in the old library. The doors being locked, I went to the little smoking-room door that does not lock; indeed it swung free as ever, and I entered, drew, and beat down their swords, enjoining them to leave the fight. I thought it must be from some ill-feeling from the war or Prospero's fresh slander, and 'twere best, meseemed, that they not draw blood without formalities."

"Ah, the war," the Emperor murmured. "Prospero has a grudge against him for the war, we have had some inkling of this before. Prince Golias was in Prospero's hire awhiles."

"That's so," Herne said. "Golias spoke of it to me, and Prospero has needled him as an oath-breaker often since."

The Emperor's face gave no sign of what he thought behind it.

Gaston said nothing.

"You may leave us, Marshal; this is a domestic matter and beyond your authority," the Emperor said smoothly.

Gaston bowed and left, still silent. Herne and the Emperor both hated Prospero, and the Fireduke misliked to leave them together sitting on this business. It would be easy for the Emperor to claim the charge of attempted rape was trumpery, to smear the girl's character, perhaps to claim she'd played coquette with now-Prince Golias, and to accuse Prospero of thereby ensnaring Golias as vengeance for the ex-mercenary's treachery. It was plausible only if one believed Prospero had no feeling for the girl. The Emperor was not beneath such rearrangements of truth, Gaston knew.

Yet if the Marshal reported what the girl had told him, it would go worse still for her: this he also knew. In the current political and social milieu, she would be dishonored; out of favor and powerless, she would suffer reprisals, her marriage to Prince Josquin surely cancelled, no scrap of dignity nor defense left to her nor Prospero. Gaston thought of Lady Miranda's body. Though named now Prince, Golias had no part of nobility. Truly Gaston had been an idiot not to suspect that it had gone worse for both of them than the visible wounds showed. He skewered his past self mercilessly: he had not wanted to suspect, had been blind to the truth of Golias's viciousness.

The Marshal, disdaining niceties of the scope of his authority, had already inquired quietly among the guards. His most trusted captain, a Landuc man named Jolly who served Gaston now in his Montgard army, had spoken with the two men who had been assigned to watch Lady Freia that evening.

They were two of Golias's mercenaries who had taken the Emperor's gold and enlisted under Herne, who'd needed men badly to fill out the ranks thinned by Prospero's war. They had guarded Lady Freia when Lord Dewar led her from her chamber to the Coronation Hall, guarded her thence when she fled her betrothal, and guarded her to the old library, where she had gone in and sat by one of the low fires that burned there to drive damp from the books.

The guards were careful; they had stood within the door, which had remained open, but had not approached nor spoken to the lady, as they were under orders not to do so unless she made some effort to escape. They had kept her under constant watch until their former captain, Golias, had come to them, beckoned them out, said they were relieved for a couple of hours to drink the betrothed lady's health below and that he'd cover her until they returned.

He had been their commander and was now a Prince. They had obeyed cheerfully, promising to drink his own as well in honor of his access of nobility.

Gaston's captain had had this from their own mouths, before they'd had any word of what had followed from their dereliction. He'd asked them amiably what they did, and they had told him, and he had said nothing to them of the result of their celebratory pot-tossing. Jolly had drunk a cup with them and returned to his commander to report.

No matter what the Emperor and Herne decided, the guards would be dead at dawn for disobeying orders and abandoning their post. Gaston himself had ordered hangings for such. A soldier who could not obey an order was useless, and Herne would watch them drop without pity.

The question must be, what would become of Golias?

⸺ 10 ⸺

FREIA COULDN'T STOP SOBBING, THOUGH IT made her sicken and vomit. Prospero had asked her what had passed before he came to her, and she became hysterical and incomprehensible, raving and clinging to him, not permitting him to leave her, terrified that Golias would appear again. Prospero sent one of the waiting-women to get a fire laid in both rooms (and that yesterday, wench), and when Doctor Hem arrived, sent by the Empress or the Emperor or both, Prospero would not allow him to examine Freia; instead, Hem was sent away again to find Dewar.

"Don't go . . . don't go . . . don't go . . ." Freia was half-wailing into Prospero's shoulder when the sorcerer arrived.

"What in all the devils' names is toward?" Dewar asked as politely as he could manage. It had been a good card game; Fortuna had stood by his shoulder and he'd relieved Fulgens of much of the weight of his purse already. But it seemed that Dewar was destined to complete nothing he began, this cursed evening.

"I trust thee and no other for this," Prospero said. "Hie thou, find that charlatan Hem and oblige him to open to thee his pharmacy. (Hush, Puss, none shall harm thee, none shall harm thee.) There fill thy hands from this list—" he handed it to Dewar, short and scrawled, blotted and jarred "—and bring the things back. She cannot be calmed."

"Why?" Dewar asked, in a tone of great reasonableness.

"I'd brew a draught, and I trust not Hem nor any of the creatures here!" snapped Prospero. "Do thou make haste ere she rave her way to utter distraction, and me with her."

"What—" Dewar stopped himself at Prospero's glare. He bowed. He left, passing a surly chambermaid kneeling at the fireplace where a sharp-faced lady-in-waiting stood over her, taking a crumpled piece of paper from the maid and stuffing it into her pocket.

Luneté, Countess of Lys, clenched her fists and inhaled carefully. Her dress was too tight, there was no pretending otherwise; or, more accurately, her dress was too narrow and her corset too tight. It could not be the heavy-sauced Palace food, the opulent banquets and fantastical dinners. Luneté knew she couldn't have eaten so much in so few days as to put her new-fashioned Court gowns all out of size. Laudine had made a mistake when she had altered the dress from the high-waisted (and, Luneté thought wistfully, more comfortable) old style of Sithe of Lys's Court years with Queen Anemone to the narrow, long-waisted newer style preferred by the slender Madanese Empress.

Though Laudine had hotly denied erring, she was now picking and restitching seams, letting fullness back into the bodices and waists of three gowns. But Luneté must be dressed, and so she suffered now in a room that seemed oppressively warm, wishing she had thought to persuade Ottaviano to crave this audience on the morrow, when the gowns would be ready.

Dewar stood gazing out a window to one side, meticulously whetting the red-handled knife he had lately obtained from Ottaviano, a small smile slipping onto his lips from time to time as his thoughts amused him. A covered table waited in the center of the room, before the small dais and throne on which the Emperor would sit; irregularities in its draping suggested a candle, a bowl, and hid the rest.

Beside Luneté, Ottaviano fidgeted with his pockets, doubtless missing the folding knife now in Dewar's hands. It had been his favorite pocket-piece ever since Luneté had known him. She would have to find him something as interesting to occupy his hands in idle or anxious moments, but the curious knife would be difficult to replace.

Dewar admired the thing exceedingly. At their meeting two nights previous, after a long wrangle in which the Countess of Lys and the Baron of Ascolet had proposed payment after payment to the sorcerer, who had shrugged off gems, money, land, a small manor-house, everything offered to him—Luneté had begun to fear he would accept nothing less than herself—after two hours of this, Otto had taken out the folding knife and cleaned his clogged pipe. Dewar had watched, and Ottaviano had expanded happily on the ten thousand uses and virtues of the thing. Dewar had tinkered with it, peering at his fingertip through its useless little burning-glass, testing the point of the awl, counting the blades, hooks, files, and incomprehensible implements. He particularly admired the corkscrew. Ottaviano had jestingly offered the knife as payment for the sorcery he needed from Dewar, and Dewar had haughtily replied that he did not sell his sorcery.

Later, after they collapsed with relief into their bed, Ottaviano had told his wife that he had recognized in that instant that they had approached Dewar incorrectly. For Ottaviano had next said, "Would you accept it as a gift, then?," and Dewar had smiled, asked whether Otto could live without such a marvellously useful thing, and Otto had replied that there were things he'd rather have that might be of more use, such as his blood-father's name. And that was that: Dewar had said he would unravel Otto's paternity, there was no further talk of jewels and money, and the sorcerer had taken the folding knife and left them to stare at one another.

"An expensive gift," Ottaviano had said, as Luneté was falling asleep. "But about the right value."

"What?" Luneté had come awake with a start.

"I've had that knife for years," Otto had said in the darkness. "It's part of me. He has me now."

"Has you?"

"Things that are intimately associated with a person can be used by a sorcerer to work on them," Otto had said. "That's why we burn hair clippings and nail parings—you know. But anything can be used if it's been near the body."

"Work on them?" Luneté had repeated apprehensively.

"Enthrall, influence, ensorcel—"

"How did you learn so much about sorcery?" his wife asked, interrupting.

"The hard way. —I wish he'd settled for a house and some land. Or the sapphires. I know he likes sapphires. He was holding out for something good. This had better be worth it."

"Dewar's our friend. He wouldn't do that."

"He's a sorcerer."

And shortly afterward, Otto had snored into a bolster while Luneté stared at the darkness, afraid of nameless things, until the great Palace clock rang the ninth hour of the night.

This afternoon the Emperor had consented to give them a few moments' relatively private audience. Luneté had arranged it through the Empress, though she had felt uncomfortable about trading so quickly on the royal favor shown her. But Otto had insisted; and the Empress had said that she would attend also and advised Luneté to find another witness. A man versed in law would be best, said the Empress, someone to counsel the Baron on what steps he might take when his father's name was revealed. Luneté knew no lawyers and few of the nobility, and so the Empress had sent to her the Lord of Valgalant: the same elderly nobleman who had stood beside Luneté in Court.

The door opened without warning and that Lord Gonzalo of Valgalant entered, garbed as before in unrelieved mourning. He bowed over Luneté's hand, greeted Ottaviano, nodded courteously to Dewar, and stood beside the Countess and Baron to wait for the others. Luneté gnawed her lip unbecomingly.

After another quarter of an hour, the door opened, the Empress and Emperor were announced, and those two individuals entered, followed by the Prince Heir, the Prince Marshal Gaston, Princes Herne and Fulgens, the Princesses Viola and Evote, Count Pallgrave, and the Emperor's secretary Cremmin.

Luneté curtseyed and stayed down, a Court curtsey; Otto bowed, and they covertly glanced at one another with some dismay. The entire royal family, excepting Prince Prospero and his daughter, were there, a far larger audience than either of them had anticipated.

It occurred to Luneté that there was surely some formula for the proceedings to follow; the Court had a formula for everything. She had no idea what it might be.

"Good afternoon," Dewar said pleasantly, and she glanced back as she rose to see him leaving the window. He had not bowed. "How stirring to see such interest aroused by a little unfashionable sorcery," he said.

Luneté wanted to slap him and tell him to keep his flippancies for light matters, such as the Baroness of Broul. She breathed slowly and deeply, damning Laudine's ill-measured needlework.

"Lord Gonzalo, the protocol?" Dewar asked.

Lord Gonzalo nodded, coughed slightly, and spoke. "I have conferred with the Master of Protocol. As it was done in Prince Esclados's case," he said, "the procedure was to establish paternity as claimed by the Prince. There has not been a case of disproving paternity, and there really is no protocol."

The sorcerer shrugged: then he would invent one. "The object of this sorcery," he said pedantically to the waiting Princes, Princesses, and the Emperor and Empress, "is to establish two things. First, to establish the truth or falsity of recent claims that Baron Ottaviano is not the son of Prince Sebastiano. Second, depending on the outcome of the first, to establish who in fact sired the Baron. I will state now—for Master Cremmin's always-useful record—that it is quite plain to me, as it is plain to anyone with proper training in the power granted by the Well, that Baron Ottaviano's father was an initiate of the Well. His mother was not, but he bears nonetheless the signs of Well-engendering."

Ottaviano was taken aback. Luneté opened her mouth to speak and closed it. Lord Gonzalo's and Prince Gaston's bland expressions did not change at all, and the others glanced sidelong at one another with the beginnings of surmises in their faces.

"What are these signs, Lord Dewar?" asked the Empress, as much to disrupt the moment as to know the answer.

"Madame, they are difficult to describe, but easy to see. Poetically, but not wholly accurately—the Baron has the requisite streak of Fire in his soul."

"Is the soul visible to you?" she inquired, managing to make the question sound curious and not contemptuous.

"No, madame. I did say, poetically. When viewed with perception in the proper—octave, the Well's Fire is apparent in the Baron." Dewar paused; the Empress nodded, and the Emperor scowled. "Before I continue," Dewar said, "all present must swear that they will endorse the truth which I shall discover in addressing these two questions. I require the Oath of Blood."

A brief silence of shock was followed by a storm of royal and Imperial outrage. "Blasphemous!" cried Pallgrave. Cremmin, faithfully taking notes for the Emperor, resorted to abbreviations. Dewar stood, arms folded, and Ottaviano and Luneté followed his example and remained quiet. He seemed to know what he was about. Lord Gonzalo stood gazing at the covered table, his expression remote and grave.

The sorcerer lifted his hand. "If you refuse," Dewar said, "I shall perform the sorcery anyway and shall broadcast both the result and that the witnesses refused to endorse it as truth. Your credit will suffer, I assure you, and denial of the Well's truth always brings its own unpleasant consequences."

"Blackmail," Prince Herne muttered.

"Prince Herne, you may leave if you do not wish to remain," Dewar said. "Which I would also make a point of mentioning."

There came still no word from the Emperor; the Empress and the others were waiting for his lead. Dewar's expression was cool, contemptuous; Prince Fulgens was glaring at Ottaviano as if it were his idea (Luneté did not think it was).

The silence ended. "I do swear by the Well that sustains me, to endorse the truth of the matter of the birth of Ottaviano, which shall be revealed here through sorcery; an I fail of this oath, let the Fire of the Well in my blood destroy me," Prince Gaston recited quietly.

Luneté realized that the Marshal had just embarrassed the rest of them heartily and forced them into the Oath. If he took it and they did not, they would look very bad when the matter came to be discussed by others, as Dewar would assure it would be. Even without an oath, the Fireduke's probity was proverbial.

The Emperor stiffened, visibly angry; but he said the Oath, almost muttering it, his expression hard.

Luncté thought she wouldn't want to be Prince Gaston later.

The others followed the Emperor, and Luneté, Otto, and Lord Gonzalo swore as well.

"For the first stage of my work," Dewar said, "I must have either a Key or some article intimately and strongly associated with the late Prince Sebastiano. As the associations of the Prince's belongings are weakened with time and disuse, and I have no appetite for tomb-openings to retrieve relics from the dead, I hope someone has a full set of Keys or can fetch them."

"I've mine," Prince Josquin said, and fished a flat, hand-sized leather case from an inner coat-pocket. "You may *borrow* them," he said with a grin. He tossed the case underhand to Dewar, who plucked it out of the air, giving Prince Josquin in return a slight bow and a smile.

"Thank you. Which is Prince Sebastiano's?" Dewar had opened the case. The objects within were unlabelled, all different, arrayed in rows.

"On the bottom, third from the right."

Dewar extracted the square-topped iron Key from the case and removed the cloth from the table. Underneath were a golden candelabrum, a tall shell-footed silver ewer, and a hemispherical gold basin. A round silver box with high sides, like a lady's powder-box, was also there, its lid hiding its contents. The candelabrum was one Luneté recognized from the banquets she had lately attended; its form was of two open circles one above the other, candles in two tiers—an epergne. At the banquets, flowers, statues, or even portraits and conversation-pieces were displayed in the circles, lit from all sides by the candles. Dewar picked up the golden bowl and put it inside the circles; it fit as if made to do so.

The onlookers watched without interrupting. The Emperor's face was hostile and cold.

From somewhere Dewar produced a little flame, dancing at the end of his finger; he touched each of the candles and they flared high, then settled into a steady burn. Their light reflected in the golden bowl and lit his face from below. Luneté felt a tickle in her belly; Gaston lifted his head as if scenting something; the Emperor leaned forward without knowing; and Otto moved half-a-step toward Dewar.

"Susceptible," muttered Dewar, or something like it, and he lifted his hand to Otto: wait.

Otto shook himself as if waking and stopped.

Dewar opened the silver box and took out something crescent-shaped that flashed in the candlelight. He set it aside on the white tablecloth. Luneté was suddenly aware that he was talking, speaking in a rippling undertone singsong, and she wondered how long he had been doing that. His expression was at once remote and ecstatic and wholly attentive. The candle flames streamed upward; Dewar lifted the ewer and poured water into the golden bowl, and it looked like fire streaming downward.

Somehow he had picked up Sebastiano's Key, and he dropped it into the bowl. It sparked and glittered as it fell more slowly than it ought, and the water did not splash when it struck. Instead, there was a deep bell-like sound.

Dewar, gazing into the bowl, beckoned peremptorily to Ottaviano. Otto joined him at the table, watching and listening to Dewar's murmured spell. Dewar grabbed Otto's arm, shoved his sleeve back, and held his wrist over the flames above the bowl, which was glowing with light now, the Key's outline visible as a dark shadow-form over it. Dewar picked up the silver sickle and paused, said "Now!," and blood gushed from Otto's arm down into the bowl, or blood and fire, and the shape of the Key remained a hollow shadow.

Luneté smelled the blood. Her stomach roiled. She swallowed and clenched her hands, biting her palms with her nails, and slowed her frightened breathing.

Dewar released Otto's wrist. Otto stepped back, pressing the cut. The sorcerer moved his hands, speaking indistinctly, and a veil of carmine-glowing blood swirled upward from the bowl. It moved around and around the shape of the Key, upward and downward like a tubular fountain, and Dewar stood with his hands to either side of the candelabrum and bowl, watching it.

He broke off his muttered incanting and said, "Is this clear?"

"Yes," whispered Ottaviano.

"No," said the Emperor.

"If Otto were of Sebastiano's line, his blood would by its affinity form the shape of Sebastiano's Key, drawn to its origin. Were I to do this with your Key, Emperor, and Josquin's blood, that is what you would see, for his is yours; he is your son."

"Ah," whispered the Empress.

"The next phase will be rather trickier," Dewar said, "as it involves using all of your Keys, balancing the force in all. You may feel a touch strange." He clapped his hands once—did they pass through the candles?—and the blood subsided. Sebastiano's Key was hanging there instead, between the candles. Dewar reached in and cupped it in his hand, lifted it out gently, and set it aside.

"This will suffice," the Emperor said sharply, beginning to rise.

"Oh, no," Dewar said, glancing at him, "one doesn't drive sorcery like a horse, Avril; it is in hand, it is moving, and it will go on. Pray you remain."

His fingers had been busy as he spoke, plucking Keys from Josquin's case and putting them, one by one, in the candle-flames, where they hovered and became little balls of flame. They moved, arranging themselves; lines of fire leapt among them, drawing two squares overlapping: an octagon, a star of white-gold fire.

The Emperor had fallen back into his chair, gripping the arms, breathing hard, and perspiring copiously. Gaston was nearly smiling, his eyes half-closed, and he made a small, contented-sounding "Hmm . . ." noise as if savoring a fine wine.

"The Well," Herne whispered, and Fulgens and Josquin both looked wild-eyed and folded their arms tightly.

Otto was shaking. "Come on, man," he moaned.

"I wonder what Esclados thinks of this," murmured Dewar, "and Father," but he took from his sleeve a slender black wand, touched with silver and gold, and moved it through the star-shape.

A line of Otto's blood rose up like smoke from the gold bowl, following the wand-tip as Dewar traced the two squares, touching each Key-light in turn.

"Gaston, no," Dewar said quietly, passing one. "Prospero, no. Herne, no. Fulgens, no."

Otto was whispering the "No"s with him, his eyes closed, concentrating. Luneté wondered what he felt; he was still shaking, and she stepped quietly closer to him.

"Yes!" shouted Otto explosively, a triumphant happy note in his cry, as Dewar's wand and the blood-plume touched a light, which flared and shot down into the bowl.

Dewar flicked the wand past the remaining lights; they dimmed and fell with metal clanks on the table and candelabrum. The Empress had cried out, and she and Princess Evote were fanning the Emperor, who half-lay now in the throne-like chair on the dais.

The sorcery was dissolved. On the table were eight candles, scattered Keys, a bowl of blood and water, an empty silver ewer. A few scarlet drops bloomed on the white cloth.

Dewar stood with his arms folded, smiling slightly, looking down at the table; then he began picking up the Keys, examining each one, and returning them to the case.

The Emperor recovered himself and pushed the Empress and Princess Evote aside.

"Well?" Princess Viola asked. "What does it all *mean*, sorcerer?"

"Mean?" Dewar repeated, glancing up at her, at all of them. A merry wicked light was in his eyes, but his face was set and cold. He put the tip of his wand in the bowl and lifted the remaining Key free, holding it up for them all to see, dripping blood. "Why, Madame Princess, it means it is impossible to hide the truth from the Well; that all things are clear in the end; that blood is thicker than water; and that the Emperor Avril is Ottaviano's father."

Luneté felt her mind leave her, flying away into comforting darkness and leaving her body to pitch gracelessly toward the floor.

Drugged, Freia allowed herself to be parted from her father and put to bed, bruises bathed and salved; but she roused often, crying out, and betweentimes whimpered in uneasy dreams. So Prospero sat by her, gnawing his nails to the quick, talking to her low-voiced, telling her tales and fables. Two maids sent by the Empress stayed sewing in the outer room; one or the other fetched him coffee, water, a towel, more candles when the Prince commanded, but they would not look at him and sidled away, at once afraid and disdainful. He read when Freia was quiet, and when the sedative's effect lessened and she distressed herself with wild talk, he made her drink the bitter-tasting cordial-laced stuff. The third time, she sank shortly after into a deeper sleep—the silver light of a wolf-dawn making her repose deathlike—and in a while, as the maids left and others came, Prospero slept too, sitting, book slipping from hand to lap, snoring softly.

A touch woke him; he started, clenching hands and body, shaking his head, casting off sleep's net.

Freia was trying to take his hand.

"Puss," he said to her, and patted her fingers. The fire had finally warmed the room, even to the windows; her hand wasn't icy-frail.

"Papa, please, let us go home."

He sighed, shook his head, and said, "Nay, Freia. We may not leave." And, as he'd feared, within two brief minutes she was halfway to hysteria again, wanting to go home, to leave the evil place and the hateful people, and he must drug her again for peace. So it went later in the afternoon; he coaxed her to eat, that time, half of a bowlful of soup one of the insolent maids brought, and in the course of eating Freia again began pleading to leave and telling him she feared Golias, stammering and weeping and speaking incoherently, and Prospero again gave her the potion he had brewed, regretting he'd not made it stronger. She was overwrought, all out of proportion to what had happened; he was near losing patience with her distress and demands and must mind his tongue.

No one came to inquire about her during the day. Prospero sat and read, deliberately reserving himself from outrage and rage, tending his daughter and biding his time. He sent the maids for food and wine, and watched the heatless light leave the clouds as he dined, and watched the stars beyond the fire's reflection as he supped. For some little while the Well was uncommonly agitated; he felt it surging and catching at him, never fastening: some sorcery afoot, but there seemed no threat in it, and soon it faded away. With a heart-pang, he supposed that Dewar was working.

Freia's own exhaustion finally regulated her; she woke, said nothing but accepted some boiled chicken and custard and kept them down, and slept true sleep afterward. Prospero, pleased but cautious, thought he had better stay a few hours more. He was surrounded by the heavy winter night; the fire and two candles by the bed were all the light. The maids left and no others came. Again Prospero dozed, his hand on Freia's wrist where beat a steady dream-paced pulse.

c— *11* —ɔ

"PROSPERO!"

Light, movement, noise: Prospero started, the image of his cavern-cell fleeting from his mind's eye, his name ringing in his ears.

"Be still, damn thy throat!" he hissed as he sat up. "She sleeps. Herne?" Prospero stood.

"Aye," Herne growled, appearing with a candle in his hand at the sitting-room door, and Fulgens behind him, both frowning.

"Your tender avuncular hearts move ye to odd calling hours," Prospero observed, scowling too, and they glared at him.

"Thy tender fatherly heart, likewise," Fulgens said. "Come."

He pointed past them to the door. "Nay. I'll not leave her; she's wracked and strained. Get out; you'll wake her with this blather."

"The Emperor desires thy presence in the instant," Fulgens

said. "Prettily enough said? Now come; nor the matter nor the Emperor admits delay."

"Nay, I say; I'll not leave my girl. She's unwell and I mistrust th' Emperor's charity."

Herne showed his teeth. "She's not thine, but the Emperor's; all thou hadst is his, Prospero, even to thy life. Wilt find no refuge behind her skirts nor sickbed. She malingers," he snorted.

"Begone," Prospero said, his hand itching for a weapon. He tensed; Herne shifted, setting the candlestick he held on the table by the door, stepping a half-step toward him.

"Shall give me great pleasure to invite thee with my fist—"

"Papa?" Light as a sparrow's twitter, the word dropped Herne's hands.

"Let's see the maid," Fulgens said to Herne as Prospero went to the bed again. "Be she ill, one of Glencora's women can sit with her."

Freia was speaking to her father, a liquid low tremulo. "So cold, so cold, O Papa, so cold, and I couldn't move—Papa, don't go—"

Seated on the bed, Prospero had turned to face the two Princes, his daughter's arms around his neck.

She made a fearful whimper as she saw them; Fulgens frowned, looked down a moment. Herne reached forward.

"Don't touch me!" Freia shrieked, a pure high thin sound of terror. "No! No!" and Prospero, wroth in an instant (but secretly pleased at her distraction) turned on them, rose up roaring and shoved Herne back.

Fulgens dodged between them, grabbing Herne's arm and keeping him from swinging again at Prospero, whose stance was defensive.

"Go home, go home, go home—" Freia was keening into her hands, knees to her chest, pressed into the corner of the bed, a sound halfway to madness even to the most unsympathetic ear.

"Be still, girl!" Fulgens yelled. "Makest noise enough for a flock of mews!"

"Get you gone!" Prospero shouted.

Footsteps and clatter came in the outer room, and someone called for Prince Herne.

"What is it?" Herne snarled, not turning.

One of the Palace Guard entered. "My lord, sir, it's the sorcerer, sir. We tried to—that is, four men went as you ordered, sir, and they, they—"

"What?" Herne glanced at the man.

"They can't move, sir," the guard said.

"Can't move?"

"They walked into the room, sir, and they, they're stuck there. They can't get him, and they can't get out."

"You sent four men to arrest my son?" Prospero said, sneering, though his blood was cold in him: a midnight arrest—an ill start to a day, an ill end to a night. "Sent four men to arrest a sorcerer, a guest, lying sleeping in a hostile house, and expect them to live? Perhaps they will—awhile. Think you he's as easily bullied as this girl? Hah!"

Freia had pulled herself into a ball and was huddled silent now, though her trembling breathing rasped loud.

There was a brief silence as all parties prepared to speak. Fulgens was first.

"Come with us, Prospero. The Emperor desires to speak with thee."

"Nay. 'Tis the middle of the night, you've set my daughter a-raving, and I shall not go," Prospero said coldly and precisely. "If you're here to prison me, I can be as easily held here as anywhere. Let some of Herne's famous guards ward the doors and windows, if they can keep the task in their sieve-heads for an hour at once, and be you gone, for I shall not go."

Herne began to speak; Fulgens interrupted. "Very well; that shall we relay to His Majesty."

Herne glowered at him. "The wench is lively enough," he said; "her own mind torments her more than anything outside it. But I concur, Prospero; canst be arrested here or anywhere, arrested, tried, judged, and—"

"Enough!" Fulgens said. "Let's see what the guards have done in Lord Dewar's case."

With a final hate-filled glare at Prospero, Herne left behind Fulgens, and the guard followed them out.

Prospero, iced with his own perspiration in an instant, sat down on the edge of the bed, his legs weak. "Freia, my Puss," he whispered.

"P-Papa?" She peeked at him above her fingers, cowering yet.

"Come; I would hold thee. No surety but that they'll come again."

Freia uncurled and slid toward Prospero. He leaned against the bed-post and hugged her, suddenly struck by how near death could be: his; hers; his son's.

"Papa," she whimpered, huddling to him, "Papa, I wish we were home."

Prospero closed his eyes and embraced her tightly. "And I, Puss," he whispered to her hair that smelled of smoke and stale air. "And I."

Dewar awoke, stretched, and lay abed staring blurrily at the stitchwork at the end of the pillow, half-asleep yet and thinking of how it was done, each stitch, and how one might get an Elemental to do it, perhaps a Sylph—

Voices. His elaborate plan for training the Sylph evaporated. It was probably cheaper to have girls embroider linens anyway.

The voices were outside his closed bedroom door. He put on a deep-turquoise quilted silk dressing-gown and tucked his wand in the pocket before opening the door.

"Ah," he said.

Six armed men stood statuelike, none closer than four paces to the door. His protective Bounds had snared them and kept them snared, speechless and frozen . . .

. . . but aware. Their eyes rested on him.

Dewar leaned on the doorjamb and looked past them at Count Pallgrave, Prince Herne, and Prince Fulgens. Prince Herne was also caught, red-faced with effort and fighting it still, attempting to draw back a fraction at a time from the sticky, engulfing suction of the spell. He was losing. Prince Fulgens and Count Pallgrave were apparently trying to pull him out without also being taken.

"Good morning, Prince Herne."

Herne glared at him.

"Uncivil of you to call so early," Dewar said. He yawned. "I shall be along in a while. In the meantime, carry on. Amuse yourselves. I'm sure you can think of something. I certainly shall." He smiled and shut the door. Count Pallgrave spluttered; Prince Fulgens bellowed threateningly.

Having shaved, bathed, groomed, and dressed, Dewar stood before the looking-glass in the bedroom, adjusted his cuffs, and took up his wand again, which he tucked in one sleeve. With a courteous bow to himself, he turned away and went to the door.

"Very kind of you to wait," he said pleasantly. As he had hoped, Fulgens and Pallgrave were now indeed trapped; their hands on Herne's arms, the spell had flowed outward to seize them as well.

Dewar wondered how many people one could link into such a daisy-chain of near-paralysis before the influence of the spell was taxed beyond its capacity; it was his version of a common variety of protective spell, designed to keep intruders alive but harmless until the sorcerer had leisure to deal with them. It might be wise, he thought, to experiment; the spider-spell normally acted only when one entered its sphere of influence, but one could also be trapped by touching someone already caught—though not reliably nor within any certain time; Dewar was unsure what the variables were. He nodded to Prince Herne and Prince Fulgens as he went by; the door had to stay open because Count Pallgrave was in the way, but that was all right. Perhaps some of the domestic staff, or Cremmin, who seemed to loathe the man, would come by and take advantage of the moment. Meanwhile, breakfast called.

"Dewar!"

"Good morning, Prince Josquin." The sorcerer bowed,

smiling in a most wicked and ungentlemanly way.

"What's going on at your apartment?" Prince Josquin asked.

"Your Highness—"

"Josquin. I asked you. Cousin."

Their eyes met; Dewar inclined his head slightly, as if it were he granting the favor, not the Prince. "Josquin, I am not sure. They don't look terribly friendly, do they? But they're harmless. If you have ever wanted to—well—Count Pallgrave may be immobilized for much of the day, and he is slightly bent forward—"

Josquin laughed. "You are evil, you know."

"Merely mischievous, and charming too. And disinclined to be disturbed by armed guards and irate princes in my sleep," Dewar said. The joking was over. "Kindly tell me what they were trying to do. Arrest me?"

"Uh."

Dewar shrugged, started away. "I'll find out from my father."

"Dewar—" Josquin pursued him as he strode away. "Your father— Damn it, wait for me!"

"If anything has happened to my father, I shall do things the Emperor will dream about for eternity in his nightmare-death," Dewar said, staring the Prince Heir down.

"It's Golias," Josquin said. "To do with that."

"Has your father somehow convinced himself that my father was responsible for Golias's attack on my sister?" Dewar asked in an unpleasant voice. The air crackled audibly.

"No. No. Calm down, Dewar! Prospero's all right; he threw a coffeepot at Viola this morning. She made a rather funny joke—about the murder and your sister. Wish he'd hit her, but it missed. Viola— He— I mean— They said your sister might— Damn! Do stop *looking* at me like that. I can't think." Dewar had backed Josquin to the wall, and Josquin felt like a bird before a snake.

Dewar's breath, clove-scented, stirred the Prince's hair. "Tell. Me. What. Has. Happened."

"You don't know about Golias?"

"I know more than I like knowing about him, enough to know that I do not intend to dine with him any time soon, although I don't mind taking his money at cards."

"He's dead."

"Dead. I am not surprised." Dewar moved a step away from Josquin, who remained leaning against the wall, not taking his eyes from the sorcerer.

"Did you kill him?"

"No. He owes me too much money for me to want to do that. Someone killed him, eh?"

"Quite thoroughly, sometime yesterday evening. He's a mess. What's left of him. He can't have died quickly. He was half-disembowelled."

Dewar thought of several witticisms on partial as opposed to complete disembowelment, but restrained all of them. It was early in the day yet.

"And castrated," Josquin said, watching him. "Before dying, evidently."

"How do you know?"

"Something about the—the wound. The surgeon said it, not I."

Dewar snorted. "Hem wouldn't recognize his own—"

Josquin shook his head quickly, once, and interrupted. "Gaston's man made the inquest; Herne insisted. He knows more than Hem about violent death. You mean you didn't know this."

"No. I didn't know, and although I am not surprised—he had many enemies—I am disappointed that I won't see the money he owed me. Thank you for the information, Your Highness. I am going to see my father, wherever he is."

"In his rooms or your sister's. He and Father went one round already this morning. Father wanted him to release Herne and Fulgens and Pallgrave."

"Prospero to release them from my spell? The Emperor has a short memory," Dewar observed drily.

Josquin reddened. "He thought Prospero might be immune

to the effects of, of whatever you did to them. I said I'd wait for you." He hurried past the awkwardness. "Father gets a little—excited."

"So does my sister, but she doesn't kill people. Not usually," he added, remembering Malperdy and Perendlac. "I'll release them when it pleases me," Dewar continued. "Tell the Emperor I said so. You could remind him—no, I will, perhaps."

"Remind him?"

"That were he not so cheap, I might not charge so dear," Dewar said. "I'll think about what I want in return for freeing them while I talk to Prospero." He smiled again, the lazy smile that Josquin had come to associate with Dewar being in control of everything.

Dewar knocked on his sister's door. There was no answer, but she never did answer and still had no maid, and so he pushed the broken handle down and nudged the door ajar.

"Freia, it's Dewar."

Was that a sound? He rolled his eyes—she was taking things too far, languishing and being theatrical about everything. Entering, he closed the door at his back. There was a fire, for a change; the rooms were warm. Good sign, that she'd gone after the servants and made them do something for her. He looked cautiously through the chamber door.

There stood the curtain-dimmed cubicle of a bed; a table beside it with a napkin-veiled pitcher and a covered tray; a cup, a glass. The fire was low, and there were clothes on the floor, a heap in the corner that was her torn dress, a dressing-gown, shoes and stockings—the usual disorder.

"Freia?" he asked, his voice hushed.

"Hm?" came very softly from the bed.

Dewar wondered if she ever left her bed before tea-time, and then as he passed he saw that the pitcher had sediment in the bottom. There was liquid left in it, but very little. He sniffed the glass and smelled bitter herbs, masked by cloying sweetness. So Prospero was still drugging her; it was strange that he wasn't here now. She would be groggy, if awake at all, and dazed and a poor conversationalist, but he ought to say hello.

"Hello, Freia," Dewar said, sitting on the edge of the bed where she was lost in an ocean of cutwork-edged Madanese linen, quilted velvet counterpane, and tasseled bolsters and cushions.

"Papa . . ." she breathed, her breath catching, her brows kinking.

"Dewar," he corrected her gently.

"Hm." Her hand moved vaguely, a seeking anemone in the pillow-sea; he clasped it. Her mouth flexed, dreaming of a smile, and her eyes never opened.

Heavily dosed, he diagnosed, and in no state for talking. He sat watching her face—the bruises around her mouth were like charcoal smudges, the tendrils of her hair swift-drawn free-hand curves on the bedding—until her hand was limp in his again and her sleep was deep.

Prospero had lashed out, Dewar thought. He had borne his defeat and its onerous conditions as gracefully as a true Prince ought; he had made shift to live by his wits and not his sorcery; and then he had been pushed too far. Had Freia finally told him about Golias's treatment of her? Probably. Attempted rape alone seemed insufficient, to Dewar, for a penalty of mutilation and death. But if Prospero had at last listened—in his already-enraged state—to Freia's tale of previous violation, he would surely snap, and rightly. If the Emperor wished to use Golias as a Prince, Golias must behave as a Prince, and he had never done so. Herne was as violent as Golias, but kept in check by honor and intelligence; so too were the other Princes, and Prospero was one of them. Golias was an unrestrained, bestial monster, and Prospero had killed him for his monstrosity.

For the first time, Dewar wondered, uncomfortably, whether he ought to have killed Golias as soon as he found leisure for it—as soon as he'd arrived in Landuc. But no—it would not have answered, to be swaggering around avenging Freia unasked, undeclared; he hadn't come here to kill anyone, but to see more of his father and to protect him if necessity required a sorcerer's protection. It was none of his duty to sort out Freia's difficulties for her: she was Prospero's creature, to manage as he saw fit; Prospero had said so explicitly when he'd asked Dewar not to take her from Landuc again. Indeed, from what Dewar had seen of Freia when he first met her, if she'd just shake off her present melancholy she'd be capable of killing Golias herself; she had soared into fights and held her own. No, to strike any such blow for her would have been presumption, as bad as removing her against Prospero's expressed wish.

Yet, Dewar thought, perhaps he could help her indirectly. He was not sure what Prospero thought of this marriage to Josquin: it was a logical alliance, certainly, if one didn't know she was a construct, but perhaps Prospero had had another match in mind.

Dewar released Freia's hand slowly and stood carefully, not moving the bed. He put wood on the fire as he left, and at the door he glanced back, but the dark box of a bed enclosed and concealed her.

Prospero shouted what Dewar hoped was an invitation to enter when the latter knocked, and so Dewar did, peering around the door before stepping in just in case Prospero was not really in humor for a caller.

But the Prince smiled and nodded amiably. "Dewar! 'Tis good to see thee. Hast broken fast?"

"No," Dewar said. The food-smells made him swallow—bread, ham, mushrooms.

Prospero lifted his cup, looked at a chair and at his son. "Why, come then, and join me; there's ample for both, as they think me a very prodigy of appetite, or perhaps two."

Dewar smiled, inordinately pleased at the enthusiastic welcome, and joined him with vigor; and they ate and talked of inconsequentialities until satisfaction slowed them.

"I went to Freia's rooms. I thought you might be there."

"Nay."

"So I see and saw. She's still sedated?"

"Aye, the wench is deranged beyond self-government, so that she'd not let me leave her all the while she woke, and I must give her sleep in a cup that could not get it any other way. 'Tis best for her now; 'twill heal her more than anything, and moreover it keepeth questioners from her." Frowning, Prospero broke and buttered bread as he spoke, each piece carefully set aside.

"I have some visitors," Dewar said.

Prospero did not look up, but his eyebrow flicked and his mouth curled his beard in a smile.

"What in Hell is going on?" Dewar asked when Prospero said nothing.

"Why, Hell indeed is where the goings-on are," Prospero said, "for they must find Golias a rare fellow in their revels. Hast heard of his passing from our merry company?"

"Josquin said he's dead, wholly and in parts. I don't know more than that." Dewar took out his pen-sized wand and began toying with it; Prospero watched from half-lidded eyes, nodded wordlessly. "Of course the Well would have killed him: but it seems that the Well preferred not to be soiled thus, and found him a fitting end."

"Aye," Prospero said, "murdered with savagery beyond belief; least one would wish it were, but there he is, truly in the flesh and now beyond it. And whereas 'twas I he betrayed i' the war just past, and I whose daughter he sought to force, therefore did Avril send Fulgens and Herne to arrest me for kin-slaughter at the 'tween-hour of the night, a siderate time well-suited to such grey undertakings; and they with their posturing and fulminating did so distress thy sister that I must sit with her the balance of the night swearing hollow oaths to her of safety."

The wand had lengthened to a walking-stick. "You do not think her safe."

"I am not sure of it. I am indeed not sure. She is a precious thing of herself, being of our house, she is even betrothed to thy dewy cousin Josquin; she hath done, can do, no harm to any; and yet I cannot be sure she is safe." Prospero spoke to the bread and butter mess on his plate.

Dewar stood and walked slowly around the table, drawing a line on the carpet with his silver-shod staff. "You don't think Jos would hurt her?"

"Hurt her, that one? Only through folly, not malice. She'd be happy with him as anyone, I dare say, an she put her mind to't, an he allowed it. 'Tis in her humor and his too to dwell tranquil at home if not abroad—"

"There," Dewar said, sitting again. A silver shimmer, visible from the corner of one's eye, now circled the table, and the crackle of the fire on the hearth was inaudible. It was a hasty job; Dewar preferred to take longer and forge such protective Bounds as to allow outside sounds to be heard within, but this met the nonce need.

Prospero nodded once. "Well done. There's a peep-hole by the chimney; in most of the rooms o' this wing at least one. 'Tis why guests are housed here, but a sorcerer hath what privacy he pleases. —For thy ears: she'll be well enough when she wakens and the drug's purged from her. Her immoderate humors have gone to crisis i' the night and found balance, and I've no fear for her soundness. As for the marriage, 'tis as great an evil as most of 'em. So you Ottaviano hath found." He snorted. "And as to Golias."

"They tried to arrest me, and they are still trying," Dewar said, smiling. "Herne and Fulgens, Pallgrave even, and some guards. A tableau vivante."

Prospero chuckled, leaning back and stretching. "Ah, good lad; I knew wouldst have some trap laid about thee, and thus I did not seek thee out, rather kept to my restless alibi."

"I won't release them without some concession from Avril, I've decided."

"Interesting notion. Hold 'em hostage i' the anteroom, dust them weekly; why, charge the public to view 'em. What wouldst thou?"

"I came to ask you that."

Prospero blinked and gazed thoughtfully at Dewar for a long time. "Hast nothing thou wouldst demand of the Emperor for thine own?" he said softly.

Dewar shrugged, embarrassed, knowing the value of the gift and the pride of the Prince. "Nothing sprang to mind at once. I thought you might make use of it better than I. He's not equipped to give really useful concessions as King Panurgus could."

" 'Twill be his death. Hm. Aye, a host springs ready-fitted to mind." Prospero opened a pomegranate, pensive.

"If I can release you from the oath—"

"Nay, thou know'st it cannot be so lightly untied. I thank thee for the thought." He ate seeds one by one. "Meseems," the Prince said slowly, "canst not ask too great a thing; he'll deny it outright. Must ask a small thing with great things to tumble after when it rolls."

"I understand."

"My preference, of all the fetters that lie on me, must be to throw off the choke-chain that leashes me to this cur's-house. Thou know'st the terms; I am under house-arrest, to fetch and carry, come and go, heel and sit, all at his behest, and ere long I'll snap, howl, and foam. Do thou get my freedom for theirs, untrammel me from that condition fully as they shall be freed by thee, and 'twill serve well."

Dewar nodded. "All right."

"He'll grudge it, say it cannot be done. It can an he will it; 'tis paper and spit, no sorcerer's vow, and can be altered by both in accord. I'd be gladly restored to myself and freed of fealty, but I'll settle for liberty of my body; 'twill answer admirably." His eyebrow twitched again as he contemplated the crimson pomegranate, smiling faintly. "Aye, 'twill answer," he murmured.

Luneté sat writing little notes of apology and farewell. She was probably permanently ruining her future in Court society, but she didn't care; she had to get out of Landuc. Laudine, behind her, packed with loud bangs and sniffs. The maid had been looking forward to spending the winter here, in the Imperial City, and had received the Countess's orders to prepare to leave with bad grace.

The door opened behind her.

"Otto, please knock," Luneté said without looking up. "I have asked you so many times." *To the Lady Quarfall, with all respect and duty . . .*

The door banged. "What do you mean telling everyone we're leaving?"

She continued writing. *"We* are not leaving. *You* can stay and you probably should. *I* must return to Lys at once." *Signed, Luneté, Countess of Lys.* Luneté sanded the note, then folded it cleverly and sealed it, then looked up at her husband.

Otto pulled the stool from the dressing-table over and sat down close beside her. Laudine conspicuously remained in the room, slamming the lid of a trunk. "Lu, what's got into you?"

"An unfortunate choice of words," Luneté said. "I'd prefer not to discuss it here, in Landuc. If you'll ride a little ways with us, I'll explain. I absolutely must return to Lys before the snows close the roads. I must, Otto."

"You must," he repeated. "We were going to go to Ascolet—"

"That was before, before my vows, before other things. Now I must go to Lys. You can stay here in Landuc, and probably you should, to try to come to some kind of . . . agreement . . . with your . . . father."

"Has that advisor of yours, Valgalant, put this in your head?" demanded Otto.

"No," said Luneté. "We will leave tomorrow before dawn. Would you please ride with me a little way then?"

Ottaviano stared at her. His calm, steady wife had become a frantic, driven madwoman. Had a certain person whispered some nasty piece of gossip to Luneté, enhancing Otto's role in the matters of Miranda and of Prospero's daughter? Was she shamed by yesterday's revelation of his father's identity?

"Luneté, why?" he asked.

Luneté took a deep breath. "Just come with me tomorrow, as far as Chargrove Inn, and I will tell you," she said. "But do not think you can persuade me to stay."

"All right," said Otto. "I'll ride partway with you and we can talk. I hope you know what you're doing, Countess."

"I do," said Luneté firmly. She picked up the pen and dipped it again. Her eyes narrowed and she began:

> From Countess Luneté of Lys to Lord Dewar, with all due gratitude and regard. I cannot depart Landuc without acknowledging the labors you have generously performed on matters nearly touching Lys and Ascolet . . .

Freia stared at the canopy of the bed. She knew its shadows and sags now, and her gaze went from one spot to another, from cobweb to frayed thread, with the attention a traveller gives to a map of his morrow's route; but her starting-place was always the same, and her route never varied, and she knew how her journey must end.

The fire had gone out hours ago. Coldness was coming back to the room, a thin trickling stream seeping down from the windows. Prospero had gone out also. She remembered him scolding her for being ungrateful and telling her he had more important things to attend than her vaporous fancies. Golias was dead, he had said, and therefore would not trouble her again, and he, Prospero, would not sit another night with her; she was old enough to bridle her nightmares, damn her, and his patience was blown. He rued the day he had sparked life in her. She had too great an idea of her importance. He was damned if she would hamstring him.

The herbs left a musky aftertaste and thickened her tongue and saliva. Freia had drunk the cupful obediently. Even as her head had begun to float and spin she had heard the door slam. She had dreamt that he had returned and sat with her, but it was only a wish-born dream; the heavy fog of the drug had dispelled gradually and she knew no one had been in the chamber since Prospero left.

Golias was dead. That wasn't a dream. Prospero had said it was so.

Prince Herne and Prince Fulgens had come and awakened her, shouting at Prospero; and that was a true thing, too. A strange man, white-haired and palely dressed, had come as she had been falling asleep again, and Prospero had stopped holding her, had put her in the bed, and had spoken a long time with the man, whose craggy, sad-eyed face had looked at her past Prospero's shoulder from time to time.

"Miranda!" Prospero had cried roughly, and "The craven whoreson butcher! I'd have flayed the rutting varlet, spilled his bowels and watched him try to gut it out, choked him with his rot-blunted sword— O 'tis fair Justice, Justice, Gonzalo, but I'd fain mine own daughter had died for thine, O Miranda." He had wept, and the white-haired man had talked, and Freia had been unable to get up and go to her father; her arms and legs were leaden, paralyzed by the drug.

Staring at the top of the bed, she wondered about Miranda. Prospero had spoken of her often through the years when they two had lived on the isle alone, saying that in her Freia would meet the best of her sex, the finest and fairest of all humanity, and Freia must study to be as much like her as possible, for there was no better model. Yet her elusive model had ever surpassed Freia, in his judgement.

Once he had explained to her that though sorcerers had no families, they kept pets sometimes, and that her father loved his daughter, and that the sorcerer was fond of his Puss. Freia had been contented by that. Now, in the detached contemplative mood that had followed her drug-muffled fits of despair and terror, two things occurred to her.

The first was that she had become a burdensome pet to Prospero the sorcerer, and so he shunned her and would be rid of her.

The second was that Prospero, here, did not exist as she had thought him to be. He was a Prince. She had thought he would no longer be a sorcerer when he renounced sorcery, but he was more a sorcerer than ever, busy with unexplained concerns, impatient with her and putting her aside, though he'd insisted she come here to hateful Landuc, and now that she was here there was nothing for her to do and no one wanted her about. It had been indicated to her in arch, oblique terms that her origins were unacceptably vague; Princess Evote had inquired minutely about Freia's mother and Freia had truthfully replied that she had never known her mother. What? No family, no kin? None. Where was she born, where were they wed, then? She had stared at Princess Evote, feeling trapped and not knowing what more to say, and a sinister whisper of bastardy had run round the Palace. She was no true member of the family.

Freia's chest ached. She wanted to go home. Prospero did not want her there. He had shaped her mind and her deeds with his lessons in everything he thought a princess should know: more than most princes would agree was necessary, and no fripperies like embroidery or dancing, but in the end she had failed him. She wasn't as fine as Miranda. She would be mated to cold and doll-like Prince Josquin and stay prisoned here, and Prospero would go to his home that was not hers. There was no wilderness into which she could escape here but the maze of her memory-tangled sleep.

Freia turned on her side, shutting her eyes and pulling the coverlet high over her head, hiding from the claustrophobic bed-hangings and the cold beyond.

ᴄ— *12* —ᴐ

THE COUNTESS OF LYS'S COACH, THOUGH of heirloom vintage, was neither heated nor plushly upholstered. Its exterior had been freshly painted for this momentous journey, in Lys, and the brave paint was spattered with the mud of the roads from Lys to Landuc. However, the coach was solid enough to stand any distance of rutted road, and Luneté had had Laudine procure extra cushions and lap-robes to make the interior more comfortable. Now Laudine, thoroughly annoyed, rode on the coach-box, and the Baron of Ascolet, thoroughly bewildered, rode inside, his horse following with Luneté's page on his back. Luneté smiled at Otto from time to time, distractedly, and was rigid as a fencepost until they rolled through the Fire Gate and left the City Bounds behind. The wheels bounced and jarred them over the frozen road.

"Better than being stuck in the mud, I guess," Otto said, to break the silence.

"Yes," Luneté said. "I'm going to have a child."

The coach hit three cavernous holes in a row.

Otto's ears rang from the concussion or the news. "You? You are?" he asked. "How? I mean—Luneté, you're sure?"

"As you may know," said Luneté primly, "there are certain unmistakable signs." She sat as straight as she could, despite the bouncing, and she looked not at Otto but at a faded painted fish on the opposite wall.

Ottaviano turned a remarkable shade of crimson. Her tone reminded him that he was not reacting as a prospective father ought. "I see," he said, and bounced with the coach to land beside her on the seat. "You want to have the baby in Lys," he said.

"Yes."

"Why not Ascolet?" Otto suggested. "We take the Eälschar Road and—"

"Lys," said Luneté firmly.

"But he'll be my heir."

"And mine."

They regarded one another, neither having any stomach for a jouncing, rattling argument.

"Very well—"

"Lys then," said Ottaviano, beating her to it. "And at this time of year it's safer anyway. Lys."

"You don't mind?" Luneté said, a quaver in her voice.

"I— Just a moment." Otto rolled down the shutter over the window and bellowed out at the coachman. "Iwen! Iwen! Stop the horses for a few minutes." The coach rattled to a halt, and

Otto sat back. "I don't mind," he said to Luneté, and he kissed her.

"I do mind," Luneté told him when they had moved a little apart. "This is bad timing. I shouldn't be tied down now—you need me at Court, and Lys needs me everywhere, and I said I would go to Ascolet—it's so inconvenient—"

"There's plenty of time later for Court and riding around Lys and Ascolet," Otto said, soothing her. It was all understandable now, her strange moods and fainting and bad digestion. "I'll return to Court now, follow you to Lys in a few months, and we'll stay there until the baby comes." He patted her stomach, feeling a nervous pride of possession. "Um, maybe, maybe we should get a better coach."

"I'll be all right," she said. "I came in this one."

"You mean you were already—"

Luneté nodded.

"Oh!" They had spent so little time together—but it wasn't the time, rather the timing that mattered, and he *had* made the most of their few hours during the wars. Otto bit his lip, and a further thought came to him. "Well. If you think it's all right, well, then. You go on to Lys, and I'll stay here awhile, see what I can do for us. Luneté, did you tell anyone?"

"No. No one. I don't want anyone to know until afterward."

"Right." Otto nodded. "Smart girl. The Emperor doesn't need the news. Not right now." He smiled. An heir for Lys and Ascolet. No, the Emperor didn't need the news, but it was very pleasant to contemplate his discomfiture on hearing it.

Dewar caught Josquin's elbow. "Look," he said quietly, and drew him along a side path into the fragrant yews. "We must talk."

Josquin smiled slightly, but did not move away from him. "I agree. I have wanted to talk to you for ever so long."

They stopped and regarded one another, turquoise-blue eyes and mist-blue-grey, both breathing a little fast, both very conscious of Dewar's hand still on Josquin's arm.

"I meant to tell you," Josquin said, his smile warming and widening, eyes still locked on Dewar's, "I'd be honored to make you a gift of a, hum, a book I've a notion you'd like, and an old piece of artwork, cartography . . ."

Dewar grinned, tried to squelch the grin, and shook with unvoiced mirth, throwing his head back nonetheless. "Thank you."

"You're welcome." They managed to look at one another again, and Josquin laughed now too, noiselessly. He touched Dewar's elbow. "Come, let's further in here. Evote was out for a stroll with that bitch-in-heat Baroness of yours."

"By all means, let's." They glanced at the opening in the yew and, as one, walked away from it, into the shrubbery, around a corner, slowly. "That wasn't what I wanted to talk about," Dewar said, his smile disappearing.

"Let us continue with it soon, then," Josquin suggested.

"Yes." Dewar glanced at him, inhaled, swallowed, looked away. "About my sister, Prince."

Josquin sighed and sobered. "The title is ill-used. What about your sister? Or should we say, the impending contracted nuptials?"

"How do you feel about that?"

"How should I feel? Eccch."

"Oh. Mm."

"Sorry. I'm delighted! Tons of joy! Charming girl. So bubbly."

"Jos, be serious. Come now. Eccch?"

"E-c-c-c-ch. I think that's how it would be spelled. Dewar, I really— I knew I must marry someday—" Josquin's lip curled, and he shook his head.

"Entirely averse, eh."

"Yes. Besides, according to what I understand of the treaties, effectively she's a pauper; the Emperor's already taken the best of Prospero's estate for himself, and the girl is just an additional item to confiscate. No kind of advance at all. That's the reason for it; he wants to put the screws to Prospero and tighten them."

"Yes, I know. It hasn't escaped his notice either, but he's bound by his word. But Freia, Josquin—"

"She hasn't had to lift a finger. Lucky girl. If she did, I'm not quite certain she'd know what to do with it."

"What do you mean?"

"She does not, pardon me for frankness, but you are a frank man yourself, convey an impression of agile wit and nimble thought. Of great knowledge or great anything. She's a rather ordinary thing. In these circumstances," Josquin gestured with his stick, hitting the hedges, "ordinary is a cipher."

Dewar nodded. "She isn't very broad, that's true. One must make allowances."

"Even with a generous allowance, Dewar, dear fellow, there's not much left after the allowance."

"Jos, have you ever talked to her?"

"Daily. I say, 'Good morning, m'lady cousin,' or something of the sort, and she looks at me, gulps, nods, and looks down again. At dinner, when she deigns to dine with us, I say, 'Allow me,' or 'May I please have the salt'—"

"I get the idea. No." Dewar thought of Otto and Luneté, of the blushing, flirting, and panting that had preceded their wedding.

"Dewar, she has nothing to say."

Dewar stopped at a junction of two paths where a bird's nest had fallen from a tree above to the gravel, tossed down by the winds of some storm and missed by the gardeners. He picked it up and looked at it: twigs intertwined by blind instinct, mud daubed neatly around, a few downy tufts of feather still clinging inside the bowl. It weighed nearly nothing.

"You think I should talk to the lady before the vows?"

"I don't know. Yes, I do. There is something about all this that disturbs me. I suppose it is just that coldness that comes with all arranged marriages, Jos, yet she knows you no more than you know her. She's in a foreign place, she doesn't always understand the language well—"

"She ought to pass the blessed Fire."

"—and that's another thing, but I think she fears it. Prospero hasn't pushed her to it, you know, and doubtless Avril wouldn't allow it—not until after the wedding, lest she run away. But, Jos, it would mean a lot to her, and it would make a very very good impression on my father I believe, if you—if you swallowed your distaste and buttered her up a little."

"My dear fellow, supposing she did uncloister herself, I daresay there'd be little opportunity for it. She won't talk at table. Fulgens saw to that."

"Fulgens?"

"Yes, when she was still dining in company he completely flummoxed her—you know how he does, it's all steam, nothing of substance in it."

"I see. She's not used to bluster, Josquin, or even to jesting. Prospero has kept her—secluded."

"And the poor little tortoise tucked in her head and is waiting for the lightning to hit."

"Do be serious."

"I am. All right. I will talk to her. I will pretend she is somebody I want to know and call on her and talk to her. For your sake, not hers."

"Thank you, Jos. It is good of you to try. I know the whole prospect of this is—most repugnant."

The Prince scowled and thwacked a few more yew branches with his stick. "It's novel that someone sees my side of it. I'm not looking forward to it at all. The very thought of—disgusting. This is generally counted a pose or a character flaw. What a pity my foundling brother did not wait to wed; he'd suit the task far better than I, if one may judge by his performance in Chenay."

Dewar nodded, touched his cousin's shoulder and then squeezed it and let his hand fall. "I know. It's a shame you're getting shoved into this—it's worse for you, although the traditional thing is to pity the girl. I think she'd be quite happy with you. It just requires a little—conciliation on your part for her sake."

"For our sake not hers, I have a suggestion."

"Go on?"

"Weren't we supposed to try fencing?"

Dewar looked from his bird's nest to his cousin, who was watching him with a nakedly hopeful, anxious expression, and Josquin colored slightly.

"Yes," Dewar said. "Let's do that now."

"Now?"

"Now. I'll tell Freia you'll call on her tomorrow. In the morning."

"If only she were chatty, like Viola. I delight in talking to Viola. She always has a nice rancid bit of gossip about someone or other, fresh from their servants."

Dewar laughed and set the bird's nest in the hedge. He tucked his arm through Josquin's, and they set off through the shrubbery toward the armory.

Josquin was at his breakfast, reading a letter which he folded up and put away in his pocket, when Dewar came in. "Hello, cousin."

Dewar paused in the doorway, surveyed the breakfast-table and the Prince Heir in his dressing-gown still. "H'lo. I think we had better practice our fencing *before* breakfast, sir." He crossed the room, seated himself uninvited.

"I am inclined to agree, sir, but breakfast is served so damnably early in the day—"

"Early?" repeated Dewar, pausing in mid-reach for a pot of coffee. The clock's hands stood at half the fourth hour.

"Early," repeated Josquin haughtily.

They regarded one another. Dewar lifted an eyebrow. "Fine. When, then?"

"You mean regularly. I suppose I could manage before breakfast if you asked nicely."

"I'm asking."

"Nicely."

"If you'd rather work up a sweat on a full stomach, all weighed down—"

"That is not nicely."

Dewar shrugged and flicked him a quick, brilliant glance.

"I capitulate," Josquin said, flushing hotly for a split second. "Before breakfast. Every day, if you like."

"Sorcerers do not ask nicely," Dewar said. He grinned briefly over the cup and then drank. Josquin, he thought, was asking for it, daring him, and if his sister weren't betrothed to the Prince Dewar would be on him now. O ye Powers of Road and Stone, don't leave him with this man alone. . . . What was it Oren used to say, about how people who fall in love reinvent it? Five or six things he'd reinvent—later. Later. Later. Dewar looked up from his cup, having disciplined his expression and body, and said, "I spoke with her last night, and she said she would be in all morning. I don't believe she actually goes out."

"Not on such a day as this, I hope. It will snow later and it's damned cold. Prospero's curse, they're calling the weather, have you heard it? I must induce the Emperor to send me to Madana. Perhaps on my wedding-journey." Josquin made a face and buttered a roll. "Try that green jam, it's some new thing Evote brought in," he added diffidently.

Dewar obligingly smeared some on a piece of bread and ate it; they breakfasted in a taut, charged silence no small talk could penetrate.

"Let us go a-visiting," Josquin said finally, as the clock struck the fourth hour.

Dewar nodded and stood; he followed Josquin out of the room and then walked beside him as they went through the Palace corridors to Freia's apartments. Dewar tapped at the door and opened it, and they went in.

"Must have stepped out after all," Dewar said, glancing around. The rooms were cold, as always; long-dead ashes and cinders lay in the fireplace.

Josquin nodded and paced, arms folded. He stopped before a small niche in the wall which contained a chipped bust of glowering Panurgus. "Damn it, Dewar. The more I think about it the less I like it."

"Tell your father."

"Hah. I have done so. I am informed that I do not have a choice. I really feel as if I'm getting a rotten bargain in this. She's utterly plain, common as dirt and stupid as wood; she can't carry on a conversation and she's socially inept; she's clumsy and awkward; and the truth is she's not very bright. Utterly unsuited to me or my position or even to her own as your father's daughter. Look at her clothes! Mother had her own seamstress and maids make them and she still doesn't dress properly. She can't carry herself; she slouches and shrinks. Imagine her in Madana! I shall be a laughing-stock. I certainly did tell my father, and he agrees with every point; she's a fool and a nuisance to boot, he said, and I'm marrying her. I believe he is getting me back for not liking women. He's hit on the most offensive creature he could find. I'd sooner have wed Miranda of Valgalant; she was an idiot in her politics, but she knew how to dress, walk, and talk." Josquin was pacing, his words fast and angry, back and forth before a small dark console table on which an arrangement of fading flowers dropped pale petals.

Dewar, taken aback by the passion with which Josquin rejected his sister, listened. "There is truth in everything you say," he admitted. "It is all quite true. She has no beauty, no fire, and her manners are coarse. Had I never known a woman in my life, I could have wished up a better sister than she, with all her earthy failings. But there she is. We all, and you especially, must make the best of her. She's molded ill, but she could be shaped by an apt hand; she's clay, not diamond, unformed, unhardened yet, There's advantage in that too."

Josquin glared at him from the other end of the table. "I'd rather turn hand to making the best of you. I cannot believe you're related; it's some monstrous jest of your father's. There are rumors, you know. Perhaps I'll alter the contracts, by your leave: I'll take her if I can have you too."

Dewar laughed, to cover the flush of desire quick-kindled,

and after a moment Josquin laughed also, throwing up his hands. He turned and plucked at the wilted flowers, showering more petals on the table, and Dewar joined him, but on the other side, across the wan lilies and withered hot-house roses.

"Josquin, may I ask a personal question?"

"Of course. The whole business is a personal outrage. No reason not to."

"No offense is meant but: have you ever—"

"No. I don't like women." Josquin glared at him again, his eyes icy. "My august and dignified father," he added coldly, "has recommended that I forgo my usual pursuits and hunt me out some pleasant brothel, for tutelage ere I'm to perform in contract." He snorted, shook his head, and laughed bitterly. "At least in a brothel I can find what pleases me; and their manners are less peasantish. Am I a Prince, and I must wed with dirt-common trash?"

Dewar laughed too, amused by Josquin's puffed-up pride. "Tasteless bastard. Indeed, Freia *is* wooden-headed and common as dirt, mortal clay to the core and sticks for bones, but console yourself—though her blood is mixed, she's compounded of rare earths, already broken to your ease, and, if you put your back to it, fruitfully ploughed and sown."

Josquin halted, staring at him, a rose crumbling in his fingers. "Indeed? A commoner bastard and no virgin? Then I need not wed her—"

Dewar waved a hand dismissingly with an uncomfortable feeling he had said too much: far too much, and a wiser and cooler head than Josquin's would have heard too much. "She's Prospero's blood. Prospero was a sorcerer, and is still a Prince; if he says she's his daughter, then that's what she is. She bears Prospero's blood as well as—the other."

The Prince frowned. "Damn. It might be grounds to dissolve the agreement: although a peasant mother is easier to dismiss from ancestry than a Prince."

"Think no more of it; it is a quirk of—construction, and

truly it is too late to cancel the wedding. Only cultivate her, and she'll study to please you."

"Why, then, I'll please to plough and sow both sides of her genealogy, noble and common, for noble issue and commoner pleasure." He snorted disdainfully. "Why the fuss over Golias then? Prospero swore she was untouched; am I to settle for gleanings? 'Twas no more than clod-breaking, and if she's already well-harrowed—"

Dewar nervously picked petals from a lily, hastening its end. "Don't be too crude, Jos. It was worse."

"Sorry. I suppose. The only benefit I see in the whole sordid business is that I'll have an excuse to see you." Josquin's voice lowered, and he fixed Dewar with a hot look. "Never mind this fencing. We should dine or sup sometime. Tonight. And this time you're not leaving so quickly afterward."

Oh, well, thought Dewar, and he began to smile, pleased with Josquin's interest and relieved to have gotten Josquin away from the subject of Freia. Why not? It wouldn't hurt anyone. It would clear the air. It would be good for both of them—possibly even better than good. "We should. Tonight, then. Yes."

At the other end of the room, behind a sofa by the empty hearth, there came a rustle of moving fabric. Both men whirled to see Freia rising from the high-backed sofa, swaying a little.

Her eyes rested a moment on Josquin, and then she gazed at Dewar, her lips parted, her brows drawn together and her eyes pinched in an expression of pure pain and incomprehension and shock.

She was there? thought Dewar, the blood draining from his cheeks. He could not look away from the betrayal, the broken trust and shattered feelings in his sister's face, could not lower his eyes, felt his own face falling into astonished embarrassment and then guilty, self-conscious unease.

Josquin, beside him, was silent and motionless.

A full minute passed among them, all agony, no respite.

Freia's mouth moved, and in a tiny, whispery voice, she said,

"You—woke me, excuse me," and she bolted to the door and ran out, her hands rising and half-covering her face as she went.

"Freia!" Dewar cried, and he took half a step after her, but could not make his feet go on.

The door banged shut.

He closed his eyes and tried to breathe.

"Eavesdropping," Josquin said hoarsely.

Dewar looked at him, shook his head. "No. No. I— She must have been asleep. She said." His ears roared. He felt as if he stood beside, outside himself; he feared he would vomit. "Excuse me," he said, and walked numbly to the door and went out.

Where would she have gone?

To Prospero? Could he get there in time to explain— Explain? What was there to explain?

He had said crude and unkind things about Freia to Josquin. He had gone along with Josquin's catty, vindictive, resentful assassination of his sister; he had said nothing in her defense; he had betrayed her for a cheap joke. He had spilled to Josquin the essence of a tale that Prospero had never intended to be heard by anyone—perhaps not even by Freia.

Dewar stopped, shaking his head, holding it; he found he was outside his own rooms, his hand on the door. He halted and turned, spurred by a sudden terror of the enormity of what he had done.

If Josquin were to tell another what Dewar had said about Freia, more and more would hear of it quickly until the whole of the Empire knew: a commoner, dirt-common, not even a virgin. And Prospero would be wroth, justly, and Dewar was no longer enough of a sorcerer not to care.

He hurried back through the halls; Josquin had left Freia's rooms, a footman had seen him going toward the conservatories. Princess Evote was often to be found there. Dewar's legs loped at an ungentlemanly gait and bore him down, around, along, to the tinkling fountain in the forecourt of the glass-walled paradise. He inquired of the footman outside; yes, the Prince Heir had gone in.

The air was thick and humid, scented green and earthy. Gravel rattled as Dewar walked along the paths, listening for voices. He wondered of a sudden if Freia had ever been here, if she knew about the marvellous year-round summer in the Palace. She would like it, he thought. He ducked under a broad green leaf as big as a card-table and saw Josquin.

The Prince Heir was just sitting down beside a four-tiered fountain of shells and fat-finned fish. Neither man spoke as Dewar sat next to him, facing him.

Josquin's face was set in the polite-nothing expression he usually wore around the Palace. Dewar studied him for a moment and then Summoned the Well, growing instantly hotter in the steamy air.

"Josquin," he said, putting the Well in the words, "I do lay upon thee geas, that thou shalt say nothing to anyone of what hath passed between us today, no word of our conversation, nor of its end."

As Dewar began to speak, Josquin turned to look at him, and the geas fell on him unhindered and potent. Josquin shook his head and blinked, then glared at Dewar from a princely face.

"I will not marry her," he said in a voice that rang hard like Avril's.

"No," Dewar said, seeing in an instant what he must do, "you shall not."

They regarded one another for a single tense moment more, and even in that moment Dewar felt himself wanting the other, the heat moving in his body and pushing him toward Josquin, who was leaning away with the beginnings of fear in his look now. Dewar stood and left the conservatory as hastily as he had entered, a gust of wet warm air flowing into the cooler dry hall with him.

He would go to Freia and offer to return her to Argylle. That was the thing to do. He would make her happy by taking her home again; she would not have to marry Josquin if she didn't return to Landuc; he would make up for what he had said; and he would annoy Prospero, but only a little, Dewar thought, because he couldn't imagine that Prospero really wished Freia to be bound to a man who loathed her. Prospero's oath required that he say and do things that he could not support in his heart. Surely this marriage was one of them.

Freia's rooms were just as he had left them—empty. He waited a few minutes, trying to suppress his foreboding, but when she did not appear, he had to admit to himself that she was not going to be back immediately. Slowly, Dewar returned to his apartment and sat down heavily in a windowseat with his back to a cold pane of glass, and his apprehension blossomed to occupy all his thought.

She had certainly run to Prospero; she had nowhere else to go. Prospero would be very angry if she had heard—everything, or even a fragment of it. He would be here shortly. Dewar breathed in and out, slowly, feeling ill, a cold dreadweight of iron in the pit of his gut. In his mind, his own voice and Josquin's echoed, drawling, bantering, the undercurrent of sex purling and rippling in every word. And then he saw Freia's expression again, and remembered Freia sitting with her head on her knees crying quietly when she was ill and in pain, and remembered that he had promised to help her once, and he saw that he had behaved like a cad for the sake of nothing.

For she wasn't unattractive or stupid or graceless; he knew that, for he had seen her in better days, before she had been taken prisoner and battered in body and soul. She was frightened and lonely and homesick, here against her will; he knew that, for she had told him. He hadn't helped. He'd been busy exercising his charm in a mating dance with Josquin. She'd been attacked by her ravager Golias in Landuc Palace itself, and nobody had quite believed, none of her urbane and witty aunts and uncles, that she hadn't brought it on herself. Bawdy jests from earthy Herne, double entendres from gossipy Viola. Prospero's hurricane anger and Golias gutted, silencing the jesters.

It didn't matter, he thought, what she looked like or how she was made or whether she were really human—and she was, oh, she was. She had trusted him with herself, and he had spit on her. That was what it came down to. Her trust and his sneering superiority.

Nothing happened.

Dewar drew his knees up and sat on the windowseat for several hours, and nothing happened. He loathed himself, his egotism and crudeness, his cruelty and his selfishness, and he wished desperately that Prospero would come and break the storm.

No storm broke; no hand slammed back the door preceding a voice of denunciation and excoriation; no knock or Summoning came. He sat in dread and shame waiting for damnation, and damnation had other work, elsewhere. Prickling foreboding made him sweat and tense, and nothing followed from it.

Dewar did not realize he had passed the whole day thus until the door did open. He jumped, paling, and saw a valet bringing clothing he had sent to be cleaned. Serenely aloof, the man took it to the dressing-room and disappeared; he returned, departed, without a word.

Shaken by this indication that the world was continuing on after such a blow to its stability, Dewar stood up stiffly. He washed and dressed to dine, thinking, as he did, that Prospero had decided to wait. Probably Freia's misery was such that he was looking after her, comforting her and perhaps informing the Emperor that the marriage was off.

The dinner hour was struck. Dewar walked slowly there, not hungry. His father did not join the party at table; the Empress said something to Princess Viola, who asked, about him being engaged.

Dewar sat across from Josquin, usually a delightful situation. He did not dare look at his cousin save once, and his cousin at that moment was looking fixedly at his plate.

"What a gloomy aspect," the Emperor said. "If you cannot do better, we would prefer that you dine in your rooms."

"It's the weather," Josquin said. "Sir."

The Emperor snorted and addressed Prince Gaston, who was evidently leaving later in the evening.

Nothing happened. Dewar ate mechanically and watched the others covertly. The Emperor was in an iffy temper. Freia did not appear; by the third course, her place was removed as it ever was, and neither the Emperor nor the Empress said anything.

Did everyone know something he didn't? Dewar wondered, and began paying more attention. Her name wasn't mentioned; they were all talking about a new ship now, a cutter Prince Fulgens meant to take south.

The meal ended, and Dewar rose to go without a word to Josquin. He was halted by Prospero, who laid a hand on his shoulder lightly as Dewar passed through the door.

"A word."

Dewar nodded and let his father steer him aside, into a small anteroom.

"Where's Freia?"

"I don't know," Dewar said, a pang of guilt curdling his meal.

Prospero looked at him, and Dewar couldn't look away. "Don't know? Hast seen her today?"

"I saw her. She—she wasn't well, this morning. Upset. About the marriage plans."

Prospero looked at him still. "Her apartment's empty," he said finally, quietly. "I've sought her all afternoon. A brace of guards and a maid said they'd seen her leave the Palace in the forenoon, and thus I essayed a Summoning for her. 'Tis null."

"Null?" repeated Dewar, wondering what Prospero knew about that morning's meeting. Was the Prince playing with him?

"I'd have thee make the same attempt," Prospero commanded him.

Dewar, perplexed, nodded consent, and they left the anteroom. The Emperor, waiting with Prince Gaston, glanced a sharp question at them.

"He knoweth naught of her," Prospero said.

"People don't just drop off the face of the earth," the Emperor said.

"Nay," Prospero agreed, " 'tis unwonted. We'll try again."

"We'll wait for your word," the Emperor said. "Damned nuisance, that girl." He stalked away. Prince Gaston nodded to them both and left with him.

"What's up?" Dewar asked, nervous.

"Surely thou'rt not untutored in what a null Summoning may be."

"Of course," said Dewar. "Concealment."

"May be."

"She doesn't know how to conceal herself; she hasn't even passed the Fire."

"Exactly. Let us make haste." Prospero went faster.

Dewar, pacing him easily, said "Not—" and didn't finish the thought, finding it too terrible to speak.

" 'Tis possible she's not concealed, but dead," Prospero said dispassionately, "but the power of seeking farther has been stripped from me. Thus I'd have thee try thy hand. 'Tis not beyond possible that I have erred." He ground his teeth. "Erred," he repeated in an undertone.

"I—Father—" Glancing at Prospero, Dewar swam again with the oppressive giddiness he had felt on facing Freia after his scurrilous conversation with Josquin. He could not remember what he had meant to say, and so he left the words hanging. They arrived at Dewar's door and he led the way in. Prospero picked up a candelabrum and waited as his son opened the closet where he had stored his tools.

Prospero helped Dewar set up the apparatus, efficient and reticent. "Use this for the token," the Prince said, and he put a wooden comb in Dewar's hand, then stood back and watched Dewar, who had to pause a moment before beginning the spell to bring himself fully under control.

The forces lay ready to hand, easily commanded, easily spun and sent whirling out from Dewar through his glass. The comb hung in the spell and colored it with something that was essentially Freia, bringing him the sound of her voice and the feel of her skin, the scent of her body and the color of her hair, and the single taste he had had of her mouth.

The Mirror of Vision remained blank. The spell wound outward, inward; it found nothing to seize on and complete itself.

Null. Dewar waited as long as he could maintain the suspended energies, and then closed the spell, aborting its search. He leaned on the table, looking at the Mirror.

"Good work," Prospero said, beside him.

Dewar shook his head, catching his breath. He took his handkerchief out and wiped his face. "I'll try Seeking her location."

"Location? A failed Summoning—"

"It shows the last detectable location of the subject," Dewar said, his mouth twitching, trying not to smile proudly. It was one of his own innovations. "As long as too much time has not passed."

Prospero's eyes flashed with interest and optimism. "Indeed. By all means then, carry on, sir."

Dewar nodded, straightened again, and relit the fire.

The Seeking worked at once, as the Summoning should have. The spell jumbled images in the Mirror, an irrational, undecipherable kaleidoscope that spun and halted. The glass showed darkness, moving.

"Where in the world," muttered Prospero.

Something white plunged into the scene; they both jumped. It was a bird, folding its wings and floating on the water.

"Ocean," Prospero whispered. " 'Tis a calmewe."

The water moved in the darkness of the early winter night. Other things moved in the scene, flying flakes of snow.

"Ah, black damnation," Prospero whispered, and turned away, biting his knuckles. "Enough."

Dewar closed the spell. Again he mopped his face.

" 'Tis well-worked, well-made," Prospero said softly, his back to Dewar. "Oriana herself could do no more."

His son looked at the Mirror, empty now.

"This Seeking told us little useful," Prospero said to his raw knuckles. "Canst discover more of the location?"

"Yes. It's just a question of control."

Dewar repeated his spell, his emotions locked away where they could not disrupt the sorcery, not considering the implications of what he saw.

"There," he said through his teeth as the images whirled. Prospero turned and stood behind him, looking over his shoulder.

A boat, a small dinghy, drifted on the waters, its oars laid neatly lengthwise inside, no one in it or nearby. The scene blurred into movement and became snowy water again.

"Lost it, sorry," Dewar said.

"Enough; 'twill serve," said Prospero emotionlessly.

Dewar closed the spell and leaned on the table again, taking a deep breath. "What does it mean?" he asked the Mirror and the firepan.

"Its meaning is: I erred," said Prospero, arms folded, turning away and walking to the door.

"What means you erred?" Dewar shook himself and chased his father, catching his arm. "Where is she? That meant nothing to me."

"She went to the sea, via the boat," Prospero said.

They stared at one another.

"Dead, I fear," Prospero said gently, putting his hands on Dewar's shoulders.

The color drained from Dewar's face. He had done this, he thought. He had belittled her until there was nothing left, and she had become nothing.

Prospero dropped his hands, turned away, started out. "Wait for me," he said, pausing, looking back at Dewar. "Wait."

Dewar blinked, still shocked.

Prospero left.

The sound of the door closing seemed to reach Dewar as from the top of a cliff. He felt his knees buckle; he let them fold and knelt on the floor.

He had done it, he thought. He'd killed her.

Freia's face, shocked and naked, would not fade from his mind's eye. He put his hands over his ears and shook his head hard; he bent forward until his eyes pressed into his knees.

I trust you, she had said not long ago.

Thank you, he had replied, a careless courtesy. The feeling of her body, clasped against him, strong and warm, flooded his nerves again, so that despite his position it overwhelmed him with its remembered brief contact. Alive. She had been alive, and now she was not, would never be, and the blood-guilt was on him. She had put herself in his hands. He had torn her to pieces. In the first hour he had known her, he had cursed her, and all the evil that had fallen on her after was his doing.

Dewar moaned, a low, frightened sound.

The oppression of her death suffocated him. There was no outlet for it here, in this room; it constricted his thoughts until he thought he would collapse inward and vanish, vanish as she had vanished. He moaned again. Freia stared at him across the room, as helpless before his cruelty as a straw against a lightning bolt. Dewar whispered, "I'm sorry. Please. I'm sorry," to the blanket of horror enclosing him. He thought of cold wind and cold water, of the tug and pull of the waves and the sour salt in her throat, of her eyes closing, of her body yielding to the hostile element and subsumed by it. "Freia, Freia, no," Dewar wailed to his belly, and shuddered. He had killed her; he had ground her under his heel in dung, and his burning urge to bed Josquin had made him a cur. She had only been kind to him, only offered him friendship, only had herself but had been generous with all she had.

It was unfair, unfair. If he could unsay it— If he could catch her, just long enough to apologize, when she ran away, repelled by the shabbiness of Princes and the perfidy of brothers—

Her death was his doing, as surely as if he had slashed her throat on the fireless hearth in her rooms. As surely as if he had held her under the near-frozen waves.

He jerked upright. The workroom seemed airless. He could

barely breathe here; he had to get out. Dewar staggered to the door of his workroom and closed it behind him; he said a word as he did, melding door to wall. He leaned against it, eyes shut, for a moment. The room was dark save for the light of the pale snow falling outside the windows.

It was still too close. Dewar felt hemmed in, surrounded. He had to get out. He lurched unevenly to the cloak-rack and took one. He crossed the room and threw open a tall window, stepped out onto the balcony, and dropped over the edge to the ground.

— *13* —

DEWAR WALKED AIMLESSLY AWAY FROM THE Palace. Somehow he got into the Gardens—later he was never sure where he had been that evening—and from the Gardens to Herne's Riding, into which they faded in growing wilderness. In the Riding he happened on a road and followed it indifferently. It could not matter where he went now, he thought. When he returned to the Palace he would confess his guilt in the matter to Prospero, and Prospero would take out her blood in his own. Prospero had killed Golias, and Golias had not murdered Freia, only made her life a torment.

The snow blew around so that he could hardly see the road. It mattered little; Dewar was not attending his steps, and so he bobbed from the edge of the road to the middle and back to the curb again, muttering apologies to Freia, whose accusing, mute face hung before him still.

"I'm sorry," he said, tears freezing on his cheeks. "I'm sorry, Freia. Please listen. I'm sorry. I was wrong. I was an ass. I'm sorry. I lied. I'm sorry."

Dewar stumbled against something as tall as he was and caught at it: a tall black stone. In the snowlight, the strange illumination that came with the chill pure whiteness of the snow, he saw the stone and it echoed, remotely, against another stone in memory. He laid his hand against a curving carving in its face.

"I'm sorry," he said again, bowing his head. "Freia. Oh, Freia. Hear me. I'm sorry." A memory of Freia, smiling shyly at him when he had been doing his utmost to win her over, to coax such a smile, came to him, and with it a wave of grief and regret crashed down. He had won her, indeed, and then what? Dewar leaned on the cold stone; he knelt before it, hugging his cloak around him and sobbing. "Come back, come back, Freia. Don't be dead. I'm sorry, Freia. It wasn't meant so. I didn't think. I'm sorry."

The snow whirled around widdershins, an opaque white curtain, and hung on the wind without falling. It thickened and circled Dewar and the stone. He closed his eyes and bent his forehead against it, feeling the throb of the Oldest power that still persisted weakly here. Far away, the heart of its realm; yet it comforted him to know that it was here in this stone as it was in the great Stone on Morven.

"Ancient One, pity a fool," he whispered.

The wind whooshed in with a thunderclap of force that drove Dewar against the stone. He fell forward, and the stone was no longer there to support him. On his face he sprawled on a surface without sensation.

"You. Invoke."

The voice, genderless, gravelled in Dewar's inner ear, ideas from outside rolling through his mind and clashing together, leaving meaning. He recognized it. Well save him, he had Summoned the Stone. The sorcerer thrashed up to kneel, hunched, but kept his face covered.

"I—Ancient One," he said, shaking, "I am half out of my wits with grief. I addressed you, but I did not mean to—"

"Invoke. You. Me. Past. Present. Reason."

Now that it had him, it wasn't letting him get away without paying. He swallowed. Long years ago, pursued by his mother's hatred, he had been desperate for his life; now he cared more for another's. "Last time I was imperilled, and now—my sister, my sibling, my father's daughter has died, Ancient One, and it is my fault for I wronged her. I hurt her and she killed herself. I grieve, Ancient One, for the loss."

"Waste."

"She was a good person," Dewar protested, and began to weep.

"Sister. Life. Desire." More ideas bouncing off one another, echoing with sharp cracks.

"I didn't want her to die! I didn't mean to—to—hurt her—" Dewar looked up, but saw only darkness.

"Sister. Life. Balance. Alter."

Hope jolted through Dewar. He stared at the darkness. "To restore her? To—bring her back?"

"Sister. Life. Return. Balance. Alter."

Dewar had an image of things swinging back and forth across abysses, a glimpse of fourfold symmetry that fleeted before he comprehended it. "From life to death. I can move her back?"

"Yes."

Dewar, who had dealt with sorcerers all his life, knew such a blessing could not be without cost. "What must be done for that to happen, Ancient One?"

"Time. Task. Exchange. Life. You. Balance. Life. Sister."

Dewar closed his eyes. An inverted pyramid. He and Freia, touching hands, swinging around, changing places. "How much time?"

"Time."

Sand running through a glass flashed in his mind. Dewar swallowed. Little time.

For once and all, he could do something good, something right, something that would change the world and better it. Freia could live. He would be dead, but it was his fault she had gone to the sea and thrown herself in.

"I will make the exchange," he said.

The darkness did not reply.

"Ancient One?" he whispered after many heartbeats had thudded in his breast.

"Sister," came the voice, and a heptagon of meaning arrayed itself. "Plateau. Balance. Seek. Consent. Exchange. Life."

"Thank you—" Dewar breathed, and then a brilliant white light flashed and he had to duck his head and cover his eyes again.

A perfect silence surrounded him. He peeked through his slitted lids and fingers to see darkness, but a lighter darkness. Cautiously, Dewar lowered his hands and raised his head. "Beware," came the voice in his innermost hearing.

Dewar nodded, waiting.

"Tarry. Long. Plateau. Remain." Four cold flat square facts.

He'd be dead, inferred Dewar, and for nothing. How could he find her? How long was too long?

He knelt now on a broad plain beneath a lightless sky. Vaguely seen figures were around him, standing, kneeling; there were stones also, and a feeling of movement.

The kneeling figures were rising slowly to their feet. Those who stood were walking away from the place, all in one direction.

These, he understood, were the dead.

He rose. The world was painted in a palette of greys, all dark. The dead were indefinite; their faces and heads were clear, but they blurred gradually through their bodies to the ends of their indistinct limbs. Their expressions were calm, neutrally preoccupied. No one looked at him.

Dewar looked at himself. His body was solid, his clothing vestigially colored in the grey light. An elderly man passed by with thoughtful paces, his eyes on the horizon.

They all looked at the horizon, Dewar realized. He turned and gazed awhile that way himself, but saw nothing there. However, the longer he looked, the better he understood the vastness of the plateau. It was covered utterly with people, all walking toward the horizon.

In the opposite direction lay darkness. It ebbed and flowed around the stones—

They weren't stones. They were people, huddled on the ground in foetal positions, tightly balled, not moving, not rising.

Dewar bent his head again and covered his face a moment. How could he find her? There were so many dead. It was a hopeless task, as hopeless as sorting a hill of beans. It could not be done. Yet there was no escape here. He must seek her, or perish forever and with him Freia; indeed, if he must die, then he would die searching.

With faint faith, he walked among the dead travellers, looking into their faces. He opened his mouth to shout, to call "Freia!," and no sound came from his throat. He observed he was not breathing; that his heart was not beating.

He attempted to methodically walk back and forth among the dead. The plain was boundless in all directions, or at least unfathomably wide. But Freia must be somewhere near the border, mustn't she? It appeared that the dead at first crouched curled womb-shaped on the ground and then slowly uncurled, stood, and began to walk. As they walked, they lost definition: their features faded into a blur, and he dared not press far from the border to see what came next. Yet some, those within the darkness and at the fringe of it, never rose, never changed: remaining as they began, stonelike lumps self-enclosed.

He swallowed and went back toward where he thought he had arrived. The foetal dead were well-defined. They faded as they moved away from the border—as they left life behind, he surmised. He looked, and looked, and looked again. None of them were Freia.

Dewar walked among the dead for an age. One part of his mind, which he shoved away and denied acknowledgement, suggested that the Stone toyed with him: there could be no chance for him to find one woman among the thousands of dead who walked along this unbounded plateau. He would not consider that and looked into each countenance, seen by none, wondering what had their attention.

Their expressions haunted him with their inhuman distance.
Freia, his lips formed, again and again. Freia! Where are
you?

He pressed into the blackness whence the dead came, where
they were all huddled on the ground. Recent arrivals? Or the
dead who do not go forward, who never cross the Balance, he
guessed. What might they be? Why not?

He bent and looked in face after blind face. The black bound-
ary flexed; it had nothing to do with whether any of the dead
moved or not, or how quickly. It was only there, murky unlight.
Dewar crawled on his hands and knees from body to curled
body. They were as assorted as the rest of the dead: Death was
indifferent, he thought. Not just. Just death would mean all
would get the end they deserved. Miranda didn't. Golias did.
That paused his thoughts a moment: Golias, dastard and traitor, here with the rest, travelling onward toward the dimly
bright horizon—Dewar would have made a disgusted noise.
The man did not deserve so much. He looked at another stony
dead person and went on.

He did not grow weary, but his mind became dulled. He
mouthed his sister's name at bowed heads and clenched arms.
His spirit flagged, and he was horrified to see that his hands
were not as solid-seeming as they should be, not translucent but
ill-defined.

Furthermore, he thought, looking up and down at the grey
dead, when he found her what must he do then? Perhaps it
would become apparent. Dewar crawled on fading legs in the
darkness.

He went into the blackest area and looked at the dead there
with difficulty, again and again, and he saw her not.

It was when he paused to stand, from desire for variety instead of physical need, that he saw a tongue of blackness recede
briefly and then flow back toward a huddled body whose back
hinted familiarity. Dewar ran to the bent-over form, jostling the
uncaring dead as he did, and dropped to his knees.

"Freia!" he cried soundlessly, seizing her shoulders without feeling.

The world changed; the blackness snapped. The dead were gone. He and Freia were alone on an ashen plain, the two of them dull-colored in the dull light.

"Freia!" Dewar shouted again, and now he heard himself, felt himself, felt her.

Under his hand, she trembled.

"Wake up, Freia! It's me, Dewar."

Her hair was loose and long, hiding her face. She was soaking wet, wearing the claret-red gown she had worn that morning. He pushed her hair aside and found that her face was covered by her white hands.

"Freia," he whispered, and hugged her awkwardly.

A rustling dry-leaf voice came from her behind her hands. "Leave me."

"No. Freia—I'm sorry, Freia. I wronged you."

"Leave me."

"I came to fetch you, sister. I came to give you my life so you can live on."

"Leave me."

"Look at me!" he demanded, frustrated, and pulled her hands forcibly from her face with one hand as he lifted her chin with the other.

Her expression was cold and hard, contemptuous. Her left cheek was marked by a reddened bruise.

Dewar released her and sat back, looking down at his hands. "I'm sorry, Freia. There isn't much time—"

"Leave me."

"Accept my life. It won't be the same, Freia—"

"Nothing changes. I've had enough of it. There is nothing there for me. Leave me." Freia folded in on herself again, bending forward.

Dewar caught her, not wanting her to retreat from him, and held her up, against him. "Please, listen," he whispered in her salty hair, against her ear. "I came to apologize and to restore you. I am sorry, Freia. I was cruel to you. I—"

"You feel guilt." Freia moved, pushing away.

Dewar wouldn't let her go. "I am guilty," he admitted. "I am here to atone. You can return to life, return home, and I will stay—here."

Her voice was dead, a monotone. "It is nothing to me. I cannot return. There is nothing for me there. I was never alive." Freia slumped, and Dewar held her up.

"Father—" he began, and she interrupted.

"He hates me," she said.

"No."

"You know nothing of it. He hates me." She trembled, still trying to pull away, and Dewar forced her to look at him. "Leave me," Freia whispered.

"Prospero doesn't hate you," Dewar protested. "He is upset that you are gone. He has been searching everywhere he could for you—"

Freia shook her head, sadly. "He hates me," she said. "He doesn't want me. He wants Miranda. I'm a thing he shaped to use, and I'm broken, useless. He likes you. You are like him, and you are useful, and you're his son. I am a dead thing. I should never have existed."

"Freia! Of course you're really Prospero's," Dewar said uncomfortably.

"You know I speak the truth. You said it. I have no mother. I was never real. Miranda is real, she was always real. I'm common as dirt. I never was better. I never wanted to be better."

"Miranda is dead," Dewar said. "She is no better than you. You can live, Freia!"

"Let her live," Freia said. "Nobody wants me there. You don't, you said so."

He looked away. Freia broke from his grip and stood, began walking away on the featureless grey ground. Every step she took seemed to stretch to the horizon, yet she moved little, if at all.

"Time." A feeling of cutting-off, of ending.

"Give me more time, Oldest!" cried Dewar, rising and catching Freia, holding her arms. "She doesn't understand! Freia, you *must* accept my life—"

"I don't want your life, I hated life, I never had life," Freia said, struggling free of him. "I will not return. There is no life there for me. There never was."

"Balance. Life. Forfeit." The world was swinging, moving off its perpetual balance; Dewar felt it, a slow sway in reality. The horizon was nearer.

"No," Dewar moaned. "No."

"Forfeit?" Freia repeated, looking around.

"I'm dead," Dewar said. "There's a limit on how long the living—" Prospero, he thought. And he pitied his father, bereft in a day of his children.

"Who are you? I don't believe you!" Freia shouted, enraged in an instant. "You're just like the rest of them, playing nasty games! Who are you, to be pushing people—"

"Freia!"

"All. Balance."

"You're taking his life because I won't?" Freia demanded.

"Forfeit."

"Bullshit!"

"Freia, shut up—"

"You shut up! You fool. —He doesn't want to die! He doesn't know what he wants."

"Exchange. Balance. Freely." Monolithically indifferent, the Stone admitted nothing.

"I bet you tricked him! Let him go!" Freia shook Dewar's arm. "He's being stupid."

Dewar, with some surprise, saw that she wept.

"Send him away!" Freia demanded. "I chose death. I was never really alive. He is. He has everything to live for."

"Freia, stop," Dewar said, touched, and embraced her. He closed his eyes with a thrill of fear. How did it happen? What did the blank-faced grey dead think? He would know, but would he know he knew? What was on the horizon?

"It's wrong!" Freia turned away from him to shout into the close grey void.

"Freia." Her sudden outrage on his behalf at once embarrassed and comforted him; he'd volunteered, though he hadn't expected to be called, and she was trying to protect him. She couldn't be so angry with him, if she was trying to help him now.

"Life. His. Life. Yours. Value. None. Refuse." Cold crystalline insult, glittering.

Dewar thought that was a rather nasty dig. "She didn't know—"

"His life is his, not mine!" Freia cried. "You can't just hand it around like a loaf of bread."

"Ignorant. Essence. Life."

"Then it doesn't just evaporate at a fixed time; it's always there," Freia said. Dewar blinked; how did she know that piece of arcana? From Prospero? Freia persisted, "You can give it back. You can send him away."

"I came for you," Dewar said. "I want you to live."

"I do not want to live! I was not alive. I didn't die accidentally. I stepped into the water myself. You have a good life. Leave me in peace. Go live."

"It was my fault you did that," Dewar said, attempting to keep the argument on track.

"You can't think of anything but yourself. Prospero—" She stopped.

Stung, Dewar demanded, "What did he do?"

"Nothing. As always, nothing," she said.

"It would make him very happy if you were there," Dewar said softly. "He loves you—"

"He hates me. He made me, and I'm a failure. He loves Miranda—Miranda is real! I'm not real! I'm useless, a stupid thing, a burden! I'm not what he wanted. I was a mistake. He wants you! You're real, really human, a real son." Freia was shouting, nearly screaming, violent and furious and not hearing a word Dewar said.

Frustration made him shout back at her. "I didn't come here

to argue about who Father likes best. If you're here, Freia, where we are now, you were alive and you are real! Do you understand? You were alive. It doesn't matter how. It doesn't matter that he made you. Miranda is dead, beyond life, beyond love. He may have loved her but he loves you too! You must live. You must accept my life!"

Freia threw his hands off her arms. "I don't care! What made you think I'd want your life?"

"Nothing," Dewar said, defeated. He turned away. A bitter ache tightened around his heart like a wire. To keep it in, he folded his arms tightly over his chest, closing his eyes. When would the Stone claim him? Or was this an afterlife, a punitive eternity of argument and anger?

"How do you feel now?" Freia asked him after a moment, behind his back.

"Useless. Worthless," he said dully. His life forfeit, for nothing: the most precious thing he had, worthless.

"I feel that way all the time," Freia told him. "All the time. Nothing I have, nothing I think, is worth anything to anyone, not him or you or anyone."

He nodded, understanding. "I'm sorry, Freia," he whispered.

"You always know you're so clever," Freia said, her voice thin and strained, "and you think you can make me do things, and you never really hear anything just like Prospero and—"

"I know," Dewar said, small before the truth.

"I'm sorry," his sister said, sniffling. "I like you. I always did. You should have stayed away."

He felt her hands touch his upper arms, and he unclenched his arms and folded them around her. "I'm sorry," Dewar said, looking down at her face; the light was growing poorer. "It's all wasted. I wish I had—done other things." If only he had done them, had even done one of them. But he had not: now he would not. He could see himself now; he understood where he had lost track of what was important in the greater scheme, of what would endure in value of the sorcerer's and the gentleman's worlds he bestrode.

Freia nodded her head against his chest, a comforting feeling. He stared at the dim ground and hugged her. She was cold
to his touch.

"Time. Forfeit. Balance. Exchange."

"No!" Freia said, exploding out of the peace that had settled
on them. "No forfeit, no exchange. Return him to his place
among the living."

"Freia, sister, I came to release you."

Freia put her cool hands on his cheeks, framing his face; her
brows drew together, kinked upward in the middle. "No.
Dewar, it's not that I'm ungrateful—but I won't take everything
you have. It's *yours.* I don't deserve anything of yours. Leave
me."

Stubbornly, he shook his head. "I want you to have it. It's
not taking, it's accepting."

"It is all you have, Dewar. Too much. Half as much would
be too much."

Dewar stared at her. An idea blossomed in his mind. "Would
you accept half?"

"What?" She lifted her eyebrows. "Half?"

"Would—Ancient One, could we not share a life?"

"Divide. Life. Essence." The concepts didn't fit together.

"Would you accept a shared life, Freia?" He grabbed her
shoulders, made her look at him through her tangled damp hair.

"What would that mean?" She frowned. "Half a life? A half-
life?"

"If life is truly an Essence, it may be divided between us, and
one life serve both."

"Past. Never." A doubt from the Ancient One, with a hint
of interest.

"It's still one life," Dewar said, looking away from her,
around at the suffocating void; it had become lightless, though
they two had a wan luminosity. "Embodied in two. It's been
done before. The sorcerer 'Adramasch of Wislaval, for example—"

"One. Life. Two. Live. Never."

"It's not that radical a step," Dewar insisted. "In the case of the Two Prophets of Bachangee—"

"Dewar—" Freia began; he put his hand over her mouth and pulled her to him.

"Balance." The Oldest couldn't balance the ideas: life, lives.

"Would you consent?" Dewar whispered to her.

Freia stared up at him, bewildered, her eyes wet and dark. He lifted his hand from her lips and touched her face, leaning close to see her. "Please," he asked. His voice cracked and broke on the word.

She closed her eyes, shook her head, and said, "It means so much to you."

"It does."

"Why?"

"Because." The reasons tumbled around; he couldn't seize and speak just one. Because it was justice; because he didn't really want to meet the horizon, not yet; because of the way Prospero had looked; because he loved her.

Freia shook her head again. "Very well," she said. "I don't like it. Very well. I will kill myself again if it is bad."

"It won't be. I won't let it be. I'll take you home to your Argylle. It's a good place. You belong there, and they want you."

"You," Freia said with an uncommonly sharp look, "don't care about Argylle, only the Spring."

He blinked; it was true. She had a discomfiting knack of perception. "I— Let me try, Freia. Let me try again. The Spring— yes, I care about that, but I care about you more. Please let me try. You consent to share my life." It sounded like a proposal of marriage, Dewar thought.

"Yes."

"She consents, Ancient One."

"Forfeit."

The darkness began to grow closer, drawing around them.

"Ah, too late," Freia said, and sighed, and sat on the ground. "Too late," Dewar heard her whisper.

"No!" raged Dewar, "you never said the time was up, you let us—"

"Balance. Life. Cost."

"What would you require to make it worth your while?" Dewar demanded frantically. "Another life?"

"Balance. Preserve."

Freia vanished, curling up again.

"Bring her back!" cried Dewar. "Are we not more use to the Balance alive than dead?"

"Past. Balance. Sister. Disrupt."

The abortion, thought Dewar. "Low blow," he replied. "Very low. She is unique among all our kind, you know that. Let her live!"

"Ground."

"That's ground enough—the Balance is the real problem, is it not? Keeping it in equilibrium?"

"Balance. All." A pause, and, "Balance. Keep. Possible."

"Make me an offer."

"Life. Other. Exchange. Life. Yours."

"I kill someone?" Dewar asked bluntly. Not Father. Please, no, not Father.

Dewar felt the Stone's incomprehension; the Ancient One didn't concern itself with means, only ends. "Exchange. Life. Forfeit. Balance."

"Whose life?"

"Blood. Yours. First. Afterkin."

Dewar closed his eyes, opened them on the blackness which enclosed him. "I see," he said, and swallowed. Two for one, essentially. He had forfeited his own life, taking too long to talk his sister around. She had ample reason for not wanting to live; her life had not been happy lately, and her future was dark. Yet—a child. To sacrifice someone yet unborn, a stranger, but his own blood as much as Freia was—

"Is this one of those midnight-at-the-crossroads affairs?" he asked.

"Choice. Yours."

Dewar thought the Ancient One was amused. "I don't so choose."

"Not," gravelled the Stone. "You. Do. Nothing. Life. Forfeit. Balance. Need."

"So you can actually carry an imbalance, so to speak, for a little while—or a long while—"

"Terms. Not. Evade."

"I don't intend so, I, ah, I just wondered." He thought of Freia; he thought of the Spring gleaming and chuckling to itself under Prospero's fortress, of his thorn-wrapped tower and the workroom there. He had much to live for: she had been right. Surely Freia could find something that mattered as much to her. "I accept your terms," he said softly.

The darkness flashed white, making Dewar throw up his hands and stagger, and his foot slipped and sent him skidding down in snow, his knee landing on a stick, the black stone snowless and ominous before him.

What had he done? Dewar wondered, and he shivered and pulled his cloak tight. His last bargain with the Stone had been more usual, more of the sort he supposed other sorcerers made or would make if they could. This was sorcerous insanity from start to end. He should never have gambled his own life, were he a proper sorcerer. Now the Stone had her, had him, and had his first child to boot. Dewar shivered again as the wind bit his face. His hair was wet with snow.

"My respects, Ancient One, and my thanks for your—boons," he whispered to the standing stone, and he bowed on his knees. Then he stood, turned away, and without looking back hurried along the road, on which his previous footprints lay fresh and new.

— *14* ⌒

"WHERE IN ALL THE HELLS OF man hast been?" Prospero demanded to know, spinning around at the still-open window.

"Went for a walk," Dewar said. He took off his damp cloak and hung it up. Beneath it, his clothes were wet through. "Needed it," he added. He'd had time to think as he walked back to the Palace through the swirling snow. There was no way to tell his father what he had done, even if he could have brought himself to speak of it. Dewar suspected Prospero would take a very bad view of such a bargain.

Prospero nodded and closed the window. "My apologies," he said to it, and twitched the draperies together. "I'd asked thee to await me here."

"I was distracted, sir." Dewar sat on the sofa. Prospero carried over a candelabrum with three lit tapers and sat beside him. Dewar stared straight ahead. He took a deep breath and released it; the flames fluttered. "Any word?"

"Naught."

Had he been duped? Had the Ancient One, with some play on words Dewar had missed, tricked him? He had looked for Freia along the road to the Palace and seen no sign of her. But the Stone could not lie; the meanings lay together, solid blocks—

"I think she's alive," Dewar said. "I think—I don't know. She can't be dead."

"She was compounded most mortal," Prospero said bitterly. "May I kindle thy fire?"

"Surely. Ah. There's wine." He was forgetting to play the gentlemanly host.

"An excellent idea." Prospero took a candle to the hearth, stacked kindling and logs.

Dewar forced himself to rise, to find a corkscrew and heavy glass goblets at the sideboard and to open a bottle a servant had brought him with Luneté's regards and her farewell note.

"Lys wine," Prospero remarked, tasting it.

"Gift from the Countess of Lys." This was better than the last Lys wine he'd had, a shallow but flavorful red. Dewar took a linen towel from the washstand and rubbed at his wet hair.

Prospero turned, watching him, and said, "A lively young woman."

He smiled. "Very. My cousin-in-law, is she now?"

Prospero drank, rolled the wine in his mouth, swallowed. Dewar watched pale infant flames catch the edges of the logs on the hearth, climbing to glory. They emptied and refilled their glasses in silence.

"I hold no hope that Freia lives," Prospero said to his goblet.

"We don't know anything, Father. All we have are hints, clues. She may— Maybe she has wandered onto the Road, or into some situation where she is not easily perceived—"

"Have faith in thyself, son. Dost so timidly endorse thy sorcery?"

"No," admitted Dewar. "I have hope."

"Hope is for fools," said Prospero, "and other things too," he said, "and belike I'd be as great a fool as any, now. There's a matter I'll broach with thee, which I'd liever have left untapped until the morrow."

"I listen, sir."

"I've spoken with Odile," Prospero said, "but recently, and 'tis mine intent to bring her to my new dwelling at the Spring." His mouth twitched slightly.

Dewar touched his lips with his winey tongue and set his glass down carefully. "I am not sure that is—wise—Father."

"I'm told of the difficulty which has existed betwixt you."

"I have said nothing of it," Dewar murmured. Odile. His hands were damp all in an instant; his feet wanted to move.

"We talked of't, she and I. At first 'twas concern for thy sister that prompted me; the girl hath no mother, no model for a woman's role and conduct, which lack hath been the root of certain faults in her. I've spoken of thee as well. Though the breaking of thy oath was a heinous start in life, thou makest strides toward redeeming thyself. Thy mother hath in her heart to grant thee pardon, an thou'lt sue for it meekly."

Spoken today? *She* willing to pardon *him*? Dewar thought, and his head jerked to stare at Prospero.

Prospero gazed at the fire, not seeing him. "It is for love of me she does so," he said. "I trust thy bearing will be amicable and suitable."

For *love* of him? Odile, love? Prospero deluded himself— "I shall bear myself," Dewar whispered, bowing his head, "appropriately." He would ride the Road and hide, he thought; he would find a hole and pull it down behind him; he would return to Oren's Company of Twelve and be there protected. "I am surprised at the suddenness of this," he went on in a stronger voice.

"It is not sudden. I've long desired to refresh the acquaintance. I am pleased to find that the rare affection she felt for me remains, as mine for her, untarnished by time or circumstance." Prospero drank again. "She is here, now," he finished.

Dewar's chest tightened. "Here? She is?" He looked around swiftly.

"Aye. In the Palace. Hath been here all the day, arrived this morn early and sought me," and Prospero closed his eyes for a moment, "and I prithee do her the honor of joining us in my rooms tomorrow for a late breakfast. I'd intended—other things. We'll wait to see if thy sister's body be found," and Prospero breathed deeply and took a quick swallow of wine, "and then begone after such obsequy as be required. She's dead, and cannot be bound, cannot be used to further bind me." He did not look at Dewar; he seemed rather to address the now-empty goblet.

"Oh," said Dewar, although he had known this. "What are your further plans, then?"

Prospero refilled his goblet. "Ere my vow was fulfilled, I sensed deep changes in the balance—"

Dewar started, hearing the term again.

Prospero spoke still to his wine. "—which hath maintained 'twixt the Stone of Blood and the Well. Alas, I had no fore-knowledge that I'd be forever kept from sounding deeper in these currents, but this much could I see from the surface, this much do I know: the Spring hath altered the balance, hath begun to disorder the flow of the Well, at the wastelands fringing Pheyarcet."

"Oh," again said Dewar, who had not only noticed the effect but deduced the cause and calculated its approximate location and strength, alone in his Tower of Thorns: which discovery had prompted him to travel in Pheyarcet and Landuc. "That's interesting." It was interesting. Prospero knew what he held in the Spring, Dewar had supposed he must, but now—banned from sorcery, what good could it be to him? And Dewar's belly tightened as he thought of Odile, and what use she might make of such power.

"I believe 'tis a natural process—the upwelling, so to speak, of Wells. Avril," Prospero said, and smiled scornfully, "who fears sorcery, Gaston who ignores it—they know naught of't. They know I drew my forces, my men, from some mighty but unfamiliar place: they've not the knowledge to guess what the truth is."

"The Spring?" Dewar half-asked, prompting.

"Avril hath an ill dawn lurking," said Prospero. "What dost know of it?"

"What you have told me," Dewar replied, which was but half the truth: with Odile in the background of his thoughts, caution governed him, and he wished to veil himself and his work and hear what Prospero would volunteer. "I only followed Freia there, and you," he added, another half-truth. "The Well seemed weak and distant."

" 'Twas a source of power," Prospero said. "I opened it, drew 'pon and primed it with the last of my sorcery. If all's worked as I wished, 'tis now a mate to Landuc's Well and the Stone of Morven: antithesis and complement."

Dewar drew his breath in and held it. "A wonder," he said softly. Exactly what he'd thought himself, waking there in Argylle after his marathon of copying. Did Prospero think him utterly blind, not to have observed the change? Or had Prospero simply not thought of it, so consumed he'd been by his other difficulties?

"More than a wonder. I do not want Pheyarcet. I've something better that's mine own, and there shall I dwell."

"This cannot have passed unnoticed by the other adepts, Father." Dewar pictured the disruption a new Power would cause in political circles, not just sorcerous—although those of the sorcerers in Phesaotois capable of finding the place could and would do much toward making it considerably less idyllic. Prospero must know this; he had driven the Argyllines to complete their city's walls before he left, and the walls had potent Bounds on them.

But what use would Bounds be when Prospero meant to invite Odile within?

"I am sure not, thus I desired to seal with Avril some stronger edifice of defense than the simple shield of words he granted on my surrender. I'd have had the better side of't; he'd no idea of what I represent." Prospero chuckled darkly. "Pity. 'Twere a pleasure to see his discomfiture, when the true state of affairs became evident: not knowing what he did, he granted Freia might hold Argylle 'mongst her dower-lands, hers alone." Prospero's laugh deepened. "Why, His Mean-Spirited Majesty stooped to quibble o'er houses I've not beheld in full four centuries, o'er estates whose very district-names are half-eroded with their lands, e'en let me dispute with him for a few of Diote's jewels, all that he niggardly begrudged the maid: but never marked a virgin woodland and a village with no manor-house appertaining, all called Argylle, lying in a vague quadrant far-flung from Landuc. He thought them without worth, though he burdened all she was to have with tithes. Incompetent."

Dewar smiled too. The Emperor deserved what he got, to let himself be so led about, pursuing the obvious and ignoring the veiled, the unseen. "And now?"

"Since the bride's gone—" Prospero shrugged. "I swore non-aggression; I'll keep mine oath. I've no interest now in Pheyarcet. The surrender treaty chafes me, but thou hast gotten me my liberty again—and thy poor sister's, for all the good she made of it."

Freia, thought Dewar. Where was she? Perhaps best out of sight, if Odile was about the place. She'd as soon poison Freia as look at her, surely. Would Odile test her mettle in the Fire? The Emperor might not allow it—

Prospero was speaking still; he paused and said, "Dewar?"

"I'm—preoccupied. It's been a day of many shocks, Father." Dewar put his elbows on his knees and his head on his hands.

Prospero squeezed his shoulder. "I ask thee to join us for breakfast o' the morrow, in my apartments," he repeated quietly.

"I—usually I fence with Josquin in the morning, or try to if he is up," Dewar said, looking up. Prospero's face was kind, care-lined. Dewar pitied him, ensnared by Odile. He would come to a bad end, through delusion to humiliation and degradation. Prospero was a fool, as he had said himself, and Odile would help him make himself an ass, as she had so many others.

"Come afterward. There is more for us to discuss. I thought to tell thee this now, 'twould distract thee."

"I cannot believe she is dead," Dewar said, truthfully.

Prospero pressed his shoulder again. "I must go," he said, "and see what word Herne's turned up, or Fulgens. Gaston could not wait; despite the storm he must ride to his Montgard on some business of his army." He paused. Dewar looked at him, at the concern in his face, and nodded. "Wilt be well . . . ?" Prospero half-asked.

Dewar said, "Yes."

"She was too mortal made," Prospero whispered, shaking his

head, "to survive here 'mongst the smokes and stirs o' the Well."

Dewar nodded.

"Good night, son."

"Good night, Prospero."

Prospero went out of the room. Dewar lifted his head and gazed at the fire. He listened to the door close and a frown drew the corners of his mouth down; his eyes narrowed.

"Odile," he said to the fire, and ground his teeth. "Damn," he whispered.

Dewar left from the sofa, took up the candles, and opened his workroom. In the bottom of a wardrobe in his bedroom, after strenuous searching, he found a pair of large leather saddle-bags and brought them to the workroom.

First he stripped off his wet clothes, dried himself, and dressed again; then, the real work began. Methodically, sometimes going to fetch a vest or socks or other clothes to pack something fragile (the Mirror he wrapped in three new shirts of fine South Madanese silk), he emptied his workroom of everything sorcerous, everything scholarly. It required that he fill an additional pair of saddle-bags and a haversack, for he had borrowed, from the Palace library, books which he had no intention of returning. If the Emperor did not value sorcery, Dewar did, and he knew what was worth studying. Two old histories of the early days of Panurgus's reign went along also.

When he was done, he heaped all he had packed on the bed. He cleaned the bedroom meticulously next, removing all traces of his occupancy, and then, regretful, decided it wasn't enough: he must scour the place the best way he knew, annihilating every atom of himself Odile might use against him. Sword and cloak he donned, and his best high boots. He judged the pile of luggage and added a rolled blanket containing two new seagreen silk waistcoats embroidered with silver stuffed into a new pair of riding boots. Such amenities were unobtainable near his Tower of Thorns.

Last of all, he took his staff.

How to depart? He might make a Way; it would be quickest and easiest, and there'd be no chance of pursuit, and he began to rummage for the little cube of stone that would lead him to his tower wrapped in thorns. And as he did he thought of Freia, and he slowed his searching and halted. Freia had not been found. She lived, though, and he fully expected her to appear soon. A feeling that she could not be far away at all nagged at him. He owed it to her not to leave her here, in Odile's reach.

Though the Stone hadn't promised anything of the sort, Dewar's sorcerer's instinct told him that he must put himself in a position to meet Freia by chance. That precluded a Way. He would have to take the Road, risk Odile and Prospero tracing him or just happening by bad luck to meet him, and trust Fortune to put Freia in his path. Fortuna had served him well before, in similar circumstances.

Dewar draped the awkward saddle-bags about his person and lifted the black staff, Summoning the Well of Landuc. He spun the staff and chanted a spell of Bounding, walking through the rooms and moving the staff along the walls, making a confinement for the Elemental he would invoke.

Having completed his circuit, Dewar stood in the center of his rooms, at the door of the bedroom and sitting-room, and Summoned again with words of power.

It exploded into the room along a line he cut in the air with his staff, hovered, limited in its scope by that staff's circling.

"Perceive the Bounds," said Dewar.

"I persssceive the Bounds," said the Salamander, a hiss and crackle.

"Within the Bounds is thine."

"I ssshall take what is withhhin."

"When all within is burned, be dismissed, and return to thy proper sphere."

"I sssshall burn within the Bounds, and return to my ssssphere," agreed the Salamander. "The Bounds are small, massster."

"Tough. That's what you're getting."

"There is greater food without. . . ."

"It's not for you." Salamanders, thought Dewar, were a greedy lot. Sprites were content to work within Bounds and rarely overflowed; the desire of a Salamander was only to devour.

"As you wisssh, massster."

"Indeed." Dewar blew out the candles; the room was lit only by the dull red glow of the Salamander hanging, contorting, at the end of his staff. The sorcerer, staff in hand, walked to the window, reached through the curtains, and unlatched it. The Salamander could not leave the Bounds he had made; Dewar stepped backward through the opened window onto the balcony and the Elemental dropped from the tip of his staff at the Bounds, exploding into light and fire. Dewar closed the window on the roar, being neat at heart, and jumped, for the second time that night, from the balcony into the snow, encumbered now by his souvenirs of the Palace.

The hue and cry was raised as he reached the stables; undisturbed, he chose and saddled a horse, Majuba, burdened him with the saddlebags, and led him out. Prospero's glossy black Hurricane stood at one end of the stalls; Dewar paused there.

"Tell him—nothing," Dewar said to the horse. "Farewell, and we'll meet again in better times, Hurricane. I'd like a foal of yours one day."

Hurricane snorted and tossed his head, as diminished from mightier things as his master and as chafed thereby. Dewar smiled a little and left the stables.

He cared not where he went, at first; the Gate of Winds would do as well as any, and he could get to the shore-road from there, to follow the ocean a ways.

At the Palace to the west, there were shouts and shrieks, bells and to-do. He chuckled. The Salamander would consume everything within the Bounds and no mortal hand could restrain it. A Sprite might destroy it and itself too, but only if a sorcerer could put one inside Dewar's apartment.

"That's me," he said, mounting. "Out in a blaze of glory. Let's go!"

— *15* —

PRINCE GASTON TOOK A LANTERN ON a pole from a rack and lit it while the groom saddled Solario and brought him from his stall. The horse snorted when he scented his master, and Gaston stroked his sleek neck and nose. He led Solario out of the stables, into the snow-whitened yard, and mounted. His road was north, into Herne's Riding. At an ancient standing stone, he would pass onto the Road and make his way toward Montgard.

The wet snowflakes swirled like comets under the lights of the Palace ways. Gaston passed through three gates, was saluted briskly by the guards at all, and settled with Solario into a frame of mind for the long, dark, damp ride through the forest before he could pass onto the Road. The cold and wind were nothing to him; the horse ignored them as well, being Gaston's animal and having absorbed something of his nature in the service. At the end of its short chain, the lantern bobbed and swung, covering the white road before them with a cycle of shadows and wan light. Solario was a horse accustomed to getting from here to there rapidly; he cantered smoothly, comfortable with Gaston's weight and light hand on the reins.

The snow thickened and deepened by the time that they had passed the seventh marker from the Palace and they were well into the forests Herne maintained, his lands on which he permitted others to ride and hunt, or not, at his whim. Herne, Gaston knew, was in the Palace, but his gamekeepers might be patrolling the road, or might not on such a foul night—they'd liever keep to their fires and ales. The snow was less wet than it had been in the city, the flakes clumps of white crystals, hexagonal colonies covering the road and black trees with a flawless coat hiding color and irregularity.

He glanced from side to side as he went, out of habit, and it was this habit which caused him to register a standing stone he knew well, the Moonstone of the Wood, which was also a Gate to the Road and a Nexus itself under some conditions. Not tonight's; the Moonstone had a white side windward and a heightening cap. The crescent graven into its blackness was half-limned with snow. Gaston's eyes looked at the stone in his swaying light, followed the light to his left to look there, and then snapped back to the right.

Solario, feeling his master's knees close on him, picked up his pace; Gaston drew on the reins, though, having tensed with startlement.

He could not have seen what he thought he saw, yet—it would do no harm to be sure.

A single twitch and leg-pressure set Solario turning carefully in the road. He walked the horse back to the stone and pulled up.

It was really there, not an illusion made of a fallen branch and the light and snow. The Prince frowned, dismounting. An arm, white under white, a bulk of body behind it heaped at the foot of the stone, all shrouded with the soft cold snow: and Gaston thought, in the brief time after he recognized it as he dismounted, of certain sorcerous practices—necromancies and worse—and his lip curled in revulsion.

No blood in the white of the snow. The lantern-light circled the arm, the body—the arm outstretched, hand open in supplication or offering, clad in a whitish lace-trimmed wet sleeve with a deep red sleeve over it.

He brushed snow from the body and cried, "No!"

His niece lay there, white as the snow that dropped on her from indifferent clouds.

Gaston, clenching his jaw, set the lantern down and brushed more snow away, looking for a wound, a bloodstain, a mark of violence. Nothing. Something dark was wound about her throat; he picked at it and found a long leaf of kelp, freezing and stiffening. Her eyes were closed; her hair was wet and frozen into thick strands around her face— Her face. It was nearly colorless, except for a fresh bruise on her left cheek. In her expression was no sign of distress; she seemed to sleep.

Gaston lifted her from the ground. There was little snow beneath her, mostly bare russet leaves. So she'd lain long so. Still flexible; despite the cold, no rigor. Still—

He frowned and laid his head on her chest, his hand at her throat. Still alive. Cold, her clothes full-soaked and freezing like her rimed hair into robes of solid ice, but she was alive.

"What devil hath cast thee here, let him have cause to rue it," whispered Gaston to unhearing Freia. He unfastened his cloak and wrapped her in it quickly after brushing away all he could of the snow, picked up the lantern, and considered what to do.

He could return to the Palace. Yet that seemed unwise. She was not here of her free will, surely. The politics and tension between Prospero and the rest had flared. Someone had done something—who or what Gaston didn't know, but it had probably been someone in the Palace or thereabouts, since that was where she had been. Therefore to return to the Palace might be folly: might imperil her afresh for reasons unknown, might waste an opportunity to find the guilty party later. Not the Palace.

But Gaston knew also that although he was indifferent, even impervious, to the winter, she would be dead of exposure in a very short time. She needed to be warmed, to be dried and revived. Inns there were none in this area, only Herne's keepers' cottages—

And a hunting-lodge. It was not that Gaston did not trust his brother Herne; he would have done so had no other chance presented itself. But there was an Imperial hunting-lodge not far from here, off the road, and it would have firewood, some food, and the means of drying her off and thawing her out.

Juggling lantern, lady, and reins, he got mounted again and urged Solario to a hurried canter. The lodge was on a track that ran northwest from the road. Gaston rode on that side and huddled Freia against him, and she never stirred save for the lame flutter of her heart.

Prospero watched the fire in Dewar's rooms from the terrace below, his arms folded. There were other spectators, but they'd drawn away from him and he stood alone in the crowd. Rumors and speculations were invented and embellished in his hearing, most of them involving the sorcerer's deserved demise at the Emperor's hand.

Avril, Prospero thought disgustedly, could not conjure an idiot-light to kindle a lamp, let alone command a Salamander of the potency required to gut the rooms in so brief a time. The creature was confined, obviously to Prospero but not so to the fire-fighting Palace Guard and servants, who were frantically wetting down neighboring chambers and throwing futile water on the flames trailing from the roaring, hissing Salamander as it devoured the place corner by corner, wall by wall.

Dewar would be gone, Prospero knew. And he had covered his tracks thoroughly, so thoroughly that no sorcerer could follow him.

With a window-shattering implosion, the Salamander departed and the conflagration vanished.

The crowd gasped and shrieked at the sudden darkness and silence.

Prospero pushed through the gawking gaggle and started toward his apartment to tell Odile. The inescapable conclusion was that Dewar had left because his mother was here. Prospero had told him of her but three hours past. It angered him that the boy hadn't even spoken with her. Prospero had, at length, when he'd visited her to enquire about her son, and on later reflection he had become convinced that she meant Dewar no harm. Perhaps a scolding, a taste of well-earned guilt and shame, but no real injury. She was his mother, Prospero thought; she wouldn't be capable of harming her own child so, though he had bruised her pride and sentiment. A mother's nature was forgiving, not destructive.

Dewar, gone; Freia . . . gone. Prospero stopped at the porch of a side door and leaned on it in the snowy darkness. Freia, gone, dead. Miranda, dead. Gonzalo, beloved friend, a half-dead wreck from the King's and then the Emperor's disfavor, which had starved him of the life the Well would have given him, and bereft now of his bright daughter. Prospero closed his eyes. If only Miranda had not ridden, O noble folly, O brave beloved woman, to tell Prospero to guard his back. A piece of him had been living for her, and it was dead now, withered after years of quiet waiting for the glance of her eye, the touch of her hand. Most radiant Miranda, dead, brutally killed by worthless Golias. She would have done such good for Freia, who had thrashed and fought what life had brought until it exhausted her.

Suicide. Prospero shuddered, and the empty boat floated before his mind's eye. He hadn't meant to lose his patience. He had never struck her before, hadn't meant to strike her then. She had barged in, damn it, he had been talking most privily with Odile, and Freia had stormed in demanding notice—he'd cursed her and told her to get out. He'd bid her leave him, scolded her importunity, said he would see her in his time, not hers, and struck her, knocked her against the door; she'd gone swift enough, her hand on her cheek, and left him, taken herself away to where he would never find her until indeed his time had come.

His remembered anger sickened him; it swirled darkly like the ocean in Dewar's small Mirror of Visions, blurring and swallowing Freia. She'd never liked the sea, mistrusted water so unbounded. Rivers, ponds, smaller lakes, well enough and she would paddle and swim as needed. But not the sea, the churning sea; not until tonight when she desired its wide and indifferent embrace. He hoped they'd never find her body, swollen and bitten; O Well of Fire, he prayed, let her be swept away to dissolve into the deep, become a part of the sea.

She was so damnably impatient. She'd no head for politics, could not see anything here beyond its being alien, not home.

And at home she had fussed at him about every blade of grass he cut, every alteration great or small. She'd no vision of the morrow, he thought, she knew only present and past and understood naught of laying groundwork for a future. He had tried to make her see that, and she had refused to accept it. And now she was out of the present, flowing away from him into the past, soon to be naught but a small trunk of worn clothes, her bows and arrows carefully kept, her exercise-books already palimpsests overwritten, a name black-bordered in exhaustive genealogies of the descendants of Primas. Died without issue.

And himself? he asked.

Still there was Dewar, gone into a sorcerer's retreat in some lair, and the Well's truth was that Pheyarcet nowadays had a rich assortment of nooks and bywaters where a sorcerer could bide unnoticed—

"Prospero."

He opened his eyes.

"A new career as a statue?" Odile asked, and with her black-feathered fan she brushed at the snow on his shoulders.

"Nay, madame, quick flesh will not stiffen sufficiently for such a purpose," he replied. "What dost thou here?"

"Seeking thee, and that done, must find some other game. What alarum was raised so?"

" 'Twas Dewar, set afire his apartment and no doubt hours gone by now. The Salamander's departed; 'twas a fine large fellow."

"Pity, I should have liked to see it. So hath he mastered Elementals," she added, half to herself.

"At least the Salamander that scoured his rooms. More I cannot say, not knowing. 'Tis cold to stay without, madame; though statuary care not, folk of flesh such as we freeze unaesthetically. Let's within."

"Indeed."

He opened the door, bowed her in; Odile's gown rustled and her scent set him tingling. They walked along a narrow tiled hall together; it was dim, lit by a few oil-lamps along its length but more by the light from the open door at its end. After a few steps he said, "I'll Summon Fulgens and ask what tidings. Mayhap they've found some sign of my daughter."

"Thy offspring are a destructive brace of curs, my lord; it grieves me to see them tear thee so."

"It grieveth me also, and I know no remedy but to have no children," Prospero said bitterly, "and my own remedy is applied to me, so must I be cured of grief."

Avril the Emperor had taken to locking things, unable to seal them as his sire Panurgus had. With a poniard Gaston broke the lock on the lodge's door and carried Freia in and up to a small chamber. He put her on the bed, heaped blankets from a chest over her, and ran down for a first armload of wood. Haste, haste, he thought, though if she'd lived so long it seemed impossible for her to die now that succor was at hand.

He had a fine blaze going in seconds after laying the wood—fires always burned for Gaston, be the fuel ever so wet or icy—and brought up more logs in rapid relays. Hot liquid, he thought; the kitchen was lean, but he set a black three-legged pot at the fire melting snow for water and a smaller one on the other side to heat a bottle of wine fortified with spices and honey.

Then he looked at Freia again. Ice-white, ice-still: Gaston considered treatments for exposure and decided that the case was extreme; maidenly modesty must be sacrificed for warmth. He took the blankets off her and opened his cloak, clasped her stony hands in his for an instant apologetically, and began stripping the wet, ice-starched red dress and other garments from her. Her shoes were gone already.

Sand fell from her clothes, grit caught in pockets and pleats and folds sifting onto the cloak and floor, and small strands and fronds of seaweeds. Gaston sniffed salt and wondered, but hung the clothes over a chair and shook four woollen blankets over her marble-veined body. Not much to do about the hair being so wet now; he put a fold of another blanket around her head to keep that warm. He sat on the edge of the bed, pulled off his boots and dropped them, took off his sword belt and high-collared coat and hung them on the post, and rolled under the blankets with her, putting her near the fire.

It was like hugging a statue of bronze on a midwinter morning. She was breathing, though softly, and still the heart was struggling to move in the cold cavity of her chest. Gaston cradled her against him like a lover, wrapping his body around hers, tucking her head to his breast and bending his face over her. The fire crackled.

When he held himself very still, the whisper of Freia's breath was audible to him. He closed his eyes, concentrating on it, and willed it stronger as children will snow to fall or sun to shine.

Gaston dozed tensely, alertly, unrestfully. A log falling into coals woke him, and he saw that the fire required fuel. Carefully, he left the bed and covered her again, fed the fire, had a cup of the wine and moved it a little away from the heat, and covered the water-pot. Then he rejoined the pallid, passive lady, pressing her against him again, trying to judge whether she were warmer.

He napped lightly, as before. A gamekeeper might scent the smoke and investigate; he would say, Gaston decided, that his horse had strained a muscle and it was his pleasure to wait out the storm here. That anyone would come was unlikely. He could hear the wind and snow hissing on the windows, in the chimney. After the second feeding of the fire, he embraced Freia again; she was warmer, yes, but not rousing. It was best to revive the victim gradually, he knew from winter campaigns, and with gentle heat: and that was this.

Freia twitched convulsively an hour or so later, as Gaston thought he should feed the fire again. He loosened his hold on her and waited for more signs of life.

"Freia, lass," he said in her ear, low.

No answer. He checked her pulse. Stronger. Her hands were not so cold; he'd had them in his armpits, hoping she wouldn't lose fingers.

"Freia," Gaston murmured again, "lass, wake thee, Freia."

Her breath caught a little and she made a small sound. Gaston could not see her face; she was deep under the blankets.

"Freia, I hope canst swallow, because thou must drink," he said, pleased at the sign of life. Gaston slid out of the bed and tucked her in, fed the fire, and prepared a cup of the spiced wine sweetened with honey and thinned with a little of the hot water. He lit a pair of candles and set them on a table by the bed with the cup.

"Here now," he said encouragingly, and moved the blankets away from her face.

She had acquired an expression: pain. Eyes still closed, her mouth was twisted, her breathing labored.

Gaston touched her lips with the spoon from the honey and they parted. He trickled a little of the syrupy-sweet, hot stuff into her throat. Freia coughed explosively, chokingly, once, gurgled a little, and opened her eyes without focusing.

"Pardon," he apologized, "but thou must swallow't."

"Eh." Freia closed her eyes again.

"Brave lass. Here."

She swallowed, working at it.

"Easier, maybe, sitting up." Gaston pulled a pillow under her head and tried again. It was visibly easier. He smiled and cheered her on in a murmur with each spoonful. The honey would provide nourishment; the wine would warm her.

"Cold," she breathed after a few minutes.

"Aye. I'm working to warm thee." He refilled the cup according to the same formula and spooned it into her delicately. Her face was white, too white. She finished the cupful and Gaston saw that she was too tired to take more. However, he had gotten nearly a quarter of a pound of honey into her thus, so she could rest for the nonce while her body fired on it. "I'm sharing bed with thee, Freia. 'Tis warmer so. Th'art too cold."

She had no objections; she was half-conscious. Gaston arranged them as before and was pleased to feel her pulse stronger and her breathing more definite. He drowsed again, finding no reason to be alert every instant. It was enough to wake a little every quarter of the long winter's night hours and see how his patient fared.

At regular intervals he rose and fed the fire, and when he did he would spoon-feed Freia more honey-wine-water. She was stronger each time, but never woke fully.

The storm abated toward morning's paling; Gaston needed more firewood and fetched it, and went again to the kitchen to search for anything that might have been left behind by the last hunting-party to house here. There were some preserved fruits in whisky, potent evil-smelling things. No meal, cheese, fruit, meat, or other mousable, spoilable food, which was too bad because honey was not really sufficient, he thought, to the task of revitalizing his half-frozen niece. He went back to the stables, saw to it that Solario was comfortable under horse-blankets, shovelled manure and scattered clean straw, and found a barrel of oats he had overlooked in his earlier haste. Solario was pleased by that, and Gaston returned to Freia.

She hadn't moved; he roused her and made her take more of his improvised restorative, then doffed his coat and boots and curled around her again. Her hair was drying slowly in the blanket. Gaston closed his eyes and napped fitfully.

Fulgens had no news for Prospero. His searchers had not found the rowboat nor had they found any trace of the girl.

"Prospero, the tide runs strong, and the weather is foul. I have recalled the boats searching," he said stiffly.

"Aye, one's enough," Prospero said.

"The water is cold. She'd not have lived above an hour in good weather, and in such a storm—"

"I know. My thanks, Fulgens. And to thy men. I've naught to give them but my thanks for't, parlous labor that such a search is. Surely the sea hath her in its bed tonight."

Fulgens said, looking away, "Aye. 'Twas fated she'd be wed to water; if not Josquin, then otherwise. So must our affinities destroy us an we let them o'ermaster us—"

"Good brother, sermon me not; I pray you keep such epigrams for sailors' memorials. My thanks to thee and thy generous hardworking men for their search."

Fulgens scowled at him, but Prospero sprinkled sand in the firepan of his Summoning apparatus and the frown vanished from the Mirror of Visions, to be replaced by his own face. He turned away, out of humor for self-admiration, and took the lamp into the bedchamber, where Odile met him with her clouds of darkness and soft arms.

In an in-between moment, Prince Gaston's nap ended and he was sharp awake. Freia had moved, was moving, jerky, spasmodic motions.

"Lass, Freia, how now," he said to her. "Nay, don't—thou'lt be cold."

"Cold now."

"Stay nigh me. Warmer."

"Papa?" Freia fought her head free and woozily looked at him, squinting in the candlelight and flameglow from the fire. Recognition came slowly to her, dazed as she was. "You . . . oh."

"I found thee i' the snow. Thou'lt be right."

"No . . ." she moaned.

He needed no strength to pull her back to him. "Aye. Stop thy thrashing, lass."

"Why . . ."

"And let us not debate whys and wherefores and insofars now. Th'art half-frozen yet. There is naught to warm thee but me, small fire, and honey in wine."

Freia allowed herself to be embraced, shuddering. "Hungry," she whispered.

"I'll bring thee some of that honey. There's naught else."

It was better this way; she managed, with a steadying hand from Gaston, to drink from the cup. "Ech," she said, swallowing.

"I'd not have it in other circumstance," he agreed. "Yet it warms."

"Mm. Just honey and water?"

"Very well." He mixed it for her, helped her drink it. "More?"
Freia downed another cup of the honey-water. " 'Nough."

"For now. More in a little while. Must keep thee fuelled."

"Rather not," she whispered, and closed her eyes. "Cold . . ."

Gaston began to move to get into the bed with her, but stopped himself. "I'll seek clothing for thee, lass; those wet things won't serve. Bide."

He tucked the blanket around her face and head and took a candle to other rooms, raiding linen-presses and pungent-scented chests and closets to turn up a few lawn smocks, stockings that had been abandoned rather than darned, and a long moth-raddled woollen dressing-gown. These he hung by the fire to heat before she put them on.

"Art warm?" he asked her.

"No."

"If 'tis not offensive to thee, I'll warm thee again." An awkward situation consciousness made: Gaston knew Freia disliked being touched at all, wincing from every hand, and he thought that to be bundled into bed so with a man must be wholly disagreeable to her.

Freia cringed and whispered, "I'm cold."

He got her another warm drink and, by the time she had swallowed it, one of the smocks was warmed. Flimsy thing, serving decorum only; Gaston helped her don it because her arms and hands and legs were unresponsive and confused. He huddled into the bed with her. Freia held herself stiffly away at first until the wonderful heat he radiated became irresistible, and then she grafted herself to him. She shivered now, and Gaston kneaded her arms and hands to move the blood. Then he lay quietly again, and she was warmer and more alive-feeling than the near-corpse of the night before, if only through the tautness of her bony back.

The next decision, Gaston thought, was how to move her, whither, and when. She was not strong enough to travel alone. He could wrap her in blankets and carry her on the saddle before him, he supposed; to be carried was less strenuous. And to what destination? His own, Montgard? To her father, Prospero, who would surely leave the city now that his son had bartered for his father's liberty? On the other hand, there was her brother, the erratic sorcerer Dewar; could he be trusted to care for her? He had acted in her interest before; he seemed a generous soul and might be willing to take her in his charge while she mended.

It was impossible to decide, not knowing what had brought her to this state.

Freia relaxed into sleep for a while; Gaston, bored, slept also, and dreamt of Freia in a grey stone maze on a winter-blasted hillside of stones and thorns. He watched her from above, seeing the blind alleys she took and the open ways she bypassed, prevented by dream-paralysis from calling out assistance to her. Her hands and feet were bloody; her clothing, the gown she had worn when he found her in the snow, was torn and muddy. Freia knelt on sharp stones and ice, bending double, weeping, and he saw that the maze was contracting, the stones tumbling and sinking or fading, until there was only a high cold wall around her: a tomb.

Gaston's grief woke him; he did not like such dreams, which told him the obvious and offered no insight, only agitation. Freia was awake too. She stirred in the cocoon of blankets and looked up at him, knuckling her eyes.

"Just a dream," he said, for both of them. His head ached from oversleep, from the confined air of the room, from the tension of the dream.

Freia nodded gravely. He studied her—she looked better, still pale but not so ghastly and wraithlike. Her eyes were still shadowy and her mouth had not a hint of a smile to it, only weary sorrow to bring the corners down and tighten its innate softness. The bruise was deep violet-black and bigger, her cheek swollen. Someone had laid a hard hand on her.

"I'll bring thee drink," he told her. He had a cup of plain wine himself and mixed the honey into another of the heated wine with a little water. Freia downed it indifferently; he sat on the side of the bed and supported her wobbly hand on the cup. When she had drunk, she lay back and Gaston tucked the blankets around her again.

"Well, lass. What shall I do with thee?"

"Don't care," she replied, whispering. "Just leave me alone."

"Nay, that wouldn't help," he said gently. "I found thee on the road and brought thee to the Emperor's hunting lodge; 'tis where we lie now. Wert nigh death."

"You should've left me."

"Freia, nay," Gaston protested. "I could not—"

"I'm too precious to just leave alone," Freia muttered resentfully, and she turned her back to him, withdrawing into the blankets and curling into a ball.

Gaston had been expecting a more welcoming answer from the lady he had thrice now picked up and patched up. He considered angles of attack and chose one. "Th'art precious, aye," he said, moving close to her again. She didn't pull away. "Freia. Tell me what's passed. How cam'st thou on the road in the snow?" And, unspoken, he added, Why the sand and the seaweed in thy clothes, and wherefore thy disappearance from the Palace, and why so sad?

"Don't know," she moaned. "Don't remember . . ."

"Thy father and brother sought thee," he said. "They're distressed."

"Hah."

Gaston insinuated his arm beneath her and turned her to face him. "Josquin inquired anxiously for thee—" he began.

Freia's small white fist shot up and hit him lightly on the nose, something so unexpected that he made no attempt to intercept it.

Astonished, not so much pained, Gaston yelped, "Ow!"

"I won't go back," Freia cried. "You won't make me go back!" She bounced to sit against the stag-carved headboard and stared back at him, fists clenched and arms crossed, wildness in her eyes and voice.

"Not 'gainst thy will, never, no," Gaston said, rubbing his

nose—unhurt, only startled. He should have guessed, he thought, that Josquin would have something to do with this: the marriage her father and his were bickering over would be as unpalatable to one as the other, for different reasons. Had she run away because of that and found greater ill? No jewelry—had she been robbed? "Freia," he went on, "I've sought to help thee. Thou knowest that. I have never forced thee, have I? Never shaken thy will?"

"No," she admitted, and ducked her head. "Don't—"

"Nor shall I. I told thee," Gaston said intently, leaving his surprised nose and putting his hands on her chill cheeks, raising her face and leaning close to look into her eyes in the poor light, "that thou shouldst consider thyself under my protection, when we met and wert afraid, and I . . . ." He did not say aloud what he had done, but she blinked, once, her eyes like stones set in marble looking into his: she knew, he knew. "By the Well," Gaston went on more softly, "that promise is still binding on me, so that I shall not leave thee here in a barren wood in winter, and I shall not carry thee back to the Palace, and I shall not tell any soul I have met thee if that's thy will. What I shall do is see thee safe, in good health, as happy as may be possible."

They regarded one another.

"I'm sick of this," Freia whispered at last, putting her hands on his and drawing them away, ducking her head again, "you don't understand, how . . . how it is . . . I'm just a husk. I'm not really alive. Not real at all. I want to die. Don't want it to go on."

"What makes it so bad, lass?" he asked, gently solicitous, cradling her cold hands in his warm palms.

"Everything . . ."

"Everything in Landuc," he suggested astutely.

She nodded. "Everything about me," she added.

"If th'art not in Landuc, 'twill be easier."

"He'll drag me back again," moaned Freia.

"Prospero. Perhaps not." Was it wise to tell her that her father thought she was dead already? "Thy father was sore troubled that thou wert nowhere found, lass. He tried to Summon thee, to bring thee to him, and failed, and feared thee beyond Summoning."

She covered her face.

"Whither didst go?"

"The sea," she whispered. "I pushed the boat in the water and rowed, until the tide took it, and I just . . . it was all grey, everywhere . . . fog and water . . . I put the oars in and I left the boat."

Gaston closed his eyes, O Blessed Well, and looked again. The salt, the sand, the seaweed, the sodden clothes— He stroked her coarsened, tangled hair. "Freia," he said, sadly, "what made thee do that?"

"Hurts." Freia's tight whisper creaked and broke into tears.

"What hurts so?" Josquin wasn't that bad, thought Gaston, pained by her pain.

"P-P-Prosp'ro," she wept. "You don' unders'and," she added.

Gaston did not. Prospero had been inscrutable of late; he had been plucking and sowing at a great rate and had had many affairs and plots ripening at once, among them his daughter's arranged match with Josquin; he had taken blows from several quarters and borne them stoically. Yet he'd seemed devoted to the girl, taking her part and attending her.

"You're too good, too good t'me," Freia hiccuped, and hugged him around his neck, as unexpected a favor as being hit on the nose.

Gaston patted her back. She felt cold yet, so he pulled a blanket up over her shoulders, holding it there as he held her to his breast. It pleased him that she did not flinch from him now: he had her trust for that, at least. "A man of much business, thy father," he murmured.

"He hates me," she said through tears. "D-d-doesn't want me. He . . . Hurts so much . . ."

Gaston couldn't presume to contradict her. Prospero had seemed, to his eldest brother, uncomfortable with the sudden acquisition of a son—although Dewar was clearly of his father's blood and uncannily like him—and that his daughter would discomfit him more deeply was all too likely. Particularly a daughter who had caused him to suffer heavy losses by being captured and used against him as Freia had. He must be fond of her, else he had not capitulated to free her; yet he might resent her and consider her an enemy partisan, though unwilling.

"I just want to die, I'm so sick of it, so sick of it, being everybody's anvil," Freia keened softly, "hurts so much, it hurts so . . ."

As when he had found her in the library, Gaston listened, murmuring, "Child, child, there, there," and wondered what he was supposed to do. Then, it had been obvious: now, it was less apparent, but he recognized that the girl was hardly able to do anything herself, and that he had assumed responsibility for her welfare by caring about it.

". . . just want it to stop," she sobbed raggedly.

"Lass, lass. What befell to hurt thee so? Canst tell me?"

"He said," she began, and broke off. "They said," she tried, and shook her head.

"Breathe deep."

Obediently, she did.

"Another." Gaston felt her ribs move in his arms. "Now then."

"It was them," she said, swallowing hard, "they started . . . Dewar and P-Prince Josquin. Dewar said . . . I should meet him, not so publicly . . . I agreed . . . he hadn't talked to me at all before . . . I didn't want him and . . . so Dewar said . . . we could meet, just the three of us, in my apartments."

Dewar had the instincts of a courtier, thought Gaston. "Aye," he said.

"My . . . my head hurt . . . I couldn't sleep all night . . . I was lying on the sofa and trying to rest when they came in, they were early, and I woke up, I didn't know I was really awake. They didn't see me, didn't know I was there. They talked about me . . ." Freia had stopped weeping, but the grief in her voice was deep and raw. "Prince Josquin . . . said . . . he thought I was . . . bad . . . he said because I'm plain-looking, and common as dirt, and stupid as wood, then he said I never say anything in company, and I can't do anything, and I drop things, and I'm awkward and . . . and stupid . . . I'm not clever," Freia whispered. "I know I'm not clever like all of you are. He said I have no taste in clothes and that his father . . . said I was a fool and a nuisance . . . and he said his father was getting him back for not wanting women."

Oh, Josquin, thought Gaston, horrified. The prancing ass. To speak thus to her brother—

She began crying again, catching her breath erratically. "Dewar said well, yes, I'm not . . . pretty, and he could've wished for a better sister having never met a woman in his life, and Josquin would have to make the best of me. . . . And he said, Prince Josquin said, he'd rather make the best of Dewar . . . and that he'd take me if he could have Dewar too . . . he s-said I'm c-common t-trash. . . . And Dewar laughed and said I'm wooden-headed. . . . I thought h-he l-l-liked m-m-me. . . . H-he s-said I'm beastly common . . . he s-said I'm m-made of dirt . . . other th-things . . . and the P-Prince . . . he t-told the P-Prince about G-Golias . . . he . . . he said he w-wouldn't . . . I'm not b-b-beautiful, and I'm not clever, and I don't know politics, and I can't do anything, and I don't know what to do with myself, I just w-want to go home and I can't, can't . . . it's gone. Prince Josquin said then why fuss about G-Golias . . . I couldn't move, I was so hurt and it . . . I wished I had a knife to let the pain out . . ."

Gaston pictured it perfectly. The girl, hazed with headache, half-awake and then horrified; the two young men flirting and gossiping a few feet away, uninhibited and frank. He knew they were attracted to one another; the effect Dewar had had on Josquin in the war-camp had been obvious, and though Dewar had veiled his own lust, he had given Josquin hot looks enough, keeping the Prince Heir fretting on edge. But Freia common? No. Were Prospero her father, and he'd sworn he was to his own harm, she could be of the basest mother-stock and still be rich enough in birth for Josquin or any Prince of Landuc—and nobler than her brother. To tell her future husband of the rape—Gaston was appalled—it was a cad's trick, knavish gossip.

"I never wanted to be better," Freia said, weeping harder, curling away from Gaston. "Don't want to be, I'm not a princess, told him so, I know I'm not, and I'm not a l-l-lady. . . . Dewar said something, I don't remember, and he said anyway, the marriage was an excuse to see Dewar. And he said they should have supper tonight. And Dewar said yes. I thought I'd be sick, I was so upset at what he said . . . what they said . . . he said . . . I was so ashamed . . . felt so, so bad. I don't know what I did . . . I got up. I stood up and they turned and looked at me, they were startled—"

Shocked to the heart, more likely, thought Gaston. Damned fools.

"—I couldn't speak, and then I said, You woke me, excuse me, and I ran out to find Papa. He couldn't know, he couldn't know how little . . . how hateful he'd be, that P-Prince. . . . I ran to his rooms and I ran in, and he was angry that I interrupted him; he—I did interrupt, he was talking to a lady in the bedchamber. I don't know what I was saying, I—I wanted to talk to him, I wanted him to tell me if it was true, if he made me like he made the others . . . dirt . . . stones . . . like Caliban . . . He was angry. He—he hit me and told me to leave and he would see me when he was ready, and I had no manners and . . . other things . . . He hit me," she repeated. "He hit me. He never hit me, ever, all the years . . . all the time . . . on the island . . . I loved him s-so m-m-much . . ." Her left hand cupped her cheek, covering the mark Prospero's hand had left.

Gaston was disgusted. No wonder the girl was miserable. A fine morning's work by all parties. If they had desired to drive her to her death surely there could not be a better way. Poor creature. He held her against him; she was on the verge of hysteria, and he made low hushing sounds and patted her back to calm her.

"Why?" Freia wailed, muffled in Gaston's shoulder. "I loved

him so, I loved him so, and he . . . he made me wither inside and I'm nothing. . . . Why did he tell him that . . . Why did Papa . . . I don't understand how someone who loved me so much could make me into so many pieces, and all of them hurt. . . ."

"Lass," said Gaston, "ah, lass. I do not know Prospero. I did long ago, but that was before he became what he is now. He changed, his sorcery hath changed him."

She shook with grief. Gaston rocked her and said nothing, thinking. He must get her out of Landuc entirely; his idea of bringing or sending her to Dewar would not serve. Since he had been riding to Montgard, he might as well take his niece with him. The place was quiet and healthful; the society was not demanding; there was no traffic from Landuc and no one would bother her there. Let Prospero and Dewar sit and study the wreckage a few crude words had caused. Now there would be more conflict, for Prospero had named the girl his heir and had renounced everything for himself, and there were treaties signed and sealed; Dewar had said he would not involve himself in such worldly matters. Yes, Prospero and Avril between them had set up a pretty house of cards, each trying to o'er-top the other's flimsy plans, and Gaston felt sadly vindicated: he had warned Avril it would be best to stay out of such entanglements, to refrain from rubbing Prospero's face in the muck.

It was out of the question that he should take Freia to Landuc again: she was too fragile, and he had promised not to do so. Get the child out of it, he thought, and let her recover her equilibrium; let her grow accustomed to the whole business, rather than shove it down her throat and kill her with it; let her be spared the sneering condescension of her relations; do all that, and Freia would make her own choices when she was ready.

"Thy arrival here was in good time," Prospero told his lover. "Wouldst agree to depart also?"

"Thou art minded to leave," Odile said, "and I have said I

would join thee on thy journey, an thou wouldst be companied."

"I'll have none an thou refuse. Perhaps 'twere better to thy liking to return to Aië, for I know thou hast but little power here, no resource but thyself."

"I find myself sufficient to the occasions that have arisen," Odile replied, smiling her slight, maddening smile, and she touched him invitingly.

He caught her hand, took it to his lips, and watched her over the smooth curve of her soft fingers. "I'd not uproot thee, madame, nor deprive thee of thy home. For where I go shall be as far again from there as is here, and worser journeying. The place is crude and without amenity, madame, and its habitants and habitations rustic. Mayhap 'twere little to thy liking, when the occasional novelty hath grown dull to thee."

"Nay, my love, I have thought long on this ere undertaking the journey," she said, "and I will travel with thee."

Prospero kissed her hand reverently. "I thank thee for thy grace," he said.

" 'Twere an ill homecoming for thee, to arrive alone and dwell alone," Odile said. "Thy bereavement will breed melancholy, an thou bide alone. I who have bided solitary for long years know this full well." Her look of tender concern was soft and wise.

Prospero took her other hand and kissed them both, his eyes closed. To go home alone, with nothing, to vacancy; nay, it was a bleak prospect. His throne, lost, and lost at great cost, in order to keep Freia alive long enough to destroy herself. His books, burned in the great fire; his daughter forever absent, and his ingrate son having plundered him, cozened his sorcery from him as he'd robbed Odile his mother— He put his face in Odile's hands and she smoothed and stroked his head, held him to her breast and offered lover's comforts.

Thus, in the dim hour before sunrise, two horses were harnessed to a phaeton by quick hands and a third saddled; and with a light whip-lash the phaeton, occupied by a well-muffled

lady, and the horse, whose rider was tall and grim-faced, trotted from the Palace swiftly, passed the Bounds without opposition, and left through a side-gate in the city walls.

Three blankets, two chemises, the woollen dressing-gown, and
Gaston's cloak were bundled around Freia. She wore three pair
of moth-eaten hose. The Fireduke had finished removing all
signs of use from the hunting lodge and saddled his horse as the
sun set in a livid stain of scarlet, guading the clouds and pur-
pling the evening sky. Now, after dark, by lantern-light and
milky stars, he set her on the folded blanket he had put before
Solario's saddle. Their breaths puffed white in the dry air. Gaston mounted behind her. Freia held the lantern. He took it
from her.

"Here, sit back toward me," said Gaston, "so, aye. Good.
Will that do?"

"Yes. I'm sorry—"

Gaston interrupted her. "If th'art uneasy in thy seat, say so."
He glanced around: nothing left behind save hoofprints and
bootprints, his only because he had carried her. It was unlikely
that they would be so unfortunate as to meet anyone. With a
nudge, Solario started away.

Freia held the blankets with one hand and clutched Gaston's
fingers with the other. His gloves were far too large, but he had
given her them anyway. He had one arm around her waist, his
other busy with lantern-pole and reins. She settled, half-leaning
on him, and when Gaston glanced down at her he could not see
her in the folds of cloak and blanket over her head.

The snow was dry and light, no hindrance to speed, and so
Gaston hurried with his passenger toward Montgard, trotting
Solario. They arrived at the megalith and passed onto the Road
meeting no one, which relieved him profoundly. Because he had
tarried a night at the lodge, he had missed a Gate that would
have shortened the journey he now must make. Gaston suspected he would need to stop at an inn to feed and warm Freia,
perhaps taking a room and sleeping awhile. Delays, delays—

unavoidable. He did not speak of time and detours to her. Prospero and the Emperor had called her a nuisance (and worse) more than once in his hearing, and in hers, and clearly she had begun to believe it.

Such a shame, he thought, an innocent, truly innocent, dragged through so much will-she, nill-she. And how she had gotten from the sea to the stone Gaston did not know, but he thought he would like to, and he suspected he never would. Some sorcerous business: the Moonstone had an aura of alienness to it, of sorcery. Gaston believed her when she said she did not remember what befell her after she stepped from wood to wave. She trusted him, had trusted him with other things already. She would have told him had she known.

So someone, somehow, had fished her out, poor lass, and dumped her to freeze in the forest rather than drown in the ocean. But why no better rescue? Why not bring her to safety and warmth? She had been near to dying, there in the wood. Had it been intended that she die anyway? An offering to the Moonstone, or to whatever it represented, he speculated, and hoped not. No sorcerers about who'd perform such deviltry: Prospero's sail was lately reefed, and he was her father anyway, and Dewar was, Gaston considered, not inclined to bloody perversions such as sister-slaughter. Breaking the girl's heart was another matter.

Freia shifted a little before him.

"Art well?" he asked her, leaving speculation.

She moved, a bob—yes, Gaston supposed. She pressed her fingers in his cavernous glove against his.

"If th'art cold, or ill, tell me," he reminded her.

Another pressure of fingers, a small movement of her whole body to lean more on him. The hazy, blended landscapes of the Road flowed by at Solario's steady, confident pace.

— *16* —

GASTON BROKE THEIR JOURNEY AT AN out-of-the-way Road junction which, to the best of his knowledge, nobody else used. The tavern nearest the place was rough and offered no luxury, but it had warm fires, hot soup, and a close-mouthed landlord who knew Gaston. A few words, a few coins, a less-desirable guest shuttled protesting into a less-desirable bed; and minutes after arriving, Freia could sit in front of a fire with mulled cider in a pewter tankard and a wooden bowl of pungent dark soup, watching bread-and-cheese toast on a fork her uncle held over the coals.

"Thank you," she said as he plopped the bread-and-cheese in the soup.

"Welcome. If th'art too warm I'll screen the fire."

"It's lovely," Freia said, stretching her feet toward the flames.

"Hast lost sense i' thy feet?"

"My toes hurt. They're blistering, like my fingers."

Gaston nodded. "Take care the blisters be not broken." A girl came in and made up the bed vigorously. Freia slowly ate two bowls of soup and sopping bread and nodded off at the fireside. Gaston picked her up and she woke, struggling, as he put her in the bed. She clawed for his eyes; he caught her wrists. "Freia, 'tis Gaston!"

"Oh . . ." Freia blinked at him. She relaxed all at once again.

"Th'art asleep, lass."

"Yes. Bad dream." Her eyes closed again and then opened with visible exertion. "You'll be here?"

He nodded.

"Cold," Freia said. "You're warm." Her eyes closed again, and Gaston comprehended: she wanted him beside her in bed again. He frowned at the idea. It smacked of seduction; yet there was no lust between them, and the tiny chamber was cold, save by the fire, the walls unplastered logs and the floorboards uncarpeted. Gaston left the soup plates on a table in the common hall where other patrons snored on benches, went to the stables to check on Solario, stopped at the latrines, and in the chamber again found Freia migrated far under the blankets, curled in a ball, shivering. He pulled off his boots and coat, spread his cloak over the bed, and climbed in with her.

"Cold . . . so cold . . ." The bed was sucking away what warmth she had.

"Hush, child." Gaston put her icy hands under his arms and hugged her bony body. He cursed himself for neglecting to get a warming-pan or some hot bricks.

Freia's teeth chattered. "So cold. Always so cold. Since I went looking for Papa. Cold. Shouldn't. Shouldn't."

"Hush, hush, lass; 'tis all gone by, cannot be undone."

"Wish it could. I wish it could," Freia said, and she cried a little before she slept.

In the morning they travelled along a Ley and turned onto the Road at a Gate which was an ancient, decayed arch, spanning the way, whose shadow fell hard and blue on a red road. Gaston nicked his thumb and left a drop of blood there at noon. He had purchased food at the tavern; they stopped once for an hour at a Gate and ate while waiting for its opening, a summery place where Freia basked and dozed in her wraps on a warm flat rock. There were no difficulties on the Road, and Solario brought them to Montgard just after sunset.

They trotted along a road toward a walled city whose curfew-bells were ringing, the flat distant sound floating over the hedged fields. Beside it and over it loomed a great fortress. The season was late autumn; the trees still clutched ragged leaves and the fields were stubbled and dark. A sliver of pinkish-gold moon adorned the indigo sky. Solario stepped higher and more briskly, snuffing the air of home.

"This is Montgard," Gaston said. "The land, and that city. The river is the Mont."

"You live here," Freia said, asking and stating.

"Sometimes. 'Tis broad; see the mountains." He gestured toward the mountains which loomed steeply to either side of them, for they rode in a wide, flat valley.

"Yes."

"Those also are Montgard. Formerly not; I've brought them under me. We go now to my castle, and thou'lt bide there. I must ride again to Landuc after some business. Shall return with the men I brought to war."

"Oh."

" 'Tis a pleasant place," Gaston assured her.

Freia's head nodded, her face invisible to him. "Dewar said Landuc was pleasant," she murmured.

Gaston pulled Solario up; they stopped at a triple-arched stone bridge.

"Freia. Th'art no prisoner, but a guest. An thou wouldst bide otherwheres, thither shall I convey thee, but cannot in this hour, this day. But I do swear to thee upon my honor: thou mayst move freely here, and mayst leave an thou wouldst, and I will help thee as I can. But first must I bring my men to their homes again."

Her voice lowered, she said, "I know. I don't have anywhere to go home to. I'm sorry."

He started to cluck at Solario again and stopped as the words and her tone turned again in his ear. "Lass, th'art welcome, full welcome. Th'art no burden, no weight to me nor my household. There'll be no such hostility here as hast found in the Palace. I promise thee, wilt be warmly met and kindly." Gaston paused, wishing he could see her face. "Dost believe me?" he asked.

She said, "I want to."

"Lass, have I lied to thee or misled thee, with words or silence?"

Freia thought about this, which dismayed Gaston, and her reply further disconcerted him. She turned and looked up at him in the blue evening light as she asked in a near-whisper, "Did you know Papa was coming back for me?"

"When . . ."

"When I was your prisoner before."

"Art no prisoner of mine nor anyone's now," he retorted, stung, and in a different tone he admitted, "I knew, aye—thou didst not know?"

"No. No one told me."

Gaston sighed heavily. He heard the veiled accusation, the hidden question she wouldn't put directly: was it all his fault, were Prospero's loss of power and her loss of liberty and peace all linked to him in the end? How could she trust him, considering what he had done to her loved father and that he had imprisoned her for the Emperor? "Lady Freia, I cannot say to thee, I deceived thee wittingly. Nor can I say to thee, I did not deceive thee. For I did not tell it thee, and I knew of't, and of the bargain. I knew it, and I would not have left thee ignorant: had I thought of't, I'd have thought thou knew it too already. Blame me an it comfort thee, but in my defense let me plead that I've spared thy father once and again from Avril's worst wrath, have walked a fine line 'twixt treason and literal loyalty, and I had liever thy father, my brother, live as he is now than that he were dead."

She said nothing, thinking about it, looking at him as closely as she could.

" 'Twas not malicious silence," Gaston went on after examining his conscience. "I swear, 'twas no intent of mine to harm thee through thy ignorance. An I have harmed thee, I crave thy pardon with all my heart."

"I didn't mean that—" Freia was distressed.

"Ah, but thou didst, for 'twas in thy question."

She looked down. "I'm sorry. You've been kind. I— You're the only person who's been—just good. Never mind it. I didn't mean that. I don't know what I meant. I'm sorry. Please let's go."

"I take no offense; hast said naught to sorrow at." He nudged Solario, and the horse walked over the bridge.

Gaston wondered who, in the end, would become the focus of her wrath, taking the blame for everything she had suffered— for sure as thunder followed lightning, she would be angry when she had recovered from outrage. Her father? Dewar?

Himself, despite—or because of—his help? Most likely it would be Avril. The Emperor had done nothing to make her love him; to him, the children were extensions of the father, to be abused (in Freia's case) or used (in Dewar's, save that Dewar had turned tables on the Emperor) as occasion permitted, and Prospero had doubtless long excoriated him in her hearing.

The many-towered city before them disappeared as they descended a small hill and reappeared when Solario trotted around a corner and crossed another stone bridge arching over a rocky brook racing toward the narrow river, which ran sinuously to and through the city. Gaston felt Freia lean more heavily against him. She must be sore weary, and he knew there must be pain in her frozen, now thawed, hands and feet.

"Not far at all," he said, looking ahead at the walls, a white barrier in the growing dark. Overhead, stars were brightening behind veils of grey-blue clouds. The air was thin and dry, an agreeable change after the dampness of Landuc.

The city gates were closed, but the watch opened them for Gaston; the city streets were quiet, but one or two men bowed as Gaston rode past toward the castle; his servants were not expecting him, but rallied at once with food, fire, and hot water; and, after a flurry of eating, warming, a soporific bath, and bruise- and frostbite-dressing, Freia dropped into a bright-painted cabinet bed and plummeted into a deep and dreamless sleep.

When he had refreshed himself, Gaston went to his niece's chamber to tell her that he would send a dressmaker in the morning. She was already asleep. He drew the lofty quilt over her shoulders, looked at her relaxed face for half a minute, and then closed the bed's latticework doors.

This was what she needed, he thought. Good food, quiet rest, change of place. He had done right.

"My lord, what is it?" asked Odile from the phaeton, for Prospero had reined Hurricane in on the crest of a low hill and sat staring.

"The city," he said. Argylle plainly had had some difficulties in Prospero's absence, and there were more concealed beneath the visible damages.

"It is not large," she agreed.

"Not large! Why, a third's gone, madame, and the river runs broader than e'er I've seen it in any season! The bank's gone, I cannot— Let us make haste, madame."

Indeed the river had risen. It had flowed out of its banks, not so widely on the near side as on the far, and buildings, store-houses, and walls were simply vanished beneath a sheet of water. That the water had been higher became clear as they descended to a mud-plain below; that it had receded as far as it would was opined by Utrachet when Prospero found him in a house newly set upon the waterfront that had been some hundred strides from it before. Mud and water-marks on the wall showed the river's course.

". . . but it has not fallen more, Lord, and it is silted, too, shallower I think. We are sounding it, I supposed you would want that done, but the channel is gone and we cannot sail the great ships up here without stranding them, so they are down at Wyemouth, at Ollol's shipyard's cove. The ones that survived."

"How did it happen?" Prospero asked. They stood now at the edge of the river, Odile a little apart with a perfumed kerchief over her face against the stink of decay that hung over the floodplain.

" 'Twas all at once, Lord. It— the Spring— I will tell you of the river first. It was at night, Lord, and I was on the island in the tower you made. I was asleep, as were all here, and that was how so many died, Lord, for the water came down under the full moon in a wall—there is a woman who saw it, she was awake that night."

"From the sea—"

"No, Lord, from everywhere, all swelling up and lifting, then rolling down, from upstream in the forest. I woke at the thunder of the water, and I looked out and saw it crash onto the banks and strike at the city . . . I saw the houses go under the wave like wood-chips, houses where people lay . . . I saw folk and animals running from the edge, and some escaped and some were caught by the water as it rose in a great swell, and it ate the land and felled the walls and devoured the bridgeworks and knocked away the storehouses yonder as they had been leaves. It was a terrible sight, and the sound was so deep that the tower and the earth trembled.

"I watched, and as I watched I felt the tower shake more beneath me, though the water had not come near to it, and Scudamor came running to me to say that below—from below water was coming up, a fountain. But it was strange water, not—not wet. It was not drowning anyone, Lord. I cannot describe it—"

"The Spring," Prospero said.

"We thought so, Lord. It had risen up like the river, though why I do not know, for it is autumn and there were no great rains. The Spring went up and up, like a fountain, Lord, as it did the night you—before you left here, and then it fell back and we all fell down with its going, dizzy and weak and ill, every one of us. And it was long before I could stand again, and when I could I helped Scudamor to stand and we went again to the window and looked out, and the river's wall of water had left the city much as you see it, and water lay on the fields.

"We have been trying to clean up," he added apologetically.

Prospero nodded. The damage was greater than his first glance had shown. The missing storehouses had been where the harvest had been kept, food for the winter, and the river appeared to have swept away all of them from the far bank.

"It is curious about the islands," Utrachet went on after a brief silence. "One would have thought they too would be washed away, but instead the tower's isle is even extended, and the others have come back a little larger."

"They are stone, not soil," Prospero said, "and 'twould be more than water that washed them away."

The water had left a thick coating of earth behind it. The riverbanks were smooth as if planed, a wall-fragment jutting from the ground here or there, fallen from the flood or having withstood it.

"How many ships survived? Did the wave flow to the shipyards?" Prospero asked, his eyes on the vacant space where the storehouses had been.

Utrachet replied softly, "Three, Lord, and all are damaged."

Three ships, of more than a hundred.

"Ollol's and the other shipyards are . . . There is not much more left of them than that," Utrachet said, gesturing at the far bank. "Lord, I am sorry."

Prospero snorted. "Were you to stand against the water and hold it back? Pah. Thy apology's folly as great as resistance were."

Someone shouted "My Lord!" and Prospero turned.

"Scudamor," he said, pushing his mouth to smile.

"My Lord! Lady Freia, welcome—ah, madame—" Scudamor skidded to a stop, halted in mid-greeting as Odile turned and looked icily at him.

"Freia is dead," Prospero said emotionlessly.

He watched the news reach them. Utrachet swayed and closed his eyes for an instant. Scudamor's mouth hung soundlessly open.

"Hath Dewar come here?" Prospero asked, to force motion on them again.

"Nay, Lord," whispered Scudamor.

"An he be seen, let me be informed in the very instant," Prospero said, "he hath spurned me and broken his word, taken what he could and may return to plunder more."

"Aye, Lord," Scudamor said after a few seconds.

"This lady is the Countess Odile of Aië, who shall bide here with me. Her will is mine. Let all be told."

Scudamor and Utrachet glanced at one another and nodded. "Aye, Lord," Scudamor said.

"Lord," Utrachet said, "if you would care to see the woman who saw the waters coming down the river, she is easily found. Her account of it is better than mine."

Prospero considered it, nodded. " 'Tis plain it was no natural flood," he said, "and I would question her nearly on it. Let her come to the tower."

"Within the hour, Lord," Utrachet said. "I will bring her myself."

"Go then."

Utrachet bowed and went up across the mud toward the remaining houses.

"My Lord, m— Countess, I will row you to the isle, if you would cross," Scudamor said. "It is a rough boat—the good ones are gone."

"I'm not surprised," Prospero said. "We'll cross."

The river was wider than it had been, and the water was churning brown; snags stuck out of the water close to the shore. Prospero made a quick excuse to Odile when he had handed her out of the flat-bottomed rowboat, and he told Scudamor to conduct her to an apartment beside Prospero's own, that would have housed his daughter. The straight-sided tower had taken no damage at all; it stood tall and clean and proud as it had on the morning of its first day, watching over the city, the river, the isle, and the Spring.

Prospero took a lantern and a few candles and hurried down.

The stairs were fine-grained black stone, the risers high, the treads wide. They spiralled dizzyingly; there was no counting the turnings. The ceiling, an arm's-length over Prospero's head, seemed oppressively close. His light was nearly superfluous, for once his feet had learned the rhythm of the steps he need not look.

He had only ascended here, never descended; and then he'd been half-carried by Freia, who had stumbled and paused every dozen steps until he understood that she was holding him up, half-lying across her back and shoulders. He'd insisted on supporting himself, hindering both of them. It had taken them a quarter of the day to come out of the darkness, from the sunken Spring to the bright door where faithful Scudamor and Utrachet had peered and waited.

It seemed more oppressively close than he recalled, and he could not feel the Spring's power seeping upward. Prospero loped three steps at a time, perilously fast in the turning spiralling darkness, and at the bottom there was the arched opening as it had been, letting onto black nothing.

He stood, listening.

Not a sound met his ears. Not a draft stirred the darkness, Caliban's great labor now to be of no use to Prospero. The place was dead air, not living as Prospero had intended it to be; a hollow corpse, untenanted.

The light of the lantern's flame was lost in the dark. All it showed him was that beneath his feet lay stone. Prospero tried to find the Spring with his senses and failed: either it eluded him or it was gone. How different it was from the hours after his great sacrifice, when the place had teemed with life's essence!

He walked with small, careful steps in what he thought was the right direction. Another pillar. No. He turned and went back, tried again.

His foot nearly went into the hole before he caught himself. Prospero leapt back, the light almost extinguishing itself as he brandished it, and stared at the place where the Spring had been.

A vacant cavity was sunk in the floor, lifeless. He held his hand over it and concentrated. Was he deluding himself, or did it stir, but faintly? He could not be sure.

Something had happened, but what? Had Dewar come and done some mischief? But they had said he'd not been about the place. Yet the drowning, or near-drowning, of the city—

Drowning. Prospero nodded. "Not Dewar, but Freia," he whispered to the hole. "For I had assigned the place to her; 'twas she who was the ruler, but for a few days. She drowned: Argylle drowns. Water leaving death behind it. Aye."

The silence answered nothing.

The harvest swept away by the waters was—

Prospero ground his teeth. Had he guessed this might be the result, he'd have undone his gift to Freia, passed the place to his son, who was suited to rule it far better than Freia; to match her nature to the Spring's had been a risk. Yet it was just as well not, perhaps; Dewar had shown his true self in fleeing Landuc. He was a sorcerer first.

He turned on his heel and left the dry Spring. As long as some little flow continued, the place would survive. Indeed Argylle was now in a similar position to Landuc, whose Well had been dark since Panurgus had made a pyre of it for himself, whose ruler was as incapable of sorcery from ignorance as Argylle's was from his vow. And Landuc persisted. Argylle would endure.

The Prince of Montgard had intended to be there only briefly, but he had been away nearly three years and had much to review. He spent sixteen days on the most urgent business, reading letters and reviewing accounts from his stewards and retainers, by and large approving what they had done. He did not appoint cheats, liars, or fools; Gaston's sense of justice required that all, great and small, be treated equally, and if he did punish harshly, the punishment would be the same be the offender a serf of one of his estates or the Lord Mayor of Montgard.

The delay gave him time to assure himself that he had done right by Freia—for he had felt a qualm that he ought to have taken her back to her father—and to observe improvement in her health. She slept two days, waking a few times to eat ravenously and then relapsing into exhausted slumber. A maid stayed by her, sewing and watching, and brought her food when she wanted it. Another few days saw Freia being measured, passively doll-like, for clothing and shoes and other necessities, fussed over by Mistress Witham the housekeeper. Her feet and hands, though blistered, were not severely frostbitten, her face patched and peeled; but she mended rapidly, without complications or complaint. Gaston observed to himself that the Well must have shielded her from the worst, though she had not yet passed its fire. He had seen men lose limbs after such exposure.

When she was able to rise, and when she was not required by

seamstresses and cobblers, Freia kept close to Gaston, saying little, nearly invisible in her stillness. If he worked in his office, she would sit wrapped in a shawl in a chair near the fire or a sunny window, her hand cupped protectively over the sallow bruise on her cheek, looking at books from his collection; if he walked on his walls, Gaston took her with him and showed her the town, or they might walk in the castle garden and look at espaliered fruit trees and the pleached arbor, now bare, and the fountain whose water was shut off for the winter. The castle garden was functional, herbs and vegetables pragmatically arranged with little art, but the weather was mild, and the Fire-duke was pleased to divert his sad, dull-eyed guest by strolling the gravelled and planked paths with her and teaching her the names and descriptions of the plants and furnishings.

Though Freia lunched and dined alone, since Gaston had much to do in the way of social and business eating, after his guests had gone he would sit with her in the solar where she would be looking into another incomprehensible book or staring at the coals and seeing other things in their place. Silent but companionable, Gaston would read missives from his deputies and reports from various eyes and ears he kept open, and he would talk if she wanted to talk, though he did not force conversation on her.

"Uncle?" Freia's voice chimed diffidently into an account of a sordid cheating of one landowner by another.

"Lass," Gaston said, after realizing she meant him: he was the only other person there. Josquin seldom called him uncle.

"Papa never told me— Why are the seasons different in different places?"

"Because," he said, "they are different places."

Freia, who sat across the fire from him, wrinkled her forehead. "I thought—" she began, and stopped, and tried again. "It seemed to me that—Papa showed me once—that it was all a—a sort of a—well, a globe— We did not go *very* far. . . ."

Gaston pursed his lips and pondered. "I'm no sorcerer nor a scholar of such matters. Maybe 'tis. But Montgard lieth on its globe, as Landuc hath its too, and so the other places. Together all are Pheyarcet. In travelling, 'tis not distance, but direction, that brings thee here or there."

Freia gazed at him, clearly trying to picture something Gaston had never thought of visualizing: all the worlds, all at once, together. It wasn't possible, he thought.

"Dewar had a Map," she said finally.

"Ah," Gaston said. "The Map shows places in relation to each other and the Well, by the Well. 'Tis no picture of the shape of the lands; 'tis a geomantic tool, not geographic."

"Then—it's not that—that someone from Landuc could—sail here."

"Nay, but 'a could, had 'a drunk of the Well and knew where the Leys and Gates and Road lay. There are Gates and Leys just as on land, and my father warded them as well. Fulgens hath made such journeys; so hath thy father, so have I. He knows the colors of the water and the ways it moves and changes, and he can read it as thou seest the lie of the earth around thee."

Freia nodded.

"But he must travel the Road to come here."

"Leys . . . ?"

"Leys do not pass 'tween spheres as doth the Road. There is a Ley from this city up to a village, in the mountains and beyond, which I use to go from here to Montjoie in short time and distance. But to ride to Landuc I must use the Road, and to find the Road I must use the Gate, and that Gate lets on many Roads, yet all are one." Prospero had kept the girl damnably ignorant; it was no wonder she had fallen foul of Ottaviano and Golias in Landuc. She'd no means to elude them.

Freia had been linking her fingers together as if playing some child's game. "I think I see. It's like nesting eggshells."

"Aye, so. Yet all the eggshells the same size. Or maybe not. I cannot swear to't," Gaston said, wondering if he had explained anything, "some larger, some smaller, some more distant than others."

Freia nodded slowly. "And sometimes they touch."

"And 'tis the Road, those places where they touch. 'Tis not always in truth a clear path."

"And the places we don't stop we see—"

"Veiled one o'er the other, dimly seen spheres, yes. A good likening, lass."

"I'm getting it all wrong." She shook her head.

Freia's uncle smiled, shaking his head too. No knowing what kind of image she had in her mind now. "Why, it sounds right enough to me."

"How many spheres are there?"

"None knows, none whom I know of," Gaston said. "Perhaps my father did."

"I'm sorry to plague you with foolish questions—"

"Nay, they are sound questions. 'Tis shame to me I'm not the man to answer them best, no scholar but a soldier, I. Thy father or brother could tell thee more, and tell't well. I'll fetch my Map anon, and thou mayst try me again."

Freia drew up her feet in the chair and looked again into a book Gaston had given her, an illuminated history in Tallamont, the language of Montgard and its provinces. He watched her for a moment.

"When I fare again to Landuc," Gaston said, "I thought 'twere of benefit to thee an I brought thee other books, that thou mightst better learn that tongue."

Freia shrugged. "I can read. Papa taught me. He said I would understand perfectly once I stood the test of fire," she said to the book.

" 'Tis true. Spoken language. Not written."

"Why?"

" 'Tis the nature of the Well," Gaston said, and smiled wryly. "Alas, thou needest a more sorcerously-grounded tutor."

"Don't—" Freia glanced up with alarm.

Gaston held up a hand. "I'll not reveal th'art here." She expected betrayal, he realized. She did not trust his promise of secrecy. She did not really believe anything anyone said, including Gaston. This pained him. He could not take it as a personal slight, but he desired to cleanse the stain of his brothers' and nephews' cruelty and faithlessness from her image of him.

A meal had been set for Prospero in his new rooms in the tower, and a bath readied and fresh clothing laid out. Prospero sighed and sat down on the bed for a moment. Food. There would be scant food this winter, in all likelihood. He must address that first, and fast.

A light rap came at the door. Odile, he hoped, and he called "Enter."

Not Odile, but Scudamor. "Lord Prospero—"

"Scudamor; good. I would have sent for thee. Here's a task, most urgent, that must be completed within this day: let a door be shaped, of two thicknesses of wood, and set in the opening of the top of the black stairs that lead downward; let it be fitted with a lock, and I shall have the key in my hand by sundown. And ever, as ever, two men to guard the door."

"It shall be done, Lord. If you will see the woman who saw the river rise, Lord, she is here, or she will bide till later."

Prospero stood, nodded. "I'll see her now, perhaps again later. Let her come in."

The Seneschal smiled and bowed again, turned away and beckoned; a woman came in past him. "Are there further commands, Lord?" Scudamor asked.

Prospero was staring at his guest, who was regarding him with serene brown eyes. "Nay," he said. "Go."

Scudamor closed the door.

"You called me, Lord Prospero," the woman said.

"How art thou called?" he asked, nearly whispering.

"Cledie Mulhoun, Lord Prospero. I do remember you." And she smiled as she had in the first light of the sun that morning beside the Spring, when he had shaped her last and best of all his folk. He had but glimpsed her since. Her shimmering hair was long, drawn back and braided, and she wore the simple tunic most Argyllines preferred, dyed bright yellow, draped to leave a breast bare and pinned at her waist with a bone brooch.

"And I remember thee, and well. Long years have passed." He had never known her name before. Cledie. It echoed in his ear with an uncertain familiarity. Cledie.

She nodded. Her smile was gone, but she was still beautiful, perfect and still.

"Where hast thou kept thyself? I have scarcely seen thee since that day, and I inquired for thee. Wherefore hast thou now returned?"

"I thought I might be needed, Lord Prospero," Cledie said.

Prospero could not take his eyes from hers. "I—"

A light tap at the door preceded its opening: Odile entered. Cledie turned, and the two looked at one another, Odile cool, the Argylle woman cooler and seeming faintly amused. Cledie looked back to Prospero, and amusement danced still on her features. "Indeed," she said, "if the Lady did not mention that we had become friends, it was to surprise you with what she thought would be welcome news. I am grieved to learn she is lost to us. I longed to see her again."

"She said naught of it," Prospero said, damning Freia in his thoughts, tight-lipped wench. "Tell me of the flood, Cledie."

"There's little to tell. I was wakeful, and I had gone to the roof to be cooler in the moonlight and breeze. But no breeze was there, and I heard thunder. I looked to see if lightning played in the hills, as it does in the heat, and I saw instead the movement of the water, dark in the light of the moon. It gathered itself up from the riverbed and more surged in behind it, until it mountained up, rushing forward at the same time with a rumble that moved the house around me. I was in Voulouy's house," she explained. "I saw the waters rolling over the city, and it so horrified me I could make no sound. I desired to fly, but fear held me fast, and I saw the mighty wave pass down through the city, tearing away houses and riverside, and onward to Ollol's and the sea. Behind the wave the waters were higher; they rolled over the banks and flowed over the city high and deep, and the rest of it surely Scudamor has told you, Lord

Prospero." She shook her head. "I would forget that hour, if I could," she said.

"It came all at once, then."

"Yes."

"There was but one wave."

"Yes, the single great one, and thenafter it was as when the river is high with rain or snow: much water, but not in a wall."

A single blow sweeping through, altering the place. Prospero nodded.

Odile was watching, dark by the door. Prospero glanced at her and then at Cledie. "Thy account's of some help to me, and I thank thee for thy words."

"A sorry gift to give you, Lord, to welcome you. I shall be here, or near, if you need further words of me." She smiled slightly at him, ignoring Odile, and opened the door and left, her step quiet.

Odile closed the door. "Who was that?"

"An Argylline," Prospero said, "that I met once, that knew my daughter well, she said."

"But your daughter did not mention her?"

"Nay," said Prospero, and poured wine for himself and drank it all in a swallow.

Gaston brought Freia the promised books from Landuc when he led his army of Montgard on the long march home from their snowy bivouac. They were glad to return; they had suffered fewer casualties than anyone had expected and they had been paid well for not doing much, by their standards. Their packs were heavy and their pockets light; most had already spent part of their wages on exotic luxuries and on mundane goods more cheaply had in Landuc than Montgard.

The Fireduke had his trusted Captain Jolly purchase the books, and by proxy thus also acquired a golden brooch, formed as a flowering and fruited apple-bough, and a new cloak of fine Ascolet wool for his niece. The brooch had caught the Prince's eye in the window of a goldsmith, beside the shop of a swordsmith whom he patronized for daggers and knives.

After sending Jolly after it, Gaston had felt odd about the gift. He had never given his sisters such trinkets or indeed any particular presents; the impulsive giving of lavish, inventive gifts had been one of Prospero's habits, long ago before Panurgus banished him. However, he thought it would please Freia. She liked the castle garden, found the espaliered fruit trees there both fascinating and unnatural. The brooch was handsomely made; it looked well closing the cloak. So he pinned it on the green- and fawn-flecked brown wool, had his squire pack up the cloak, and determinedly thought no more of it.

At the Palace, when he inquired offhandedly when his nephew Josquin would be wed, the Fireduke was given to understand that the bride was presumed dead.

"Prospero said the sea had her, and he would leave it at that," the Empress told her brother-in-law. They strolled along an exterior gallery, a pleasant place for late-winter perambulation with its southern exposure and for private conversation in any season.

"And there shall be no tomb?" The omission was more than discourtesy or insult; it was blasphemy. The girl was Prospero's own, Panurgus's blood through him, entitled to a place near the Well though her body be lost to the sea.

"That is all he said. He made no arrangements. Prince Gaston," the Empress lowered her voice, "you did not meet this Countess Odile. . . ."

"I did not." Something Dewar had once said, and the way he had said it, about Odile came to Gaston's mind, and his hands prickled. From Princess Evote, he had learned that Dewar had fled the Palace the night of his sister's drowning, the same day Countess Odile had arrived. The events could be interpreted a dozen ways.

"A gracious lady," the Empress said, "but—different."

"A sorceress," Gaston said.

"Well. They are never less than—different," the Empress agreed. She changed the subject. "Jos is gone out to Madana."

"Aye, Admiral Bolete sailed with him aboard, Viola told me." Viola had emphasized that the Prince Heir had incurred Imperial disfavor for neglecting to inform his father before leaving.

"Yes. So much has happened in just the few days you were gone. That poor foolish girl. Perhaps it is just as well. I do not know what we were supposed to do for her, Marshal, that was not done—"

"The failure," Gaston said, stopping at the red balustrade and gazing across at the bulk of the New South Wing of the Palace, "was ours, not hers." Absently, he studied the ornately carved pediment, the high, elegant windows of the ballroom, the patterned terraces, the gilded flames that adorned the roof. He had never liked the overwrought, unbalanced effect of the decorations on adornments on embellishments; Panurgus had erected it for Queen Anemone. Against the dingy snow, the building glared.

The Empress said nothing.

"We, all of us," said Gaston, turning from the Palace and looking at the Empress instead—altogether a pleasanter sight— "are answerable for all, from her abduction onward; for any could have, had he chosen, exerted him for her benefit. What you've said is of a piece with the rest of't: that all that could be done for her, was done; 'twas not. She was not protected. She was ill-treated; I've heard her mocked, then and now. She presented us no demands nor benefits of association, and we offered her naught because there was naught to be got from her. We of the Well pride ourselves on our power to shape the world to our requirements. All becomes what we would make it, and her we made nothing."

"You are very harsh on us," the Empress said stiffly.

"I include myself," Gaston said. "Do you truly believe you did all needful?" He thought of Freia in the Palace: absent from meals, ignored by the servants, rudderless in her father's stormy wake. He had not noticed either. She had been hungry, a Prince's daughter in the Emperor's Palace, and cold, a stone's throw from the Well, and he had not noticed, nor had anyone else. It ought to be a scandal.

"Obviously, you believe I did not. I admit the possibility of a lapse, although I made many attempts to bring her out. She was a sullen child; her own father said so."

"Perhaps bringing-out was not needed," Gaston said. "I fault you not, Your Majesty. You've lived all your days in Court. 'Twere unreasonable to expect you to be other than what that life hath made you."

"Prince Gaston, I do not know which I find more aggravating: your arrogance or your condescension," the Empress said. "You censure us for lacking something, and then say that we cannot but lack—"

"Perhaps I should not include you, then," Gaston said, "and limit my judgement to my siblings and peers."

"There you are again. There is not another man in Landuc as lofty as you, Fireduke."

He looked down at her; he was taller than she by the length of his forearm. "I hope that is not so, Your Majesty," he said. Nothing would come of it, he thought; there was no reason to find fault now.

Glencora stared up at him, perplexed as to what her response should be. Gaston held her gaze a moment, his attention elsewhere, and then, counter to protocol, began walking along the marble once more, leaving the Empress to lag a few steps.

Gaston dined only once at the Palace, and he observed then that the Emperor was in a perpetual foul temper and that almost everyone was out of favor, including himself. Late winter storms were taking a heavy toll on the fleet and the countryside; diplomatic problems from every quarter of the wind were keeping Pallgrave and Baron Broul at one another's throats with conflicting counsel and solutions; Josquin had gone to Madana without craving permission, which the Emperor would have been minded to deny; and, despite the subjugation of Prospero, the Well's fire remained withdrawn and the coming New Year looked to be colder and wetter than usual. After Gaston dined with him, the Emperor desired the Prince Marshal to remain in Landuc. The Prince Marshal excused himself with a reference to the cost of maintaining the Montgard levies away from home, for so long, at such steep wages, and inquired whether Prince Herne were deemed in any way inadequate. Prince Herne, at the same table and in earshot, glowered. The Emperor ceded the point ungraciously, seeing that Gaston meant to leave and desiring to avoid both the indignity of losing an argument and the necessity of appeasing Prince Herne.

The Fireduke bought his niece the cloak and the brooch and hastened back to Montgard as swiftly as his men could march along the Road.

Freia tended toward solitariness. Her habits were silence, introspection or a kind of glazed emptiness that was neither inward nor outward, quick tense movements, and dislike of attention; she would sit in reverie for an hour together, right hand cradling left cheek. Her uncle understood enough of human nature to guess that whether or not they had been in her character before she came to Landuc, in Landuc these things had become ingrained as part of her desire not to be there, and now, as the snows of winter flew through Montgard, they were in danger of setting permanently and shaping her forever into a ghost.

With the excuse of teaching her the language of Montgard, he was able to make her talk to him each day, or to read aloud as they sat before a fire while the wind outside drove bad weather down the valley to pasture. He had thought of getting her another tutor, but she was shy of strangers, barely speaking to even the household servants whom she saw every day. It would not do to force her; he supposed she would open in her own season. Besides, Gaston took pleasure in teaching her to make letters with a pen, to read the different scripts used around the area, and to compose in the forms adhered to for correspondence.

Mistress Witham did not quite approve of a woman being

taught reading and writing, but Gaston's niece was exceptional and the housekeeper kept her mutters belowstairs, where Captain Jolly heard them and repeated them with amusement to the Prince. Curiously, there were (in Jolly's hearing anyway) no debates on how the Prince, who had never shown family to Montgard in all the years he had lived there, had suddenly acquired a niece. Gaston had feared a little that the appellation might be made a synonym for "concubine," but this never happened. Freia's physical frailty and timidity were noted, Jolly reported, and it was generally taken that Gaston had removed her from some unfit guardian who had ill-used her.

Gaston never mentioned the truth of the matter, and the fragments of it known to the men who had been in Landuc were sufficient to pad out the story and make Freia a figure of deferential interest and mysteriously romantic provenance. The Prince's reticence, moreover, forestalled direct inquiry, and there it rested: his niece lived with him in the castle and watched the garden fill with snow when she was not bent over her letters or reading slowly from books or her slate to her attentive uncle.

Freia learned quickly; she heard words once and remembered them, and her ear distinguished between the accents of Gaston's servants, Montgard's merchants, and the knights and landsmen who came to the house. Gaston praised her aptitude when he realized how far she had gone by midwinter.

"It's nothing but parrotry," she said, shrugging, making little marks with her chalk. "Surely anyone can learn fast when it's all he hears."

"Most take longer."

Freia began to say something, and stopped herself and lowered her head instead. The sunlight falling from the solar's small-paned windows sparked in her hair. She wore it in two beribboned braids, the local style for unwed maids. It made her look very young.

"I've a new book for thee," Gaston said, changing the subject and taking the book from the drawer beside him. " 'Tis from Sir Blanont's library. I recalled he had it and borrowed it." As he spoke, he capped the ink-bottles and put his pen aside. Freia watched him set the book on the cleared desk: a thick red-leather-bound manuscript, triply clasped. Gaston unfastened the clasps and gently opened the book.

"Flowers?" Freia said.

"An excellent herbal, with another book bound in on husbandry and farming. But this first hath many plants. 'Tis a famous work, by the bye; I've Bonlest's own copy at Montjoie," Gaston added, and told her about the surgeon Bonlest who had made the book two centuries before at the Prince's commissioning, an herbal of all the plants in Montgard and nearby.

"Papa had books about flowers," Freia said, the light in her face fading. "He used to let me look at them. I liked them. They were pretty books. From all the worlds, he said, and they told all about all the plants. He burnt them with his other ones. But they weren't sorcery. He burnt all the books."

Gaston paused; he could think of nothing to reply to this. " 'Tis arranged seasonally," he said, passing over black close-written text of dubious medical value. "Here, the plants of spring. Hm, 'tis not so fair-made as mine. This is an astel."

"Astel," Freia said, softly, experimentally.

"That's also a maid's name."

She nodded and wrote the word down on her slate. Astel.

" 'She bloometh in the snow,' " Gaston read in an undertone, " 'and the root is of good nourishment ere much foliage appeareth. . . .' Do thou read. 'Tis ill-written and some words will be new, but practice is good for thee."

Freia peered at the text and began reading haltingly. Gaston listened and corrected her sometimes, praised her as often, and helped her discern the words.

Page by page, spring went in review before them in the thin warmth of the midwinter sun.

— 17 —

THERE ARE FEW CHOICES OPEN TO a person believed dead, no matter how powerful or insignificant one is. All of them sum to one of two ends: to continue as dead, cut off from those living, be they loathed or beloved, who are familiar with one's countenance and manner; or to reveal the optimistic or embarrassing error, either as soon as the error is apparent or later at one's leisure, perhaps after other business more conveniently accomplished dead than alive is brought to fruition. Allowing oneself the luxury of attending one's own funeral and revealing oneself there is stressful for loved ones and enemies alike; the latter may seize the moment and attempt to rectify one's condition to conform with popular report. On one's reappearance, no matter when it occurs, one's friends assume the uncomfortable onus of having to return small keepsakes from among one's belongings and are burdened further by uncertainty as to whether their eulogies or jeremiads on one's departed, now revenant, character will find their way to one's ear.

If one is believed dead as a result of a suicide attempt, the situation becomes more complex, because one has clearly, if ineptly, expressed a preference for a state, and one has not quite succeeded in attaining it. This is why it is best not to leave a note.

If one's suicide attempt was, rather than a cri de coeur for succor in one's darkest straits, a determined and wholehearted act of sincere self-hatred, one is faced, on failure of the suicide, with all one's former problems again, as well as with the difficulty of being supposed dead.

Some are enlightened by their near-death ventures and go on to accomplish feats hitherto beyond their abilities; others are weighed by a further sense of failure and incompetence. Some of the latter make sure of success and have another go at death, and others lose their taste for death as well as for life and endure in a state partaking of both.

The Fireduke's niece was burdened, in her continued life, by a feeling that she was not allowed to try death again. She had done her best and had distinctly felt certain that she had perished, yet somehow she had not, and now the life that animated her felt borrowed and ill-fitting, remote from her own desires. She had been kept among the living by heroic and selfless efforts by someone whom she did not entirely trust and for whom she felt neither liking nor disliking. She did not know how it was that Gaston had found her and revived her, but he had done so, with the kindest intentions. She was now obligated by the generosity shown her. Like the food she had been served at the Emperor's table, it was not at all to her taste, yet taste she must, and chew, and swallow, and digest the stuff and live on it, no matter how it stuck in her throat and roiled in her bowels.

Unpalatable though the thought of it may be, the most unwelcome of viands or the most unwanted of lives may, by dint of great effort, be made more attractive to the reluctant recipient when a knowledgeable and benevolent hand seasons either.

Thus Prince Gaston chivvied Freia gently, coaxed her with outings and books, and tried to teach her draughts. She was very bad at draughts, but better at other stormy-day games, and he allowed her full liberty to ride and roam. He improved her seat on horseback and presented her with a gentle white-socked mare and maps and directions, trying to assure her that she was no prisoner. He taught her the use of his Map of Pheyarcet and its companion Ephemeris and let her pore through them trying to find her home, but she found nothing that seemed right and nowhere she wanted to go.

The Countess of Lys, on the morning after her lying-in, dictated three letters to her clerk. The first was to the Baron of Ascolet, who had ridden to Ascolet some sixteen days previously to go round the wool-markets and see his people after waiting out most of the pregnancy within an arm's length of his wife. The second was to the Emperor Avril, and the third was to Lord Gonzalo of Valgalant.

In the afternoon she composed an additional letter to the Empress Glencora, and all the letters were much the same. The Countess of Lys had been lightened of a healthy girl-child, on the night of the New Harvesters' Moon. The girl would be presented at the Shrine of Stars in Champlys and named Cambia on the next suitable naming-day.

Here the letters differed: for Luneté said nothing more to her Emperor; suggested to her husband the Baron of Ascolet that he might exert himself to be there for the infant's presentation and naming; begged of the Empress her understanding for Luneté's keeping the event secret until it had occurred and begged also any advice the Empress might care to send, particularly regarding the child's status in the Imperial family; and of Lord Gonzalo of Valgalant Luneté requested that he might visit her, as he had promised to do, so that she might take counsel with him regarding this and other matters.

After sealing the letters, Luneté lay back in her bed with her hands on her newly-emptied stomach. Her breasts seemed to have become even larger and heavier, annoying her. She had gained flesh while carrying the child; she had no desire to run to flab and fat as some did on bearing. Now that it was done, she could eat like a woman instead of a sow and look like a woman again. "Laudine," she said after a moment.

"My lady." Laudine, seated beneath the window, looked up from her stitching on something small and white.

"I shall have some new clothes from the goods we brought from the City. Cut in the new fashion. A riding-habit laced like Lady Quarfall's that her maid showed you; for I shall travel around Lys this autumn. I must see how Lys fares after such a bad year as this has been—though Otto claimed we have had the fairest weather of all the Empire, still it has been most foully wet, and I have perforce been neglecting Lys."

"Yes, my lady," said Laudine. "Will you require a new gown for the presentation at the Shrine?"

"No—yes. Yes. In Lys's colors. Yes," Luneté said. "I am quite sick of dragging around in sacks and draperies. Let the wet-nurse finish those things for the child and start on the new gowns at once."

Through the winter, though Freia's command of the language improved and her physical debilitation was replaced by wan and listless health, she remained withdrawn and nervous. Gaston spared her the social life of Montgard; at this season it consisted largely of banquets, dances, and weddings, with regular sleighing- and skating-parties for outdoor exercise. In order not to offend the Montgard burghers, nobles, and their wives, he had Freia dine with him in select company, at home, several times. The invitees' sharp-eyed ladies saw for themselves that she was unwell, nearly an invalid, and exhortations to come dance or roister were superseded by tactful presents of preserves, fortifying cordials, and hot-house delicacies.

Freia found the summer fruit in midwinter astonishing and asked Gaston, with the first signs of liveliness he had seen in her, where it came from. He showed her, when they walked along the city walls, a glass-walled hot-house that might be glimpsed from there and, when they returned to his castle, drew a diagram of one upon her slate. He had no hot-house himself; to desire one had not occurred to him. For Gaston the seasons passed quickly enough that the presence or absence of strawberries or apricots was hardly noticeable. They went, they came again. If there were none, soon enough there would be.

"Didst thou not see the Palace hot-houses in Landuc?" he asked her. She had said she'd had a garden, once, and Gaston had gradually discovered that if any subject had the power to engage Freia's attention, gardening and plants did. He used this cautiously, conserving its strength, but truly in winter there were few chances to speak of gardens.

She shook her head, sniffing a strawberry. "A whole house made of glass," she said.

"Aye, with vents and stoves, that in warm days it may be cooled and in cold seasons heated; for the sun's strength is too little, in midwinter, to keep the tender plants alive. But perhaps thou hast used a bell in thy garden."

She had not, and Gaston bade her fetch her cloak and took her to a gardeners' outbuilding, where he showed her the glass bells. He took one outside, into the sun, and set it on a bench for some few minutes, then bade Freia put her ungloved hand beneath it.

"It is warm now."

"Aye. Now mayst thou see that a seedling set thereunder in earliest warming of the year will be so warm, or warmer, by day, and by night warded from the coldest air. For the heat of the sun's light is caught and held beneath the glass."

"The seedling will be bigger and stronger than the others, much sooner. This is a very good device," Freia decided.

"A hot-house doth the very same, but larger," Gaston said.

Freia looked at the bell, nodding. "For many plants," she said. "Always summer." She held her hand under it again, feeling the focused sun. "It's so cold here," she said.

"The season changeth, lass. 'Tis not forever winter. In sixteen days, or twenty, thou'lt see the gardeners placing these in certain beds, to encourage the plants there: and the true spring is never long after that."

Spring thaw came as promised and expected. Gaston took Freia walking outside the city walls and let her find the first astels clustered at the bases of trees, and when the astels were succeeded by gaudier, later flowers and foliage he put her on horseback and removed with her from the town to the mountainside, to his compact manor-house Montjoie, where snow still lay in the violet shadows.

The journey took ten days; they rode slowly, on a scenic route winding upward along the sides of the mountains, both to spare Freia's strength and so that the baggage and household servants would arrive before them. Freia halted her uncle again and again to ask about this flower or that bird or what animal had crossed their path or even what a stone was called. He answered what he could. Her face brightened with interest; her eyes closed and her cheeks reddened as she snuffed the warm damp valley wind pushing spring higher. Gaston showed her plants she had studied in the herbal, and Freia proved to have learned more than he had thought in her tenacious silence. She sometimes did not recognize the real plant, because the drawings had been unlifelike, but always remembered names, characteristics, uses.

For her uncle, it was like watching someone wake after a quarter-year's sleep. Freia did not liven to the extent of laughing or smiling, but she softened and was less melancholy and detached. Gaston felt unburdened; her continued depression had worried him. He reckoned that her poor health might have been worsened by the unnaturally long winter she had lived in— most of Landuc's, then all of Montgard's.

On their last night on the road, they halted at an inn on the shoulder of Montjoie itself which commanded a view of the mountains, the valley, and the sky above, all resplendent with color as the sun set. Freia watched the spectacle, wrapped in the cloak Gaston had brought her fastened with the apple-bough brooch. He stood with her at the edge of a pasture occupied by the landlord's cattle, his hands behind him, watching the last molten-gold tracery around the edges of the clouds tarnish and darken away. The first stars of the evening pricked out among the dusky clouds before either of them moved to go in. Freia looked up at Gaston and smiled, shyly but brilliant in the twilight, and Gaston was so astonished by the alteration that he stared at her dumbly for a second before responding with the warmest, most heartfelt smile he had ever found in himself.

"*Now* it's summer," Freia said.

Within five days of the sending of Luneté's letter, the Baron of Ascolet had returned to Champlys by roundabout but speedy way of several Leys and a brief stint on the Road. He arrived at the city gate just before closing and spurred his horse to hurry through the narrow, crowded streets to the castle. The whole town was decorated; banners and buntings hung from the houses across the narrow streets or down in fluttering falls of color; flower-boxes adorned even the attic windows, and fresh paint was everywhere. Had he missed the presentation? He hadn't misread his Ephemeris, had he?

His horse staggered to a halt under the castle's portcullis, where Otto dismounted and handed him to a groom. Empty trestle-tables were ranked in the front courtyard: so he hadn't missed the day. They'd feast here till midnight and after when the baby—his baby—Cambia received her name at the Shrine. Otto went less hastily into the castle, running his hands over his hair and straightening his clothes as he climbed to the solar.

Luneté was there, standing on a stool with three women kneeling around her; they were doing things to the hem of her dress. A minstrel, decently out of sight behind a carved screen, was playing sprightly dance tunes, but the music stopped and all stared at Otto as he paused in the doorway.

"You're just in time," Luneté said, looking over her shoulder.

Otto smiled. "Did you think I'd miss this?" And then, realizing he had indeed missed the great event—having reckoned that the baby wouldn't arrive for another twenty days or so—he went on, stepping over a maid's feet and taking Luneté's hand, "I'm surprised to see you up." He kissed the hand.

"I'm very well, thank you, my lord. No, don't—you'll spoil the hem—perhaps you should go bathe, dear. I can tell you've had a, ahem, strenuous journey."

Rebuffed, Otto backed away. "Where's baby?"

"With her wet-nurse," said Luneté patiently, straightening and squaring her shoulders. The maids resumed pinning.

"Which one? You hadn't decided who it would be," Otto persisted.

"Vita," said Luneté. "Cambia is with her at the mill."

"At the mill? Not here?" He looked around, realizing that he saw no cradle, no infant's attendants, none of the white-frothed lace stuff that had been erupting everywhere for the past months.

"Of course, at the mill," Luneté replied. "Vita will bring her tomorrow for the procession, don't fear. It's all arranged. *Do* have a bath, Otto."

Ottaviano opened his mouth and closed it. He bowed to his wife's back and left the solar, where the music began to play again as he shut the door.

Not everything in Argylle was lost to the sudden flood. Some crops of fruit and later-ripening barley still remained to be harvested, and Prospero and Scudamor calculated soberly that on lean rations they could all survive the winter. Prospero went to the cove where his three remaining ships huddled out of reach of the sea and dubbed them fishing-boats. The necessary modifications took many days. When at last the boats ventured forth, the fish they brought back were not numerous; the fishermen were inexperienced with prey and tackle both.

The sun shone, though, and the weather stayed hot and clear—too hot and too clear. A great hot dry wind blew steadily for six days, and at the end of them the standing barley was so much straw, and Prospero could hold a stalk and rattle kernel in husk. The soil of the cleared lands became dry, too, and blew around in stinging dust-devils. A hailstorm followed the heat and laid flat the grain as well as punishing the fruit still ripening, and what was not battered from the bough was hard and sour. The banks of the river eroded and the fields gullied and rutted.

That winter they lived on meager fish and game, though the game was not so numerous as it had been and many folk disliked to eat meat—a peculiarity Prospero had hitherto respected, but now found over-nice. He sent hunting expeditions out to take the best-furred animals from the wood, and when he had a shipload tanned and ready he voyaged on an ice-rimed ship and found, after much uncertain wandering on the unstable outer Roads, a place far from Landuc in Pheyarcet where he could trade the skins for seed-grain.

Spring came but reluctantly—if it came at all. The scant snow melted too quickly in a rapid flash of late-coming hot weather, and the runoff crumbled away the riverbanks and more deeply gullied and stripped the fields' topsoil. But Prospero distributed the seed and it was planted, and it sprouted and withered in the heat without rain. Blossoms faded on the trees and fell, fruitless, and the river's fish were elusive. The weather was wrong, and the earth was barren.

"Damn her selfishness," Prospero whispered to himself every day as the place grew dry and deathly around him. People slipped away from the city, faring in small parties into the wilderness to hunt-and-gather a living there, and golden Cledie disappeared with such a band. Prospero had seen her in company many times over the winter, never alone though he had sought subtly to contrive it; she had always been courteous but cool to him: as if he had wronged her, but he knew he had not, and he thought she must blame him for Freia's death.

He had said nothing of how Freia had died. Let it be known to have happened, he thought, and that sufficed; that she killed herself was evil and ill-omened.

And that she had killed herself had cursed the land he had bestowed on her when the Emperor had forced him to renounce it. He thought of Panurgus's death, poisoning the Well and wounding Pheyarcet, and wondered how long Argylle could continue without its Spring's sustenance. The Argyllines scraped and scrabbled and starved onward, through another winter, and Prospero felt the Spring's pulse weakly when he put his hand over it.

Once again he journeyed away and bought seed and once again they planted and again drought killed what rot did not. The summer was harrowed with windstorms and lightnings that sent fires racing through the tinder-dry forest, and the river was choked with fallen trees and drowned animals that had taken refuge from the flame. The water smelled foul, and nobody dared to drink it or swim in it. The cleared lands deteriorated further; they were little more than gravel now, the good earth gone, and the trees at the edges of the clearings began to die back, blighted. What the weather failed to provide, Prospero thought to get from the wells he'd had the Argyllines sink, but those dried one by one as they drew on them to irrigate the fields.

Six more years of drought and death marched after those first two. The world was twisted, a source of death instead of life; the Spring was gone. Though they cleared more and more land to replace the destroyed fields, the weather would give no quarter nor even hope. Once-rolling hills were become steep and forbidding. Thickets of tough brambles sprang up at the edges of the forest, making the work of clearing more difficult, and the fields sprouted little thorn-studded weeds that stung the hands. Even smiling Scudamor went hunched, gaunt and silent, about his duties; Utrachet hunted and brought Prospero bleak tales from the forest highlands—animals starved or vanished, birds unheard, streams and springs dried or filthy. There was always famine; it seemed that they had not eaten for twenty years, and the few children who were born were sickly and died.

Prospero began to believe that Dewar was hiding in Argylle, working to destroy him. Odile pointed out that the Spring would attract Dewar and that he must inevitably attempt to overthrow Prospero to gain control.

"He is a sorcerer," she said, "and power, gained by any means, is all his desire. He hath cozened much from thee already, as he did from me; he will not stop with less than all thou hast, my love."

⸺ *18* ⸺

AT MONTJOIE FREIA FOUND HERSELF MORE in company than she had been in the city of Montgard. There were many manor-houses like Gaston's on the mountainsides; guests passed to and fro among them, and the households themselves would visit back and forth freely, riding or driving in coaches, picnicking and dining in groups. The custom was for ladies to gather in a garden, occupied with a dainty piece of needlework, sometimes with music and instruments, and to amuse themselves with gossip, stories, and songs through the afternoon. Often gentlemen were included in these parties as well; sometimes the gentlemen spent the day in other business deemed better suited to their sex, and sometimes the gentlemen just stayed home. Prince Gaston was careful to attend his neighbors' fêtes occasionally, but not so often as he was invited; it was understood that the work of government commanded his time. Once in a great while he would host such a party himself, usually with an underlying political bent. And as he had in his reign so improved Montgard, which had in their ancestors' days been an isolated town bickering cyclically with its neighbors over water-rights and tariffs and which now ruled the whole of the mountain region, traded with the great states of the south and east, and weighed much in the considerations of the rulers of the world, the prosperous, proud folk of Montgard were inclined to leave him to his treaties, fortifications, reservoirs, and diplomacies.

When the beautiful and vivacious Lady Ofwiede persuaded the Prince to make a meeting with a handful of eminent Montgard landsmen the occasion for a summer pleasure-party, Gaston passively consented, allowing Lady Ofwiede to arrange everything as it pleased her. It was simpler, to his thinking, and perhaps also more agreeable, to let the party be planned and its guests entertained by another's wit while he pursued strategy and ore elsewhere in the house.

Freia had not been to such a gathering before. Gaston had kept her from them, having little time for such things himself and considering that her health would not stand the heat and trooping about. She found herself dizzied by the three dozen bright-clothed strangers when they arrived. She could not remember their names, and after they changed their clothing she could not distinguish them at all. The women flashed gold and gems; they wore little mitts half-covering their hands, and their breasts stood high over tight-laced waists. Freia's gowns were not so brilliantly colored, nor so highly tailored. The men wore patterned skin-tight leggings and snug hip-skimming tunics with heavy gold-trimmed belts; it was a fashion Gaston did not bother to follow too closely in his own wardrobe. They all laughed and talked, voices ringing in rooms and halls usually empty and still, and Freia stayed fast at Gaston's elbow as he greeted and spoke with them, a word or two to each; but now he instructed her with a word and a nod to go with the richly-dressed, high-coiffed ladies and the loud-voiced young men who hovered around them, and Freia went, bewildered but trusting him. The company proceeded to an arbor-shaded corner of Montjoie's small garden, in order of rank, each lady paired by one of the young men, the whole party trailed by servants with workbaskets, refreshments, musical instruments, and whatever else had been deemed necessary. The benches, each big enough for two, were arranged; a quiet competition for certain places was settled with subtle looks and gestures by the young men; and everyone sat down and began to pass the afternoon pleasantly, with songs, stories, and embroidery of the most delicate sort.

Freia had no talent for needlework. Prospero had never taught her more than simple knitting and a straight seam, and that had sufficed to construct such clothing as she bothered herself to make: for, lacking sisterly examples of vanity and covetousness to prompt her, and Prospero being mostly indifferent to her appearance, her clothing was functional and served no grander social purpose than to conform with her father's standards of modesty. She had not touched a needle in Montgard; the maids of the house sewed, and a maid brought her some gown or other to put on each day. The ladies of Montgard appeared to Freia to be stitching spider-silk on scraps of fog—whitework was all the fashion then—with invisible stitches. Several of the ladies, and the mischievously unhelpful gentleman beside her, set at once to remedy her ignorance, and Freia was endowed uncomfortably with some spider-silk (that would tangle, no matter how careful she was, and then it became dingy from her fingers) and a scrap of fog (that soon lay limp and unresisting, resigned to mutilation) of her own.

The tall young gentleman beside her on the bench leaned over to examine the fate of the doomed embroidery, offering observations on the music being played or encouragement and critical remarks at nearly every stitch she took. Meeting little response to these forays, he took up another subject: herself. He asked her if she liked the mountains, if she had seen this or that outlook or view, did she find the park at Montjoie agreeable, if she would be long there, if she liked her uncle, if the house in the city was as richly furnished as they said, if she knew this one or that one who lived here or there, if she cared for another one at all. Freia drew away from him, edging toward the very end of the seat, her head down, staring at the wretched shred of fabric in her hands; she whispered a few yeses and noes at first in reply to his prattle and then answered nothing, finding the probing unanswerable. When she gave no answers for most of the questions he began asking others, closer to the bone. When had she come to Montgard, was it really only last winter, where had she lived, and with whom, how old was she, where was she from, was her father yet living, was the Prince her guardian. . . . Under cover of the songs, all insouciantly suggestive or throbbing with love-lorn lamentation, his questions bore at her.

"Whatever are you about there, my dear brother?" Lady Ofwiede interrupted the young man, after singing a parting-song and finding his voice an unsuitable burden. "Have a care, Heiko, you shall compromise the maid if you will flirt with her before us all."

"That's true," said Heiko, who was become annoyed, "we ought to leave and flirt privately; I might have better success. Or perhaps I shall go flirt with the fountain; it would have more to say."

"The essence of flirtation is conversation," said Lady Ofwiede, laughing at his consternation. "If the maid says nothing, your flirtation is a failure, Heiko dear. Or do her eyes speak?"

The young man leaned closer still to Freia, pushing his face in her averted look. Freia jerked back, away from his breath, his heat.

"They are lowered with proper modesty," said Heiko. "I suppose some would consider that a recommendation." A few of the young men laughed loudly, among the mock-protests of several ladies.

"Dear girl, it is most incorrect to sit among us saying nothing," said Lady Ofwiede. "Perhaps His Eminence has neglected the social arts—it would be like him, I fear his mind is too much on higher things. Come, converse with Heiko! It is a great honor that he should sit talking only to you, you know."

The whole company laughed at this, and Freia shuddered before the noise. She felt Heiko beside her, threateningly near; the area was thick with voices and bodies; she was trapped. Her heart began to hammer in her breast. The blood seemed to have left her hands to become numb and ice-cold; she was hardly able to breathe.

"Good Lady Ofwiede," said an older woman, "this seems rather a dull pastime; let me sing next, instead."

"No, no," insisted Lady Ofwiede, standing and walking gracefully across the lawn to stand over Freia and her brother, "conversation is a noble art, and it is a seemly one for us all to practice. Now, Heiko, put your question to the maid."

"Why, sister! But I have not spoken to her uncle yet," said Heiko, prompting more shouts of laughter.

Freia was rigid, still.

"All right: pretty maid, tell me all about yourself," said Heiko, surly at his sister's badgering.

"Now you must answer," Lady Ofwiede commanded.

The hammering heart in Freia's chest became erratic: it skipped, fluttered, and then raced faster. A boiling heat began to rise in her body.

"What's your name?" asked Heiko, when Freia said nothing.

"Say your name now," said Lady Ofwiede. "It cannot be a secret, child!"

"Where do you come from?" asked Heiko, folding his arms and letting his annoyance show openly, no longer veiled with flirtatious courtesy.

"To that you should reply with your birthplace," Lady Ofwiede said. "Don't sit dumb as a stone, dear. Speak."

"What's your father's name? Where lie his estates?" asked Heiko, throwing his hands in the air and looking round at the others for support in his exasperation.

The gesture flashed past Freia, and the paralysis that had seized her since the start of the inquisition left. She struck at Heiko with the hand that still clutched the dingy embroidery, rising to her feet and roaring "No!" with a voice of rage such as she had never used before in her life.

Heiko, whom she had punched in the eye, rocked backward, and Freia shoved him and the bench over as he shouted "Hey!"

Lady Ofwiede was crying out something shrilly, and two or three others had risen to catch hold of Freia. But they stopped: Freia had turned on Lady Ofwiede, fixing her with such a look of hatred and anger that Lady Ofwiede was struck dumb and motionless by the sight.

Freia was quivering with fury, and with fear, and with consciousness of her own utter impotence here. She could not set on the woman and the man both; some part of her mind was conscious of Prince Gaston, of her being in his power and these being somehow favored by him. She had no words in Tallamont or any language she knew to express her loathing and hate. Her heart beat once. They weren't setting on her; she could flee.

"I never want to see or hear you again," Freia whispered, the loudest she could speak with her throat nearly closed from emotion, and she ran, jostling she knew not whom, lifting her skirts and sprinting away from the place.

She ran, and she was sick once, violently, on a pile of clippings and twigs some gardener had collected, and then she ran again, hampered by the hated stiff, laced-up dress, away from the house and the garden and the barns, with a stitch in her side in no time for she had not run in ever so long now, uphill along a dusty lane with stone walls and low trees to either side, between fields of green corn and staked vegetable-vines and other things she did not see for running so hard, past people working in the fields, past a boy with two donkeys with empty baskets, her plaited hair untying and unbraiding and knotting as it bounced, as she ran and ran.

She could not run very far. The dress, the heat, and her own body limited her. There was an open woodland a half-hour's walk up the mountainside from the house, and in half that time Freia was there, leaving the road and cutting across a pasture. She staggered. She caught at the trees to support herself as she crashed through the undergrowth, entering the wood. Her side hurt as if a hole had torn in it. Her mouth tasted foul. She pulled sweet-flavored leaves off a low bush growing on the verge and chewed them, spat, chewed more, spat again, and took the tinge of vomit from her tongue.

Her head pounded synchronously with her side. Freia stumbled over every irregularity on the ground, sticks, rocks, and roots, and blundered her way to a small stream. The road bridged it a stone's throw away, but she didn't know that; the stream curved and the trees and bushes were thick. Freia pushed her hot face in the water and drank, then, gasping, rubbing her side, sat by the stream and leaned against a tree-trunk among a pile of ferns.

Something had happened. That man's questions. Like being in Landuc again, a prisoner. Like being tied and watched, while Otto asked questions and questions, while the sorceress Neyphile asked questions and questions. Her breath roughened. Questions. Startling her, her eyes filled with water and she began to weep, long slow voiceless gasps for air and hot tears. Questions. The man, leaning over her. Golias, and Ottaviano asking questions.

"No," whispered Freia to the water. "No, no. No." Questions. She closed her eyes, opened them, wiped her face on her sweat-soaked sleeve, then fiddled with the front-lacing on her bodice and untied it, loosening the outer gown to air her smock and the wilted underbodice. Cooler, better. She pushed the memory of questions away from her thoughts, but it would not go.

Had her uncle meant that to happen? Why had he sent her away? She hadn't expected that; she'd begun to follow him out of the room where he had received his guests, and he had bidden her softly to go with the others. Had he planned that they would ask questions, though he did not? The man was like Ottaviano, watching and talking and pushing at her. Like Dewar, too; Dewar had prodded at her, but then he had stopped. Ottaviano had not stopped. Nor had Neyphile. Then Golias's questions and violence. The questions, the same questions, again and again and again, and Golias. That woman didn't look anything like Neyphile, but she was like her, so like her that Freia feared and abhorred her as much as she did Neyphile. She didn't think she had ever met anyone before who was so like someone else. Gaston had said the people here weren't like the people in Landuc. He had said she wasn't a prisoner. He had lied. They were the same, the same people, the same questions.

Freia lay back in the ferns. She was away from them now. She was safe here. Her head thumped; her side ached when she breathed. She closed her eyes and tried to push aside all that had happened that day. Forcefully, she slowed her panting, calmed her pulse. The brook gurgled to itself thoughtfully. It was nearly like home.

The lowing of cattle and clanking of bells woke her some little while later, breaking a dream in which the brook's bubbling had turned into a voice that had talked and talked in her own language, the language of Argylle, but said nothing she could keep on waking. The aches in her head and her side had gone. Freia lifted herself on an elbow in her crushed bed of ferns and looked around, disoriented: then she placed herself, and remembered. Where were the cows? She realized she could not be far from the road, along which animals were driven from one pasture to another, and she held very still until the noises of the cattle's passage had stopped.

The sun was tilting through the trees, cooled from the white-hot of midday to a softer amber color. Freia splashed more water on her face and observed, a little distance down the brook's meandering bank, that there appeared to be strawberries growing on its flood-steepened slope. On investigation, she found they were indeed fingertip-sized ripe strawberries, and she began picking and eating them, thinking of nothing but their sweetness melting in her mouth, her fingers busy and efficient as she browsed her way downstream. There was no next moment; there was no previous moment; there were berries, water, and the trees.

While she gathered berries, the sun's hue deepened and the woods began to darken. Freia collected a last handful and sat back on her heels. For the first time, she considered what to do. Without a weapon—without even a knife—she doubted her ability to forage. There were a great many people hereabouts, but they never seemed to go into the forests, and Freia supposed that she could live there as she would at home. Her clothing was utterly impractical. She knew she was physically soft, and she dispassionately doubted her endurance; merely running here had winded her. But memory pressed her: the woman, like Neyphile; the man, like Ottaviano, like Golias. She shuddered. She would not go back.

A dog barked no great distance away: chasing round the animals in a pasture, she guessed. Then there came crashing noises. The dog was in the wood.

Freia almost disliked dogs, which there were none of in Argylle. Gaston's dogs were all working dogs—war-dogs, hunting-dogs—heavy-jawed and hot-eyed, trained to obedience and, to her mind, parasitic. To have an animal kill on order, as the dogs did here, fouled the animal, to her thinking. The dog bashed about, making a strangled yelp-sound. It was quite near. Freia tensed. She rose to her feet swiftly, still cupping the strawberries in her palm, and her pulse quickened. Sticks, rocks—nothing big lay handy, and she seized a half-broken dead branch and snapped it off; it might do to keep the dog away. Flee, or fight?

The dog made another strangled yelp, and Freia stiffened, still undecided; and as she braced herself to receive the dog, it burst into sight among the ferns and trees. And behind the dog was her uncle, Prince Gaston: the dog was leashed and muzzled. Doubtless the noisy passage had been more his than the animal's.

Gaston jerked the dog in and bade it sit as soon as he saw Freia. It obeyed, whining, panting. Freia fancied that she could smell it where she stood. She neither spoke nor moved, waiting.

"I knew not thou hadst left the house until we sat to dine," Gaston said. "Tell me what befell, to drive thee forth." His voice was neutral, without the undertone of storm she expected. Freia hesitated, unsure. "Some account have I had," he said, "but to none shall I lay full truth but thine."

Freia looked at the pulsing, breathing dog.

"I knew not how to find thee otherwise," said Gaston. "Though Jan did say he saw thee running hither, as I crossed the field but now." He waited, and urged her again. "Speak, lass. Tell me what's passed."

Freia watched the dog pant as she said, "You said it's not like Landuc and it is."

"How so?" Gaston prompted her.

The wood was becoming blue and dim. "What they say, how they are. Just like Landuc. Just like them." She could not hear the bitterness in her voice, but Gaston did.

"What did they say?"

Freia felt the boiling feeling begin to simmer again. "That, that Ottaviano, that Neyphile," she said. "You said they aren't like that here and they are. Just like them. Questions. Questions and, and they won't stop."

"They shall go," said Gaston.

"He wouldn't go away. They wouldn't stop."

"They shall leave Montjoie tomorrow," he said. "Which woman was it, Freia?"

"The one like Neyphile," Freia said. How could he not know what she meant? Hadn't he controlled them, their questions?

Gaston hesitated, then said a name, another, another, and Freia stopped him. "That one."

"Lady Ofwiede."

"She's just like Neyphile," Freia said, trembling. "Maybe she is. Maybe she came here."

Gaston said slowly, "Nay, she's not Neyphile. I've known her many years, indeed since she was a babe. She is not Neyphile, lass, though mayhap she hath some of her ways."

"She talks like her," Freia whispered.

" 'Tis long since I've met Neyphile," Gaston said, "and I do believe thee, that there's a semblance I cannot see. Thou wouldst not say so lightly. The man who pressed thee, was it not her brother, Landsman Hinrick?"

Light had gone from the wood, leaving thick dusk.

"Come. Let us go to supper," Gaston suggested, after a short silence.

Freia didn't move. She couldn't run away. He would follow her with the dog. Anyway, she was unready to support herself. But Golias's shadow lay over the house; Lady Ofwiede had become entangled with the sorceress Neyphile in Freia's mind, and she could not willingly go near them. "He's there," Freia whispered, half to herself. She wanted to go home, a very sudden, painfully deep desire to be safe and far away.

"Thou needst not see him again," Gaston assured her. "He shall go. No harm shall come to thee, Freia, upon my honor."

Freia was stone-still. Gaston had promised her that before. But he had sent her off to the garden with that man, and the others, the Neyphile-creature. But he promised to send them away. He might be like Otto, like Golias, after all. But she couldn't escape him; she had met her limits today, and they were frighteningly near. She sensed he wasn't going to let her stay here, alone; he would insist on her returning to the house, walling her in. He said she would be safe. Could she believe it? "Please don't be lying," she begged him, her voice quavering.

"I promise thee, Freia, I shall send away both Landsman Hinrick and Lady Ofwiede on the morrow. I promise thee, thou shalt not see them nor speak with them again. Doth my word suffice thee?" Was that firm, sharp note in his voice anger?

Freia made a small, frightened sound, which Gaston took for consent.

"Come then, lass, along to thy supper," said Gaston, and he said something to the dog and started forward. Freia stood like a post until he touched her arm in the grey darkness. " 'Twill be easier to follow the stream to the lane, than to beat the bushes by night," he said. "Come, lass."

Freia let him take her elbow and steer her before him. She still had her strawberries in her hand, warm now and damp with her sweat; she dropped them into the leaves and ferns. The dog panted hot breaths at her thighs, snorting from time to time. Gaston ducked under branches and stepped in the brook once, a sliding splash followed by a sigh. Freia turned away from the brook and pushed out of the undergrowth a few steps above the ford, where the brook flowed shallow and wide and the ground was marshy, even in summer. Gaston stepped from stone to stone—there was moonlight enough to see by—and came to her where she waited, passive with an air of despair.

"Come, come this way," he said, and guided her along the road toward his house.

Gaston's interview with his niece at nightfall in the wood had startled him, more for its incoherence than for anything said. He had expected a more vigorous accusation, a vengeful female tale of insult and offense, and instead Freia had flinched from him and said, in a voice that had disarmed him with its hollowness and fear, that they were like Ottaviano and Golias and Neyphile.

He knew something of how Golias and Neyphile had treated her, having himself seen the surgeon Gernan salve the girl's galled wrists and ankles and treat her bruises, burns, and fractures. How Lady Ofwiede and Landsman Hinrick had managed to achieve anything resembling it in the company of a dozen others without laying a hand on Freia was an uncomfortable mystery. So as Gaston led Freia back to the manor-house (a side door, she was so dishevelled that he would not have her seen, and on the way he gave Gram the dog over to a groom) he repeated her answers to himself. Lady Menillan had given him an accurate-sounding report on the afternoon's proceedings, and Gaston had concluded that Freia had been offended in quite a different way: at the condescension shown her, perhaps, or the impertinence. But it seemed that was not at all Freia's objection. *Questions,* the girl had said. *They wouldn't stop.* And then she'd pleaded with him not to lie to her! *Questions.* Like Ottaviano, like Neyphile, like people in Landuc—

Unseen by his household or guests, Prince Gaston guided Freia up a back-side stairway that was usually used for domestic task-work. He touched her shoulder (sacred Well, she winced and he snatched his hand back) and told her to change her dress, wash up, he'd have supper sent up to her. Freia, avoiding his eyes, slunk into her rooms. She closed the door quietly. Gaston went on through the dark-panelled narrow hallway to his office, where he rang for a footman and ordered food for his niece. Then he sat at his writing-desk, poured a tumbler of clear, pepper-flavored distillate, and gave himself half-an-hour by the one-handed clock in the corner to consider the problem.

People in Landuc. Ottaviano had questioned Freia. Yes. Neyphile, Golias, Ottaviano, the Emperor, others in Landuc had all put Freia questions, constantly: about Prospero, herself, his plans, his whereabouts. She could not bear such questioning, not yet, perhaps never.

Landsman Hinrick had certainly been rude to Freia, and Gaston had already decided that he must reprimand the nobleman and his sister. Yet he had promised Freia she wouldn't see them again and he couldn't very well demand that the child confine herself to her rooms until their twelve-day visit was ended. She'd think herself a prisoner. Now he must ask them, which must mean their sister's husband and the husband's brother too, to leave the house, which some would call discourtesy surpassing that shown Freia. Had it been directly done to him, Gaston would have acted differently, but evidently Freia was ill-prepared to bear rough treatment, even simple teasing.

It perplexed Gaston and it disappointed him. He had thought her nearly mended. She seemed well. She had put on flesh and her lackluster look had brightened. She talked sensibly enough of healing-herbs and gardening with anyone who'd listen, or who'd tell her more: the gardeners, field workers, and old wives of the estate were bemused by her eagerness and attention.

Were Freia a man, Gaston thought ruefully, his task would be as easy as administering a short, firmly worded lecture on good manners, cowardice, and stoicism. He knew the girl had bottom; he had seen her out-face Avril privately when he questioned her, taunt him publicly (though perhaps she did not know how insulting she had been, in Court), and although she was mad to try to kill herself, that took a kind of courage too. She had overcome physical abuse that would have snapped many men—indeed would have killed many. He couldn't very well tell her to put her chin up and stiffen her backbone; she would have done, already, if she could. Something else was needed.

Freia sat in an armchair drawn up to a round table on which her supper had been laid. The food was untouched. Three candles stood on the table, and others around the room, their flames steady and still. Her hair had been untangled, her dress removed, her muddy shoes tched over by Helma, whose duty it was to look after such things. When the supper had come, Freia had told the maid in a whisper that no, she would need nothing more, and now she waited, ignoring a baked trout stuffed with crumbs and herbs, a brace of partridges roasted golden-brown, warm bread in a damask napkin, a cress salad, a little dish of haricots and bacon, and a bowl of berries with soft custard. Freia bit her fingernails instead.

All the candle-flames bowed as Prince Gaston tapped at the

half-open door between her sitting-room and her bedchamber, where she sat. "Freia, dost wake yet?"

Freia stopped biting her nails and looked up, dread-filled. He came in, shut the door, and brought another chair to sit beside her. Freia huddled into herself, looking at nothing, arms crossed, her right hand holding her left cheek.

"Lass," Gaston said presently, "that Landsman Hinrick will be gone on the morrow, and his kin. He bore himself with unseemly discourtesy toward thee, and thus toward me, and carried himself far other than a guest ought. I have told him so, and he shall leave." A brief interview had secured this. Landsman Hinrick had sought to dispute the matter, and Prince Gaston had asked Lady Ofwiede if he spoke falsehood in his reasons, and the lady, cowed and embarrassed, had murmured that there was surely a misunderstanding, but that it would be best not to argue with their host.

"You're angry," Freia whispered then.

"Nay! Wherefore?"

"Helma says you want to marry her."

"That is false rumor. I am not marrying anybody," Gaston said, more annoyed by this in-house gossip than he would have thought he could be.

She seemed not to have heard him. "If I could go home, I would. I don't know where it is. But I will go away."

"I will not hear of thee going thus," said Gaston, "driven by an ill-mannered lout who is naught to me."

Freia said nothing, and Gaston was sure he had not said enough, or not the right word. He sorted again through the broken threads of their conversation in the wood.

"I fear thou thinkest thyself a prisoner yet, but I cannot hold thee here: though I say, I would not have thee leave, 'tis not to say, thou mayst not leave. Th'art my guest, unfettered." He contemplated a crime and decided for it. "Wouldst thou have me bring thee covert to the Well? For then couldst thou travel on the Roads, everywhere in Pheyarcet as thou list, and seek thy father and thy home."

"The Well?"

He nodded.

"But nobody can go there. Papa said so. He said the Well is weak."

" 'Tis forbidden, but such a ban may be evaded; indeed, I know't hath been done. The Well's as it ever was—I've no doubt the Fire burns quick as afore, properly invited."

"I wouldn't be able to find home," Freia said, her shoulders slumping. "Dewar couldn't even find it when he wanted to. He had to make a sorcery for it."

This was news to Gaston, and disheartening news at that. "Well—"

"If it is forbidden and the Emperor found me, wouldn't he be angry?"

"Aye."

"He'd lock me up again, or make me marry the Prince, or kill me," Freia said. "Prospero said the Emperor kills people he doesn't like. He might kill you."

"Nay, I think 'tis unlikely."

Freia thought about it; Gaston could see her becoming occupied with the problem, nearly against her will, her face reflecting each idea: fear, pain, resignation. Gaston waited. "It burns people up," she said.

"Only the unfit, the pretender, the false. Th'art of Panurgus's blood. Hast nothing to fear."

Freia shook her head. "No."

Gaston nodded, accepting her word. "An thou shouldst change thy thinking, lass, do thou but tell me, and we shall go."

She looked at him for the first time and shook her head again.

"I'll not hold thee to it," he promised her, smiling a little. It was early for her to be refusing the Well. He looked at the dishes, lifted a cover to see the meal untouched. There was little profit in entertaining proposals of adventure on an empty stomach. "Do thou eat, lass."

Freia looked at the glaze-eyed fish, which Gaston had uncovered, and she looked from the table to Gaston, who was leaving.

"Uncle Gaston."

He halted, hand on the door, and half-turned.

"You aren't angry?" she asked in a whisper.

Gaston shook his head slowly, lowering his hand from the door as he regarded Freia, still hunched in her chair. "Wherefore would I be angry?" he asked.

She said nothing, but her look was apprehensive. Her fingers touched her cheek again, commemorating past pain.

"Thy running to the wood," Gaston said, and Freia shrank inward, "that was no crime, Freia." He left the door and went to her chair. There was something he almost understood: something that almost made sense to him. Gaston sat down beside Freia again. "Wherefore would I be angry?"

"Papa used to be angry when I ran away," whispered Freia.

He nodded, slowly and deliberately still. Prospero. "I am not Prospero," he said.

An expression of perplexity began to wrinkle Freia's forehead.

"Didst thou run away from Prospero often?" Gaston asked, in a soft friendly voice.

She looked down, then back at him; she shook her head and then nodded, frowning now a little, as if concentrating. "After the people were there, I didn't like them and he was always busy with them," she said, "so I would go away, and he would be angry with me."

After the people were there, thought Gaston, and he guessed aloud, "At first thou and thy father lived alone."

"On the island," Freia said.

"I see," Gaston said. "Then later, there were people."

"I didn't like them."

"Why?" He suspected he knew, if she had been reared in such isolation.

"They were too many," she said. "We didn't need them."

He nodded once. "Hadst not met folk before?"

"Papa has books—had books with pictures of many people. They all looked alike," Freia said.

They regarded one another.

"Perhaps 'twere easier for thee to take them one by one," suggested Gaston.

"When I met one of them, just one, in the forest, that was better," Freia said. "I didn't like them all at once, but she was different."

He nodded again, once.

"Papa was angry with me for not liking them," Freia said.

"I am not angry with thee for disliking people," said Gaston. " 'Tis all too true, that most are difficult to like. And 'tis difficult to like many people met all at once. One alone is better."

Freia nodded. "I know," she said, "I noticed that, that when I talk to only Scudamor, or only Utrachet, or, or," and her voice faltered, "or only Dewar, then it's not so . . . frightening."

And so 'twas until she came to Landuc, thought Gaston, and must face a world of faces, and no way to hide from them. "Thou needest not go into company here in Montgard again," he told her. "An it give thee no pleasure, I cannot require it of thee. But even here, some folk are good to know, one by one."

"Not—not him—"

"Landsman Hinrick has shown otherwise, I am in concord with thee."

"The people in Argylle are not like that ever. Not like the Landuc people."

"Yet thou didst flee them."

Freia looked down at her hands. "I wouldn't now," she said. "They, they never—they always want to be kind. Prospero made them do bad things, cutting down all the trees and going to war, but they never do bad things, themselves."

Gaston saw a tear glitter, falling on her hands, and he pitied her. Prospero had badly served her, rearing her in isolation so that the only person she was sure of was himself. Parted from him, she had done her best in a confusing world: but the evil she had met taught her too well and too soon to retreat at any cost. "There are many cruel folk in the world, child," he said, "and many unkind, and many who care naught for naught. But still there are some as tender toward their fellows as toward themselves, even in Landuc."

"I don't understand how to know. The good people look just like the bad."

"Alas, child, this knowledge cometh only with labor: from intercourse with all manner of men, wilt thou learn to discern one from another, and to treasure the good scattered among them."

"Some people are good and bad both," said Freia.

"Aye, 'tis so."

"Dewar did things that were good, and then he did horrible things. . . ." She looked at Gaston imploringly. Could he explain this?

Gaston rubbed his chin and thought, and at last said, "Dewar is a mixed man and sorcerer, that desireth to be both; his man's heart prompts him to do good, but the sorcerer's habits of mind inspire him . . . not to evil, perhaps, but to do what must harm others, whilst it serveth some intent of his own. I deem he hath not the character of the man who is cruel by design, rather giving pain thoughtlessly."

"That man," Freia said, "meant to hurt me . . ."

"I fear 'twas so."

". . . and Dewar did not," she concluded, half to herself, and Gaston nodded his agreement. Her brows were knit together as she concentrated, thinking about this new insight—and then she shook her head, as if banishing some idea, and said, looking up at Gaston suddenly, "You are very kind to me."

"I do but wish to see thee well and strong," said Gaston. "And hence, would have thee eat thy supper."

For a moment longer she gazed at him, and then Freia nodded, uncoiled herself and set her feet on the floor, and took up the knife and fork to eat.

Gaston bid her good-night and rose and left her, and he went slowly down the hallway, to go to his guests and complete the night's social tasks. But as he went, he revolved again and again in his thoughts a sentence Freia had said: *The people in Argylle are not like that ever.*

Argylle. Prospero's hidden center, from which he had attacked Landuc, to which Gaston was certain he had now retreated, had a name.

ᴄ— *19* —ᴐ

GASTON TOOK FREIA TO THE FOOT of a glacier before they left Montjoie at summer's end, and its cold breath followed them down the valley to the high-walled castle-watched city. Freia walked the ice-fringed walls with her uncle, knitted an elaborate jacket and gloves and bonnet under Mistress Witham's tutelage, and puzzled through antique manuscripts in Gaston's solar. She liked Gaston's kind silence; unlike Prospero, he never demanded account of her time or her reading. The days grew brief, and she dozed in the short afternoons' colorless light, rousing to eat a small supper, then sleeping again.

Gaston watched her with covert interest in the unconscious slowdown after her restless summer. His brother Herne was like that, sluggish and irritable in winter, unbounded in activity in warmer months. Herne would act in winter, were he forced to it by circumstance, but he hated it—and Prospero had surely taken that into account when he had planned his war. Freia, curled napping on a divan with her yarn and needles fallen to the floor, resembled her forester uncle more than she would have liked to know. She stirred and looked up at Gaston as he fed the fire.

"I've been here for a year," she said.

"Aye," he agreed, and sat on the footstool beside the divan. "Mayst go, an thou wouldst, lass; I'd not keep thee 'gainst thy will, nor guide thee where thou wouldst liever not go. I did offer thee the Well before, and 'twas no mayfly gift, but hath outlived the summer and awaits thee yet. Say but the word, and I'll help thee go, an thou wouldst leave." He waited, watching her face.

"Where?" she said sadly, and she put her head down again and pulled the lap-robe up near her face, concealing it. "I am sorry, I am a nuisance."

"Nay. 'Tis pleasant to have thee here. Art unhappy?"

"I don't know," Freia said in a small voice after considering the question.

Gaston nodded. "I did not think thee happy, but I hoped thee not unhappy. 'Tis not thy home, I know. 'Tis strange to thee. Yet th'art full welcome here." He thought about it more, and tried, "Is aught lacking, lass? Hast only to ask and I shall provide it. Art at full liberty to come and go as thou wouldst, an thou wouldst." A half-year ago, Gaston had decided not to pursue the scrap of information Freia had let fall. He desired that she should trust him, that she should not see him as another of the enemies who had hurt her so; in the long run, Landuc would gain most, he thought, if some foundation for friendship and confidence were laid between Prospero's excluded family and the Palace. The realm and the Emperor would best be served, deemed Gaston, by his protecting Prospero's daughter now. So he had set aside that name that he had heard her say, and stayed in Montgard, and Freia did not seem to have noticed her own slip; she was as careful after as before.

Freia shook her head. "I don't know where, and it's not in your book," she said, and emerged a little from the lap-robe again, eye-to-eye with Gaston, who leaned on the head of the divan. "Have you heard anything about Prospero?" she asked.

She had never asked before. "Naught, lass. Nary a word. The Emperor's hot thereat; by the terms of the treaty there's a tithe due him each quarter-day, and payment of war-reparation, and none hath come all these three quarters that hath passed in Landuc. 'Tis said by some, he's fled to Phesaotois, but I misdoubt it."

"A tithe?" Freia asked.

"A tax," explained Gaston. She nodded, but her expression was still perplexed, and he went on, "A tithe's a portion of the produce of the land, to be given to the Emperor, as the Well's representative, returned to him as it is provided by the Well to the landholder. 'Tis money, gold or silver."

"But—" Freia stopped herself, understanding altering her perplexity to alarm.

"Now Prospero holdeth yet some few lands of the Emperor," Gaston said, "that were to pass to thee on thy marriage, which hath not been performed."

"I thought he gave it all up," Freia protested.

"So hath 'a done, but he bargained with th' Emperor to bestow some scant holding upon thee: a dowry, to be thine alone, should Josquin die. The terms of the wedding-contract forbid that thou shouldst inherit anything of Josquin, but dowry's different: 'tis the woman's own, come what may, to support her. Thus did those lands—I misremember what they were—remain nominally in Prospero's hands: 'twas intended that it be for little time."

"All that was forbidden by that judge. He said Papa couldn't give me anything."

"Nay, dowry's not the same as the land-titles bestowed on thee, with which Prospero sought to protect himself."

"If it's mine, it can't be the Emperor's."

"In Landuc all cometh of the Well and belongeth to the Well, and the Emperor is the Well," said Gaston. "And the tithe doth confirm that, dost understand?"

"But—" and Freia stopped herself again and sat a few minutes thinking. Gaston did not interrupt her. "So this tithe, it must be given to the Emperor," she said slowly, "because he made Prospero give him everything he had. That's their agreement."

" 'Tis bound to the land: whoever holdeth the land, must pay the tithe. And it must be tendered quarterly, unless the Emperor grants some special boon."

"The time is different here. There. Where they are. I can feel it."

Gaston nodded. "So did I suppose to Avril, and it pleaseth him ill. For Prospero slipped away, e'en as thy brother did, ere the Emperor or anyone learnt where his lair lieth. I'm not asking thee!" he interjected, seeing her begin to protest.

Freia bit her lip.

" 'Tis now a matter of great enquiry by the Emperor, with rich reward to the one who telleth him where Prospero's hid. Panurgus our father would never have need done such a thing, but the Emperor hath not our father's mastery of the Well."

"Papa didn't like him," Freia said.

"Panurgus. Aye. Nor was Panurgus easy with Prospero, and meseems now that 'twas the sorcerers' rivalry that overrode the father's affinity for his blood and the son's respect for his sire. The King won in the end, by banishing thy father, yet he was deep-grieved to do it and it sped his death on him. An 'a had not fought Prospero, rather embraced him as thy father hath his son, Landuc must wear another face today. Such controversies can only work to our diminishment," he said, half to himself, and rose and began to pace, thinking about the matter for the thousandth time. "Such rivalries the Well fans in us, an we let it rule our tempers," the Fireduke went on in the same tone. "Aye, thy father and Fulgens, there's another."

"Fulgens?" Freia asked, confused.

"Aye, in sooth; for Prospero was master of the King's navy for centuries 'fore Fulgens," Gaston said. "And some still think he was the better, for he knew the currents and watercourses as well as doth Fulgens, and could whistle up wind i' the deadest calm, for all winds were his. No vessel e'er was lost in storm, in Prospero's day. But that is gone by; Panurgus dubbed Fulgens Admiral of the Fleet when he banished thy father."

Gaston stopped pacing. He stood at one of the narrow windows looking down into the long courtyard, where twenty-four of his men were shooting at wands and hay bales set up in front of the earthen fortress he had replaced with this building of stone. Freia sidled up beside him.

"May I have one of those?" she asked timidly.

"Why, thou couldst not pull it, lass. 'Tis a man's thing, not a maid's."

Freia watched the men, chewing her lip.

"Uncle," she asked, "why do you keep an army when you say you prefer peace? Who would attack you?"

His mind seized the second question first. "Lindfluss," he said, "I defeated an hundred years ago and threw down their prince, and some there among his descendants resent the deed yet; Logreia hath a young and ambitious queen, much heedful of Montgard since her accession. Or Cazador, whose four sons fight 'mongst themselves and who seeks some outlet for their belligerence, hath sought to make quarrels 'tween us. To have peace, one must be ready for war. We have peace now because they know that I'd answer swift and hard any raid or slight."

Freia frowned, watching the men fire two dozen arrows each, swift and hard as Gaston said, and the arrows buried themselves in hay or passed through it to stick in the stubbly hillside. Long-bows, not crossbows; in Argylle she had had one shorter than those, but they looked much the same. The last bow she had used had been the crossbow Ottaviano had taken from her, but that was just for hunting. "It seems to me," she said slowly, picking her way through her thoughts as she spoke, "that it all starts when someone . . . when someone decides . . . it's going to happen . . . that someone's going to attack him and he gets weapons. And then even if nobody was going to do that, the others all arm themselves because now they're afraid of him . . ."

"Well—" Gaston started, smiling.

". . . and then, of course, when they all have swords, they have to fight, because they've gone to so much trouble for it," Freia said.

"Wouldst ban swords, sticks, stones even from the hand of man?" he asked her.

Freia shot him a quick irked look. "It's that first bit that's the problem, isn't it?" she said. "When someone assumes that there must be a fight and that he must kill people to win it."

"Well, lass," he said, pleased by the argument from her (old though it was to him), "never have I seen a place where men lived in perfect amity, where never hand was lifted in violence, where never was anger nor dispute. Men quarrel; men have always quarreled, everywhere in every world I have known. They may wish to live in peace, but their wills clash and their desires cannot all be satisfied, and to forestall such a fight it hath worked best to my advantage to be always the victor in wars and in peacetime disputes. And this is done by being strong enough to either push battle from the other's thoughts, and so to win, or to win the battle he demands. I do not strike where there is no threat to me, yet if threatened I'll not permit me nor my holdings to be impugned."

His niece shook her head. "We didn't used to quarrel," she said, sad now. "Nobody did. The only fighting anyone ever did was Prospero's fighting against you."

Gaston smiled a little. "Truly? Then isn't a very paradise, a place of peace hitherto unknown, and thy father were wiser, perhaps—" He stopped himself from saying *never to have gone there,* and instead said, "—never to have left it."

"That's what I said," Freia said. "That's what I said, when he started it all."

The Baron of Ascolet was crawling about on his elbows and knees in front of the miller's kitchen fire, a long grey woollen sock on each hand. The socks were yapping and barking, pursuing a roundly diapered infant in circles on the smooth slate floor. The kitchen cat had retreated flat-eared to the top of the dresser, and the miller's red-faced wife was wheezing with laughter at her washtub in the yard outside the door.

The hound-hands leapt and seized the squealing baby. Otto made loud devouring sounds as he tickled her in his lap. "Cambia crunchy munchy juicy! Ahhh, all gone, no more baby . . . wait . . . what's this? It's Cambia!" Cambia crowed triumphantly, having won the war a half-year since by losing all the battles, and tried to stand up; she got halfway before sitting down emphatically again in Otto's crossed legs. "Where's baby's other sock thing got to, I wonder," Otto asked her, kissing one bare-toed foot.

Cambia blinked lilac-blue eyes at him and grabbed his nose.

"Ouch." Nobly obliging, the Baron of Ascolet made a duck-like honking sound. "Cambia, don't you ever get upset?" he asked her as she half-stood and fell again, this time forward on her hands.

"She don't," said the miller's wife, Vita. "I never saw such an easy baby, Your Lordship, such a sweet-natured thing. Never a tear. My own two were such yellers I thought I'd be deaf by 'em, and she never much as peeps. Hardly natural, it is, I'd swear oath she smiled from the day she was born."

"Is she Daddy's sweet little thing, then?" Otto asked Cambia, and expounded for several minutes on her sweetness, her beauty, and other good traits. "That's why I spend so much time with you, lambkin," he told her. "If you bit and scratched, why, we'd send you out to pasture with the goats."

Cambia sighed. She was falling asleep, draped over Otto's thigh. In the firelight, her hair was reddish, like Luneté's; wet, it was much darker, downy curls in abundance peeking out of her cap. She did have bad traits—she had already shown herself to be stubborn and persistent, difficult to dissuade of any idea—but when her will wasn't crossed, she was so genial that it was impossible to be cross with her.

Otto picked the baby up and laid her belly-down in her cradle on the Ascolet lambs'-fleeces he had brought for her. He tucked the covers over her and transferred a kiss to her ear with his fingertip, then stood. "Did the Countess come yesterday?" he asked Vita, pulling on his gauntlets in the doorway, fastening his cloak.

"No, my lord," said Vita, thumping diapers. Her breath steamed over the cauldron of white cloth.

"Ah. Thought she might; she was heading this way. See you tomorrow, if the snow holds back."

Spring again brought new vitality to Freia, drawing her more strongly than before; as the days began to lengthen she couldn't stay still. She stretched and stirred herself a little further each day, riding out alone along the Mont or into the foothills. When they travelled to Montjoie, she was ever eager and impatient, ever hurrying, walking in the evenings after they had stopped, tiring herself to exhaustion before she slept every night, rising at birdsong.

Her restlessness continued in Montjoie, where she rode or walked out on long day-trips, so that soon she was burnt from the strong mountain sun, hard from exercise. There were no house-parties this year. She collected unfamiliar plants, bringing them back to be identified and to have their uses explained. Gaston wondered whether she would return, some days when she was out before sunrise; but he thought she would tell him if she meant to leave for good, and she said no word of leaving, only of the mountains and the wild lonely places she had been.

Freia had, with a stinging fear of discovery, been doing more than wandering. She had happened on a boy shooting with a longbow in a meadow, and she had bartered for it and his arrows. She had traded him a brooch—not the apple-brooch, she'd refused him that—a silver one, and a good knife Gaston had given her, and a belt with a silver buckle. It was outrageous, she knew; she had kept upping the ante and prayed as she did that nobody would notice the loss of the three costly (she thought) items, which she had considered as being lent to her. Any metal was precious in Argylle, and her ideas of purchase and exchange were naive, inexperienced, and anxious.

But she had to have the bow, and when she had it she cached it in a hollow log in the wood wrapped in a hide she was supposed to have had made into heavy riding boots—another purloinment that weighed heavily on her. Three or four days of practice instead of riding, and she had the feel of the bow in her arm again; a few more days and another knife to replace that she had traded away, and she was making her own arrows, tipping them with chipped quartz and fletching them with feathers from birds she had netted. She didn't think beyond the summer season; she carried the bow under her cloak and took it to out-of-the-way places and, once and then again and again and again, when she was out late past meals, she would hunt the long-footed mountain hares and the nodding, fat stone-hens and feed herself.

She didn't know why she wanted to do it, but she did it. She loved the stalking-games, the tension and release of shooting, splitting wands and putting arrows through marmots' eyes. It was not as good as being at home; she dared not run too far, too wild, but it satisfied some piece of her that missed the great dark forests that surrounded Argylle and were its threshold and its heart at once.

On a day which had passed the cusp from late summer to early autumn, she set out for her cache-place after breakfast. The previous night a man had arrived to see Prince Gaston; thus her uncle's planned ride with her had been postponed. Freia rode out alone and went to her bow-log. From there, bow beneath cloak as concealed as it could be, she went to a meadow called the Hareground. The meadow was long and pan-shaped, and Freia had used the slender arm of it between the trees for her practice.

She knew they would be leaving Montjoie soon. The season was turning, yellowed leaves and grasses already gilding the colder slopes. She hadn't thought about that time, deliberately; she would have to get her bow into the house somehow and hide it. Sneak out at night? Hide it in a barn? She didn't know. She wouldn't be able to bring it with her; that was clear. Gaston didn't approve of women with weapons; he didn't think she could pull a bow at all, and he had said so when she'd asked for one last winter. She had expected him to say that, but it had disappointed her nonetheless. Prospero had told her that Landuc people didn't approve of ladies hunting as she did; sometimes he would scold her for it, saying Lady Miranda would never be seen blood-spattered in a short tunic, skinning a wood-elk—but they did need meat, and he could not forever be forsaking his studies to ramble with her.

It seemed to her that the ladies of Landuc, Lady Miranda too, must have dull lives.

Freia picketed her horse in the lower part of the meadow and walked to the upper end. She strung the bow, nocked an arrow, and stood waiting for a hare, a hen, or a marmot, not moving a muscle.

The marmots had learnt wisdom under siege. They ducked into their burrows at the first approach of the horse and stayed out of sight now as Freia held still. Arm extended, bow ready, she waited.

Below her, out of sight beyond the dark fringes of the trees, her horse snorted and blew very loudly. A marmot's nose flicked back down its burrow. A hawk passed overhead, hunting also. Freia waited. A bird screamed rawly in one of the trees. A hare, moving from tuft to tuft of grass, emerged from the undergrowth around the meadow on her left and lolloped cautiously across. Freia didn't move.

The sun had moved across the downslope lane of trees to her right, so that the panhandle of yellow grass was darkening.

A rustle; a whinny from the horse. The hawk folded her wings. A hare bounded into view from the lower, larger meadow downslope and froze silhouetted against a tuft of grass. Freia aimed and shot. The hare tumbled up, over, twitching, red-spraying, the arrow driven through the skull. Freia lowered her bow, smiling faintly, pleased. She trotted forward to claim the prey from the hawk.

The hawk dropped just out of sight beyond the trees, though; she'd gotten her own dinner, Freia thought, and came out of the lane of trees, glancing down at the hawk and her horse—

And Gaston. There on Solario, who whinnied as he saw her, sat her uncle.

She froze, guilt-struck.

"A fine shot," he said.

Freia stood, faintly sick with dread. What would he do?

"Well, pick it up, lass," Gaston said. " 'Tis thine." He dismounted. Freia went to the dead hare. An eye shot. She favored them because they killed at once, and she took pride in the accuracy required. She drew the arrow out and pulled grass, cleaning the blood-drenched shaft.

Gaston was coming; he was there. She didn't look at him as he lifted the soft limp body by the ears.

"An excellent shot," he said, allowing admiration to show in his voice.

"Thank you," Freia said in an undertone, scrubbing at the arrow. It was one she had made, red-fletched, stone-pointed. Gaston was looking at it as she worked, from arrow to skin-bag quiver to hare to the bow now leaning on her shoulder.

"Would you like some?" she asked, not knowing what else to say.

"Aye, indeed. He's a fat pretty fellow, far better than yon stripling Gina's got."

Gina was the hawk, Gaston's hawk that had brought down a marmot and was mantling it now with her wings, glaring about. Freia glanced at Gina and then at Gaston.

"I've picnic goods with me," Gaston said, "but he'll be a welcome betterment of bread-and-cheese." Freia pushed her hair back and looked at him face-on, hard and as closely as the difference in their heights allowed. Wasn't he angry?

Gaston could see the apprehension in her eyes; though he was injured at her duplicitous reticence in hiding the bow and her expertise, he wanted to know why. "Lass," he said, "mayst practice on the butts, an thou wouldst."

"Thank you," she said again, watching him.

"Wherefore the secrecy, Freia?" he asked bluntly. "Hast no need of shame, of hiding."

"I asked you—" Freia began, and stopped at the expression on his face.

Stricken by memory, Gaston was embarrassed; he had recalled the incident already on seeing her with the bow, and now he understood. She had asked for a bow, and he had brushed the request aside. "Ah," he interrupted her. "My foolish word made thee covert."

Freia looked down. Prospero would have been angry at such disobedience. Gaston's calm, she suspected, preceded a storm. She waited.

Gaston reached for her hand that held the arrow, turned it palm-up. Calluses and scrapes marked it. He released her hand but took the arrow from her, examined the point.

No storm broke. "I should have thought ere I spoke," the Fireduke said slowly. "Indeed, should have thought better ere now. I heard tales of how thou fought'st at Perendlac. Th'art no novice with that weapon, nor with others. Aye?"

"I didn't like hurting people. And I only use the bow," Freia said low-voiced.

"Hast little need of other. Freia." He put his hand on her shoulder, touched her chin so that she looked at him warily. "Forgive me for ill-grounded reason. Let me never damp thy joy in aught. An it please thee, shoot, walk, aye speak as freely as thou wilt. I would not bound thee."

⟨ 20 ⟩

THE LINENS WERE CLAMMY WITH SWEAT. His own voice still rang in the air. Dewar pushed the bedclothes away from him and lay panting, staring at the rain-spattered window across the room. He strained his ear for noises; only the rain and his own life-sounds were there. Waking in confusion, he had been certain someone was in the room with him, that Freia was beside him, that he lay in some waste place with her as they had when they were searching for Prospero.

It had been a night of long and vivid dreams about her. He had grown accustomed to them; she had been the dominant figure in his night-thoughts since he had left Landuc. He dreamt of others from time to time, or of nothing at all, but nearly every night Freia would pass wraithlike through his dreams, usually silent, and his dream-self would pursue her and be lost in grottoes of inexpressible thought until he woke, wanting her.

This morning's dream was different, and he lay close-eyed below the dark-timbered ceiling recalling its particulars. In this

dream, she had noticed him. Always before she had been indifferent. The setting had been one dream-familiar, a dark forest lit by tilted columns of sunlight spearing through the trees
to brighten the ground briefly, just like the forest around Prospero's Argylle. The trees were hung with mosses and ferns, and
the place was ancient and weary.

Freia stood very still by one of the trees, a drawn longbow
in her hands, the arrow nocked and ready to be loosed. She
gazed fixedly at something Dewar couldn't see. Her clothes
were plain and sensible for hunting or riding; high boots, divided skirt. Dewar, in the dream, moved to stand at her shoulder to see what her quarry was, but she lowered the bow and
turned her head to stare at him.

In the dream, they were eye-to-eye, though he knew she was
smaller than he, and her look was penetrating and unavoidable.

"Can you forgive me?" he asked her in the dream.

"You want me to forgive you," she said.

"I think of you often," he said. "Tell me where you are, Freia.
Tell me how you fare."

"You forced me to live for your sake, not mine," she said.
"The Balance must be kept." She lifted the bow and drew the
string and arrow back again lightly, smoothly, and loosed the
arrow, and Dewar followed its flight to see it strike Prospero,
who stood as a tree at the other side of the clearing, and Freia
shot quickly again and again, liquidly graceful, her draw and
release flawless, and the trunk of Prospero was a very pin-
cushion of shafts. Dewar grabbed at the last arrows, which he
knew were meant for Prospero's eyes, and Freia seized them
back and said, "All must go home," and when he tried to keep
them from her he knew that the only way to do so was to put
them where she would not take them, and so he drove them into
his heart.

Dewar woke.

He had never dreamt persistently about anyone before, not
even about his hateful, raging mother when he had fled her
house and her curses in Aië. Day and night Freia fretted at the

corner of his thoughts; he could close his eyes and summon up her image in any instant, hear the sound of her voice in his mind, no matter what other business he sought to concentrate on; and when he slept she ruled his dreams. Was this the price he would pay for endowing her with life? Was this what half-a-life meant, that each shared all of the other's? He wondered whether she dreamt of him, wherever she was.

His fascination distracted him from his sorcery. On this wet morning, alone in the tower, he lay staring at the glistening rain-trails on the pane and indulged that part of him that refused to let go of her. He recalled her sweet voice, her generosity; he conjured for his senses the softness of her cheek and the ripe curve of her lips. She was a masterwork of the Art, so surpassing Art as to befool Nature, and so surpassing the common run of Nature as to require no artful enhancement.

But she was not Art, but Nature, now. More than merely existing, she lived, felt, reasoned. If she had ever been nothing more than a sorcerer's cleverly-constructed experiment, she had changed; she was genuinely human, truly alive, and Dewar suspected she had been for a long time—if not always. She had a soul, that had persisted and been reclaimed.

Reclaimed, but lost again: where was she? He had half-expected to find her as he left the city; he had followed the shore road and crossed the icy, perilous causeway. He had seen only snow and ice and water, and he had gone on expecting to see her any instant, anywhere, as he rode to his retreat, the Tower of Thorns. Seasons had passed and he knew nothing of her; he feared to seek her actively, for what he might find and for what might find him. She never came, but the dreams made her a presence.

Once he had sealed a few drops of her blood in a wax-sealed crystal bottle, spherical in shape; that blood had been the basis of the precarious spell he had shaped to bring Freia home, when he had freed her from Landuc. He'd saved the sphere, of course. Dewar had put it in a little wooden casket in his work-room and he had not touched it, hoping that Freia would find her way to him—guided perhaps by the Stone. But the dreams were becoming too distracting. He had to know more; he had to see her face, hear her voice, behold her living.

Dewar swung his legs out of bed and went purposefully to the workroom, pulling on his dressing-gown as he went.

Freia's cheek stung still when she thought of Prospero, but pleasant though Montgard was it was not home, and as kind and courteous as Gaston was, he was not Prospero. She wanted her own hearth in winter, her own bed, her own trees and flowers. Prospero was intertwined with all these things, his storm-growl voice or zephyr-soft whispers, the flash and darkening of his eye, the movement of his hands. Freia yearned for the quick illumination of his stories and observations and the slow, savorous way he recited poetry and gestes to her. His anger was terrible, but it was a familiar anger, whose rhythm of rise and fall, swift and violent, was familiar also. Surely he had not meant to strike her.

Snow came early, falling as she and Gaston arrived at his castle in Montgard the city, and Freia retreated to her winter napping. Mornings were when she most thought of her home. Something about languid waking, about her winter habit of lying curled half-dozing for hours after sleep was finally lost, made everything about Montgard more foreign when she finally rose and looked at it. The square stone geometry, the mountains crowding on every side, the tilled fields and rutted roads around the town, the tower-bells that counted time, and the bright-clothed people teeming everywhere were all strange to her eyes wanting high trees, the dark river, stillness.

In a few days she would have been here two years. Two years of Gaston's kindness, of his comfortable hospitality and the warm, soothing domestic feeling of being beside a low-burning fire in a safe place. Two summers in Montjoie, on the steep-sided mountains that were like and unlike the ones at home.

Two years from home, and more counting all that time, nearly a whole winter, in Landuc. If she ever got home again, she would stay there, Freia swore to herself. Standing in a patch of midday sun, she poured hot water from the heavy ewer to the warmed silver basin and bent over to wash, untying the neck of her nightdress to sponge her shoulders and chest. As she towelled her face dry, her reflection floated in the water and shimmered in the rocking water. The image changed, darkening; the sunlight gathered into a ball at the bottom of the basin and popped like a bubble.

Dewar gazed at her, straight-on, biting his lip.

"Freia, this is sorcery, a Lesser Summoning, by which I can get sight and sound of you and you of me," he said.

"Dewar?" she whispered, her eyes wide.

"Yes." He had shaved off his beard; he appeared boyish without it. His voice rang metallic from the edges of the basin. She saw him as she might through thick glass, slightly blurred. "Freia, I'm sorry about what—what happened. What I said, what I did. It gnaws me."

Freia leaned forward, gazing down into the water at Dewar. He had done this vision-making before, when they were looking for Prospero. But how had he found *her* this way?

"I'm sorry," he said again. "It was an evil thing for me to do, betray your trust and turn on you."

She still said nothing, spellbound by the wonder of the sorcery.

"Should I stop speaking to you now?" he asked finally, tormented by the tension.

"No," she whispered, and later she didn't know why.

"Thank you. I—I wanted to know you were—are—all right. That's all. Don't—I hope you're happier than you were in Landuc."

"I'm not home," Freia said to his image.

"Don't go there. I believe Odile is there. She's poisonous; she has Prospero in her net, and she'd do horrible things to you, Freia, if she could reach you. Stay away."

"I want to go *home,*" she replied softly.

"I know. I'm sorry, Freia—"

"I can't. I don't know the way," she said, and swallowed tears and the ache-knot below her throat. She twisted the linen towel in her hands.

Dewar moistened his lips and swallowed too. "Dear sister, I do not want to take you there now, not with Odile there," he said again.

"You—" Freia began—and she jarred the basin. The image broke apart in ripples and was gone.

She waited for it to happen again, and the water remained water and the basin remained a sunlit silver hemisphere with no other activity than the rocking of the water within. Dewar had Summoned her as he had Summoned Josquin and Golias when she had been searching for Prospero with him. Could he be watching her as they had watched those two? Would she know if he were? Freia revolved slowly, looking at the windows, the door, the bed, the cupboard and chests and furnishings.

"Talk to me more," she whispered to the air.

Nothing happened.

The door moved; Helma came in with a fresh-brushed gown, and Freia dressed, her inner senses straining to hear Dewar.

Freia heard nothing more from Dewar through the whole of the winter. She said no word of the Summoning to Gaston. He had, after all, been her jailer in the Palace, and pleasant and honorable though he was, kind even, he was still oath-bound to the Emperor Avril, and he might deem Dewar's whereabouts as important as Prospero's.

And now Dewar edged into her dreams. Often as she woke she would be confused, having just dreamt of him lying beside her, his arm around her, his breath against her neck; or she dreamt of flying on the gryphon Trixie's back, conscious of the unfamiliar hardness of his body against hers. Often before she'd dreamt such dreams, which had always become terrifying rehearsals of Golias's brutality or projections of Ottaviano into Golias's role, but these latter dreams were innocent, flying over strange or clouded lands and waters, often leaving her with a feeling that someone had been speaking lovingly to her as she slept. She wanted to dream deeply of home and the forest, but instead she dreamt of Dewar and flying, though Prospero and Cledie and other folk of Argylle flickered through.

His brief conversation with her had told her much. Freia extracted every hint of meanings from it, fermenting it in her homesick heart through the winter. He was not with Prospero himself, as she had thought he must be, favored son and heir. Someone named Odile was, and Dewar thought Odile was to be feared. That Dewar would fear anything was novel. Who was Odile? Someone Prospero preferred to Dewar—that was incredible to Freia. Surely after allowing Dewar to see his precious books, Prospero would do anything to keep him there.

And Dewar apologized, freshening the ache of his insults and betrayal. Freia had passed two years barely thinking of him, and now he dominated her thoughts. She had thought of home, of Prospero—not of Dewar, the alien interloper. Interloper indeed—he had said he could not take her home now, and that implied that he could take her home, but chose not to, and it galled her that he could go home to the island and chose not to, and she wanted the place more than she wanted to breathe and could not have it.

Cambia had three words: "Taddy," "Muvver," and "Duck." "Duck" had come first, in the miller's yard where the large spotted ducks loitered and nabbled. Cambia was passionately enamored of ducks, and she followed the flock around until it seemed that she had become a duck *honoris causae* herself. She had been doing exactly that—following the ducks as they investigated a rain-puddle—when her mother arrived for one of her rare, usually brief, visits.

"Oh, there she is," Otto said, pointing. "Playing with the ducks again."

Luneté followed his finger and then stiffened. Cambia was filthy. Her hair was a mess of muddy knots. Her shins and knees were black. Her clothing was made of the solid, fine-quality wool and linen Luneté had provided, and the child looked like a peasant.

"Playing with the ducks again," Luneté repeated in a cool voice. "She does this often?"

"She likes ducks. I told you. I gave her the duck on wheels because she likes ducks."

"I didn't realize she had adopted them as her preferred companions," Luneté said. "Cambia! Come here."

"Taddy!" Cambia obeyed happily. She fell only once, despite the uncertain footing. Luneté wrinkled her nose on seeing the fresh green smears.

Otto, grinning, swung down from the saddle and swung Cambia up and around in a swooping circle. "Upsy-daisy!"

"Eeeeeee!"

"Here's Mother to see you, Cambia. Say Mother." Otto had had a lot of trouble teaching Cambia to say Mother.

"Muvver. Duck."

"This will not do," said Luneté, staring at her child.

"The ducks—" began Otto defensively.

"The dirt. It is time to bring you to the castle, Cambia. We shall find a proper nurse for you."

Accordingly, Cambia was borne back to the castle on Ottaviano's saddle-bow. On arrival, she was bathed under the pump, stripped, carried naked indoors and bathed again in the hot baths, had her hair clipped, and was brought back to her father when she was free of duck-muck and tangles.

Otto took Cambia from Laudine, who had scrubbed her, and held her, leaning against the solar's mantelpiece. "All clean and pretty like a princess," he told her.

"That is more suitable," Luneté said, coming in to them. "Hm. Her hair is getting darker."

"It's just dark when it's wet. I think it's going to be your color." The baby-down was nearly black now, very pretty against Cambia's fair skin and striking with her blue eyes. "You're going to be a pretty lady like Mother, aren't you, pet?"

"Taddy. Duck." Cambia twisted in Otto's arms, staring

around at Luneté, and suddenly grabbed at the Countess's necklace: a rope of pearls, given to her by the Baron.

"No!" exclaimed Luneté, and Cambia yanked back as her mother tried to pull the pearls from her fist; the string broke, and pearls bounced on the floor. "Don't! Oh, you naughty girl!"

"No, no, Cambia, that's Mother's," Otto chided her, moving away from Luneté; Laudine, tsking crisply, was picking up the loose pearls, gathering them into a handkerchief with the broken necklace. "I bet you're hungry, lambkin. It's dinnertime. Laudine, see if you can find her some food, would you? A coddled egg and bread, maybe a baked apple. She'll get fussy soon. As fussy as she gets." The maid curtsied and left.

"We must have someone to look after her at once. Her manners are atrocious," said Luneté. She was fond of the broken necklace.

"Who did you have in mind for a nurse?" Ottaviano pried at Cambia's still-closed fist and extracted two more pearls from it.

"Duck duck duck Taddy duck," carolled Cambia.

"I hardly know, but I won't have her rolling around in the mud like that," Luneté said. "Hm. Sir Matteus has a granddaughter just widowed."

"That girl whose sot husband fell from the bridge. Are you sure? She didn't act too clever when I saw her." Otto shifted Cambia, who was squirming.

"She has no children of her own," Luneté said, "and no husband to distract her. I think she'd do very well. Do you know anyone better?"

"Duck Taddy."

"Not here," he said. "In Ascolet, yes."

"I want her where I can watch her."

"She's Ascolet's too, Lu. Don't lose sight of that. The Emperor could award her either or both—depending on her siblings."

"I don't want another child now," Luneté snapped. "This one has been more than enough trouble."

"Duck," said Cambia loudly, and Otto let her down. Naked, she pattered over to the bag of toys and clothes hurriedly packed at the miller's house and took out her wooden duck. "Duck," she said again, offering it to Luneté.

"Goose," said Luneté, shaking her head.

The animal's wings were wide and russet-bronze-gold. It was ripping apart a black-striped Montgard hind, tearing skin and flesh, crushing bones, and swallowing all, its beak red with the prey's blood. The feathers were spattered with gore, and the eyes were a hot, angry yellow.

The gryphon shrieked, bloodcurdling and raucous, and a replying sharp whistle preceded the emergence, from the trees surrounding the landslide-meadow, of Freia. Smelling blood and the strange animal, Freia's horse tried to rear; she kept her seat and put her cloak over the mare's head. Then, the mare stilled but shivering, Freia dismounted and dragged her horse to a tree, looping the reins, never taking her eyes from the gryphon.

The gryphon was crouching now, its neck parallel to the ground, warbling softly.

"Trixie," Freia said softly to the gryphon. Her voice shook. Could it be Trixie? There were no gryphons in Montgard—

It crooned.

"Pretty Trix, pretty Trixie," Freia said, edging closer, "see, it's me, it's me—"

Trixie's hind legs folded; she sat, still mantling her kill, and burbled unbirdlike.

"—did you look for me, Trix, as you looked for Papa? Ooo, fine kill, well done, pretty Trix . . ." More cajolery, and Freia was smoothing the gryphon's throat-feathers, scratching her, talking to her in a rippling patter of repetitive flattery, and Trixie fawned and preened and warbled at the attention.

"I saw you, pretty Trix, saw you flying, yes, today, and I followed you, brave Trixie," Freia whispered, "and they won't like you poaching here, no, and that foot doesn't look well. What did you do, poor silly thing, hm, a bite I'd guess. . . ."

Her mind raced as her mouth rambled. She had to hide the gryphon. She would hide Trixie, take care of the infection in her foot, make a harness for her, and—and—

And what?

If she could find Freia, could Trixie find Prospero again? Find home from here? Freia had never been sure how she did it the first time; the creatures of Argylle all seemed to be able to follow him and find him, and she had relied on that when she'd used Trixie to venture after her absent father. Captured by Otto, Freia had sent Trixie to find Prospero alone, and when she'd returned to Argylle with Dewar, Scudamor had told her that Trixie had come, stayed long enough to eat once, and flown away again.

Now Trixie had come to her. Would she be able to find Argylle again? However she did it, could Freia persuade her do it once more?

It was worth trying. Freia didn't know the way home herself. Dewar had taken them there with sorcery, through a Way, but he wasn't helping now. She couldn't get there with Gaston's help, either, willing though Gaston might be to assist her. Trixie must have been wandering around looking for her, all these seasons, all these years.

"Poor Trixie, poor Trix," crooned Freia. "There's a wood I know where I'll hide you now, for the while, and you must lie quiet there. . . ."

Planning the theft of a considerable quantity of leather and chain from Gaston's house, Freia stroked Trixie's soft feathers and soothed her agitated temper.

Ottaviano was in Ascolet again. And yet again, the Countess of Lys was unable to join him, due to the demands Lys placed upon her. Otto had flared angrily before going this time.

"Why do I always have to come here? You haven't visited Ascolet once. Why don't you and Cambia come to Ascolet now?"

"I can't, Otto! I'm needed here."

"The place got along without you for years," he said. "Who says you can't go away for a while? Valgalant?"

"Are you jealous?"

"Of *Valgalant*?" yelped Otto. "Lu, I asked why you can't leave Lys!"

"And I told you! Lys needs me."

"What is so all-fired important that you can't leave it to look after itself for the summer?" he demanded, exasperated.

"I'm reviewing the tariffs and duties now," Luneté said, "and there's the problem of those graziers wanting more range but I don't know if it's really profitable to Lys to allow them to take land out of wheat, and the canals are being refaced, and—"

"None of that is life-and-death essential!"

"Neither is going to Ascolet!" Luneté shouted back, and she realized what she had said when Otto's face went white and cold.

"Madame, I leave you," he replied formally, and he bowed and was out of the solar before she could soften her words.

"Otto—" she said, but the door had closed.

Biting her lip, Luneté sank back in the chair. Lys needed her. She could feel it, needing her. Lys wanted her here, not in Ascolet; she had vowed her life to serve Lys. She couldn't run off to Ascolet half the year. It wouldn't be right. Ascolet didn't matter to Otto the way Lys mattered to her, she supposed, or he wouldn't make such unreasonable suggestions. He didn't understand her bond to Lys. Why, he wasn't really of Ascolet blood; the Emperor had thus far said nothing of rescinding the title he'd unwittingly bestowed on his bastard son, but Otto had only been able to claim the title at all because it had been Sebastiano's. Otto wasn't what he'd said he was; that was why he didn't understand Luneté.

The Countess of Lys squared her shoulders and straightened. He would be back, probably before the summer was out, full of aqueducts and roads and wool.

— 21 —

FREIA IMPROVISED A HARNESS FOR TRIXIE, poulticed the gryphon's injury, and writhed with indecision about telling Gaston she was leaving. She wanted to tell him, and she said nothing. In her heart, she feared he would hold her from going, perhaps even take her back to Landuc.

Smuggling heavy clothes and some food and utensils out of the Montjoie manor-house and hiding them was easily done during the five days she tended Trixie's foot. Freia spent those days with deer-hide and chain, hastily stitching harness for the gryphon. Gaston's Montjoie steward conducted an inquisition among the servants to discover who had purloined the chains that drove the well-pump.

The foot improved rapidly. Trixie groomed herself back to glossiness and ate well and crooned when Freia spoke to her, all normal behavior. On the seventh day after finding the gryphon, Freia donned warmer clothing than the season warranted and went riding out with her bow, a saddle-bag of food, and a troubled conscience. Gaston had brought her a book, a romance with pretty margin-pictures from Lindfluss, and he had mentioned that he would like to ride up to a certain view-point with her on the following day, and he had been as kind as he ever was, or better, and Freia nearly told him about Trixie. Nearly: fear kept her tongue silent.

That day she finished the harness, shot a young buck for Trixie to eat, and picked berries. She would wait until twilight to fly.

At dusk, Freia loaded the gryphon with the saddle-bags from the pretty white-socked mare and stood a long, indecisive moment before untying the horse. If she sent the horse home without her, they would think she'd had an accident. Perhaps, she thought, they would think she was dead when they didn't find her. She looped the horse's reins around and around her fingers, considering. Gaston would be angry with her for running away, but what if he thought she was dead? He wouldn't tell anybody in Landuc about thinking her dead in an accident in Montgard, because they wouldn't believe him—or if they did, they'd blame him for not telling them she had been alive. Thus if she let the mare go back without her, she would be safe from Landuc, and Gaston couldn't follow her.

She looked at the ground. The mare tried to toss her head, and Freia made her stand still.

But the things Gaston had done . . .

He had given her the horse, and he let her go anywhere—not that it mattered, because he knew she couldn't leave here and go home—but he had said he would take her home—had he meant that? Had he truly meant that? He had shown her the book of routes and places and the Map, explaining how to use them together. He had told her things her father never had. When she was sick, after Golias had stabbed her, Gaston had talked to her gently and never lost patience with her silence, and he had brought her good food and kept her prison-chamber warm and forbidden the Emperor to throw her in a dungeon again. He didn't ask questions, not like Dewar. He didn't make her do things and not do things, not like Prospero.

But would Gaston keep her from leaving? Would he have stopped her this morning?

He would be worried if she sent the mare away; Freia knew that. She imagined him searching and making all his people search and call for her, all over the mountains, as they had when two shepherd boys were lost in a late snowstorm last spring. Gaston wouldn't give up. He never gave up. He would fell the forest, she thought, or at least look in every tree and under every bush. He would be worried and unhappy, and it would be her fault; he would feel as she felt when Prospero went away and told her nothing.

She shouldn't have ridden this morning; she should have

walked here. Well, now she would have to send the horse away with some clear sign that she wasn't hurt or lost.

She tied the mare up again. Trixie fidgeted and croaked, impatient; Freia took out her flint and steel. Squatting on her heels, she cleared a little space on the ground and, after a few false starts, made a twig-fire, small and restrained. There was a thin-barked log by the mare, and Freia used her knife to cut the bark, peeling until she got a largish piece off.

The fire had nearly burned out; she began offering it twigs and pulling them out half-charred.

She hesitated. She had never written a letter. Gaston had taught her all the ways people here wrote letters, but she didn't have enough bark or sticks for a formal address or the courtesies and bombast which formed half the body.

Uncle, she began, and chewed the stick's unburned end, thinking. The letters were neat enough. She thought he'd be able to read it. What should she write?

I am not hurt, she scratched out carefully, stick after stick. *I found a way to go to P. Thank you.*

All the letter closings she knew were too long. There wasn't room on the bark for them.

F.

Would that be enough? Freia thought so. It seemed a very good letter to her, even written on bark in smudgy charcoal. The top words were bigger than the ones toward the bottom of the bark, but she didn't want to try writing it again all one size. She rolled it loosely, tying it with a long blade of grass, and squeezed it between the mare's saddle and saddle-cloth.

Then Freia untied the mare again, slapped her rump, and shooed her onto the homeward path. When the hoofbeats had clipped away Freia took Trixie's bridle and led her out of the forest to a clearing.

The sun was behind the mountains; the thin air was cold. Freia waited under the dark trees as the clouds changed colors. Trixie crouched, alert, knowing departure was coming. The stars began to come out behind the clouds, and she found constellations Gaston had taught her, bright chips of light above the dark fringe of treetops. Night: they could fly unseen. It was time to go. She guided Trixie from under the trees to the open clearing.

Trixie lifted her head, lashed her tail, looked around.

Freia stopped in mid-gesture and listened, wary.

"Freia!" someone shouted, very near—Gaston. Branches breaking and a disturbance in the forest accompanied his voice.

He had gotten the letter. He *was* angry. She'd better go.

The gryphon twisted and misbehaved as Freia tried to mount, squirming and jumping away like a cub, and Gaston yelled "Freia!" again, now at the bottom of the meadow. Trixie squalled angrily.

"Freia?"

Freia yanked Trixie's bridle and stood still, holding the gryphon's beak closed with her arms. A horse whinnied; Gaston said something to the horse; she saw him come out of the darkness toward her, a tall lantern-lit shape blotting stars.

"Bright World! What—" he began saying, and stopped, holding the lantern high, and the light flashed suddenly from the long blade of his sword.

Trixie thrashed, threw off Freia's grip, and screamed. Freia hung on the bridle with both hands and used all her weight to pull the gryphon's head down as she tried to bolt.

"Don't—"

"Freia!" Gaston lunged forward, lifting the sword as Solario carried him closer; another horse, released, galloped down the meadow.

"She's scared; get back!"

Solario wheeled and Gaston retreated, lowering but not sheathing his sword. "Freia. Th'art unhurt? What beast is this?"

"My gryphon," said Freia, panting, holding Trixie's head down. "Please, I'm all right, please put your sword away, I think it scares her."

Gaston sheathed the sword, still peering at the ill-defined shape of the gryphon in the dark, beyond his lantern's range.

"I found thy horse a-wandering. Did that beast start her? Hast met no mishap?"

Freia saw now: he had ridden Solario and led the white-socked mare, but the mare had fled down the meadow away from the gryphon. "No," Freia said. "Didn't you find the letter?"

"Letter?" Gaston repeated, his voice rising.

"I put a letter on the horse," Freia said. "Under the saddle. A piece of bark." She was insulted. She had gone to considerable effort to write the letter, and he hadn't even looked at it.

Gaston said nothing. Trixie made a low rattling noise in her throat.

"I did, I put it under the saddle," Freia said, aggrieved, "I knew you'd think I had an accident if she came back without me."

Gaston dismounted, keeping watch on the gryphon distrustfully; Trixie glared back. "Well," said he, lifting the lantern to half-light Freia and the gryphon, "I confess, lass, I'd not thought to look there at once. Wherefore didst thou not tell me this morn that 'twas thy intent to leave? Hast found this, this gryphon but today?"

"I found her a few days ago," Freia said. "She was hurt. She was looking for me. She's mine, I trained her at home."

Gaston, lamplit, nodded understanding.

"I thought you wouldn't let me go," Freia said. "I'm sorry, but I did, I thought—"

Her uncle drew breath to speak; he stopped and sighed. A pause; he thought, studying her. "Freia," said Gaston then, "didst thou think I'd keep thee here by force, having told thee th'art free to go and offered thee aid without reserve?"

Freia looked down. "You did say that," she admitted, "but people here—people say things, offer to do things, that—that they can't do."

"I have not betrayed thy trust in aught," said Gaston. "What I have promised thee, what I have given, is thine without reserve."

"It's not that I'm ungrateful," she said, her voice trembling. She was grateful; she was bowed with gratitude. Not a day passed in which she did not thank Gaston for something great or small, and not a day passed in which she did not labor to think of something she might return him for his kindness. There was nothing, not even meat or vegetables and fruits of her garden, such as she had offered Prospero; Gaston needed nothing from her, and all she had for him was gratitude.

"Gratefulness is naught of't," Gaston replied, coming a few steps nearer.

Trixie made a hissing sound. Freia cuffed her, out of patience with her bad behavior. "Friend!" she said.

"So have I sought to be," Gaston said, "as much thy friend as thou wouldst let me be."

The pain in his voice was audible; Freia, dismayed, understood in that instant that she had wronged Gaston. It wasn't gratitude that he wanted, nor obedience nor the subjugation of her will to his; unlike Prospero's or Dewar's gifts, Gaston's gifts such as cloak and horse, books and brooch, were given, not to require that she produce something he wanted in return, but because he wished her to have them. He offered them as her friend. Was it truly possible that Gaston wanted to be her friend, with nothing more to it? Prospero had said so much about the evil people of Landuc, and she had found nothing good in them herself—yet Gaston had asked nothing of her and had given so much—

"I'm sorry," Freia said in a small voice.

"Lass—" Gaston began, surprised, but Freia interrupted him.

"I'm sorry," she said again, "I didn't mean—I didn't think— I haven't—" She stopped, looking down at her feet. "I haven't had friends very much," Freia explained. "I'm sorry."

"How now, lass," Gaston said quietly. "I meant not to accuse thee."

Freia met his eyes again and was reassured. She believed

him. Gaston was kind to her and he listened and he was never angry, and he wanted to be her friend. That was why he had not taken her back to Landuc nor told anyone there about her: he was being her friend, and she hadn't understood.

"I like you," Freia said. "I didn't mean to hurt your feelings."

"Nor I thine. Freia, I'm not wroth with thee," Gaston said. "An the gryphon can take thee to thy father, then 'tis well thou go. I know he's ever in thy thoughts; this is not home for thee. I'd not prevent thee going. Nor returning."

"Returning?"

"An it please thee to return, lass, art always welcome here." Gaston was smiling, his eyes warm and his mouth barely curved, his underlying seriousness adding weight to the invitation.

Freia smiled, warmed by a rush of relief.

"And I will never keep thee 'gainst thy will," Gaston promised, the corners of his mouth creeping upward.

Freia's smile vanished. "Thank you," she said.

"Dost believe me?" he asked, his own smile leaving him, now grave and intense.

"Yes."

"I thank thee," Gaston said, softening his look. "So thou'lt leave now, tonight. How? Hast studied th' Ephemeris and Map?"

"No. It doesn't matter about the Well. Trixie will know where to go."

"A clever creature, that can find her path 'mongst the Gates and mazy Roads," Gaston remarked, turning toward Trixie.

"She did it before. She takes a while sometimes, but she gets there. She found her way here to me all by herself."

"Well. Art provisioned for thy journey?"

"I have things," Freia said. "Some food and a waterskin and my bow."

Gaston nodded, looking at the gryphon by the lantern-light. "Wilt accept more? I'd not see thee go without the best I could give thee."

"I don't really need much—I— Uncle, it was I that stole that chain. I needed it for her. I'm sorry."

He stared at her, amazed. "It was thy doing?"

"Do you still like me," Freia asked, her throat tight.

Gaston put his hand on her shoulder and squeezed it hard. "Yes."

The saddle-bags were heavier when Freia rebuckled them just before midnight. Gaston had persuaded his niece to wait a few hours and had ridden away. He'd returned with larger bags stuffed full of food, a cooking-pot, a warm leather jerkin, extra socks, other things he considered needful for an indefinite journey. Freia demurred, embarrassed to accept so much from him, and Gaston need only stand, hands on hips, looking sternly down at her, before she said, red-cheeked, that she must pay him back someday if he insisted on giving her such a good pair of bags and a fleece-lined jerkin and all.

"I wish with all my heart that thou hadst been to the Well and stood the Fire," Gaston said, after she had buckled the new bags on. "To set off so, Mapless, with no notion of direction—"

"It's only complicated in Landuc, in Pheyarcet," Freia said. "And she found her way here, so she must know her way home. I'll be all right, Uncle Gaston."

"Th'art wise and resourceful enough that I believe thee," Gaston said, taking Solario's reins. "Remember th'art welcome here always, lass."

Freia nodded. "I have to go home," she said. "I'll come visit you, though."

Gaston inclined his head, mounted Solario. "Be careful, lass," he said.

"I will."

He lifted his hand, not smiling, serious and ruddy-gold in the lantern's low flame, and turned Solario to the path again. The hoofbeats receded into the night forest. Freia whispered, "Thank you," after Gaston again. Should she stay?

Trixie tossed her head and stamped.

Freia scrambled up on the glossy, smooth feathers. Trixie fidgeted and danced, unused now to a rider, and for a few minutes Freia must wrestle her into compliance and keep from being shaken off.

They settled who was to be mistress, and Freia leaned forward to the gryphon's ear. "Prospero," she said. "Find Prospero, Trixie. Home to Prospero."

Trixie stamped uncertainly. Freia repeated the order. Trixie shook her head and tossed it back, trotted a few steps, crouched, and leapt upward.

Gulping, Freia closed her eyes as the ground spun away under them; gryphons ascend in a spiral when they cannot drop into a glide, and for a woman who hated heights one was as bad as the other. Trixie went up and up, circling steadily, and then struck off toward a pass Freia had not been through before. On glimpsing the direction, Freia bit her lip and closed her eyes again; she hoped Trixie knew what she was doing. Gaston had said there was only one way into and out of Montgard on the Road, and it wasn't that pass, the Gatmon Pass where a trio of mountain streams joined and plunged in a seasonally spectacular cascade, a pass which she knew led out of Montgard to Logreia. But she had to trust Trixie's instinct, which had led her to Prospero before, and so Freia hung on, glad not to have eaten, and the gryphon arrowed through the gap as the moon set behind them.

Freia's head spun. She gripped Trixie's harness tightly and dared another peek at the world. The world was hazy. She seemed to see three or four images at once, superimposed and shifting in dominance. She closed her eyes. It was the Road; Trixie had done it, and Uncle Gaston had a Gate he didn't know about. Freia squirmed cautiously to half-lie against Trixie's back and outstretched neck, and Trixie's wings went up and down.

The Empress Glencora had written regularly to Luneté of Lys, dispensing advice and cautions and liberal dollops of fashion and gossip. Luneté had written back faithfully, assuring the

Empress of Cambia's good health, of Lys's good estate, and of Luneté's thoughtful implementation of the Empress's and Lord Gonzalo's counsel. Luneté wrote the Empress three letters for every one received, but that was all right; the Empress was understood to be busy and Luneté had taken seriously the Imperial suggestion that she write often.

The Empress, therefore, was well-placed to detect a note of disharmony in Lys's letters. On a delicately spring-tinted late-winter morning, she set down the latest with a little frown. Something was absent from this letter, and the letter was so complete and self-contained that the Empress could not at first think what it was. After a moment, she sent her secretary to bring her all the letters from Lys, which was quickly done. The Empress riffled through them rapidly, skimming for a name, a word, paused pensively over a smudged, once-creased note carefully smoothed and flattened. When she had gone through them all, she set them aside and thought.

It was news, she thought, that the Emperor would be pleased to hear. He had only grudgingly blessed the Ascolet-Lys union, and when the hotheaded young Baron had turned out to be his own bastard by his late brother's late wife, the subject had gone into a freeze, neither man nor realm to be mentioned in the Palace. There was no question of Dewar's veracity. The sorcery was true; it had been done with the Well, and there was nothing but truth there—the Emperor had not even tried to deny it.

The Empress, directed not to recognize the relationship, had taken no special notice of the bastard Baron. He was a handsome fellow, and she privately thought he took after his sire, finer-featured in a way that recalled Cecilie, but even more after Panurgus himself, tall and passionate and immoderate. The Empress knew very well that an able bastard will often supplant an incompetent legitimate son, and she feared for Josquin in the future of politicking and jockeying that had not yet begun. Ottaviano was under a cloud, but clouds were known to break apart.

As did other things. The Empress set the matter aside for a few days, until she chanced to see Josquin starting off into the gardens on a mild morning's walk. She sent one of her ladies to detain him, and Josquin found himself strolling with his mother on his arm, his own plans diverted.

"To what do I owe the favor of your company, Mother?" he asked, wondering if she had somehow found out what his plans were.

"I do not see much of you, dear, not when you're in Madana," said the Empress, "and you have only dined at home once in the past sixteen days."

"Ah, well, Father doesn't look fondly on me when I do, you know," said Josquin.

"You are his heir," said she. "He expects certain things."

Josquin blinked. "Mother, if this is about marrying—"

"No," said the Empress. "That will look after itself for now, I'm sure. We'll find a suitable match in good time. Of course we can't have you marrying too far down. Your cousin was just right, as far as rank goes."

"I thought we weren't talking about marrying," Josquin said, a little desperately.

"We weren't. But you cannot be deaf to some of the talk I have heard about Ascolet."

"Ah," said the Prince, understanding. "He is admired, yes. Marries in Sarsemar's nose, gets her pregnant in short order and presents the Emperor with a joint heir-presumptive to Lys and Ascolet—albeit a girl—loses all his wars and keeps his title, and now he's revealed to be the Emperor's by-blow. Quite the makings of a popular hero. Is Father going to acknowledge him?"

The Empress stopped on the flagstone path. Sometimes Josquin was too frank, but on the whole— "He's said nothing of it to me," she said, "and the Baron of Ascolet has, thus far, done nothing to please him so much."

"I gather he mostly chases round after his wife and his livestock. Funny to think of him playing the doting husband; I assure you he wasn't during the war. Wild fellow—people said Dewar was wild, but the Baron's far over him there, and a mean streak too judging by what happened to poor Lady Miranda. I suppose it all depends on whether one is seen or not."

"I suppose," the Empress said, not wishing to drift into an etiquette discussion. "Josquin," said she, "I feel a great anxiety about the Baron and about you."

Josquin squelched several hearty retorts to this. "You think he could supplant me?"

"It's possible."

"Not without Father recognizing him," said Josquin. "And he won't do that while Madana matters two straws. Think, Mother. You're Madana. I'm Madana. Is Father going to insult you and all of Madana by admitting to an indiscretion with his dead brother's dead wife? Not Father. The Baron's got all he's going to get. He's got Ascolet and Lys—by proxy—and if he starts ogling anything more, one might posit Sarsemar, Father will whip him back quick. He's too ambitious to be given any indulgence. I may be a brainless fop, but I think that much is obvious even to me."

"Lys and Ascolet. He has much already," the Empress said. "More than enough."

Josquin shrugged. "Let him keep what he has, for good behavior," he said. "If he can."

⸺ *22* ⸺

PROSPERO CLUNG TO ODILE. HE COULD lose himself in her yet, though despair smothered him. Eight years of harvesting hunger and slow death had left him famished for any glimpse of joy; though joy was fleeting or unattainable in his desperate, violent coupling, he pursued it all the more frantically for that. Odile entertained him with her games and devices, novelties and old tricks and elegant arrangements of sensations. He hoped that Odile would conceive; perhaps a child out of her by him could redeem the place. But she remained slender, and he said nothing of it to her, though he talked to her of everything else.

In a frenzy of self-abandonment, he made love to her during the late-summer storm that screamed in from the sea to denude trees of leaves and uproot trunks, smash boats to kindling and lift houses and roofs apart, and Odile received his attentions passionately and listened as he cursed Dewar.

The storm passed. Prospero rose, sponged himself, went forth to face its ravages. The gaunt Argyllines came out and stared at their stripped wood and the tumbled trunks, the flattened gardens and fields and the ruined boats. It was the storm of storms, the hand of the Element battering its passive opponent earth; it scoured every sign of cultivation from the fields with its floods and winds and drove a dike of earth and debris up to the city walls.

Prospero walked and looked, numbness settling in his soul.

"If only the Lady were here," he overheard, never for his ears. "If only the Lady had not died. All was well when she was here, before the war." Prospero ground his teeth and hoped that his ingrate daughter's soul suffered.

The trees which had not lost all their leaves to the wind now quickly lost them to the salt which the storm had carried, and the grasses were yellowed and wintry before time. A few sheltered trees still bore fruit, and Prospero said they must pick it unripe and compost it, a hard thing for starving folk to do. The inexorable sun shone again on the land, and the arid wind blew, and the mud baked to brick.

Nearly half the town's remaining population began to ready for journeys. Prospero forbade anyone to leave the place; only by all working together could the fields be salvaged, and the fishing-boats would be crewless if so many departed. The city gates were closed and barred by night, and by day the slow-moving, famished field workers were watched from the walls. Prospero persuaded, and whom he could not persuade he commanded, and whom he could not command he forced, still dominating them with words and will. None left the city, but the silence that hung inside the walls was as still as emptiness: a dull waiting silence, unbroken by protest or lament.

Ten days after the storm, the full moon rose, then darkened. At first no one noticed, and then a woman fetching water cried out and pointed at the bent shape of the moon's sphere overhead: one edge had corroded, was caving inward. Soon the whole populace had left their long-houses and stood on the common, staring at this fresh distortion of natural order.

The shouts and shrieks attracted the attention of folk on the island, at Prospero's tower, and they too stared. Prospero and Odile, on the top of the tower, watched too, neither speaking. The moon dimmed, tarnished, reddened.

"An omen," Prospero murmured at last.

"A sign," said Odile. "Dewar's at work, I doubt it not: a threat, or challenge, my lord. Would that I might aid thee better to meet it."

A boat pushed off from the mainland and hurried to the isle; two people left the boat and ran to the tower, ran up the stairs to Prospero as quickly as the hunger-weakness allowed. The door rattled open; Scudamor tripped on the threshold, gasping, and fell on hands and knees, jostled Odile and Prospero.

"Cloddish oaf; beware lest thou remain thus," hissed Odile. "What—"

Behind Scudamor, even in the deep night-dusk, Cledie glimmered. She gazed, serene as always, at Prospero, then at Odile, then at Prospero again, and Prospero felt a cold, unhappy discomfort settle on him. She had returned, but he felt her draw away, repulsed. Odile did not finish her question.

Scudamor picked himself up, dusting his skinned knees, moved back, away from Odile. "Lord Prospero," he said, "the folk are afraid of this night-in-night, and I beg you give me some words to comfort them."

"The moon hath two halves, bright and dark, fair and cold," Prospero said; "this night her darker face is shown. She'll turn again. Fear not the dark; the mutable moon's a tricksy bauble, in light and dark inconstant. Let them be calmed: 'twill brighten anon." He halted; he could not think of more to say, though his words rang unconvincing to him.

Scudamor waited, as if expecting more; Cledie said nothing,

her expression indistinct now in the gloom. "So shall I tell them, Lord," said Scudamor at last. Cledie disappeared entirely in the darkness and the Seneschal followed her down. A torch-light flared in the stairs as the door closed behind him, sharp and yellow in the night.

Prospero returned his attention to the moon, nearly gone now; and he tried to think, despite the sudden pain he felt at glimpsing lovely Cledie: he could command her stay, but to what end? "The moon," he said softly, hardly knowing he spoke aloud, "doth shine with borrow'd fire, lent by the resting sun: without that charity, her face, unveil'd by light, must show its true complexion."

" 'Tis artifice," disagreed Odile. "The moon's light is hers by ancient right, now clipped by jealous earth; without unnatural shade, illumined fair she rides her course. She shifts her aspect inasmuch she shifts her stance, and that's full natural, for there's nothing in the world appears the same from every side."

"That's true," conceded Prospero.

"And see, dear lord, e'en as we speak, she gleams again: own that's her true face, as she turns to gaze on us once more."

Prospero stared at the slender, long-limbed crescent, steadily broadening, that marked the waxing circle of the moon. Had he not forsworn sorcery, he knew he'd feel great changes in the world. Such events were not causeless, nor did they simply end. " 'Tis her true face; her wonted pallor shows she's Queen of Night. We, though, dwell in the day; and paint her as she would, I'll not take her to mistress, nor longer gaze and howl her majesty's praise." He turned away and went to the door, pulled it open, and went down in the torch-light; but Odile stayed behind to watch the moon.

The wind shifted that night. By morning, it had changed quarters and warmed, then fallen off altogether; no rain fell, but the air was milder, nearly summer-like. Three days passed, and a curious mist came to Threshwood. A greenish shimmer clung to the trees and bushes. New growth burst out to replace lost leaves, and flowers began to bud and blossom half a year off-step.

Prospero disbelieved; it could not be true; some greater, final horror must follow this hope.

The strange weather went on. Songbirds absent since the first hard winter now rehearsed liquid arpeggios among the untimely flowers. Some trees, the protected few whose fruits Prospero had spared, bore fruit and flower both at once, a strange sight; the rest blossomed abundantly. Mothweed grew everywhere and perfumed the air, springing up in cracks and nooks and waving delicate white flowers in the moist breezes.

Odile was not pregnant. Prospero could not find explanation for the second spring, and he prognosticated that it would end with a sharp frost and a long, hard winter.

But the trees hurried to turn time back to early summer. The thorns that had sprung up became softer—they bore flowers and then berries, small swelling red clusters. Opportunistic surviving seeds burgeoned in the fields, crowding out the weeds, and the Argyllines watched the crops and urged them mutely to grow.

Prospero, confounded, went down to the Spring, turning the key and descending for the first time since he had locked the door on it.

His eye found a faint glimmer that he could not be sure was not merely his desire's invention. His hand, over the Spring, felt a firm, seeping pressure. It was not what it had been in former days, but it was there, more there than recently. Yet no water had risen, and he stood for a long time in the dark with his hand in the flow of power, wondering at its alterations, and returned to the upper world with a soothed serenity in his face that greatly reassured Scudamor and Utrachet.

These two were of the private opinion that the Countess was ill tidings and that the improvement in Argylle's fortunes must be due to the return, in hiding somewhere but in Argylle, of Prospero's son.

"He was a kind fellow," Scudamor told Cledie and Utrachet

in an undertone, as they stood on the tower watching the freakish spring greenery wave in a mild autumn breeze. A party of workers was digging unenthusiastically at the half-buried city walls.

"Kind to my lady, and good to my lord," Utrachet agreed, "and a student of his father's Art, and it seems we do need to have one."

Cledie said, "The Countess likes him not at all. I've heard her."

"She has no good to say of our Lady Freia neither," Utrachet lowered his voice more. "You know—"

"I've thought—"

They looked at one another and gulped.

"Best not discuss it," decided Scudamor.

"I miss our Lady Freia," Utrachet said softly. "She was one of us, wasn't she. And she never wanted to leave us."

"She did not leave us of her will," Cledie reminded them; "Lord Prospero carried her away."

"Something happened to my lord in that war," Scudamor murmured. "He never had time for her after that. She was always chasing him, poor chick, and we were all working on the walls then, day and night."

"We built well," Utrachet said.

"But why?" Scudamor whispered. "She didn't want walls."

"She didn't want the war," Utrachet reminded him, and they glanced at one another for an instant before looking determinedly both outward at the Jagged Mountains to the north, where a veil of rain, the first since the terrible windstorm, was greying the whiteness of the peaks and working its way down among the forest's blackened trees, toward them.

When later memory blurred history and compressed it, The Year There Was No Winter somehow became the first year of the world, in spite of everyone knowing about Prospero's War and all that had happened before it. But people often think two things at once, and so that year, when the weather following the

Great Storm held mild long enough for a small harvest of fall-sown vegetables and continued subdued and soft until spring came again in its proper place in the seasons, got mixed up with the year after Prospero's Making, and blended itself with other events, until only the few survivors who had been Made by Prospero had a remote chance of keeping the story straight. Fortunately, one of these was Hicha, who kept a chronicle of all that happened for Scudamor, and she reported on the confusion and repeated the proper order of things in her account. So it was written down correctly, but never remembered.

The Year There Was No Winter puzzled Freia.

The journey to Argylle was long. Trixie haltingly felt her way, and Freia clung to her back and let the gryphon choose the route. They backtracked three times before attaining the wasteland Freia well recalled crossing with Trixie in search of Prospero, with Dewar on their way to find Prospero, with her father on their way to Landuc. Now she crossed it with Trixie again in search of Prospero and Argyle. It was wider than she remembered; there was no water to be found, so that she and Trixie both trembled with thirst before they reached a waterhole in the steep hills on the other side. There had been no hills before, and she thought she must be recrossing it in different places each time. It seemed the only reasonable explanation. Prospero had described to her how mountains were made. These didn't look as if they had been pushed out of the earth recently, nor were there the hot rocks and black smokes that he had said made other mountains.

Reaching home from there was easy, Trixie flying straight and fast. Hunting was poor. Drought and heat lay on the fields and forests, growing worse as Freia neared the isle and the city. She slept beside Trixie, hungry, longing for rain to soften the aridity and green the slopes.

Trixie flew over a wide swath of blackened desolation nearly as broad as the wasteland, but this had been made recently by fire. The trees were stark charred sticks, the ground black and baked, the waters—such as they were—silted and undrinkable.

Passing this, they came at last to a once-lovely place in the high, jagged mountains Freia knew well, and it too had suffered; great ancient trees, burnt by fire and toppled by storm, lay with their roots exposed to the desiccating air. Their branches were dry, rattling bonily in the wind. Trixie landed reluctantly.

"Oh, poor trees," Freia said, walking through the fallen forest, shocked. The smell of old smoke bit her throat and nose. Here she had hunted, eaten, slept, many days and nights; it was one of her favorite places, and it was dead. Soon she was black with soot and char. Had Prospero done this in anger? She had seen him do such damage before, but never on so vast a scale. This place, the whole countryside, were spoiled. Why would he ruin his own Argylle?

She went back to Trixie, who was drinking at a mucky brook, and mounted again. Trixie, though, wasn't interested in travelling; she wanted to hunt, and Freia had to allow her to land in a water-meadow whose pond showed drying mud above its low waterline. The fires and storms had not crossed the ridge, and here the forest was still standing and alive. She had taken the season to be autumn, from the stars and other signs, but here the trees were budding out spring-green in fresh autumnal litter, and Freia examined them, puzzling over this, after the gryphon had gone off to catch her dinner.

Freia followed the pond's stream up the hillside. The landscape began to feel familiar; the angles of trees, the tilt of the earth evoked comparisons in her memory, an effortless sorting that finished abruptly when Freia came to a cracked reddish rock shelf over which the stream spilled. Here, yes, and above, onward, up another creeper-fringed cracked rock; this was the place she recalled indeed. Another half-hour's clambering, and Freia found herself in an agreeable camping spot where the water spilled in a lacy veil over black rocks and green ferns and mosses. There were pools of cold water dammed by stones that she had pushed and hauled and caulked with leaves and sticks in the long summer days, years ago. Now her rough-crafted obstruction had become undistinguishable from nature's work, modified by the impulses of the water over time. Happily, feeling at home, she undressed and splashed herself clean, then sat drying in the single broad shaft of sunlight that penetrated the gloom of the karial trees. These were fully in leaf, their trunks patchy red and their fronds long and luxuriant. Freia pulled on her shirt, lay on her stomach on a flat-topped rock to watch the pool of water for fish, and dozed.

Her back was cold, and someone was calling to her.

She woke reluctantly. Who was that? Nobody knew she was here. Unless Trixie had told. Gryphons couldn't talk.

"Freia." It was only a whisper, in the sound of the water. A dream? "Freia," the water whispered again.

Freia pushed herself up and looked around, bewildered. The sun had left the clearing; now only deep-angled streaks of light fell on the water and the fronds. She saw movement in the water and, forgetting the dream, leaned forward with an arrow to try to spear the fish. The sun-spatters vanished, overclouded.

No fish. Light shivered across the pool's surface and swirled.

"Freia," said Dewar, a dappling image, ever-sundered and ever-coalescing in the stirring water.

Freia lowered the arrow.

"I thought you were a fish, or a dream," she said, shaking her head. Still dreaming?

He smiled and the waterfall said, "No, but—what is this, a brook? Moving water?"

"Yes. A waterfall. And a stream."

"It's difficult to work with," he said. "It may not last. Freia, where are you? I have been looking for you."

"I'm home," she said.

"Did Prospero—"

"I was—away. Trixie found me and brought me home," Freia said.

"Clever Trixie. Freia, you mustn't stay in Argylle. Odile is there. I—"

"Who is Odile?" Freia demanded.

"My mother," Dewar said. "A vicious sorceress. Avoid her, as you love life."

"I don't," Freia said tartly, and turned her back on the waterfall and the pool.

Dewar said other things, rushed words in the water-rhythm. She stopped her ears. The waterfall ran on wordlessly and then whooshed; spray dampened her back and head. Startled, Freia turned around in time to see Dewar lose his footing and fall from the moss-slicked rocks of the pool.

No watery vision: Dewar, solidly there.

She stared without speaking as he regained his feet and, soaked and green-slimed, climbed onto the boulder beside her, holding her gaze with his own fixed on her.

"You're very difficult to talk to," he said. "Or perhaps I say the wrong things."

"How did you do that?" she whispered.

"I'm a sorcerer. Freia, I wish to offer you help if you want it, but I suppose you don't want it. But you could at least *say* no." Dewar's voice was low and unsure; he rubbed at a mossy stain on his white shirt cuff, unbuttoning the cuff, nervous.

"I don't need any of your help," Freia said. "I got here all by myself with Trixie. What do you mean, you were looking for me?"

"I've been trying to Summon you for days. Freia, please—I don't know where you've been hiding, but I'm worried about Odile being here. If she has gotten at that Spring, we'll really have trouble. I'm afraid she has her claws deep into Prospero. You'd be safer if you came away and stayed with me." He spoke quickly, but clearly: emphasizing the danger and the safety.

"What's it to you whether Odile does anything to me, and why would she want to?" she asked crossly.

"You'll be in her way if you stay, she will hurt you or kill you, and I like you," Dewar said, eye to eye with her.

Freia tossed her head, glaring at him. What right had he, a stranger here, to tell her to leave? When had he done any kindness for her that did not help himself as well? She was wiser now than to believe him. "You don't. You're a sorcerer and you don't care a rat's turd about anyone else. You want to use me for something, yourself; you'd never speak to me otherwise. Go away and let me be!"

Dewar's face went blank with shock. He began to speak; he said nothing, stunned by the cold anger ringing in her voice.

Was it so? When had she ever lied?

The waterfall tumbled over the rocks.

"I'm sorry," Dewar said finally, and he slid off the rock, waded across the pool, and stood under the waterfall. It thrummed on his head and filled his ears.

A Way, he thought; he'd open a Way through the moving water and leave her as she wished: but the water soothed the pain that had shot through his heart.

"You are mad," Freia said, watching him, but she knew he wasn't, and she wondered what to do for a long time while he stood with his back to her, his hands braced on the rocks. He couldn't just stand there. It wasn't right. Perhaps he meant it this time, meant to help her without seeking something hidden for himself; perhaps he wanted to help Prospero, if Prospero was in trouble. Now she had hurt him, just as he had hurt her, and the balance of insult wasn't a pleasant feeling.

Freia splashed after him and stood out of the water's reach. He ignored her. "I shouldn't have said that, Dewar."

"It's true," he said to the water. "And what benefit have you gotten from me so far? I have harmed you as much as, more than, any man dead or alive, including that bastard Golias. You don't need me: it's true." His voice was punctuated with the rush and rhythm of the falling water.

"How can you stand that? Get out of there, please. You're giving me an ague just looking at you." The water was cold. Freia's feet were numb already.

"I like water," he said.

"I like trees. Come sit by one. You can still see the water.

Dewar, please. People don't stand under waterfalls. It's cold. Please."

He shook his head, but he pushed himself away from the water-polished rocks and turned to look at Freia. She was warily waiting for further irrationality from him. Dewar pointed to a tree; she nodded. They picked their way out of the stream to scramble over rocks and sit under the fronds of the patchy-barked tree, on a lumpy bed of moss.

"It's soft," Freia said, patting it after they had sat for several minutes.

"Lovely stuff," he agreed, stroking it delicately with his fingertips.

"What are you thinking?" she asked after another silence.

"Lot of things. I don't think you want to know them all—" He ran his fingers through his soaked hair, squeezing water out.

"I guess I didn't ask, then," snapped Freia.

"I think you don't like me second-guessing you," Dewar said, and he caught her eye and made her smile. He went on, taking heart, but halting often to find a word. "I don't want you to be hurt, Freia, but I see now that I've been the agent of much pain to you, and, and if it could be undone I'd do it. And I wonder if I should stay away from you, although I want to protect you. I don't want to be only a sorcerer. If I help you, I can fight that. So perhaps I do want to use you, to that end, to better myself—to protect myself. But I do like you. I always have. I have given you grief and never joy, and perhaps you had rather I never meddled with you again. Do you want me to go? I will." He waited a moment and whispered, "Do you hate me?"

Freia answered at once, "I like you. When you're not being greedy or a—a sorcerer or standing under waterfalls you're, you're, I like you." She could not comprehend *hating* Dewar. He might be cruel, or selfish, or simply oblivious of her, but she could not hate him, she knew; for in the same moment he might be tender, or openheartedly generous, or meet her eyes and smile, somehow making her smile too. No matter what he did, she knew she would always like him, would always help him if she could; and she could not remember what it was to not know him. He was a piece of the world, a piece she had missed without knowing what was lacking. She did not want him to go.

"If you'll please tell me about the first when you notice it, I might keep from the second," Dewar said, "and as for the third, well, I do love waterfalls. Not to everyone's taste. You don't enjoy swimming?"

"No." Freia was preoccupied with an odd warm, liquid feeling surging up in her body. She was acutely aware of Dewar's proximity, of his damp, clean smell, of the unevenness of his breathing. He was agitated; why?

They stole glances at one another and decided to continue the conversation.

"How do you know that?"

"You didn't want to swim at the sea," Dewar said, "but I thought it was because you were sick."

"Waves are terrible. I don't mind watching them, but they're too, too rolly and big and thumpy and dangerous. They make me afraid."

"They're predictable, though," he said. "They just go along like the waterfall, and they wouldn't happen, just like the stream and the waterfall, without the earth and stones to shape them."

"Really?"

"I could draw you a diagram, but I fear you'd think I was being an idiot."

Freia shook her head, thinking of pushing the rocks together to make the pool, and looked sidelong at him again. Dewar was looking steadily at her. She was wearing only her shirt, and although it covered her to mid-thigh, it was wet.

"I wouldn't think you were an idiot for explaining. I like things explained."

They regarded one another.

"We like different things," Dewar said, "but they're not exclusive. The trees need water."

"They do," Freia said, taking the general case for specific. "It doesn't seem to have rained here much, and there were fires, over that way a ways." She gestured.

"It feels very weak and life-poor," Dewar said. "Speaking as a sorcerer. I'm sure the place has missed you, if you weren't here. It is yours."

They had moved closer together without noticing it, leaning, turning, shifting.

"I missed you," Freia whispered. "I was so angry at you, but I missed you. You were so sweet, so friendly when we were travelling. Then you did such cruel things. Why did you change?"

"I did. I—I was angry at myself," he said, and looked down. "I should be flayed for treating you so. Blind, self-centered, deaf too—I should have taken you home again when you asked me to in Landuc. I have wished that at least daily since. You were right about that; you've been right about everything. I've made you deathly wretched, and myself too, and I only want to give you good things, you ought to be happy, someone should do that. And I've missed you, Freia, and I've been worried about you—"

"Dewar—"

"I'm sorry. If you had rather that I left and never troubled you again, I will do that. I've done little to deserve another chance with you. You trusted me, and I hurt you." He snapped a fallen frond in small and smaller pieces.

"Dewar." Freia touched his chin and lifted it. "You're sorry, and I'm sorry, and can we both try to be, to be—better?" She searched his eyes, brilliant blue-rimmed black pools.

"I'm trying," he said. "Water isn't much without the earth around it to shape it, Freia. I need you to make me better. I take direction from you; you guide me without knowing you guide, command me . . ." His voice trailed away. He was lost in her eyes. "I want you to be happy," he whispered. "Forgive me. Let me stay. With you."

She said, or only thought, "Yes." It seemed to her that she could feel his body as well as her own; she was conscious of herself from within and without—the pressure of her legs on the

moss, the coolness of her hand against Dewar's cheek. She
stroked his smooth face, longing to comfort him and extinguish the sadness in him. It was beyond words, what she wanted
to say; it came out in gestures, in touch.

Freia's fingers moved lightly along Dewar's jaw, touched his
wet hair, his neck. Her chest rose and fell in the damp linen shirt;
she could feel his body's heat. He reached up, found her timid
fingers—they curled around his, and he brought them to his
mouth and brushed his lips, then his tongue, over them—
smoothness, warmth. Her breath caught. Freia said something
soundlessly, a faint movement of her lips as she leaned toward
him, and then she drew his hand toward her and pressed his
palm against her mouth, a light kiss. Dewar helped her settle
against him, enfolded and supported. He closed his eyes and
embraced her, his lips on her temple, her eyes, her cheek. Freia
made a sweet, startled sound, then another, pleased, tasting his
soft mouth; another kiss, a delicate unexpected touch, and she
moved against him, sudden, hard.

"Slowly, sweet love, so," he whispered, and set the pace with
his hands: slowly, and her body loosened as she sighed and en-
trusted herself to Dewar.

The sound of the waterfall poured over them and the moist
moss cushioned their elbows and knees as he rolled onto his
back. Rain began to fall, so that the fronds moved and rustled
under the water-drops and the moss made a light pattering
sound.

" 'S raining," Dewar sighed, feeling the drops on his face.

"Need rain," she whispered, and licked the water away. "Oh,
please *oh*—"

He shivered and clasped her, suddenly inside her body trying to find his way into her soul, and some detached part of him
lectured on rulers and realms and linkages and lives, and the
rest of him ignored all the complications of the Art and danced.

"How do you feel?"

"Lovely."

Though wet, they were beyond cold. The rain was falling softly and steadily, a gentle but determined downpour. The waterfall was louder; the moss, soggy. Dewar sighed; Freia turned her head and looked into his half-open eyes, dark in the dimming light.

"Just then," she said, "it felt as if I dissolved, and you dissolved, and we weren't—separate." She stroked his face with a fingertip, smiling shyly. "I wish it had lasted longer."

Dewar gazed seriously at her, more alert. "Complete."

Freia nodded, framing his face between her forearms.

"Yes," he said, "it was like finding something I lost, only for an instant. Sweet love. Oh, love." He kissed her, his arms against her back pressing her tightly to him. Dewar wanted that thing, whatever it was; its absence had been plaguing him for years, and he knew now that the thing he had lost was Freia. The empty ache from the missing piece of him had started after her suicide; it had made itself felt as he walked along the snowy road, away from the Moonstone where he had bargained for her life and then for his own. The Stone had protected her, child of earth that she was: his prayers had been granted, at considerable expense. Was the consequence of sharing one life between them to be a perpetual preoccupation with her? Or had that already been there? He wasn't sure. It didn't matter now. It was there, and he could not remember what he had been like without it.

The closer he was to her, the further the ache receded. Sometimes his dreams of her had subdued it. It had been gone completely for a moment, and he could barely remember the missing-piece pang now. He kissed her neck, then her throat, then the smoothness of her chest, marred by the white line of a scar; she relaxed her hold on him and let him touch her freely. Her own touch was uncertain, and he tried to help, guiding, encouraging. Now they lay in the wet moss caressing, whispering further confidences, fears and pleasures and kindnesses offered in turn. Presently, "Was that it?" Dewar whispered, and Freia answered by pulling him on top of her and wordlessly demanding his cooperation. He moaned and sighed and swayed with her for, it seemed, hours, until he passed his endurance and collapsed into her arms in self-annihilating hot dissolution. She shouted with him, urging him on and on, and he laughed breathlessly when he could laugh.

"Oh, Freia. Sorry. Lost my head."

"I took it."

"You did. Grabbed it and wouldn't let me have it back. Unfair. Holding it just out of reach like that."

"You found your tongue anyway," she giggled.

"Hah. Yes, here it is—"

The rain fell and night drew close around the trees and water.

"I want you forever," Freia whispered in his ear in the rustling darkness. Now she had him: she wished to keep him unchanged, to lie beside him and curl around him, to think what he thought and be what he wanted and let him soak into her skin until they were inseparable. What made her happy overwhelmed him with joy; what made him happy sent her into near-painful ecstasy. An unending plateau of happiness stretched before them.

Dewar kissed her neck, murmuring, "I want you. I dream about you every night. About looking for you. I should have made love to you on that haystack."

"It would have been cold and prickly," Freia whispered, "and hasty. But I wish you had. I was afraid to—I hadn't ever. I didn't know—but this is—good, this is what I thought—what I wanted so much, always, but better." She sighed, shivering with aftershocks of pleasure, even as a few silent tears—old pains, flicked awake—startled her.

Dewar thought of things that might not have happened had he indulged desire then and delayed their journey to Perendlac, and he kissed her eyes as she spoke, tasting salt. "You're probably right," he murmured, and then, understanding why she'd been tense, taut, hesitant, "Dear love, dear Freia—" And memory arced through his sex-fogged brain. He froze for an instant.

The Stone. His first-born. He was a fool.

What had come over him?—but he knew: nothing he could do would avoid or delay the Stone, the working of the Balance.

"What's wrong?"

It would be fitting, neatly fitting—she would pay with him—"Ah. Freia, ah, damn me, I should have been more careful—I didn't think—I hope I, we, didn't— If I've made you pregnant—"

"Wrong time for me."

His sigh of relief embarrassed him an instant later as her voice purred on in his ear, sweet-toned with longing, "I'd like to have a baby this way."

"I can't think why. I'm a proven fool." He touched her body, apologizing to it with a gesture. She had just offered him a tremendous compliment, and he didn't know how to answer. Of his will he would not make so obvious an offering to the Stone as that. Yet he loved her; she loved life; he wanted what she wanted, and if new life was what she wanted he would give it to her despite his sorcerous instinct, which screamed against such endangerment. "But if you wish," he offered recklessly, courting the precipice.

Freia shook her head, tucked herself against him. "I don't think this would be the best year for it." It didn't feel like a good year to start anything; the blighted forest was visible advice.

"And Prospero would be perturbed." At the very least, Dewar thought, wrying his mouth. Prospero was a possessive man, and Freia was his.

"He'd be very angry," Freia muttered darkly, and she stretched and turned so that they were face-to-face on their sides. "I'm getting cold," she said, and then softer-voiced went on, "Would you stay here? Tonight? With me?"

Dewar smiled, and his voice held the smile. "You're nice to sleep with, Freia. Cuddly. It's wet and chill, though. May I offer better accommodations?"

"A tent?" she suggested hopefully.

"Come to my tower with me, and we can return here later."

Leave Argylle, with Dewar, for a safe place, undespoiled, to lie beside him—to sleep in his arms, to hear his voice in her ear, the dear warm note melting her bones in her body and every sadness in her soul—to listen to the language of his hands—to rest a night, a day, before going onward in the ashes—she desired it; she desired him.

She touched him in the darkness, water running over her arms onto his chest, his throat, his face. In spite of her own heart's desire, she thought, and Prospero's shadow, invoked by Dewar, dimmed hope and lay cold over her.

"If I went away with you now, I'm afraid I'd never want to come back," Freia said.

"I'm a glutton. I want you all to myself, all the time," he admitted, "but, Freia, only if you want that too. I can never keep you against your will."

"I wouldn't have any will left." Freia pushed her face into the warm, damp nook where his neck and shoulder met. Dewar curled around her, saying velvet words that were only reassuring, meaningless sounds. "It's not fair," she whispered, "I don't need a brother—I need *you*."

Dewar held her with one arm, gesturing with the other in the darkness, stretching and reaching. "A moment, love. A moment," he said, and murmured something more. "That will keep the rain off us awhile. —You're right, Freia, sweet love, it isn't fair, I know, I want you to be something else, but you're my father's daughter, and we cannot—"

"I'm not really your sister if I'm not really Prospero's—"

"You are, you are, though, Freia. You are of his blood, your soul in a body of odd engendering, but you are his—you are, Freia." He held her.

"You said—you said I'm not. You said I'm common clay— a thing Prospero made—like Caliban."

He realized it with coldness in his back: she did not remember their meeting with the Stone, or she would not be saying this. If she did not remember—no, he could not tell her, burden her with what he had paid for her life. It would be blackmail. "I was wrong," Dewar said miserably. "I was wrong to speak thus to Josquin, but, Freia, how your body began is unimportant: you are Prospero's blood, Prospero's daughter."

"Then *why*—"

"Because I was less than human myself. That you live now proves me wrong, for if you were not alive, alive and human to the soul, you could not be here now. Whence you came is nothing; what you are is all that matters. I have wronged you, and I beg you to put away from you all the wrongs I did you that day and let me make amends—now, for all my days—" His voice cracked with the strain of sincerity, and he whispered, "I love you. Will you come away with me?"

"He'd kill me," Freia said. "We could go away from here and never never come back again, that's all. And I don't want to do that because this is home. It's the only place I have. I missed it so much," and she seemed to be pleading now.

Dewar licked her eyes and her salted cheeks, whispering. "It belongs to you, Freia, and you belong to it. You couldn't stay away forever. It would come looking for you."

Freia thought of Trixie and smiled in spite of herself. "It did," she said.

"There. See? We'll stay here. That's settled." Dewar kissed her mouth.

"You'll stay? You will? Here?"

"Yes." He kissed her again, promising.

Freia sighed, feeling the liquid movement of his muscles, the slick smoothness of his skin. "I like being near you," she said.

"I like being near you, too. The sea loves the shore, wave by wave," he whispered and Dewar this time was kissed. "Are you cold, still," he asked after a while.

"Yes. I have blankets in my saddle-bags."

"I think we shouldn't sleep here. This is the stream's bed, not ours, and the stream is rising to fill his bed."

"So he is. It's too dark to wander around."

"Stop that, or we won't get anywhere. I'll make a light, love, and we'll find your blankets and higher ground."

ALTHOUGH THE BARON OF ASCOLET WAS out of favor, the Countess of Lys was not. This curious contradictory state of affairs was noted by the Court when the Countess arrived, at the Empress's invitation, for a springtime visit. She brought a small entourage with her, and notably present was her daughter, a charming black-haired child in leading-strings, whose smile never failed and whose sweet good humor commended her—and her mother—to everyone she met.

The Baron of Ascolet, learning somehow that his little family was at Court, appeared at the Palace gates just after sunrise about twenty days after the Countess's arrival. The guards, who had no orders to bar him from the place, admitted him, and Fortuna would have it that the first person he met as he was leaving the stables was the Empress, who on fine days enjoyed an early ride.

Of course, an Empress does not ride alone; six ladies were with her, and four amusing gentlemen.

"Your Majesty, good morning," said Ottaviano, and he bowed as gracefully as his all-day, all-night ride would allow.

The Empress considered for a lightning instant ignoring him and his greeting; her courteous conscience would not allow it, though, and she said, "Ah, the Baron of Ascolet."

"Yes, Your Majesty," he said, straightening.

The Empress granted him a nod and continued in through the high-arched gate that led to the stables' courtyard; he stood aside for her and her retinue, and she supposed the meeting was over. But when she came out, mounted and leading her attendants, he was still there.

"Your Majesty!"

Having noticed him once, she couldn't cut him now. The

Empress drew rein and looked down; it was not very far down, as he was a tall man and she was on a small horse. "You have something to say, Baron?"

He glanced at her ladies and lords, behind her, and said, "Just a few words, privately."

Empress Glencora considered it, letting him see that she weighed it as a great favor to him. Then she held up her hand, walked her horse two steps, and stopped again. "Speak," she said.

"Your Majesty, I heard that my wife, the Countess of Lys, is here at Court," said Otto. "Is she?"

"Yes," said the Empress, and his tone drew her eyes from the aigrette on her horse's head to his face—sunburnt, a sleek un-fashionable red beard contrasting with his blond hair.

"And Cambia too? Is that true?"

"Yes," the Empress said.

He nodded once. "I know I'm not particularly welcome in the Palace, Your Majesty," he said, "but I haven't—seen them in a while and—and I very much wish to. I'm telling you this so you know why I'm here. I'm here to see my wife and baby."

The Empress looked at Otto for a long, long moment. He swallowed, becoming uneasy with the examination.

"The Emperor," Empress Glencora said slowly, and in a tone not pitched to be heard by any but Otto, "did not see me, or the Prince Heir Josquin, for nine years after the Prince's birth."

Otto's brows drew together. "That may be all right for some people—"

"Be welcome here," said the Empress.

His mouth fish-flapped, and he said, "Thank you."

"There have been some difficulties between you."

"Well, maybe, I mean I—yes." He looked down.

"The Countess is very devoted to Lys."

"Yeah. Yes, Your Majesty, she is."

She studied his head, his shoulders, his stance. "We wish you a pleasant and profitable visit, Baron," she said then. "I believe the Hunt Rooms are vacant; Teppick will show you to them. Perhaps you and the Countess would join us tomorrow at our reception in the South-East Parterre."

Otto looked up, a grateful and burning look, and as he thanked her, bowing again, Glencora smiled, lifted her hand, and rode slowly away.

Freia woke on her back, confused by the view overhead. She wasn't alone, she was under a thick stand of karial trees, and she was wearing only her shirt. Birdsongs were pealing from the dark leaves; they were Argylle birds—

She had come home. Yesterday. She and Trixie had woven their way through passes in the mountains that circled Argylle like a wall, and she had stopped to rest and sent Trixie off to hunt. The forest was a mess of tumbled trunks and ashes, and it had rained, and— Freia turned on her side and stared at Dewar, who was going to wake up and complain that she had taken all the blankets in a moment. She rolled back toward him and covered them both. Dewar, complaisant in his sleep, hmm'd happily and put his hand on her rump to hold her close; Freia pressed her face to his chest, moving her legs to clasp him, inhaling their blended smell.

He moved some time later, withdrawing slightly and then halting.

"Freia."

"Mmhm."

"Were you trying to . . . ?"

"If you . . . oh."

"I will if you do that," Dewar invited her, moving against her. "You won't mind if I sleep for another hour, hm?"

She pushed him on his back and straddled him, kissing and nuzzling his stubbled neck and jaw, smoothing his day's growth of rough short beard with her cheeks. His skin was so soft, save for the beard; his arms were softer than his cheeks, nearly. . . .

"What a nice dream. I'm never going to wake up." He smiled, eyes closed, pushing his hands up her thighs.

She laughed. "I'll make you."

The damp blankets were discarded as unnecessary and Dewar was fully awakened by the time the sun had brightened the air.

"May I ask a favor of you, my love?" he said in her ear, rocking her on his lap.

Freia sighed, opened her eyes. "Yes."

"I want your shirt."

"This shirt?"

"This shirt covering you."

Freia sat back, looked at him to see if he jested, and pulled it over her head. "Here it is."

"Thank you." Dewar set it aside and drew Freia toward him again: all skin now. He touched her, sighing with pleasure. Save the best for last: this was the best. "And thank you."

"You're welcome. I feel, mmm, more than alive." She was smiling dreamily, eyes unfocused.

"I know. So lovely, Freia." He braced himself to dispel the glow around her. "We mustn't let anyone know."

She twisted her mouth, blinked back two tears. Just for a moment, she had been truly happy, wanted and wanting, holding and held. But there was no point weeping over it: she knew he was right. His "anyone" meant Prospero, and she knew Prospero would disapprove. "Of course not," she agreed, falsely brisk.

Dewar stroked her face with both hands, seeing the tears. He kissed her eyes slowly, wanting to weep himself. "And it—we'd better not let this happen again."

He was right, and she knew it. Prospero had been at great pains to explain it to her and, later, to the Argyllines. Blood-kin mustn't mate. It wasn't done, shouldn't have been done, and couldn't be done again. And he had been at great pains to explain to Freia, on several occasions, that she was not to mate at all, not until the proper partner had been found for her. Were he to learn of any of this, his wrath would fell forests. She gulped. "I know." A long, mutual gaze, each memorizing the other, followed.

"But you'll stay," Freia whispered, despair seizing her. If he did not, how empty, how lonely . . .

Dewar nodded. "I said I would," he said. "I want to stay. If you want me here, here I am."

Another silence fell between them as they sat, breath-to-breath.

"We'd better get dressed," Freia said, still sad, "and eat something, and do things."

"Like talk about what things there are to do."

She nodded and edged off his lap reluctantly. He leaned forward and kissed her mouth as she moved, letting their lips separate when their bodies had parted. Lifting her hands, he kissed each of her fingers quickly and lightly in turn, then picked up her shirt and donned it.

Kneeling on the leaf-litter, Freia looked at him with her head tipped to one side. *"You,"* she said, "are a romantic sot."

Dewar laughed. "And *you* are a eunuch's torment. Go put on some clothes." He found his own wet shirt and tossed it at her.

The Emperor of Landuc sat on a golden throne on a crimson dais beneath a white awning, his Empress ivory-and-gold beside him. The awning was topped by a gilded flame, its bottom tasseled gold and crimson, and it glittered on the groomed grass of the parterre, and the gold and gems on the Emperor and Empress glittered within its bright shade. They sat and watched the Court amuse them and itself; favored intimates clustered around the thrones and lounged on the foot of the dais, juggling witty anecdotes and badinage, wagers and boasts. At the other end of the green, musicians played a sprightly springly dance and the younger members of the Court skipped through the steps, laughing.

One might reasonably have expected the young Countess of Lys and her handsome husband to be among the dancers. They were not. Forgoing the other games the day offered, they were engaged in the strenuous pastime of not having a public argument.

"You may come to Lys whenever you wish," Luneté said, strolling between two low hedges, going further into the parterre.

"You could come to Ascolet." Otto paced beside her, his hands knotted behind his back.

"We have already discussed that."

"If you have time to dally around at Court, you have time to come to Ascolet."

"My business at Court is for Lys, not pleasure. Perhaps you should spend more time at Court yourself, and improve your standing with the Emperor."

"My standing with the Emperor is my own concern, madame, and another of my concerns is my daughter and you."

"Then you should visit Lys, where we are, more often."

They had rounded a corner and descended into a sunken part of the garden where a four-tiered fountain cascaded. No one had followed them; no one seemed to be in earshot. Otto stopped and caught her elbow, halting her.

"Luneté, why do I have to come to Lys all the time? Why do you refuse to even visit Ascolet? —And don't tell me that you have business in Lys, or that this trip is all business. You've drawn it out beyond the two or four days of business there was, and you know it and I know it. Tell me the truth."

Luneté straightened, subtly disengaging her arm. "I have given a great deal to Ascolet already," she said. "I do not wish to utterly lose myself in it. You, you are not really Ascolet; you don't know what the bond of Lys is like to me, how it feels, how the Well in Lys beats like a second heart to me. You're an outsider, appointed by accident! You have no blood-ties to Ascolet, as I do to Lys. You've no idea what that is, and you seem to think I can just walk away from Lys whenever I wish, as you wander away from Ascolet."

"In other words," Otto said, "the ancestral burden of Lys is more important to you than, say, your husband."

"No—"

"That's what you just said."

"Then that's what I just said, very well, yes. *You* never considered Ascolet as anything but a strategic asset, and Lys was an ally. You could rule Chenay as easily as Ascolet, it doesn't matter a whisker to you as long as you profit."

"Is that what you think," said Otto, with a dangerous glow coming into his face.

"Yes. And it's the truth. I've heard of the way you switched sides, back and forth, during the war, Baron, looking for the best advantage, and about how you used and murdered poor Lady Miranda, and then Lady Freia the same—stabbing her to silence her—"

"I did nothing of the sort! Golias—"

"Oh, certainly," said Luneté, "blame it all on dead Golias, your good friend, and that's just as—as ignoble and ungentlemanly as admitting it. *Everyone* knows, Otto. I've heard the tale from several people."

Ottaviano stared at Luneté, anger and insult seething in his gut. So he was being pilloried for Golias's crimes, all around the Empire no doubt, wherever tongues wagged.

"It is not true," he said levelly.

"Then why did she go mad and kill herself," Luneté asked, and the momentum of her fury seized her and carried her on. "How many love-notes did you send her afterward? Don't you think that was in poor taste?"

"What?" he yelped.

Luneté opened her pocket and took out a piece of folded, once-crumpled paper. "I was rather shocked to receive this," she said. This morning she had found it in a plain, plainly-sealed envelope among the rest of her letters. She unfolded the letter and held it so that he could see it.

His own hand.

To the worshipful Lady Freia, with most respectful greetings. We have met and parted in vile and harrowing circumstances, and since then my heart is deeply weighed . . .

"Where did you get— Give it to me," Otto demanded, and she kept it from him, darting back.

"You admit it, then."

"I admit nothing! Who gave that to you?" Dewar, he thought. It had to be Dewar—he had been hot after Luneté since they'd met, flirting, teasing—

"Is this not a declaration of love, here? 'For I do love you as my cousin and as the most courageous and right noble lady in the Well's great realm of Pheyarcet?' How convenient that your affection should have turned to her as she was proclaimed Prince Prospero's heir and successor to his lands!" Luneté folded the note again, returned it to her satin pocket, glaring at Otto. "How convenient. What a pity she did not welcome your attention. Of course, our marriage had not been acknowledged yet, had it? And Prince Prospero's daughter is certainly more profitable than Lys."

"She's, she was a nice girl! I was trying to, to, to—"

"The letter speaks for you very well, Baron," Luneté said icily. "It needs no explication."

"Tell me about Odile," Freia said. "She's your mother?"

"She is," Dewar said. They were sitting on a sunny gravel flat in the midst of a broad stream, an hour's walk from where they had slept. Upstream, four waterbirds worked the stream bottom, clucking to one another when they popped up from under the water. Freia had shared her food with Dewar, and now he lounged against a recently fallen tree-trunk washed up on the gravel spit, Freia sitting beside him. He wanted to put his head on her lap, but refrained. They were struggling with distance and intimacy, and he would make it more difficult.

Freia waited for him to continue. He didn't. "Dewar, I'd like to know more than that. Tell me about her."

Dewar glanced at her. "Her malevolence is endless."

"And."

"Freia, I don't like to talk about it."

"When Trixie gets back here—"

"Trixie?"

"—I'm going to the city, where he must be, and if this woman is there too—"

"—you'll be dead in hours."

"I don't care," Freia said. "I want to tell Papa I'm all right. I—I think he must be upset. And it looks like things haven't gone well here."

"It does." Dewar slid down against the log and let himself edge over to lean on Freia's shoulder. She didn't understand how dangerous Odile was, how deadly and how merciless. She had probably never met anything so utterly hateful and evil, he thought, not even in Landuc. He closed his eyes. "I ran away from her house in Aië when I was very young," he said. "She was angry with me; I'd tried to transform back some of the men she'd turned into swine and cattle and horses. That's her specialty, transformation; I suppose that's why Prospero sought her out. She keeps her women shaped like peahens and geese and other birds until she needs them for something, then turns them back afterward. When I realized what she was doing, I hated her. Some men came to her to do business or something— I never knew why—and she changed them all. I was watching from the shadows. She'd been teaching me a little sorcery, dribs and drabs, and so I filched one of her books and tried to restore them. They'd been kind to me. I'd never seen men before, only women, Odile and her bird-women."

Freia's heart was a steady thud under his cheek. Her arm was around his shoulders. The sun was hot on his face. Dewar kept his eyes closed and continued, "I got caught, of course. I didn't know what I was doing. Odile took the book away, told me she'd transform me to a calf and geld me, and turned me into a calf. She left me that way for a long time. It wasn't enjoyable, I assure you. Three times she tied me up and made all the preparations, but she didn't castrate me; instead, when she got tired of the game, she turned me back and set me to sorting a pile of beans. If I could do it all and get it right, she'd let me stay human and whole.

"I didn't believe her. When she had left me there to sort the damned hill of beans, I kept at it until dark and then went into the house. The Temple, she calls it. She has a vast opinion of herself. I knew how to get into her workroom, and the birds didn't raise an alarm. She must have killed them for that after I got away. I stole four of her books and fled the house.

"When I passed her Bounds she detected my going and pursued me with Sendings and storms. I ran for my life as far as a crossroads, where I took protection under a thornbush at a standing stone, an outpost of the Stone of Blood. When she paused to rest, I ran again, at first erratically through Phesaotois to try to shake her, then inward. After a few years, I came to Noroison and Morven where Paracelsus dwells, and I apprenticed myself to him. For it I gave him three of the books, which I'd copied, and I still have the fourth and the copybook."

Dewar listened to Freia's calm heart. "I stayed a long time in Morven. Odile had set curses on me, which I'd been screened from—I won't go into that—but Paracelsus lifted them and put me under his protection while I was his apprentice, so that Odile would be picking a fight with him if she struck at me. She wasn't willing, probably wasn't able, to risk that, and so I passed sixteen very pleasant years there, pleasant as apprenticeships go, far pleasanter than the first sixteen had been. There was another fellow, Oren, who was doing some advanced studies—he was a journeyman, not a proper apprentice—and after some initial spatting, we got along passably. When I finished my apprenticeship, Paracelsus booted me through a Way into the middle of nowhere, and I looked up Oren and found out he was Paracelsus's something-or-other nephew—in the line of Primas through Proteus, so we're actually cousins in some terribly remote degree. I must tell him that sometime. He's keen on family connections. He was a congenial chap when he wasn't being a journeyman; he invited me to live with him and I did awhile. That was pleasant, too. But Odile was always out there, and I always had to be on my guard because of her attempts

against me. For that reason I left Phesaotois and went to Pheyarcet. And it is a great evil that she has come here, with Prospero." Somehow Dewar had slumped round to lie in her lap,
after all.

Freia stroked his forehead, comforting and affectionate, ad-
miring his inverted nose and brows and smoothing the tight
lines there. "You are afraid of her. . . ."

"Oh yes." His eyes were closed.

She considered this. "Do you mean to kill her?" she asked
softly, not to challenge him but to prepare herself for the horror of such a thing, if it happened. She realized, thinking of it,
that she had never seen Dewar kill anything, or anyone, despite
the violence that had surrounded them.

He shook his head, a confined rolling movement on her legs.
"You don't understand, Freia, you don't understand how it is
with sorcerers: one can't kill one's blood-kin, not without hurting oneself. That's how it is in Phesaotois, and I see no reason
for it to be different here. Blood is blood. I cannot kill her; the
destruction would turn back on me."

"But you said she wanted, wants, to kill you."

"No, I did not. She wants to harm me as much as she can—
and she can harm me greatly—without killing me. If she cannot do it by sorcery, here, she will do it otherwise. You have
never known anyone like Odile, Freia. She will be poisoning
Prospero against me, subtly, secretly, with a word, another
word, day upon day. She will be painting me in blackest colors
to him, and he will hear her, for I stole from her and he will believe I stole from him. Sorcerers do not give something for
nothing, ever, and he gave me priceless knowledge by letting me
copy his books."

"Where are the copies?" Freia asked softly.

"In my tower. Safe. She'll not find them, or it, I warrant. I
suspect she has not passed the Fire at the Well—Avril's in no
mood for granting such favors, even if he had the ability to deliver them—but she may have drunk of your Spring."

"I wish I had let you drink, taken you there and given it to you," Freia said. "I'm sorry. I was so afraid Papa would be angry with me for having you there at all. He made me swear never to tell anyone from Landuc—at least you're not from Landuc. I wish I had done it then."

Dewar cleared his throat. "Well . . ."

Freia looked down at him, shading his eyes with her hand. "Did you—" she said, with instant certainty that he had.

"He left with you," Dewar said, looking up at her, "and he hadn't said *not* to, you know, and, and, Freia, I had been searching for it for years. Literally years. It has been the whole focus of my work, and I'd even begun narrowing it down to an approximate area to search for it—I simply had to drink. Besides, I couldn't have made my Way to Landuc if I hadn't. I wonder if Prospero has realized that," he added in an undertone.

His eyes pleaded for leniency.

"Oh, Dewar." It wasn't supposed to be funny, but it was: Freia smiled. She should have guessed.

"I'm a reprehensible and amoral gentleman, or a very good sorcerer," he said unhappily.

"I'd change that around."

"Helping oneself to the finest from one's host's cellar in his absence is ungentlemanly, madame. But thanks for your mercy."

"I told you I bathed in it," she said, still smiling, teasingly now.

He smiled, then laughed. "You didn't. I bet Prospero took a fit. Whatever inspired you to do that?"

"I was tired and hot and dirty, and it was water. It was just water seeping out of a rock and making a nice little puddle, so I had a drink and then a bath. It was refreshing."

"I'm sure it was," he said, awed. "Did you tell him?"

"No." She stroked his hair away from his face. "I learned later it was special. Funny; I ran away too. Prospero was cross with me, and I ran away and didn't go back to him for seven years."

"Why did you go back?"

Freia shrugged. "I was lonely. There wasn't anybody else here, then. I liked it better that way. Not that some of the people aren't good people, but—I liked it empty. And now I've come back again. Maybe he truly doesn't want me here, though, Dewar. I'm just something he made, like Caliban. People might rather I was dead. I'm not one of them. I'm not much use to anyone."

Dewar sat up and embraced her. "When you are there, I think you'll see you've been missed," he said, "and if they try to pretend they don't need you, you can come away with me, after all."

"What a choice you offer me."

"If Prospero and his people don't know what's good for them, I certainly do," Dewar said.

The garden-party duel between the Baron of Ascolet and the Countess of Lys had heated in a few words from dull red to white-hot and altered its terms from first blood to the death. They had each taken wounds and given telling return strikes, and a moment of breath-catching silence had followed the Baron's last expert and damaging sally brandishing the Countess's behavior vis-à-vis a certain sorcerer of their acquaintance. Possibly he would have carried the day, were they not interrupted by a pair of servants with messages that both Countess and Baron were wanted most urgently at the Swan Summer-house.

In the silence of suspended hostilities, then, Luneté and Ottaviano left the sunken parterre and followed the two servants to the swan-crowned, swan-friezed, swan-flocked summer-house, which was in another part of the grounds away from the Empress's reception. Yet the music had become brighter and the party merrier, and the beat of a Madanese changing dance could be faintly heard even at the summer-house a quarter-hour's walk away.

There was a small crowd at the summer-house, visible to the

Baron and the Countess as they came down the slope toward the water. The swans were clustered on the other side of their pretty pond, hardly disturbing the flat-leaved ornamental weeds and flowers that floated on its surface, bright in the sharp afternoon light.

Someone among the crowd of people was sobbing loudly, half-screaming.

Otto began to hurry, perceiving Doctor Hem among the group, and when he glimpsed the Empress, he trotted, leaving Luneté to catch up as best she might in her thin-soled slippers on the gravel path. People drew aside as he came near, and he saw the Empress rising to her feet, saw Doctor Hem approaching him bleating something, saw a young woman in a dishevelled nursemaid's dress half-collapsed in shrill hysterics on the steps of the summer-house, and saw a little wet bundle on the summer-house floor that he did not at first recognize.

Then Otto did know the nose, the plump cheek, the curly nearly-black hair of the unchildishly still body, and he began shouting.

Dewar persuaded Freia not to approach Prospero alone, but to wait in the forest for him while he returned to his tower to prepare to face Odile. She agreed, reluctantly; he repeated his invitation to join him, and she refused with less sureness than before.

"Please don't tempt me. I would. I would go."

He had a fleeting vision of an idyllic life with her, his sorcery and her roaming and returning, constant union and reunion. He knew it would take but little pleasurable persuasion for her to throw off Prospero's teaching against incest, and he cared nothing for it himself; already, an ache of hunger, of loneliness, was throbbing in him. It wasn't fair of him to tempt her, no. She wanted to say yes, and she feared to; she was bound to Dewar with her heart, and she was bound to Argylle by Prospero's gift and her own inclination. She would suffer if he induced her to renounce Argylle, and there was no reason for him to do so but his own desire; and that was not sufficient.

"It's there if you need it, Freia. Just ask if you ever do. There's no bar to leaving, and I won't force you to come there." His voice was level, serious, and true.

Freia looked up at him and smiled a little. "Someday."

Dewar lightened his voice, bantering. "When you have time for me," he said. "When your other businesses are all concluded, your appointments kept, your audiences held, debts discharged—"

"Silly! That wouldn't take much doing," she said, laughing. "The only appointment I have is with you!"

"You have one with Prospero, madame, but you have not yet set a term for it, and it shall be a long and involved business the two of you undertake, I am sure of it."

Freia's laughter had faded; she heard a note of something firm and immutable under Dewar's half-mockery. "Don't make it sound so, so permanent, so much like forever— You'll be here, won't you? I'll wait for you!" She was frightened; missed meetings had meant such ill before.

"I'll be here," Dewar promised, and he felt the words as he meant them and the words as she meant them turn and twine and net them both. She would lead; he would let her channel and shape him. "I'll wait on you, and wait for you, and wait with you," he said, trying to lighten himself. He clasped her shoulders, then embraced her. "I'll be here," he said again.

Clean and dry, gowned in stiff gold-threaded brocade that weighed more than she did, wax-white Cambia lay on a crimson-draped table surrounded by flowers and candles. The casket would be ready in a day, and then her grieving mother, the Countess Luneté, would return to Lys with her, to place her on the family pyre at the Shrine of Stars and then entomb her ashes there.

Whether the Baron of Ascolet would attend was a matter being settled over Cambia's bier.

"I told you she was an idiot," Ottaviano said to Luneté.

Luneté sat, straight and composed, at the empty fireplace. "It could have happened to anyone. She is punishing herself; I have no desire to make her suffer more. Moreover, her family has served mine well for centuries, and I will not be the one to break—"

"You don't want to break it off? Luneté, the woman was flat on her back in the bushes under a groom while Cambia drowned! You don't think that's grounds for some response? Branding? A whipping? Drowning? At least public recognition that she failed her duty?"

"I will not alienate Sir Matteus and all his kin," said Luneté. "It is none of your affair, what I do or do not do; this is an internal matter, Lys's own."

Otto, momentarily dumbstruck, turned and punched a red-lacquered cabinet. His fist splintered a large hole in its front. He stared at the hole and then shrugged, turned on Luneté again. "You seem to be forgetting that Cambia's my daughter too," he said, more quietly.

Luneté's expression changed, at last; she looked down, away, a flush creeping over her cheeks, and her mouth moved to say something. She stopped herself, clenching her hands, looking back at Otto, who was standing at the bier now, watching her over Cambia's closed eyes and slack cheeks. "No," said Luneté. "I do not think vengeance is right, here. We need not exact pain for pain, death for death. Another death cannot bring her back."

"Is that what your advisor Valgalant tells you?"

"It is common sense," said Luneté, cold again.

"And if I wanted to take her to Ascolet and put her there, beside her Ascolet kin, you'd say she belonged to Lys, wouldn't you. Common sense."

Luneté said nothing.

"You wouldn't come to the funeral if I did take her to Ascolet," Otto went on, "because it would mean being out of

Lys." He thumped the foot of the bier softly with both fists—
a few flowers slid off noiselessly—and, his expression a mask
to match Luneté's, left the room. The door echoed around and
around the ceiling, and then the room was still.

⌐ 24 ⌐

BARON OTTAVIANO OF ASCOLET HAD LEARNED, in one swift lesson, that many matters were best not committed to ink. Better
to keep them as insubstantial and unsubstantiable as breath. He
sat on his heels outside the stables now, waiting for the Empress
to appear with her entourage for their morning exercise. Dawn
had found Otto in the Royal Tombs, where night had led him
after a long detour around the Sea Gate's ale-shops. He'd
passed the stews and brothels by, preferring his own company,
and, after attaining a state of self-detachment hitherto unknown
to him, had decided he preferred even more the company of the
dead King Panurgus and his predeceased offspring. The Wards
around the Tombs had let him enter, and he had walked up and
down, climbed the little hills and scuffled down, until the drunk-
enness was left behind. Yet for all the walking there he did, he
never went near Sebastiano's tomb.

Unshaven, unbathed, he rose to his feet on hearing the soft
chiming of ladies' laughter on the other side of the hedge; a gate
opened and there was the Empress Glencora, trimly kitted out
in a pale-blue riding costume, and there were her attendants
around her, stopping, eyeing him distrustfully. Two or three of
the gentlemen's hands fell to their dress-swords' hilts. Otto
bowed, his face showing no apprehension.

"Your Majesty, forgive my impatience, but I could not wait
to schedule a private interview with your secretary."

The Empress considered him; he wore the same clothing she
had last seen him in at the summer-house, the worse for a
night's hard wear and the Well knew what physical exertions.

Yet his demeanor was sober enough, and it would look ill if she denied audience to a man not a day bereft of his child. She gestured with her riding-crop, said, "I shall call you when I want you; wait here," to her little flock of hangers-on, and crossed the courtyard to Ottaviano. "Come," said she, "let us take a turn about the stable-yard; it is uncommonly to advantage in this early light."

He bowed again, still bland, and followed the Empress into the stable-yard, followed her as she turned right and walked slowly along the wall. A groom led out her horse, on the other side; she held up her hand to him and he halted, waiting.

"Speak freely, if you would," the Empress said.

"You've been kind to us, to the Countess of Lys and me," Otto said. "Far kinder and more helpful than many might expect, all things considered. I know the Countess has much to thank you for, for herself, and I am grateful too, for the courtesy you've shown her and for your hospitality toward me."

"You and the Countess are both of peculiar interest to us here," said the Empress, pacing evenly. They turned left, along the side wall, and continued to walk.

"Thank you. I am here to ask a great favor from you, Your Majesty, one which will afford the Countess a happier life."

"Be counselled, Baron of Ascolet, against interfering in Lys's governance," the Empress said. "It is a matter of considerable concern to the Emperor, that Ascolet and Lys, though close and allied, not be driven too closely in tandem."

He ground his teeth once and swallowed. "I know. In fact, she may already have approached you and asked about this— last night—before then—I don't know. It has nothing to do with Lys's government, but with Lys's person."

"Continue," the Empress said, when he paused.

"I am convinced, Your Majesty, that the Countess is greatly burdened by the obligations our marriage places on her. I wish to ask you if you could intercede with the Emperor on her and my behalf and persuade him to annul the bond."

"Annul your marriage. This is a change of view, Baron."

"I know it must seem sudden, Your Majesty, but for some time Her Grace has not welcomed my presence or my attentions, and the death of our daughter has removed the most weighty and troublesome manifestation of those attentions. If the Emperor is anxious to forestall collusion between Lys and Ascolet, annulling the marriage will remove one of the more obvious ways the two places can be linked."

"You are convinced that this request accords with the Countess's will?"

"I haven't talked it over with her, but—every sign seems to point that way, Your Majesty. The Countess considers herself beholden to Lys, before any other worldly bond. I can't compete with the County of Lys. She isn't interested in Ascolet."

The Empress turned again at the juncture of side wall and rear wall. Otto's steps, in time with hers, echoed softly from the arched passages they now passed.

"An annulment is not a light business, Baron. Are you certain you wish to pursue this step, yourself? Surely you are aware of your prerogatives under the law?"

"I know, I know. Leaving other considerations aside, Your Majesty, the Countess is a peer in her own right, which complicates those prerogatives. If I pursued them too hard she might end up declaring war on me or something. I'd rather stop now than forcibly exercise my rights."

"You are uncommonly considerate," observed the Empress. "If you wish to request an annulment, you must have some ground on which to base the request."

"I'm sure the irregularity of the marriage would provide ample ground for the Emperor. He acknowledged it, but he can unacknowledge it too. Panurgus did that."

"More than once. The most common ground for annulment, Baron, as you must be aware, is witnessed infidelity, during the engagement or during the marriage."

"I have no evidence of anything of the sort. Your Majesty, it's not that at all, it's just—Lys is more important to her, and I can't keep running back and forth between Lys and Ascolet, and she won't come to Ascolet. There's no point to it."

They turned again, warmed now by the sun reflected from the wall onto their heads. The groom and horse were still waiting for the Empress in the center of the courtyard.

The Empress tapped her crop lightly against her hand. "It is difficult to say how the Emperor will receive such a request, Baron. It is a great boon to ask of him; he may well refuse it and require that you take the customary route. He will certainly not act without a formal petition."

Otto nodded, watching her face; she didn't look as though she meant to refuse him. "I understand. I want to know how the petition would be received. He's entitled to be angry about it, after all that's happened, but I can't think it'll be unwelcome news."

"Very well. If you are determined, and are willing to trust my discretion—"

"Completely, Your Majesty."

"Then I shall proceed as seems best to me." The Empress halted and extended her hand; the interview was over. They had not quite completed a circuit of the courtyard. Otto bent over her hand, a formal bow, and followed the Empress out through the cold dark shadow of the gateway again.

Freia waited, watching the peculiar and exuberant growth in the forest. On the second day after Dewar had left her, Trixie returned, skittish and inclined to gross disobedience. Freia petted the gryphon and used her to travel, in a circuitous route, along the mountains toward the south, toward the city, the Spring, and Prospero.

She had promised Dewar to avoid any area that might be frequented by people, but people were in the mountains, in the forest, everywhere. She heard shouts at times, glimpsed movements, and smelled smoke. The people, if they were there, eluded her. She tried to creep up on them, to find their camps and spy on them as she thought they spied on her, and they scattered away whenever she thought she had them.

It was annoying. Trixie was frisky and difficult, because of the odd weather; Dewar was taking too long to do whatever he had been doing; and now there were people in her forests hunting and digging roots and leaving messy camps behind when they moved on. They seemed to have horses with them, too—unshod hoofprints were everywhere. There were knapping flints and broken arrowheads littered where they stopped.

Piqued, Freia began tracking them in earnest. She wrangled Trixie into cooperating and flew as low as she dared over the trees, a flight pattern not at all to the gryphon's liking, watching for signs of trespass in the clearings and through gaps of the branches, circling. Lying on the gryphon's back, she was mostly concealed, unless the observer noted the harness under the animal's feathery fur, and she had no helm to reflect the sun and give her away.

Twelve days she passed this way, each day more worried about her brother—what if he didn't return?—and each day more irked by these elusive intruders. When she found them, Freia decided, she would tell them to get out of her forest. Prospero made them, and he made his city for them, and they could damned well stay there. This was hers.

On the evening of the twelfth day she was looking for a camping spot for herself in the high, dry forest of the western leg of the Jagged Mountains, a place to sleep and to let Trixie off to hunt. Trixie's hunting trips had grown longer and longer; Freia cooed and praised her warmly when she returned, afraid of being abandoned by the gryphon as well. Trixie was irritable, snappish and sullen, disobedient and gnawing her harness often; Freia wanted a game-rich area for the gryphon, so she wouldn't stray too far from her mistress. The high meadows were attractive grazing for wood-elk, and Freia now was looking for a meadow with a brook and an open place to land.

They dropped over a clump of trees and toward a boulder-strewn meadow, and Freia hauled Trixie upward abruptly. Trixie screamed protest and fought.

The man on horseback below them glanced back and turned

in an instant, a perfectly executed sinewy curve, raising a short bow and nocking an arrow.

Freia hissed, "How dare you!" at the gryphon as much as at him and yanked Trixie's head. They swerved and the arrow missed.

Trixie was angry now. She had learned about arrows at Perendlac, and she wasn't letting this one go by unanswered. Ignoring the yanking and throttling of her harness, she folded her wings and dropped.

Freia had a moment to wish Dewar had come back so that she wouldn't have been doing this and to hope that she didn't break any bones in the strike. She braced herself and they hit the ground.

The horseman, whose mount was more obedient than Freia's, had whisked out from under the gryphon's wing-shadow to halt and wheel again a few dozen paces away. He was drawing his bow again, Freia saw, and, her teeth still rattling from the force of the landing, she grabbed her own bow, strung it, nocked and drew, and pointed it straight at him.

In that instant she saw that he wasn't a man on horseback, but a man with a horseback.

He froze too, perhaps wondering if she and Trixie formed a taxonomical blur like himself, and she could see him frown.

Trixie hissed and pounced. Freia half-fell off her smooth-feathered back. She grabbed the bridle-chain, dragging the gryphon's head down and to one side and wishing she had a cloak handy to throw over Trixie's head.

The man didn't shoot, but he held ready still, watching, as Freia scolded Trixie in a scalding, furious undertone.

"You have it pretty easy, you know," she snarled at the gryphon. "Who fixed your foot, huh? You'd have gangrene now. Forget that, huh? Disobey me? I'm in charge here. You do what I tell you! Stupid bird! Fatheaded feather-arse! You want to see what it's like on your own again? You want to starve when the hunting's bad and I'm not around to get you game? All by yourself? You want that? Get out of here! Go! Go on, go!" Freia yelled, and grabbed her saddle-bags from the gryphon's back and slapped her across the head. "Go, go, go! Go!"

Trixie, glaring balefully back at her for an instant, gathered herself in a pounce-crouch. Then she bounded upward, into the air, disdainfully flapping away.

Freia watched her go, horrified at what she had just done, as the gryphon rose out of sight beyond the trees.

A thump drew her attention back to the horse-man. He had stamped one—hoof, impatient. Was this another of Prospero's sorcerous accidents, like the gryphons? Freia wondered. There were others, half-people with deer-like lower bodies, but they had two legs only, and they kept to the south. This one was half man, half horse . . . a man's torso where the horse's neck should be. He had lowered his bow, amused probably by the sight of a disobedient gryphon getting the better of her mistress.

"What are you looking at?" Freia demanded, and she picked up her own bow and quiver, and shrugged her saddle-bags across her shoulders. "And what are you doing here? This is my forest!" She tossed her hair back.

He moved toward her cautiously, like an uncertain horse, watching her hands. Freia set them on her hips and glared at him. He stopped.

"This is our forest," he said slowly.

"It is not. I've never seen you here before, and I know these mountains well. I've been through them in every season, and you don't belong here. Where did you come from?"

"Here," he said, stomping again.

Freia frowned.

"Where did *you* come from?" he countered.

"Here," she said. "I was here before anybody but Prospero." It was hers. She didn't want interlopers hunting in her mountains, running down her game, making fires in her forest. No doubt their fires had been the cause of the great destruction in the north.

"Prospero?" he repeated.

"Prospero is my father," said Freia, "and he made Argylle and gave it to me, and it's not yours."

They stared at one another on the darkening mountainside.

"You have a bow," he said.

"And I can use it well," Freia retorted, lifting it again, putting an arrow to the string.

"Your boasts are as great as clouds," he said.

"I'm not bragging. I was here before anyone and the stones themselves know the truth of that."

"Would the trees know too?"

"Mind your tongue," Freia said, with a rush of boiling rage, and the feathers of the arrow were by her ear.

"I challenge you," he said. "I am Sire of the Clan, and I challenge you. We will choose three targets. The one who shoots best at all three speaks truth. This forest is ours, and we will not be forced from it."

"It's mine," Freia said. She would show the bastard. One of Prospero's rogue inventions, wandered wild now. She wouldn't stand for it, for horse-people polluting her forests and meadows and mountains— "I'll take your challenge," she said, "and the truth is that I was here before you, and that Argylle is mine." She lowered the bow. "Who picks first target?"

He looked around, seeming nonplussed. Freia thought he hadn't expected her to take him up. The light was failing; they'd have to shoot quickly or wait until morning.

"There," he suggested, and pointed at a single white-trunked tree gleaming in the dusky fringe of the forest.

"From here," Freia said, stamping once.

"Yes," he agreed, and slowly came toward her again. They eyed one another distrustfully. He snuffed audibly when he was closer, reminding her of Prospero's Hurricane taking stock of her Epona, and stopped a few steps away on her right.

"You may shoot first," she said.

He stamped and gave her a quick glare, then drew his bow— it didn't appear to have much stronger pull, if any more at all, than hers—and aimed and shot.

They heard the arrow thock into wood; branches quivered.

Freia turned, drew the arrow back to her ear and looked at the white tree, loosed her breath softly, and loosed the arrow. *Thock.*

Without speaking, they walked to the edge of the forest.

Freia's arrow was in the trunk of the tree. The man-horse's had pierced and was stuck in a greyish sucker-shoot coming out of the ground to one side of the white trunk. He had missed by a hand's breadth, and it shocked him. He stamped and pulled the arrow out.

Freia decided to leave hers where it was. "I will choose the next target," she said, and looked around the meadow. "Let us go to the middle again," she said, "and we will both shoot at once at the first bird to pass. The darters will be out soon."

He grunted and they did that and stood, neither speaking, waiting.

The first darter of the evening cooperated by appearing not long after, its erratic path taking it here, there, left, right, up, down after insects swirling in the evening air.

Their bows sprang back; the arrows flew out. The darter fell, transfixed.

Freia's arrow was through its heart; the other's had passed through the bird's wing and fallen to the grass some distance away.

"Poor thing, I'm sorry," Freia said, looking at the soft body distorted and transfixed by the arrow, the seeping blood, the beady dead eye. "I'm sorry," she said again softly. "You choose the target," she said, resolving to bury the bird when they were through with this game.

The man-horse stamped. "Whatever comes from the forest there, in the instant it's first seen by either," he said, pointing at the other side of the meadow.

"All right," she agreed reluctantly. A live target meant that another death sentence had just been passed, for no reason other than a bet, on whatever animal, great or small, was foolish enough to move next. But this would end the argument; she was right, and she knew it, and she knew her aim was better than his. And if it was a wood-elk, she could feed Trixie, if she came back.

They stood, arrows nocked and bows ready, as they had before, silent and waiting. The man-horse's tail flicked his flanks, then stilled, and nothing moved. The darters were avoiding the place, and so was everything else.

The moon was rising now. Freia's eyes stared into the forest fringe, watching; her ears strained, listening.

The moon had cleared the trees by a good stride when rhythmic snapping and crackling came from the forest. Something large was coming through the fringe-brush.

Freia felt, rather than saw, her companion draw and begin aiming. She drew herself, holding ready.

Movement in the trees' shadows—recognition in her mind, and a panicked change of intention—but her muscles were already moving as Dewar came into the meadow, and she shot as her companion shot.

Her arrow struck her challenger's and sent it skewing off into the grass and Dewar shouted in anger all in an instant as her tumbling off-course arrow grazed his sleeve and stuck in his cloak.

"You ass, that's my brother!" Freia turned on the man-horse, drawing again and taking a bead on him. "Get out of here. Get out of here; go away, go where you came from and stay there, and stay out of Argylle!"

"You spoiled my shot!"

"You were going to kill him!"

"What the hell are you doing?"

The man-horse swung round belligerently and half-aimed at Dewar again; Dewar had a staff in his hands and it had little lines of light running down it, flickering and cascading and gathering.

"You have not won!" the man-horse cried. "The shot is mine!"

"Don't even think about it," Dewar said. "Freia, what is this?"

"I don't know. One of Prospero's creatures."

"I mean, what the hell are you doing shooting at me in the dark."

"I am Bellonius, Sire of the Clan," said the man-horse, "and the agreement was to shoot what came from the forest—"

"So you shot at me?" Dewar's voice went up. It could be one of Odile's workings, he thought, to kill him by Freia's hand, his own blood to spill his blood.

"I shot at his arrow," Freia said, his anger changing her own to conciliatory fear. "I saw it was you and I aimed at his arrow," she explained, "not at you—"

"Somebody hit me," Dewar growled, and showed the blood on his sleeve.

"My shot," Bellonius said.

"Liar!" cried Freia.

"Blood to blood!" cried Dewar, exasperated, holding his staff sideways in front of his arm, and something hissed and thunked into the staff, barely penetrating, bouncing. "Whose arrow has striped feathers?"

"Mine," Freia said.

"You hit me," Dewar said; "the blood on the tip proves it." He took the arrow from the staff and ran his hand along his staff, making a fist at the top as he summoned an ignis fatuus and bound it there. The ball of fire showed Bellonius staring fearful but defiant. "Blood on the point," Dewar said coldly, and showed it to him. "Ware lest I call your own arrow back to you unshielded," he added. "That is one of the most foolish wagers I've ever heard of, Freia. Never—"

"I didn't mean you!"

"Of course you didn't mean *me*! Nor did this Bellonius mean to kill *me* either, but someone's curse could use such a bet, you fool! What inspired you anyway?"

"This one says we, my clan, must leave this land, and we will not go," Bellonius said.

"We agreed that whoever shot best in three shots won," Freia said. "I won, three of three," she added firmly.

Dewar rubbed his chin, studying his sister's face by the flickering ignis-light, and inquired, "Freia, why must they leave?"

"They're making a mess," Freia said, "and it's mine, and I don't want any more people making a mess in my land. Killing things and burning and cutting trees."

"Did she shoot best?" Dewar asked Bellonius.

Bellonius reluctantly said, "Yes, but the last shot was unfair!"

"She blooded me; does that satisfy you?"

Bellonius stamped; his hindquarters danced sideways and he stilled himself. "We live here," he said.

"Do you know who she is?" Dewar asked him.

"She said, but it meant nothing to me. I do not know her sire."

"He's Prospero," Dewar said, "and he made this place out of nothing and gave it to her to do with as she would, to govern and shape as it pleased her, all the world. And if she's telling you to leave this part, you'd better go."

"There is nowhere to go; this is where we live," Bellonius said.

"Freia, they cannot evaporate," Dewar pointed out to her, as gently as he could. She was very angry with this fellow, he could see, and she wasn't thinking the matter through.

"They can't stay here. I won't have them here in my forest. They make a mess."

"Then give them someplace else."

"What do you mean, give them someplace else?"

"It's all yours. You decide where you want them to go. You can't just tell them to disappear—well, you could . . . remove them, but I think you'd rather not go for genocide, hm? More war?"

"No," she said, giving him a dirty look, her eyes flashing. "All right, you can go west. There's plains out there beyond the tablelands. Plenty of game, too. You can go there and stay there." She tossed her hair back again, watching Bellonius. Sire of the Clan, indeed. Men. "And get moving tomorrow morning."

"This is not fair," Bellonius said.

"Fair!" Freia said scornfully. "You said you'd abide by the game, and then you don't like losing! Is that fair?"

"Freia," Dewar said, and he touched her arm to keep her from starting a war on the spot. "Bellonius, it seems reasonable to me. Argylle is already settled. If you do not go west as Freia says, you will soon be in conflict with others who are even more . . . defensive of their lands than she is, and less inclined or able to give you an accommodation. It may not be perfectly just, but it is wiser to put distance between you and the people already settled here. Surely you can see that. There are empty lands and she has given them to you. Take them and thrive."

Bellonius and Freia glared at one another.

"The consequences of not keeping to your word would be far worse than honoring the agreement," Dewar said persuasively.

"If we perish, it will be to your account," Bellonius muttered.

"If you perish after what I saw today, you'll have been muffing your shots deliberately," Freia said, as gracious a compliment as she could manage.

Bellonius snorted. "A strange clan you have, if *she* leads it," he said to Dewar, beginning to turn away.

"It suits us," Dewar replied.

"I will lead the Clan to these plains," said Bellonius.

"Safe journey to you all," Freia said, more courteously.

Bellonius made no reply; he sidled away from them and then turned and walked away quickly across the meadow. Under the ignis-light, Dewar and Freia watched him go.

"Come over here and help me dig a hole," Freia said, when the Sire of the Clan was out of sight among the trees.

"A hole?"

"I have to bury the poor little bird," she said.

The Empress Glencora sent for the Countess of Lys to attend her as she ate her second breakfast of fruit and a few crumbly little butter-horns and a cup of manly black Madanese coffee. Such meetings were afforded only to the Empress's most intimate and favored acquaintances, Luneté well knew, and as she hurried to keep the appointment, she wished with all her heart that a hastily made grey mourning-gown had not been delivered half an hour before.

Still, the honor was hers, and she was left alone with the Empress (and a pair of maids sewing busily at the other end of the room beside the window) and offered a cup of coffee and a butter-horn just as if she had been the Baroness of Olm or the Dowager Queen Anemone. Luneté accepted, but she found the butter-horn an untidy thing to eat, and after one bite settled for sipping at the coffee cautiously. On one side of the tray were the Empress's letters in a pile with her silver-and-gold letter-knife, just as anyone might have them at the breakfast-table.

The Empress watched Luneté, chatting of light matters, and waited until the Countess had taken several sips of coffee and set the cup down before serving her the meat of the meeting.

"My dear, I must ask you a question which will seem quite impertinent," said the Empress, "but you must answer me wholly truthfully."

Luneté, recognizing the change of mood from social to Imperial, straightened in her chair and nodded her assent.

"Are you pleased with the Baron of Ascolet?" asked the Empress.

Luneté's breath stopped, then started; she lowered her chin and met the Empress's gaze. "No, Your Majesty," she replied.

"No. Then perhaps it will not come as a great shock to you to learn that he intends filing a petition for annulment of your marriage."

Indeed it came as a great shock. Luneté paled. She stared, wide-eyed and foolish, at the Empress, and Empress Glencora watched her, waiting for her to collect her wits and say something.

"Your Majesty," whispered Luneté when she found words, "I had no idea—" and she stopped herself. It was not true, that she had had no idea that Otto was discontent. But so discontent as that—as to dissolve their marriage, make it never have been, to part utterly and forever— "I would never have thought he would do that," said she.

"Indeed," said the Empress, "it is surprising, considering the trouble he went to to make it come about. But I suppose," she said, lifting her cup, "it was not quite what he expected."

"No," said Luneté. "Not what I expected either," she said, attempting to be witty, and laughed a little. The laugh was wrong; the Empress looked sharply at her, and Luneté swallowed a mouthful of coffee, trying to thaw the ice in her stomach. "I assure you he has no grounds for an annulment," she said, setting down her cup with a ringing tremor. Unless Dewar had betrayed her—but he would not—but men boasted—but Otto would have accused her to her face, not this; he was direct in all things. That letter was certainly astoundingly direct, she reminded herself.

"I believe it can be sought on procedure, rather than conduct. The marriage was highly irregular. Certainly there will be a number of weaknesses to support an annulment. You do not find the idea attractive."

"Attractive!"

"You have spent little time with him," the Empress said, "and the double burden of Lys and Ascolet is a difficult one to balance."

"He blames me for Cambia," said Luneté.

"I am sure he is too much a gentleman to say anything of the sort," said the Empress coolly. "Of course it is in your power to stop him, I should think, if you wish to remain married."

"There hardly seems any point," said Luneté, suddenly angry. "If he does see annulment as the most reasonable thing to do, I should not like to oppose him. I am sure I should never compel someone into a marriage who did not wish it with all his heart. It was Otto's idea. If his feelings have changed, and I can think of many reasons why they might, then I hope he proceeds with the petition, and that the Emperor hears it quickly and grants it."

"Very well," the Empress said. "I shall certainly let the Emperor know your side of it, Countess. I quite understand how it must be." She smiled and patted Luneté's clenched right hand, and asked how the arrangements went on for the sadly sudden journey the Countess must undertake.

"I shall be very glad to be home in Lys," said Luneté, when the meeting was done. "I shall have Lord Gonzalo keep me informed of—matters here."

"I do not think there will be any delay about it," said the Empress. "I am sure it is for the best, my dear."

"Yes," said Luneté of Lys.

Prospero's dreams were fraught with meanings; they gave him no peace. They darkened his nights and shadowed his days, and he damned them and wished them on their agent. He attributed them to Dewar, to a Sending or curse the young sorcerer had laid to harry him in his tower, and he fought them by walking, waking, late night and early morning when they came the strongest.

He would rise from beside the dark and fair Odile and dress quietly, then go down from the tower and outside and make the circuit of his isle as he was wont to do in elder days. The isle had changed. Its trees gone, Freia's garden overlaid by mud and even before then a wild ruin, it was not the pristine green paradise he had first seen on coming here. The banks to either side were scarred and denuded too, and the river was busily reshaping them to suit its new humor, so that to build on them for a few months or years, before the river's course had stabilized, were folly.

As Prospero walked he would think on his plans, his buildings and his futures. He walked in the mild unseasonable night air, knowing morning lay some little time ahead, and listened to the late-summer insects choiring and cheering.

These hours were his alone; he had the world to himself again, no disruption of daughter or other creatures to jar his thoughts, and he cherished them despite the loss of peaceful sleep that occasioned them.

So Prospero stole forth one foggy morning and quickly came in his walking to the downstream end of the isle, and he stopped, because someone was there before him.

"Who's that?" he asked softly.

"Papa, I miss you," Freia said, turning to look at him.

He stared, fearful and amazed. She was dripping wet, dressed in her hunting-clothes, and he could see the mark of his hand on her cheek beneath the tears that ran from her pleading eyes—

Prospero sat bolt upright in his bed and cursed. The dream had felt so genuine, he'd have sworn he wore his cloak. Nay, 'twas a dream, and he'd waked Odile with his start.

"What troubles thee, love?" came her voice, a dove's fluting croon, in the dark, and her arms followed it and drew him down.

"But a dream, madame, that doth double ill in waking thee as well. 'Tis naught." Prospero embraced her body, naked beside him, and felt her hands on his shoulders, his back, his thighs.

"Tell me thy dream," she said.

"I did but dream I saw Freia," he said, "as she were drowned, naught of subtlety to't."

"She seeks to drag thee after her," Odile murmured, "and I will not let her; she seeks to drown thee in her folly, but my arms shall keep thee. Thou evil restless ghost, begone and leave the living to lie in peace."

" 'Tis but a dream," he said, "her ghost, if it walks, would walk the waters in Landuc and beckon sailors to their deaths, not here."

"Think'st thou so? Then perhaps 'tis some other Sending, from some enemy that would prey upon thy sentiment."

"I've none able to reach me here, so far as I have discovered, and that's what hath preserved me so long," he replied.

"Dewar could reach thee, if he have drunk the waters of the Spring," whispered Odile, "and he'd know the shape to give thy daughter's seeming, to deepest stir thee."

"Aye, 'tis possible."

"My lord, I would protect thee with mine Art if I could. Hast me for handmaiden in lesser matters; wilt not accept more?"

"I'll accept what thou canst give, madame, and no Art hast thou here, only thy native nature. And that hath been of great aid to me."

Odile lay some while with him in wordless colloquy, and whispered again at his ear. "Dear love, I am troubled by a sudden thought: as I bemoan my own powerlessness to give thee any gift of substance—"

"Thou art thyself thy greatest gift," he murmured, preoccupied.

"—did a puzzle upraise from the disjointure of will and ability. If I may not travel from Argylle, to Pheyarcet or Phesaotois, without thy kind indulgence and escort—"

"Thine in any instant," Prospero said, half-listening.

She turned in his arms to interrupt him, commanding his attention as she spoke. "—then how did it come to pass that Dewar did join thee in Landuc, did make his Way to the very Palace steps as I was told? Saidst thou not, hadst left him here?"

"Aye," said Prospero, holding himself still and reckoning. "Aye, so 'twas; he was ill from laboring o'er the copy-books and did sleep when we rode forth."

"Perhaps he had some aid of thy daughter," suggested Odile.

"Nay. Nay; had he drunk o' the Spring when they two first came here, I'd have seen it in him, as 'twas ever clear to me in myself and Freia, different from the touch of Fire or Stone." He thought, lifting himself on his elbow and staring into the morning-greying chamber. "In Landuc—why, I know not how he came to the Well, but that 'twas done is evident, for he's able as a sorcerer should be. I noted no alteration in his substance— yet I did not look for't, had other matters in mind." He sat up, and Odile rose too and knelt half-covered against his back, warm and smooth. "An he'd drunk of the Spring after I left him here," Prospero concluded a minute later, " 'twere nowise obvious in Landuc, for the Fire might well mask the change in him. Indeed 'a must have done. He cannot have come to Landuc in any other way; he'd no means of doing it. Freia followed by her gryphon's affinity for me, a freakish and uncertain method I'd never have countenanced. Dewar had no gryphon, assuredly. Scudamor would have spoken of't."

Odile watched through half-lidded eyes as Prospero thought aloud. She could see him frowning in the dawn light, suspicion waking and driving out repose.

"Must have done it," Prospero said softly after another pause. "Ah, the sorcerer compleat is he, and in no part a son."

"Surely Scudamor would have told thee of it," Odile said. "Why would he not speak, an he knew?"

"An he knew, he must have told me. I'll think on't further. Trouble thyself not o'er this, Odile; 'tis not thy affair."

Odile murmured acquiescently and said, "Let me then divert thee from thy affairs to mine."

And Prospero smiled and was diverted.

Scudamor waited for Lord Prospero to explain what was amiss.

"Scudamor, my friend," Prospero said, "for so have I thought of thee, thou hast done me an ill turn in thy liberal hosting in my house." The high black stone chair-back was cold on his spine. He gripped the arms, also cold, and felt his hands becoming chilled.

"My Lord, howso?" Scudamor asked, taken aback. "Tell me what wrong I have done, and I shall strive to right it."

"There is no righting this matter," Prospero said. "When I departed for Landuc, Dewar was left behind; is't not so?"

"Aye, Lord, he slept." The Seneschal gazed at Prospero earnestly.

Prospero damned the man's ingenuousness. "How long slept he?"

"Four days, or less by some hours," Scudamor said.

"And what did he on arising?"

"Why, and he bathed in the River and walked about and ate, and slept again and ate—" Scudamor tried to remember. "He talked to us," he offered, "about the River and the fish in it. We did offer him all hospitality, Lord Prospero, as you commanded ere you and Lady Freia left."

"Ah. All hospitality didst thou offer him, and all hospitality did he have. Did I not remind thee and Utrachet as well that none was to approach the Spring, and bid you two set guards upon it lest any come in my absence?"

"Aye, Lord, and that we did."

"Yet by clear signs I do understand that Dewar hath been to the Spring."

Scudamor's expression became blank, then aghast. "My Lord, we did not think . . ." His voice faded as his apprehension grew.

Prospero's mouth hardened. "You did not think; nay, you thought not at all, none of you! I said none, you thought to better my command! He was allowed to pass, then!"

"Aye, my Lord. You—you had so favored him, by look and deed, and named him as your son and—"

"And gave no word that he was permitted the Spring."

"Nay, Lord," Scudamor had to agree softly. "That is so."

Prospero eyed him icily. "I'll think further on this," said he. "Go."

Betrayed by one he had trusted most, the first-made of his Argylle men, Prospero stalked bile-humored from the hall, whither he had summoned Scudamor, to the tower. He could not allow the failure to go unpunished. If he were to rule Argylle—and Fortuna had placed it again in his hands though he had tried to pass it to his daughter—he must rule unwaveringly. Prospero strode through the tower's double door and paused, then went to the stair and climbed up to the very top of the building. He would think better there, able to see the place spread out as on a map.

He opened the door that led outside and a scent tickled his nose: Odile's. She stood at the parapet gazing out toward the sea, veiled, one arm draped gracefully over a corner of the stone.

"Madame," Prospero said, and closed the door behind him.

"My lord," she replied.

"It is a sorry world I have made, and a sorry people," he said, standing beside her. "For the simplest order do they disobey. Must have learnt the trick from my daughter, who'd argue the color of the grass or the sky." A twinge of conscience panged; he knew Freia had not been so contrary as that. Indeed, she had accepted his will in most things. Yet she had balked and failed him at the test, and so now had Scudamor. "Now we've great evil afoot indeed, for Dewar hath partaken of the Spring, and he's set against me."

"I feared as much, my lord, but thou hast allowed thy desires to color all thou seest, and wouldst not see his perfidy at all. But 'tis e'en what I fear for thee, that he would plunder thee of all and then dispossess thee of thy life."

Prospero stood staring at the mountains to the west, lower than the great southern peaks and more distant, but visible on this clear bright day. The carpet of forest spread from the fields' boundaries to infinity, to the feet of the mountains. The faint green of the unseasonable spring was stronger now, the sharp branches softened and purpled by comparison. The sound of water rose to his ears; it was inescapable since the drought had broken.

He would not believe Odile, yet what she said rang true. Dewar was a sorcerer, and power was a sorcerer's existence. Surely Dewar would do whatever he could to possess himself of sole use of the power here—such as it now was. It was fully possible that he lurked in the realm somewhere, watching. Prospero would have expected him to take the place in Prospero's absence, but perhaps Dewar knew he'd get little good of raping it. No, it must be transferred with consent, or at least without murder.

The question was, should Prospero resist transferring the place to him or not, and—Prospero's eyes were hard on the inoffensive horizon—was Prospero even empowered to do so? For he had made the place over to his daughter, and Landuc had claimed his daughter ere she died, and thus was Landuc in dominion here? It had been among her dower-lands, and so perhaps it had reverted to himself. Or might it be considered, by the normal laws of heritance, to have passed to her brother, Dewar?

The Emperor would not allow it to happen so. Though he be ignorant, and corrupt, and ill-fitted to guide Landuc and command the Well that made Pheyarcet exist and Landuc thrive— he was still the Emperor, the ruler, and his will would be law.

Nor Avril nor custom would permit Prospero to inherit what he'd lost.

Prospero flinched from the obvious conclusion: that on Freia's passing from the mortal realm, the Spring and its surrounding infant lands had become Landuc's. Yet this could explain the straitened flow of the Spring: it was being dominated and destroyed by the Well of Fire. If it was so, then nothing he could do could revive the Spring, nor was he here legitimately, and this present resurgence would soon fail. He doubted that the Spring would accept governance by someone wholly of Landuc, as Prospero was not; the two places must be mediated.

He smiled as another thought occurred to him: if this realm truly belonged to Landuc, to Avril, then was it not Avril's duty to hold it against Dewar, when Dewar returned to wrest it from his father? Then Avril would indeed rue his disdain of sorcery.

"My love, an thou hast found amusement, I prithee amuse me too."

Prospero glanced at Odile; he repeated his thought.

She shook her head. "Meseems better that thou shouldst hold it for thyself, by thyself, for now thou'rt here and Landuc cannot find thee."

"An there be truth of the Well in the oaths that have been sworn around this place and all my lands, then 'tis Landuc's, and Landuc must find and claim it inevitably." They must cross the widening desert to do it, but find it they would with Fortuna's favor on them and Prospero's own web of oaths and promises to support them, his protections become weaknesses.

And among those, Scudamor. What penalty could Prospero impose upon this fool who presumed to second-guess his will? If he whipped him and spared his life, the example would be harsh but salutary to others who might not obey Prospero's commands. If he did that and left Scudamor in his position as Seneschal, Scudamor might use position and occasion to plot against him, becoming a still weaker link, and his position was too high for Prospero to tolerate his failure.

Best thing would be to take humanity from him and send him to dwell in the woods, but that now lay beyond Prospero's ability, thanks to Freia's disobedience. Prospero ground his teeth.

Imprisonment was risky; the Seneschal was well-liked and his friends might foment against Prospero, given the living martyr as a symbol.

Death. Prospero could hang the Seneschal for insubordination, and there'd be a strong lesson to the others and an end to worries about plots and treason from that quarter. He would be forgotten, as the dead always are, as Prospero's allies executed by Panurgus and later by Avril had been, and there would be an end to it. Argylle would remember it as an abstract, past event: disobedience of Prospero's orders had caused Scudamor to be hanged.

Yes: what he had done could well cause Prospero's own death. Let him die for it now rather than benefit from it later.

Dewar's luck at fishing was better than his sister's in the hunt. When she returned to their campsite, he held up a string of stripe-sided fish he had hooked during the brief autumn afternoon.

Freia dropped a handful of thin yellowish roots before him: her day's contribution to their sustenance. "I've never seen hunting so bad. Those horse people have chased all the game away. We should smoke a few fish and keep them; they won't last otherwise." She sat under the cut-bough windscreen they had made that morning. After a moment, she took her arrows from the quiver, one by one, and squinted along each to see if it were straight.

Dewar began scaling the fish. "Freia, it is uncommonly warm."

"That's why I said to smoke the fish."

"In other words, is weather so warm, this late in the year, usual? Is the climate so mild as this?"

"No, not at all. Usually by now it's colder, and leaves are down—I can't imagine why they're still on and green—and things are withered, and animals have winter coats and so do I, and it's nearly snow-time. Yes, this is strange. You picked up wood." She tested the tip of the arrow under scrutiny with a finger.

"I thought not to be wholly idle," he replied, and grinned at her to soften any sarcasm she might hear in the words.

The smile failed. "I tried," Freia snapped, glaring at him. "I spent the whole day finding nothing, nothing in these woods. Hoofprints, old droppings, nothing. There aren't any greens— just leaves and buds on the trees, and they're no good to eat. I was lucky to find the paste-roots."

"I meant no slur, madame," Dewar said.

There was a taut pause. Freia looked back at her arrows. "Sorry," she said to them. "I wish Trixie would come back."

"Smoking this won't be easy," he said, setting the fish aside. "I picked very dry wood to make the least smoke. We'll just have to eat it tomorrow, cooked and cold."

Freia shrugged.

Dewar built a small pyramid of sticks and sparked flint and steel to light it. It would be as practical to summon a Salamander and bind it while the fish cooked, but the wood-fire was pleasant; moreover, the wood-fire was familiar to Freia, unlike sorcery. Apparently Prospero had used wood-fires for everything she had ever seen him do, and Dewar was chary of appearing too alien to her. He glanced up, checking the smoke, and saw the tops of the trees still gilded with sunlight. It fled as he watched. The fire wasn't smoking.

"Dewar—"

He looked away from the heavens, at her. She was intent on him, her expression troubled and preoccupied. "Yes, Freia?"

"You said," she began, and halted.

"Tell me," he urged her after she had been quiet too long.

"When you were talking to—*him*," she said, watching Dewar's face in the blue dusk-light, the ruddy fire, "you said— something you said—"

He waited, and then said, "Say it."

"Prospero never told me," she said, looking now at the fire. "But what you said, and things he said, used to say, some-times—I'm like Caliban, aren't I."

"Who is Caliban?" asked Dewar softly, caught by the unexpected current of the conversation. She had mentioned Caliban before, he recalled.

"Prospero's, one of his creatures. He digs. He's made of stones and earth. He doesn't like the sun, and he's not quick, not like Ariel."

"A bound Sammead, I suspect—unbound from Prospero now, as Ariel was."

"Am I a Sammead?"

Dewar was cold with sweat and apprehension. If he said something wrong or false now, it could never be mended. He swallowed and told her the truth. "No. You're a human woman. You're not a, an assemblage of stones and earth ani-mated by an Elemental presence. No. You have a soul, dear heart, Freia, and a life. You're Prospero's daughter."

"How do you know?"

"I know. It's—it is sorcery, partly. And if you were a Sam-mead, you'd be very different: no matter how brilliant a sorcerer your father was, he couldn't change the nature of an Elemen-tal. You're not an Elemental. You're a human woman. Alive. I promise you it is so." He clasped and unclasped his damp hands nervously.

Freia considered this, and him, for a few moments. "How did you know he made me?"

Dewar closed his eyes to escape her gaze. He opened them, looked at the fire now. "It was in one of his books: how it was done. I read it when I was copying."

"He gave it to you," she whispered hoarsely, drawing in a breath.

"No. No! Freia, no. He did not. He—I helped myself to that one and put it away again. I was curious." Dewar had to meet her eyes again, watching the thoughts and emotions flickering through her. He was afraid. "He never told you this," Dewar asked.

She shook her head, mute, her eyes looking at and through him. She looked older: it might be a trick of the light, but her canny expression aged her face. "He—there were things he would say. That he shaped me from base beginnings. I thought he meant, from infancy. Now I see. He never said who my mother was. They asked in Landuc. I have no mother, if he made me out of dirt and sticks like Caliban."

"Well—no. But you have him. You're flesh and blood, Freia, whatever your origin. He's your father. I'm your brother. You have kin, Freia. You're not alone that way."

Freia's arms were wrapped tight around her knees now; she was a gold-lit statue across the little cook-fire. "I don't care about kin. He should have told me."

"Would it have made some difference to you? Would you have understood it?" Dewar wondered.

"I don't know," Freia said thoughtfully.

"You should think about that, Freia. Would it be different?"

"I wish I didn't know."

"I'm sorry. I am sorry, Freia. It is . . ." Dewar looked for a word, could not think of a fitting one. "It is another regret. I am sorry. —Freia."

She attended, her face drawn into an introspective, remote expression.

"You are human. You bleed; you—you could not be proven

otherwise, by any method." He moistened his dry mouth. "You conceived," he whispered. "You're human. More so than many of us."

To his surprise, Freia's look altered. She lowered her head, half a nod, and then nodded once slowly.

Dewar nodded too, twice. He began arranging the coals of the fire.

"We're very close to the island," Freia said as he set out the fish.

"I know. I can feel it," he said, thinking of the tower and the Spring.

"How?" Freia couldn't.

He glanced at her, his eyes dark in the shadows from his cheekbones. The twilight had gone, and the sudden forest night had come. "Because it is there," Dewar said after a moment.

Freia's regard held something distinctly irritated; she said, not bothering to soften her voice, "If I were half as smart as you, I'd never have gotten in a quarter as much trouble."

"Probably," Dewar agreed before he could stop himself.

Her mouth set in a tight little line, and she returned her attention to her arrows, which needed none.

The fish cooked quickly; the stringy roots roasted for a few minutes in the coals. They ate without further talk, Freia using her hunting-knife and fingers and Dewar using more elegant utensils from his bag. He watched her covertly as she ate. Her face had taken on that closed expression he recalled from Landuc, and her posture was hunched and protective. Was she brooding still on her humanity? Why had she become suddenly so quarrelsome and difficult now, after ten days in which they had travelled in good harmony toward the island from the mountains? The hunting had been bad for the whole of the journey, and Freia hadn't complained; the weather was warm and unseasonable, but she had remarked on how pleasant it was. Dewar puzzled over what could have caused the alterations in her, but found no answer.

When they lay down to sleep by the embers of the fire, Freia left an arm's-length distance between them. Dewar left the space and the silence unbridged and closed his eyes, but he was irked; they had slept close-lying every night until this, chastely but companionably. He resolved that in the morning, after she repented the chill and snuggled against him during the night, he would ask what was biting her.

In the morning he woke as he had stretched out the night before, alone, and when he lifted his head and looked about he saw that he was indeed alone. Freia had gone.

— 25 —

THE BARON OF ASCOLET SAT IN the apartment he had been given in the Palace of Landuc, in the position many troubled men have assumed for time out of mind. His head was supported on his hands; his eyes gazed down at a polished tabletop without seeing the delicate ivory flame-shaped inlay border or the fine grain of the reddish wood. The Baron was seeing, instead, something that was not there: the note his soon-to-beformer wife had brandished at him in the thick of their argument last month, on the day Cambia had drowned.

How had she come by it?

Ottaviano dismissed out of hand the possibility that Freia herself had given the letter to Luneté. Poor Freia had not shown any talent for scheming or vengeance, much to her own harm he thought, and he doubted that Freia had ever even met Luneté. Moreover, Luneté could not have had the note for very long. She would have said something about it.

He had given the note to Freia in a bouquet of flowers, a peace-offering left in her rooms. Ugly rooms, he recalled. Probably some of the servants' quarters were prettier . . . not that he had done better for her . . . anyway there she had been put, and there he'd left the flowers and the note.

Either Freia had seen the note or not; either someone else had seen it or not. If he set aside the idea that she might have sent it to his wife herself, as he must for various reasons, that left someone else sending it. Dewar and Prospero had both been in and out of Freia's apartment, surely; her brother and father were probably the only people in the Palace who had visited her. Freia had had no tiring-woman, no maid. Thus it must have been one of them, perhaps acting through an agent who forwarded something blindly. Perhaps they had acted together. Dewar had stuck to Prospero like a burr, bartering for him, doing his sorcerous work.

Otto frowned. Perhaps Dewar had done some of Prospero's unsorcerous work as well, though it seemed more likely that Golias's murder was Prospero's doing. Prospero had probably killed Golias as much, or more, for Lady Miranda's death as for Freia's injuries. Dewar was finicky about bloodshed. Perhaps the sorcerer had punished Otto more subtly than the Prince punished Golias, repayment for taking Freia hostage and for Otto's part in her suffering.

A gentleman would have burned the note and said nothing; would have struck openly, with a challenge to a duel. "Bastards," whispered Otto.

A coal of vengeance began to glow in his breast. He would pay them back somehow. They'd both slunk off now, skipped town the night the poor girl died (Otto pushed away a recollection of her face in front of the Emperor's throne) and neither heard from since. Probably the Emperor would be just as happy never to hear a word about Dewar again, but Prospero owed tribute and tithes. Ottaviano had too realistic a grasp of his own abilities to think he could find Dewar, and he wasn't about to enslave himself to Oriana of the Glass Castle. Dewar cared about Prospero, and Prospero was what the Emperor wanted.

Otto sat and stared at nothing and thought long and hard all through that long summer morning, picking through scraps and threads of information about Prospero, and at last in the high hours of afternoon, when the sun shone flat and bright on the lawns and terraces of the Palace, he rose and walked slowly to a certain room, where he knocked.

"I wish to speak with His Highness," said Ottaviano to the bright-eyed squire who answered the door, and he handed the boy one of the newfangled name-cards Luneté had made him get last year.

"He has just arrived, sir, and may not see you."

"Please ask him."

The boy shrugged—of course he would ask—and left Otto standing by a closed door for a few minutes. Then he popped out again. "My lord will see you," the squire announced, not keeping surprise from his voice. "Come in, sir, this way," and Ottaviano followed the boy into a kind of foyer, whence led three doors, and was led through one to a room where the Prince Marshal, Gaston, stood, reading a letter in his stocking feet.

"The Baron of Ascolet!" announced the squire.

"Robin," said Gaston, looking up from his letter, "boots."

"Oh, sir," gasped the boy, shocked, and fled the room—to fetch the boots, Otto suspected.

"New squire?" asked Ottaviano.

Gaston nodded. "Thy errand?"

"I didn't know you were just arrived, sir—thought you must have been here earlier. I'm sorry to interrupt."

"As yet, there's naught to interrupt," Gaston said drily, "therefore hast chosen thy hour wisely."

"Sir. I have an idea—"

Robin came in and the boots were presented, approved with a nod, and Gaston sat down to pull them on, telling the squire to go. Otto waited until the boots were donned and the Fire-duke on his feet again.

"Thy idea."

"It's about Prospero, sir. Is there any way I could obtain copies, or look at copies, of the surrender treaties and the stuff that would relate to his daughter's marriage?"

Gaston frowned. "Surely 'tis among the Muniments."

"I don't think just anyone would be allowed to see them, though, sir."

"True. What's thy idea?"

"I want to see what he gave up."

"What he gave up," repeated Gaston, and he studied Otto closely.

"Once I look at that, sir, then I can tell you more. I might be entirely wrong. It's a kind of vague hunch, sir."

"A hunch. Well." Gaston looked again at his pile of correspondence. "As I said, Baron," he said, reaching a decision, "hast found me at the best time: for hereafter, these next days of the Summer Court, must I hither and yon. Let us go to the Muniments Chambers and lay thy hunch, or feed it."

Otto smiled. "Thank you, sir."

They walked through a maze of corridors and down many flights of stairs to the Muniments Chambers. The room to which they were admitted by a stooped clerk with thin reddish hair was unprepossessing: a cube, lined with cabinets and studded with many lamps, that had a door at the other side. The clerk had a nervous habit of twisting his hands together, and he spoke slowly and raspily, with a lisp. Otto wondered if the clerk ever left these rooms. His skin was so pale as to seem greenish, even in the lamplight.

"Your Highness. Your Highness. Your Grace. Your Grace. What service, sirs? What service, sirs?"

"Those treaties that Prince Prospero signed, and such documents as pertain to his surrender," said Gaston, "would we review: bring them to me."

"The copies, sir? The copies, sir?"

"Nay, no copies: all the first matter."

"Very good, sir. Very good, sir. I shall send them—"

"We shall take them away with us now," said Prince Gaston, and he repeated, fixing the clerk with a look, "Now."

The clerk wrung his ink-stained hands for a moment, nearly fizzing, and then bobbed twice and pattered out through the other door; Otto glimpsed more cabinets as the door swung closed.

He was gone a long time. Gaston stood, waiting, watching the door. Otto, as quietly as possible, paced from side to side, eyeing the cabinets, not daring to open one and peek. He'd had no idea this was all here. How large might it be? If every letter, every treaty, every dispatch and memorandum from Panurgus's long reign until now were filed here, how large would the place have to be to hold it all? And in some kind of order, too. There was a smell of dust, but it was not oppressive: the air was hot and dry, from the lamps Otto supposed. He looked up, around the tops of the cabinets, and saw gratings dimly in the darkness below the ceiling.

The clerk returned at last lugging a wooden box. It was locked, and on top lay a ledger and a set of keys.

"Sirs. Sirs. Yes. Yes," panted the clerk, and set the box down with a thud. "Now then. Now then. You must sign, sirs. You must sign, sirs." He took a stubby, chewed steel-pointed pen from his pocket, and a bottle of ink. Muttering rhythmically to himself, he set them on one side and opened the ledger. Pages after pages, columned entries . . . at the end were blank pages, blank lines.

"Have all these people taken out this box?" asked Otto, amazed.

The clerk stared at him and then, after a moment, laughed, a dry rhythmic rustle. "Oh, sir! Oh, sir! A notion, indeed! A notion, indeed! No no, no no. The box has its number, sir. The box has its number, sir. So. So." And he pointed, and Otto saw a long number on the box, and the clerk was writing that number in a column of the book. "Sign here, sign here," he said, pointing and lifting the ledger up to them, and Prince Gaston bent and signed, and Otto dipped the pen and signed also. "I sign as well, sir. I sign as well, sir." Otto watched over his shoulder as he did just that—but only once, not twice as Otto hoped: *Fidelio, Keeper of the Emperor's Muniments.* And the date. Very neat and legible writing, and small, with one restrained, intricate flourish.

"There you are, sirs. There you are, sirs. The key, sirs. The key, sirs." Fidelio, Keeper of the Emperor's Muniments, handed Prince Gaston a single key off the ring, with brass tag on it that had a number: the box number. "Two days, sirs. Two days, sirs. Holiday tomorrow. Holiday tomorrow."

Otto stooped, hefted the box; the clerk opened the door, bowing, muttering his farewells, and they left him.

Back up the stairs, and along corridors and hallways; a short-cut through an empty ballroom Ottaviano hadn't known about, and another flight of stairs, and Otto said, "Prince Gaston, sir . . ."

"Baron."

"This probably won't take long, but I won't want to be disturbed—"

"I will assist you," said the Fireduke. "What is your notion, Baron?"

"It's not very . . ." Otto tried to shrug, holding the box. "Just an idea, based on what I know about Prospero, sir, which isn't really much."

Gaston looked at him, and waited for an explanation.

"My idea is, sir, that first I want to list the locations of all the places Prospero tried to give to Freia, with that trick of emancipation."

Freia walked away from softly-snoring Dewar in the dull predawn light, threading through the undergrowth. She stayed close to the stream, which would soon empty into the broader river that held Prospero's island. She made little noise. Perhaps she'd get lucky and see something worth eating, but she doubted it.

As the pearly light grew stronger, she went more quickly, and soon she reached the flattened area where the river had flooded, where trees hung with snags lay uprooted and a layer of sandy mud spread over the banks a goodly ways into the forest. The mud was pierced here and there by spears of new grass. Freia paused, thought, and avoided treading in the mud. The fringes of the forest were full of old flotsam cast up by the flood waters—it must have been a terrible flood, unlike anything she had seen before—but just outside them she could walk quickly, not leave footprints, and get closer to the island. After sunrise, she thought, she would have to move into the forest and circle away from the river, which might be travelled.

In fact it was travelled now. Freia saw and heard the muffled oars of a boat. She froze still by a tilted tree, hoping to be unnoticed.

Two people were in the boat, a flat-bottomed rough-made rowboat, one rowing strongly, the other riding in the stern.

"We must be 'most on it," said the rower; his voice carried clearly to Freia, and she knew him: Scudamor.

"I think it is there," said the passenger, and she pointed to the confluence of the smaller stream and the river. Freia knew her also. "Yes. I see the break in the trees, the light grows better. Let us go near the bank," said Cledie, "get out, and push the boat off; then we can wade up the stream a ways and get away from the flats. Our footprints will betray us else."

"Speak not of betrayal, I beg you," said Scudamor, pulling on his near-side oar and turning the boat.

"Friend, I know that what I have done is right, and that what you did is right, and that Lord Prospero is not incapable of error, though this error is not his," Cledie said, "but this is no hour for debate."

Freia watched them, tense with curiosity. She knew them both well; she thought Scudamor liked her, and gentle Cledie had been Freia's first friend among the Argyllines, found while Prospero was pursuing Landuc's crown. Scudamor was Prospero's man, his Seneschal and first before all others. Were they running away together? Scudamor, like all Argylle, had made no secret of his admiration for Cledie. But why run away?

They reached the shallows of the river. Scudamor rowed against the current to hold them and Cledie, rising carefully, left the boat first; she wore loose trousers rolled up over the knee and they were wet to mid-thigh. "It is deeper than one might think; wait," Cledie said, and dragged rowboat and Scudamor in toward the bank. "And mucky," she said. "Give me the sack."

"I'll carry it." Scudamor said, and shrugged it onto his back. "Your sandals?" He put the oars into the bottom of the boat.

"I put them in the sack. Come."

He crouched, balanced, and left the boat also. Together they shoved it out and away from the bank, and it bobbed, indecisive, before the river caught it and carried it away.

Cledie turned, looking up and down the banks, and Scudamor also, and their eyes lit all at once on Freia, for the light had grown stronger with each minute.

"Lady . . ." whispered Cledie.

"Lady," breathed Scudamor.

Holding very still was useless. Spotted, Freia sighed and left the shadow of the tree, moving toward them on the trackless leaf mold, her steps rustling. She stood before them on the shore, and they remained knee-deep in the water while the light paled around them.

"You're alive?" Cledie asked, and then she said, smiling, "You're alive."

"There was a, a mistake," Freia said lamely.

Scudamor was smiling too, jubilant. "I never believed it! Another of the Black One's tales—"

"You're leaving the city," Freia said.

"Yes," Cledie replied.

Freia looked inquiringly at Scudamor. "Why?"

Scudamor swallowed, shamefaced. He said nothing.

"Lady, to speak honestly, our journey is away from Prospero's city, by reason of his great displeasure with Scudamor," Cledie said then, "whom I have helped to freedom by betraying Prospero's trust."

"Why?" Freia asked again, puzzled. Scudamor, displeasing to Prospero?

Again Cledie spoke. "Lord Prospero did declare, Lady, that Scudamor should die—"

"What?" Freia said.

Scudamor, acutely miserable, began, "Lady, I—"

"—for that he permitted Lord Dewar to drink of Prospero's Spring, and Prospero considers that one his enemy," Cledie said, speaking over Scudamor.

"He's mad," Freia said. "Dewar, his enemy?" A thought crossed her mind, and she said, "Let's leave this place, move further in," gesturing up the smaller stream with her chin, "and talk there."

"Day comes, and discovery," said Cledie.

"Then we'll go. Come. A little ways on the bank is rocky and you'll leave no traces." Freia turned and went upstream, and Scudamor and Cledie sloshed behind her.

They had food; Freia had none, but Scudamor and Cledie insisted she share their meagre supply of nuts, smoked meat, and dried fruit when they reached a cluster of gigantic leatherbark trees whose discarded needles muffled every sound and hid their footprints too. The three of them sat in a triangle, Cledie and Scudamor leaving a small distance between themselves and Freia.

"So Prospero thinks Dewar is his enemy," Freia said, "and he's angry with you for allowing him to drink from the Spring?" This was not the news she would have expected.

"In a nutshell, Lady, yes," Scudamor said, not meeting her eyes. "For he enjoined me to allow none to approach the Spring—the first command ever he gave me—and I—I did permit Dewar to pass. It is just."

"It is not either just," Freia said. "He let Dewar copy from his books; why not drink from the Spring too?" And then, as what Dewar had told her about his mother came back to her, she went on slowly, "Is there a woman named Odile here?"

Cledie simply nodded: Yes.

"What's she like?"

They glanced at one another.

"I think, Lady—" Cledie began.

"I asked you before to call me Freia! I'm not a lady no matter what Prospero says."

"Freia," Cledie corrected herself, dipping her fair head, "I cannot be asked fairly to assay this Odile, for I have seen little of her. Nor much of Lord Prospero. And Scudamor has been abused by her agency, I am convinced, and therefore he will say that he's not unbiased."

"You don't like her," Freia said. Nobody seemed to be saying anything straightforwardly.

"She is not what she seems to be," Cledie said.

"She is not one of us," Scudamor said, "not from Argylle; she is like those folk Utrachet met in Landuc, but worse. Prospero drowns himself in her."

"Has she drunk from the Spring?" asked Freia.

"No," they said together, and looked at one another, and looked back at Freia.

"I fear, Lady Freia, that there is much you have not heard," Scudamor said.

Freia's mouth sagged down in a frown. She propped her chin on her hand and her elbow on her knee. "I never do," she said. "Tell me what's been happening."

They told her of the floods and the famines, the droughts and disasters and the dry Spring. Scudamor even haltingly explained that most people thought it was all because of Freia being dead, and then he stopped, confused.

Cledie smiled. "A false report, and its falsity shall be joy to us all," she said.

Freia bit her lip and shrugged. "I—it was a—mistake," she said lamely. "So people have been moving away."

Scudamor nodded. "Yes, mistress. Over the hills to the Haimance, where the rivers did not flood, and south to the mountains where there is more game. Though the ground is bad for growing things there, it seemed better than the lowlands. I suppose they wander there, searching for food."

"And the strange weather . . ." Freia began and stopped, unable to fit a question around the weather.

They told her about the storm and the second spring that had followed it, and Freia fell into an uncomfortable silence as they did.

It seemed that the weather had improved just as she had come into Argylle. She counted days mentally, reckoning as carefully as she could, sorting the time gone past, and it did seem that her return and the warm weather coincided.

Dewar had said that she was all that stood between Argylle and destruction and she had pooh-poohed him, laughing. He had tried to explain sorcery-sounding things to her and she hadn't paid much attention. It was nonsense. The place was the place and she was herself and that was that.

"Lady Freia?" Scudamor said.

She could never get Scudamor to call her just Freia; Prospero had told him to address her thus and he wouldn't change.

Freia chewed her lip. Maybe it was really Dewar, though, she thought, and she knew it wasn't. The weather had been spring-like and mild since she had arrived.

She didn't want to think about it. "Scudamor—Prospero imprisoned you and he was going to kill you?"

"Yes," Scudamor said.

"How did you get away?"

"Cledie contrived it," Scudamor said, "all without my knowing."

"He would not leave with me at first," Cledie said, shaking her head, smiling. "My Lord Prospero will be as displeased with me as with his Seneschal, for I did beg a boon of my lord, that he would allow me to pass the night with my friend, and this kindness did Lord Prospero bestow upon us, and even consented that the hours be passed in a room more comfortable than that where he had pent Scudamor."

"Pent," Freia repeated.

"On the island, my lady," Scudamor said, nodding. "I did not understand why they moved me, nor why they assured me Cledie Mulhoun would see me soon, and I feared it meant that she too was to be killed, though I could not think why except that the Black One dislikes her."

"I discovered which room of the tower it was to be," Cledie said, "and brought some rope with me, and we took that and the ropes of the bed and left through the window. 'Twas dark last night, and we launched a boat and fled."

"Where are you going?"

Cledie smiled and spread her hands open, shrugging. "In all honesty, we reached the end of my plan when we reached the Wyebourne, and I do not know where we shall go now."

"We are at your mercy and your command, Lady," Scudamor said.

Neither idea pleased Freia. "I'm not going to do anything to you and I'm not going to tell you to do anything," she said. "Prospero must be mad, to try to kill you. You are his people. It is not like him."

"It is his will," Scudamor said.

Cledie sniffed.

The two women looked at one another and Freia said, "Or somebody's."

Cledie nodded. "One hears things, Freia."

"One does. What is this Odile like?"

Cledie raised her fair eyebrows. "Ever present, ever watching, ever whispering in Lord Prospero's ear."

"She does not like Dewar," Freia said. "I have never met her, but I know that. Is Utrachet there?"

"He is still there, unless something has befallen today," Scudamor said.

"What does he think?"

"He thinks as I do," Scudamor said, "that Lord Prospero has been a changed man since he returned from Landuc with the tale of your death in his mouth and the Black One at his side, and that the change estranges him from our counsel. He never asks for it, now."

Dewar's cautions and forebodings about Odile came again to Freia's mind. She pushed them aside. The right thing to do was obvious.

"I am going to the city," Freia said. "I was anyway. You do as you think best for yourselves; you might be safer in the woods for now. I am going to have a look at this Odile and see my father. He wasn't lying—he believes I'm dead—and I am going to tell him I am all right."

Prince Gaston led Otto, via a circuitous route through little-frequented corridors and halls, to his apartment. At the Prince's command, Robin the squire arranged pens, inkwells, stacks of fresh paper, and sand-trays, and waited by the table expectantly until the Fireduke dismissed him.

They divided the work; although Ottaviano assured Prince Gaston there was no need for him to take part, the Marshal had no urgent duties elsewhere. Prince Gaston read through the documents, as he was already familiar with most of them, and reeled off names. Otto wrote the names out, two lists: one in letter-order and one in number-order by the coördinates, looking up each place-name in the Prince's Ephemeris. Proceeding thus, it went very quickly, and most of the time seemed to be consumed by Otto shuffling through loose paper or through the Ephemeris. The Fireduke's presence made him nervous. He had no certainty that anything would come of this notion of his; he had no wish to make an ass of himself in front of Gaston—again.

There were many pages to each of the lists: Prospero had wished to settle a great deal on his daughter. Midway through, they encountered a difficulty.

"Those coördinates can't be right," Otto said, pausing as he wrote a word on the letter-list.

Gaston repeated them; Ottaviano shook his head and went round to look over the Fireduke's shoulder.

"Those numbers are nonsense," Otto said. "See? This one's impossible, and that zero makes no sense. He made a mistake! Well. Probably a transposition. Hm." He hunted through the Ephemeris.

The Fireduke watched the younger man as he frowned at the book and went forward and back a few pages.

"It's not in here," Ottaviano said, shaking his head. "That place isn't in the Ephemeris."

"Perhaps it is too small."

"Must be. I'm going to put it down anyway, and those bogus numbers at the head of the list here. Could be it's under another name, or something. Funny about the numbers, though."

"Well, it will be clear in the end," said Gaston, sounding the name out slowly for Ottaviano to write. "Let us go on." And they completed the lists of the riches that Prospero would have bestowed on his daughter as the afternoon became evening.

"Now, the list of lands that he forfeited to the Emperor," said Ottaviano.

"We want light," said Gaston, and he rose and left the room, returning with a burning spill with which he lit four oil-lamps. Then he sat and, saying nothing more, began to read from Prospero's treaty of surrender, tonelessly. Otto began a second pair of lists, and these two but scantly filled a sheet each. Each new name Otto checked against the list of the lands deeded to Freia.

There was no overlap between the two collections of names. "It's obvious his stratagem was to hand the lands he wanted to really keep over to her," Otto said, looking at the disparate lists. "Since he'd emancipated her, he probably planned to continue controlling it all anyway, through her. I bet he never thought that the Emperor wouldn't honor the emancipation. But since the emancipation wasn't upheld, everything she was supposed to get has passed to the Crown. Right?"

"The legality of the affair is moot," Gaston said, ambiguously.

"Is there anything regarding her marriage to Josquin?" asked Ottaviano, surveying the table. There were four tidy piles of documents before him. He massaged his pen-hand.

"Belike 'tis another box," said Gaston, but he rustled through the papers, setting some aside, and then said, "Ah."

"What we want is her dowry. The lands she would have kept, if she'd lived and married him."

"Much was said of that, and little done," said Gaston, and he studied the dowry-papers. Indeed there was little settled on

Freia, directly on her, compared to Prospero's first generous intention. He read slowly, revolving other thoughts in his mind than the words before him. "This is not large," said Gaston, half-aloud.

"I didn't think it would be," said Otto.

"His Majesty was loth to grant the girl anything. He and Prospero argued it full bitterly, but usage is that the woman must be left something of her own. And so it ought to be."

"Exactly. Suppose they wed, he dies—could happen—and she has nothing to live on, nowhere to call home. It's only right. What would have been left to her, sir?"

Gaston shook his head, reading Cremmin's regular, smooth-flowing script. "Some jewels. Any gifts presented in the course of . . . hm. Ah," he said, and turned the leaf. It must be done: he could not oppose the Well; it would destroy him. "There is land."

"I knew it," said Otto, and he grinned. "Prospero's last trick."

"A manor-house in Landuc, lying—"

"Skip it. Lands that are not in Landuc are what we want now, sir."

Gaston looked up from the list, met Ottaviano's eyes, and nodded slowly. "I believe I see, Baron." They stared at one another; Otto was bright-eyed, sensing the quarry; Gaston was unmoved, examining Otto. Then the Fireduke returned his attention to the list, and Ottaviano dipped his pen in the inkwell. Four estates were left to Freia, had she wed Josquin, four estates lying in Pheyarcet, scattered from the center to its barren outlands. Ottaviano stood with the last sheet of paper before him and the Ephemeris open on the table's edge, flipping pages, beginning to frown.

"And that is all." Gaston dropped the paper back in the box.

The Baron took out his handkerchief and wiped his perspiring face, then his hands. "Warm in here."

"I had liever keep the door closed."

"Of course." Otto stood, looking down at the open

Ephemeris, the list of Freia's dower-lands, from one to the other. "Argylle, a wilderness," he read aloud.

Prince Gaston waited, watching the Baron of Ascolet, his hands folded on the table before him.

"It's the same as the place with bad coördinates!" Otto exclaimed, and he smacked his right fist in his left palm. "We've got him! He's there—wherever there is."

"What is thy plan, Baron?"

He hesitated, then said, "It's about the war, sir. And Prospero. He, well, he's hiding somewhere now."

"Aye, so't seems."

"And nobody knew where he was during the war, or where he came from."

" 'Tis so."

"I've been told Prospero would never lie," said Otto. "The list of things he wanted to put in Freia's control is the important one, you see: if the Emperor hadn't messed that up by declaring her his ward, and therefore taking possession of everything she might have had, it could have worked. Prospero included this Argylle in the emancipation list. Since the emancipation failed, he had to get it into the dowry-list, and he did. That's the place he cares about most. I can't believe nobody cross-checked the lists before, or looked up the numbers."

Gaston nodded.

"Now the numbers," Otto said, tapping the dowry-list with a finger, "the numbers aren't right. The zero, there— Well, the zero there, sir, if I understand the way the coördinates work, that means it's outside Pheyarcet. But it can't be, unless it's in Phesaotois; and if it's in Phesaotois, it wouldn't come under the Emperor's eye, and Prospero would never have mentioned it. There's some error. I can figure that out later. —What happens to a dowry if the bride dies?" asked Ottaviano suddenly.

Gaston shrugged, waited.

"It doesn't change hands," the Baron answered himself.

Gaston picked up the dowry-list, read it, and put the paper back.

"So he still has title to the lands she would have held."

"Perhaps not. By treaty, he has yielded his lands to the Emperor, Baron."

"I think he'd read it the other way: that these lands were accidentally left in his hands. When he surrendered his lands, he had already given these away to her. If the emancipation weren't void, then he'd hold now whatever she held title to when she died, both the dowry and these other lands. It would be a hard case; I can argue either side, and so can anyone. He'd owe tithes, but that's better than owning nothing."

Gaston nodded agreement.

"If Prospero is in Pheyarcet," said Otto, "I will wager anything that he is in one of these places. His dead daughter's dower-lands. And now that we've found this one, this that isn't in the Ephemeris, that no one's heard of—he must be here, in this Argylle place."

"Indeed 'tis possible," said the Fireduke, and he looked again at the short list under his fingers. *Garvhaile, or Argylle, a small village, no manor-house, a free-flowing spring, forest (not measured)*. He went on, slowly, "Thou hadst best prepare to explain this to the Emperor, Baron. Meseems 'tis well-thought-on, and reasonable, and he'll receive it with much interest."

"If we can find that place, we'll find Prospero," Ottaviano said. "Now the men he brought from there spoke strangely: it must be far out in the wastelands, very near Phesaotois. And maybe, if his army was raised there, that's why: the area might be so Well-poor that, that they aren't quite creatures of the Well, not the way normal people are." He was excited; he spoke quickly, loudly, assuredly. "There's new Eddies, new places, spinning into being all the time. Most of them don't last. Probably Prospero found a good stable one and now he's hiding out there. We just have to find it. Simple."

Gaston nodded, once. "The Emperor will be pleased, if so," he said. "There are tithes owed."

"Prospero hasn't begun to pay his debts," said Otto.

— 26 —

PROSPERO SLEPT NOT AT ALL WHEN he laid himself down, despite Odile's best efforts to beguile him to rest. He rose and went to his study, drank there a few glasses of whisky he had brought from Landuc, and still his mind raged over and over rehearsing the events of two days past: Scudamor's treachery, Cledie's treachery, and his own trusting folly. He would not let himself be so befooled again by Argylle's folk. He'd thought they knew little of cunning deceptions, but they had taught him otherwise. They were men, with all the evil of humanity in them. When his searchers brought the two traitors back he would hang them together on the same rope they'd climbed down on.

Seething, he dressed and went out, disregarding Odile's calling after him drowsily. He climbed up the citadel and stood there long hours, staring at the darkness and the stars while his anger glowed; and then as dawn dimmed the stars he went down and walked slowly around the isle. The air was cool, without a snap of frost to it. It was high time winter came properly. Not even the seasons kept their places. Prospero crossed over the framework of the new wooden bridge into the city.

The sight of the restored walls comforted him. He went up a narrow stair and began walking along the top, from the downstream side to the upstream, all around the curve, his pace rapid enough that he soon came to the upstream end and descended the stair on that side. The work was not yet complete. It had been slowed by the need to rebuild all the other buildings, houses and warehouses. Soon they would build a stone bridge to the citadel's island, extend the wall along the riverbank, and enclose the city. Later as the city grew he would bridge the river, up and down, with two fortified bridges. . . .

Prospero, soothed by his defenses, crossed back to the tower and walked around the island again. Smoke-smells and sounds were in the air now, Argylle waking up around him; the sun would rise soon. He strolled to the upstream end of the island, where the stolen boat Cledie and Scudamor had abandoned, evidence, lay hauled up and turned over.

A log was being carried toward the island on the current, not so common a sight as it had been in the wake of the great storm. Prospero stared at it and absently calculated the current's speed.

The log split apart as he watched.

Part of it went past the island, long and low, and part moved across the current toward him, utterly contradictory to nature, but unmistakable in the grey, bright predawn light. For a second Prospero was astonished, but then he felt weak and fearful: a delusion of his unrested mind, to be sure—

"Papa?" Freia said, climbing over the rocks and staring at him, as astonished as he. How had he known she was coming? Sorcery?

There was an uproar somewhere, indistinct shouting in the city behind Prospero. He was deaf to it; he shook his head sharply and blinked. He'd wake instantly, surely.

"It's me, Papa," Freia said, sopping wet, on her back a tight-wrapped bundle that was bow and arrows protected from the water, appearing as she always did after swimming to the island from the forest, as she did in his dreams, not in Landuc's finery but rough hunting-clothes.

The forest was not behind her; the cleared far bank with the single warehouse remaining was.

"What foul apparition art thou? Begone!" snarled Prospero, and he turned and stalked away.

"Prospero!" Freia cried, dismayed, and, shrugging off her bundle, she darted after him to grab his sleeve.

Prospero, enraged in an instant, shook his arm free, turned on her, and lifted his hand.

"Papa!" and she flinched and her arm came up to ward her from the blow.

Prospero halted, staring at her in the new day's earliest light as she stared at him, the horror and dismay on her face that which his worst nightmares showed him. Something exploded in the city, but neither of them heard it, and the top of the tower moved and made a long croaking sound.

"Be thou dream, or apparition sent to torment me, or fouler being still," Prospero said hoarsely, and he lowered his hand, "matters not, I'll not sin the same twice, goad me as thou wilt. What's thy mission? Speak."

"I'm not a ghost or anything else," Freia whispered, still guarding herself, "I'm me, Papa. I'm truly me."

"Thou'rt dead," Prospero said. "This I know. Think not to bewray my thought so simply, spirit. Art Dewar's creature, a thing of his making sent to jeer me? Go, and tell him he—"

"Prospero, I'm *me*," Freia said. "Why would anybody do that to you? I'm *me*."

"My daughter's dead, spirit," Prospero said; "tell thou thy master that. Hast something of her seeming, but the likeness is imperfect—"

"Papa! I'm here. How can I not look like myself?" Exasperation covered a tremble of fear: what if Prospero would not believe the truth? If he could believe Scudamor would betray him, couldn't he believe his daughter would come back?

"Nay, my girl was not so lean as thou, nor her hair so dressed, nor was her voice thus, nor her eyes so colored." Prospero turned from her and began walking away; there was some commotion at the bridge, a noisy knot of people.

"How could you forget— Papa!" Freia seized his arm once more.

"Release me, thou false copy, ere I abandon the courtesy I bear thee for the sake of thy original," Prospero said, and he pried her hand from his arm and pushed her from him.

"Prospero," Freia said to his back, quivering with fury. How dare he disbelieve her?

The tone of her voice stopped him; Prospero paused but would not look round.

"Go, then, Prospero," Freia said, "and you need never face

428 ——> *Elizabeth Willey*

this piece of failed work again. I would do anything to please you, and you never allowed it; you called yourself my father, but you are a sorcerer, without sorcery now, and no part a father. If I am a false copy it is because you made me so, an artificial thing like Caliban, neither human nor alive."

Prospero stared at the tumult before the tower, not seeing it, and coldness weighed his limbs and stopped his throat.

"If you go, Prospero," Freia said, "if you refuse to believe me, to let me come home, I promise you, Prospero, I shall leave you, you shall succeed in driving me from you as you never could before, and I shall leave this place and I swear I shall never return."

She went on, "You drove me away once, and I came back; and you would have left me in Landuc if Scudamor and Utrachet had not made you return for me; and if you will not believe I am here now, then you're all sorcerer still, with no heart, and I have no reason to call you father, and you can stay here and perish with your Argylle! And good riddance to you and it both. You'd rather that I be dead than admit you're wrong."

"I was never cruel to my daughter but once—" Prospero said in an undertone.

"You told me nothing, nothing of Landuc, nothing of importance, nothing but what you wanted me to know, and you never listened to anything I said—" Freia pulled herself up short, took a trembling breath, and said, "Go ahead. Go, Prospero. I was a mistake, unreliable, weak, and badly made, and you'd rather forget me than live with me. Go. Go—and I'll go."

Prospero's blind gaze had fallen to the ground before him. Her words dinned in his ears. He grappled with them, made himself understand them, and with understanding came rage. He turned on her.

"Insolent creature. What knowest thou of sorcery, of the Art that I mastered better than any? I captured a soul and pent it in a form of my making, that lived and breathed; what other hath done so since Primas's day? Ungrateful and contrary thing, upraised from basest Elements to best, defiling them with bestial baseness!"

They glared basilisk-glares a long moment, till Freia's anger left her, the fire blown out by his fury. "I shouldn't have come," she said, and her shoulders slumped. "You are always right and I am wrong, and there is no place here for me because it is yours, and you don't want a daughter who was a pile of dirt and sticks and I will never be anything else, anything better, anything real."

Prospero's throat worked. No answer came.

"Forget I was here," Freia whispered, and she took two backward steps and turned away, walking toward the water.

Dewar leaned on his staff and looked up at the high gate.

"I said open it!" he roared. "What the hell are you afraid of, wood-elk?"

"Not until after sunrise, by Lord Prospero's command, do we open the gates," a man shouted through a loup-hole.

"Lord Dewar—" Scudamor said in an undertone.

"Stand back. I'll waste no more breath on this witling. What does he mean, locking gates in an empty country? When Freia comes home, will he leave her outside in the night? I want to talk to him now, not after sunrise." Dewar had a long black staff he'd not been holding a moment before; bluish light trailed it as an afterimage when he twirled it in the air.

Cledie Mulhoun took Scudamor's arm and drew him aside. "It is not our affair," she said, "but theirs."

"Lord Prospero will take it ill—"

Dewar struck the gates with his staff. The gates boomed and an arrow buried itself in the ground at his feet. He swung the staff upward, muttering, and other arrows bounced away, striking an invisible barrier and rebounding. Scudamor and Cledie ducked, though the barrier protected them as well.

"All right," said Dewar, "the hard way, then."

He stood, eyes closed, holding the staff vertically between his hands, his lips moving soundlessly. All at once he spun on his heel and hit the gates again, and the gates tumbled down, shattering and rumbling, the tree-trunk timbers collapsing slowly inward. The arrows ceased falling.

"Lord Prospero will take it ill," Scudamor repeated, a mournful statement of fact.

"A fine discourteous welcome, Castellan," Dewar said to Utrachet, who stood across the wood-pile from him. "Are you at war? What do these closed gates mean?"

"Prospero has ordered it so," Utrachet said.

"And he wonders why his Spring is recalcitrant?" Dewar asked the air above Utrachet's head. "Accompany me to my lord father, friend Utrachet. There is a little matter I wish to discuss with him."

Utrachet glanced at Cledie and Scudamor; Cledie shrugged eloquently and stepped daintily through the wreckage, and Scudamor clambered over it far less gracefully and joined them. Utrachet's guards moved back, aside; veterans of the war with Landuc, they had a great respect for what a sorcerer could do. Besides, he was the Castellan's problem now.

"Er—clear this lumber, here," Utrachet told them, looking back, and they set to it. A small knot of spectators, attracted by the dispute, followed and grew as Dewar and the others made their way through the streets toward the bridge to the island, where stood the citadel, flat- and unreal-looking veiled in the mist of morning.

Dewar said nothing more to anyone; he walked so swiftly that his companions had to half-run to keep up with him.

At the skeletal bridge to the Citadel's island there were six guards, and Utrachet had to command them to permit Lord Dewar to pass, despite Prospero's past orders. He spoke with a feeling of reckless terror, knowing that Scudamor, who stood phlegmatically beside him, was condemned to die for countermanding Prospero's will; yet there was a feeling of inevitability, too, for if he forbade Dewar to pass the bridge, Dewar would cross it anyway, and Utrachet's heart felt that that was not, in itself, a bad thing, though something bad might follow the crossing.

Prospero lunged after Freia, his body moving before a thought commanded it, and he caught her at the river's stony edge.

"Freia, stay, stay," he said, holding her arms.

She shook her head, not looking at him, twisting away, and they grappled until he took his cloak, one-handed, and threw it round her shoulders, and then put his arms around her.

"Thou art my Freia, my daughter, thou'rt real. I do believe it. Shalt not depart so lightly." He stared into her face, fearing now that she was a phantom.

Freia, restricted by his cloak and arms, gazed back at him, still angry. "I'm not real," she said. "I know. You don't have to pretend any more."

"Real? Thou'rt real. How not?"

She said nothing, and the silence challenged him.

Prospero now looked away, and said, "Well. Thou'rt more than dirt and sticks. Who hath told the elsewise?"

"Dewar."

"Water-brained spratling! Whence had he the tale, I'd know. Thou'rt real, Freia, as real as he or I. Hast heart, mind, soul, indwelling in thy body; hast sensibility and sentiment, intelligence and instinct, compounded perfect and imperfect as any human creature's."

"I'm a copy of a human creature. You said it yourself. I was never real and you never believed I was. You made me to show how powerful you were, not because you wanted me. If I were really your daughter, you wouldn't hate me."

Again Prospero's words were seized in his throat, choking him, and he clutched Freia the harder for the lack of reply. At last, he said hoarsely, "Did I hate thee, Freia, what were thy fate when thou wert hostage in Landuc? Did I hate thee, had I delivered myself to them, eviscerated my mind and indentured my soul to free thee? Did I hate thee, had I kept thee in my house, at my side, all the years we dwelt together? Did I hate thee, I must hate myself. Thou'rt mine own blood, Freia, my daughter as Dewar is my son, perhaps the more so for I chose thee, shaped thee, made thee purposely to live. So might'st thou say I shaped the other folk of Argylle: but they are not my blood, them I did not nurture season to season in my heart as I did thee, and them I love, aye, but I love thee, my child, better, for thou'rt a piece of mine own life. That thy origin is in sorcery and not in some wench's womb, let it not trouble thee: for 'tis all the same, earth and water cradling life, will-spark, and soul. O, thou'rt more than earth and water, wood, breath, and Art; thou'rt a true human creature, Freia, and let never a doubt otherwise assail thee. O' that we need speak nevermore. The Spring bore thee, an thou wouldst, and thou'rt more near it than any other creature here. Here is thy place. Here is thy home. I have given it to thee in deed, and it is thine before any other's. Stay."

Freia listened, not fighting him now, grave and intent on him, and when he stopped she regarded him a long time before she spoke.

"Do you love me," she asked.

Prospero said, "I do love thee, Freia."

"You said, when you hit me . . ."

"I—" and he stopped, remembering. He had struck her, he had ordered her begone from his sight, and there was a piece of him that wanted to mist over that and say it had not happened, that she had run from him willful and ungrateful, and yet his arm still remembered the blow and his eyes the horror of her face— "I struck thee in madness," he whispered, looking down. "I beg thee forgive me. 'Twas blackest humor and foulest deed o' my life, and I've lived my darkest hours since. Thou hast returned, perhaps canst not forget, but let me earn pardon, if pardon there can be."

Freia touched his cheek, making him look at her. "Landuc," she said, "it is all Landuc, everything evil and murderous and ill comes from there, doesn't it. Everything here was well enough until you went there, making war, and nothing has been right since."

"It is not so simple, Puss. There are parts of good and evil immixed in everything."

"The war was wholly bad, Papa. What good has come to us from it?"

He began to speak, to argue with her, and the weight of mishap sunk the words before he framed them. In an instant of self-knowledge he hated himself and, meanly, her, but the feeling fled as soon as he knew it, and it left sad recognition of the truth of what she said. She was the Spring's creature; the Spring moved her tongue, and the Spring's truth was in her words. Prospero looked away again and said, "No good. Indeed, naught of good at all, and centuries of ill. Perhaps—perhaps you've the right of't there. 'Twas unwisely done. Aye, and you did counsel 'gainst it; I cannot pretend not."

"I know I'm not clever like Dewar," Freia said, barely louder than the river. "I'm never going to be as good as he is at anything, but—I try, Papa. I try so hard to do things, things for you. I know he's more useful, better—but I want to do things too."

"Dewar is no better than you, Freia," he said sharply. "Indeed—"

"He wants to help," she said, looking into Prospero's eyes. "Please could you not be angry with him, please, Papa. I want him to come home here. He doesn't have anyone to be home with. It's bad to be so alone."

"Well, Puss. 'Tis not so simple, for he's another kind of creature, different from you. We'll speak of that anon."

She nodded.

"Where have you been?" he asked.

"So far away, and lost, and travelling," said Freia, "and always, always I wanted to be home."

Prospero studied her face, the set of chin, the anxious line at the brow, the firm, determined gaze. Full human creature, this, no will-bound thing—he had wrought finer than he knew, surpassed his own ability. "Have you been long i' the country," he asked.

"Not very long, but some days. Before that I was lost; until Trixie found me and brought me, I couldn't find the way to come here."

"Time is, I taught you o' that," he admitted, thinking of the uncanny softening of the weather, the springlike renaissance around them: some days. "Come now; you're wet, 'tis cold air though unseemly warm withal, let's dry and warm you and find us breakfast too."

Blinking, Freia nodded again; it would be as it had always been, the two of them eating bread-and-honey and walking and talking, and she smiled and hugged Prospero's neck. "I was afraid you wouldn't want me back," she whispered as the fear fell away from her.

Prospero closed his eyes, embracing her, damp and solid in his cloak. "Nay, be welcome, Puss. Welcome home."

At the tower, Dewar stopped. In the open doorway stood the Black Countess, who had been seeking Prospero since he had left her bed. His arbitrary wandering had confounded her search, and she had returned to the tower as Dewar's destruction of the gate thundered over the city. Knowing it for no natural sound, Odile had strained her dulled senses to perceive the sorcery and prepared herself for combat as well as she could.

Utrachet took Cledie's arm and drew her back, backing into the crowd and forcing them backward, his skin prickling, the hackles on his neck stiffening. He smelled a fight. Scudamor stayed where he was, seeming to compact and thicken, bracing himself. The onlookers whispered, hissing sounds; alien Odile was not liked, and Dewar was Prospero's son.

"Odile," Dewar said softly. He had not forgotten her. Her gestures, her stance, her features, all were graven in his memory, and seeing her physically before him made his skin crawl with fear. He thought of Freia. Odile must be dealt with before

Freia arrived: confined, crippled, stilled—kept from Freia, who was defenseless and inexperienced. Cost what it may, he must protect Freia.

Odile, her face a mask without expression, gazed down on him from the tower's steps. She had not laid eyes on him since he was a stripling boy. He had grown broad-shouldered and long-legged, and even though she could not work the Spring here she could feel the power he held, a smothering, cold pressure.

"What do you seek here?" she asked; the crowd watched her and she must say something.

Dewar gestured, nothing casual. Odile felt the force unseen in his hand pushing her back, and she recognized it and grabbed at it: he drew on the Stone! Here! How?

Dewar laughed, a sharp note and triumphant, and before Odile could sap and shape the power he controlled, he withdrew it, and Odile stood with a hand outstretched clawing at nothing.

"I dislike killing," he said, "and though I may deplore my father's taste, I honor his threshold and his house. I have come to see him, and I do not wish to see you. Move aside."

"You have come to murder him!" Odile cried, watching the people behind him.

There were gasps and voices swelled.

"You have stolen from him as you stole from me," Odile went on, "and you are a sorcerer who would kill anyone for the power to be had here, as you killed your sister—"

Cledie laughed, high and merry, and began whispering brilliant-eyed to Utrachet.

"A lie!" shouted Scudamor.

"I killed my sister?" Dewar repeated, incredulous. "Is that what you've been telling him?"

"Water is his element," Odile cried, not to him but to the crowd, "and water is his weapon; he drowned her to take the realm that was to be hers, destroyed your town by flood, and now he comes to murder Prospero!"

"Odile, this tale is thinner than the air you make it of," Dewar said. "Get out of my way. I'm here to see Prospero."

The third time would be the challenge, she knew and he knew, and Odile tried again to catch the crowd, who were whispering among themselves. Cledie was aloof and amused now, and Scudamor was speaking to a small group, gesturing.

"Or have you murdered him already?" Odile demanded. "He haunts Prospero with evil dreams and punishes all Argylle with famine, flood, and storm! Where is Prospero now? He has been missing since last night! How can you let this bloodstained traitor stand among you? He is mortal, and for the murder of his sister alone he should die!"

"Stop this senseless raving!" Dewar shouted over her last words, taking two steps forward, lifting his staff. "Stand aside, viper! If any here would kill Prospero it is you!"

"There's Lord Prospero," Cledie said, clearly, over the sudden roar of the crowd.

They were silent. Craning necks, leaning, jumping, they followed Cledie's pointing finger.

Dewar stopped. He lowered his staff to the stone; its metal heel clinked. He waited.

Prospero, bareheaded and in his shirt sleeves, was walking up the narrow stone-flagged path, and someone smaller was behind him, bundled in his long cloak against the dawn chill. The sun crept up, shining into the tower's dooryard so that the stone glittered with the light, and the mist from the river was gold.

"What manner of deputation's this?" Prospero said, lifting his eyes from the path and seeing the people, surprised. His preoccupation had been so deep he had not noticed them until he was nearly among them.

They drew back, aside.

"Dewar," Prospero said. He halted.

"Did I not say, my lord, that he would come to murder thee?" Odile cried, leaving the door, stepping down a step or two. "Did I not warn thee?"

Very softly, but quite perfectly audibly, someone said, "Lies."

Dewar heard it and recognized the voice and the speaker, soaking into Prospero's fine silk cloak behind Prospero, and he twisted his mouth to keep from laughing with relief. She'd stolen a march on him, no more, no less.

A long inhuman scream came from high above—a gryphon was on top of the tower. Odile saw heads go back, mouths drop; but she would not leave her position on the steps to see.

"Gryphon," said Utrachet, seeing the head against the sky.

Others murmured the word too, agreeing. It was strange. Nesting, maybe? This strange weather had confused everything; if birds sought nests, why not gryphons? They looked back at Prospero.

Prospero saw Scudamor now and Cledie beside him. "You dare return," he said.

"My lord, canst thou not perceive this plot?" Odile pressed on. "These creatures are Dewar's!"

"Nay, they are mine own," Prospero said drily; "for I shaped them myself. Dewar, what would you here?"

"I came to visit my father," said Dewar, "and here I find a harpy whose old wounds would be best salved by his blood and mine. Blood-kin need be no curse, you once said to me, do you remember? But here's cursed blood-kin, cursed and cursing, that would twist every natural bond to hatred and hang us with that rope."

Father and son gazed at one another. "What tale is this?" Prospero asked in a voice dangerous by its mildness.

Dewar lifted an eyebrow. "Odile," he said, "did you not just assure these people that I drowned my sister and that I am here to murder Prospero?"

"What?" Freia tossed her head; the cloak-hood fell back and she moved up past Prospero. Her hair was drying, but still ten-drilled with the wet; the sun caught in it, sparked in it, warmed her face to deep-gold. She shrugged the cloak from her shoulders.

The crowd sighed her name, a single gust.

"It is a plot, Prospero! Canst thou not see past the deceit?"

Odile cried, coming forward again. "Thy folk are turned against thee, and this is some shape-molded spirit Dewar hath set to snare thy trust and betray thee!"

"Who are you?" Freia demanded, although she knew.

"She is Odile," Prospero said, his gaze moving from one to the other, Freia, Dewar, Odile, opposing forces he could not facilely balance.

The gryphon on the citadel screamed again; this time the folk who glanced up shouted and jostled, trying to get out of the open area. Prospero looked up too and saw the gryphon diving, as on prey, brilliant in the fresh day's light, bronze legs outstretched and dark claws reaching, and he had time to think that the beast was mad before it spread its wings and broke its fall into the dooryard.

"Trixie!" Freia exclaimed. "You came back!"

Trixie made a low crooning noise and folded her wings. Her expression was jaunty and smug.

"Welcome home," Dewar said, smiling, for Freia had worried about her runaway Trixie.

Freia ran to the gryphon, and Trixie crouched and warbled, lashed her tail cubbishly and, very gently, preened Freia's back once with her deadly beak, as Freia stroked her feathers and scratched her chest.

Odile had backed to the door as the gryphon plummeted, but now she moved again a few steps from it, and her tone and face were disdainful as she said, "Prospero, art so beguiled by thy doting memory that thou canst not penetrate this sham?"

"Nay," Prospero said, "no seeming, no spirit bound and tutored could this be. Thy love for me prompts thee to extremes, madame, and I beg thee to let go thy dread and rejoice, for here is my daughter home again, and all this world from the sun to the earth revived must welcome her as its very mistress."

Odile shook her head. "Oh, my friend, thou seest thy death before thee and fearest it not? Is this not the sorcerer who arranged thy downfall and stole thine Art from thee, who sapped thy Spring and slew thy daughter? My lord, thou knowest well thy daughter's dead; her bones are in the sea-bed of Landuc! This cannot be she! Dewar hath stalked thee and hath now come to complete thy death, and wilt thou not believe me? He is a sorcerer!"

"And a Prince's son," Dewar said coldly, "a gentleman."

"I never heard such nonsense in my life," Freia said, leaving Trixie to confront Odile. "When did Papa wish for a story-teller to bother him with imaginary plots? I met Scudamor and Cledie in Threshwood and they told me what you did, twisting the truth into a rope, and I hardly credited it." She shook her head at Odile. "Do you believe this woman?" Freia turned and stared at Prospero, expectant.

Prospero frowned at Freia. "She's heedful of my safety, and she speaks out of love for me; over-careful, but not false—"

"*False!* She said Dewar drowned me! I assure you that's not true! Do you believe her?"

"Dewar is a sorcerer," Prospero said measuredly, with a feeling that he walked hoodwinked in a maze, "and a sorcerer's life is power—"

"Papa, this is Dewar we're talking about. Dewar. Judge others by yourself, or by her—she is a sorceress and surely she is here for the power herself—but I know my brother, and he is not here to kill you or anyone. If he wanted to you'd be dead already. You cannot believe her lies."

"He toys with thee, Prospero, and his puppet seeks to cloud thy thought," Odile said.

"She lies," Freia said flatly. "Are we going to stand out here all day? You said we would eat something, Papa." And she tipped her head to one side and regarded him, beseeching.

"Let us go within," Prospero said, "and break fast, for truth is easier found on a full belly." He started toward the door; Freia was behind him, and Odile beside her watching her sidelong coldly from half-lidded eyes, and there was a scuffle.

"See!" Odile cried.

Prospero whirled.

A knife: in two hands, Freia's and Odile's, pushed this way and that, its blade flashing blankly.

"She sought to stab thee!" Odile said.

"You lying viper!" Dewar shouted.

"Unhand me, creature!" Odile wrenched her hand, and Freia's grip broke, and Odile's hand with the knife struck quick, inward—

Freia twisted; Dewar jumped forward, staff raised, and in that instant Trixie sprang between him and Odile, her beak wide, her claws extended and swinging, and Odile's hand with knife grazed Freia's arm and thigh as Dewar's staff—too fast for him to halt himself—smote the gryphon's head as the gryphon's clawed foot and beak raked at Odile, Odile contorting, leaping away.

"No!" Dewar shouted. Freia yelled wordlessly, staggered. "Hold!" Prospero bellowed, seizing Dewar's arm too late. "My lord, help me!" Odile shrieked at Prospero. Trixie screamed and jerked and convulsed, falling on Freia and Odile. The gryphon shuddered, her beak gaping, and her head thudded to the ground.

"Freia!" Dewar yelled, and he shoved the dead gryphon's soft-feathered forequarters off Odile, off Freia. Freia stared up at Prospero and Dewar, dazed.

"Ouch," Freia whispered. The knife was buried hilt-deep in her thigh. She gripped Dewar's arm and tried not to faint. Odile. He had warned her about Odile. "Keep her here, don't let her go," Freia said, as loudly as she could, and more softly, almost a moan, "Oh, Dewar." He moved her away from Trixie, supporting her against his body.

"O Prospero, do not be fooled! That spirit and the beast will murder thee!" cried Odile.

People were rushing forward now, the instant of horror past. Insistent voices, hands, movement tugged Prospero's attention from Odile. Someone seized her arms, pulling her away. Scudamor was helping him to stand, and Utrachet; Cledie knelt beside Dewar and Freia with Hicha the record-keeper. Freia looked up at her father; his eyes met hers, and he felt sick, shamed. He had let this play itself out before him. He was not sure what had happened—he felt dizzy, off-balance—but Freia was hurt, and should not have been hurt, and he had been not an arm's length from her when it happened.

"I'm sorry, I'm sorry," Dewar was saying again and again, holding Freia, "I'm sorry, it was too fast, I couldn't stop, I'm sorry—" until she turned her face and pressed her cheek to his, hard. Then he buried his face in her hair for a moment.

"Trixie," Freia said in a tiny voice. "Papa, Trixie."

Prospero lowered his head, lowered his eyes. "Forgive me," he begged her in an undertone. Had Freia, the gryphon, the staff moved slightly differently—he closed his eyes.

"Lord, come, come sit down, sit," Scudamor was saying.

He shook his head, shook the Seneschal off, and knelt again, taking Freia's hands from her brother's arm and holding her cold fingers in his that were just as cold. "Forgive me," he asked her again.

Freia's face was white with shock. She swallowed and took a trembling breath. "Papa, it hurts," she said.

Prospero nodded and focused on her: flesh wounds, bleeding but not gushing, and she weakened with cold and not eating and the anguish of the gryphon's loss. Sorcery was the best surgeon, rapid and sure. "Your brother shall aid you. Dewar," he said, "Dewar! Know you the way of binding blood?"

"Of course," Dewar snapped, and, with cloth and words touched by the Spring, he stanched the gashes, drew the knife out, and soothed the damaged flesh. Blood flowed, slowed, stopped. Freia sat stoic, eyes closed, breathing slowly, her free hand gripping Prospero's until his fingers whitened. "Better," said Dewar after but minutes, though it seemed longer. "It needs a proper bandage, though."

"Help me up," Freia said, rising to her feet, leaning on Prospero, steadying herself on Dewar's shoulder.

"Careful," murmured Dewar.

"Come, let us go in and—" began Prospero.

"No," Freia said, and she released them both to stand alone, looking at Odile. Prospero turned and stopped himself from contradicting her. There was purpose in her face, an intensity he hadn't seen before. What would she do?

"Prospero," said Freia, still looking at Odile, who was mask-faced and unreadable, "you gave Argylle to me, you said."

"Said and did." He glanced at Dewar, but Dewar looked puzzled too; not some idea of his, then, but her own. " 'Tis yours, as much as it could be anyone's."

"What do you mean, Freia?" Dewar said, swallowing. "If it's hers—" he looked at Prospero. "Landuc's by treaty, but hers by gift . . ."

Prospero nodded to Freia. "Then, albeit without oath of fealty, she's ruler here, and I daresay th' Emperor could find no other, nor impose his own will on the place. 'Tis mine inas I founded it, but I did give it to her, entailed with conditions of Landuc's making." He felt the cold claws of fear closing on him. What did she mean to do?

"Then it is mine." Freia stood, her hands closed in fists, breathing quickly. "I will not have this person here," she said.

Dewar's eyes flicked from Prospero to Freia.

"She is my guest—" Prospero protested.

"She's an outsider!" Freia said. "She doesn't belong here."

"No more doth Dewar!" retorted Prospero. "The lady is my guest."

"She has said nothing but lies in my hearing," Freia said, "she has just tried to kill me, she is an alien sorceress with no loyalty to us or Argylle, and you would keep her as a guest?"

"Yet wouldst thou keep yon parasite about thee," said Odile, "that hath made it his habit to prey on his hosts everywhere, across the worlds?"

Freia turned her face toward Dewar, over her shoulder and up, and they exchanged a long look, reading one another's features it seemed, and she smiled at him, a small movement that came and went. Then Freia looked again at Odile, and shook her head. "This," she said firmly, "is Dewar's home."

"A sorcerer hath no—" began Odile.

"You do not hear me, I think," Freia said, cutting her off and gesturing sharply with her right hand. "Dewar is my brother, and Argylle is his home. Here may he dwell when he pleases, and here we will always welcome him. You, however, have done nothing to recommend you to me as a guest. I'll not have you here."

"I came here under thy father's protection," said Odile contemptuously. "I pity him, that thou shouldst so little honor him as to overthrow his will in so minor a matter."

"My father's will must I respect," Freia said coldly, drawing herself up very straight despite her wounded leg. "You I do not. Hold your tongue. You have spoken not one true word today, and such a false creature does not belong here among us. You have not behaved as a guest should, and there is no reason for us to treat you as one."

Prospero's jaw tightened, and he said nothing. He thought he knew what must come now: Freia, jealous, injured, newcome to heady power—

"I don't like killing people," Freia said, as if she knew his thought. "Hateful though some of them are, I don't like killing them. There has been too much death. I don't want to be like those people in Landuc. She came from somewhere," Freia half-asked, turning again toward Dewar.

"Aië," said Dewar softly.

Odile's eyes were on Prospero, her expression supplicating.

"Let her go back there," Freia said, "and, Prospero, if you desire her company so much, this Odile who lies and murders and says poisonous things about everyone, you can go visit her there in Aië; it must be as foul as Landuc, or worse. She shall not remain here."

"If 'tis true that you'd respect my will," Prospero said then, slowly, with a rumble of storm-anger in his voice, "my guest shall stay, and yon sorcerer, yon dishonorable hyena come to pick my bones, shall go."

Shocked, Freia stared at Prospero, who regarded her unrelenting, his face hard. Odile was silent; perhaps a trace of a smile was on her lips. No one moved or spoke; the very air was stilled. Freia looked from her father, to her brother, to her father, and again at Dewar: suddenly, painfully wrenched.

"Freia," said Dewar, not loudly, "I have promised I will serve you in any way I can, and to divide you again from your father would serve you badly. I'll leave."

Freia trembled on her injured leg. She seemed unable to speak.

Cledie Mulhoun darted forward, took Freia's arm on hers. Cledie shook her head at Dewar. "That's not the Lady's will!" she said.

A murmur went around the gathered Argyllines, agreeing. It was not the Lady's will.

"No," said Scudamor, slowly, thinking aloud. "She said, you may dwell here, Lord Dewar, and we shall make you welcome."

"And she said, this one must go," said Utrachet, gesturing at Odile with a jerk of his chin.

It suddenly seemed to Prospero that he was surrounded by eyes: the eyes of the crowd, Scudamor's impenetrably dark, Utrachet's narrowed, Cledie's adamant and unwavering.

"Lord Dewar's home is with us, so the Lady has said," stated Cledie. "Lord Prospero, why do you not agree?"

Prospero held himself stiff, aloof, meeting Cledie's regard though he was conscious of a sinking, cold feeling in his heart.

"Lady," said Scudamor, "you did say you respect Lord Prospero's will, and so do we—but your will must we obey."

"I don't want—" Freia cried, protesting.

"You belong here," Cledie interrupted her, "and you are ours, as we are yours, Lady. Lord Prospero declared it so."

"Lady," said Hicha, who had only watched thus far, "what is your will?"

Freia swayed slightly, putting more weight on Cledie's arm, and her eyes met Cledie's. Beyond Cledie stood Dewar, withdrawing, ready to depart in a moment. "Dewar, please stay," she said then, nearly whispering, and she held her hand out to him. Dewar hesitated, then crossed and took her hand, kissed it, bowing to her, saying some words too soft for any to hear. Freia's voice gained strength as she turned to Prospero to continue: "And Odile must go: she is his enemy, and there'll be no peace if she stays here. I—I will not have it so."

Prospero looked at his daughter, leaning on fair Cledie's arm, Dewar poised beside her, and he heard the unspoken corollary: If Odile remained, Freia would not. And he knew he could not risk losing Freia again, for this time he would lose all, for all.

"This is hasty judgement," he said.

"Trixie would have killed her," said Freia.

Prospero held her gaze, tried to, had to glance down. "The gryphon's a blood-minded beast," he said. And his daughter was not: made of better matter.

"Dewar," Freia said, turning to her brother again. "Will you, can you, banish her from here, send her where she came from?"

"I can." Dewar spoke very softly.

"And she won't be able to return."

He shook his head. "Only if someone were to bring her."

"I don't like killing people," Freia said again, earnestly, as if trying to explain something to him.

He smiled a little and nodded. "Nor do I. It's wasteful and difficult to undo."

Freia nodded, too. They agreed on this, Prospero saw, and he wondered what other agreements they had forged, leaguing themselves together.

"I'll do as you ask at once," said Dewar, and he glanced at Prospero with pity in his face.

"Prospero, Papa," Freia said, and she waited until he looked at her. "Let's go in and break fast? And you can tell me about this tithe we're bound to send Landuc and all that's happened here."

"Aye," Prospero said, and slowly bowed his head, consenting, to her will.